Tears of Tay Ninh

A Novel By
Thomas A. Hutchings

ISBN: 1-4392-2805-1
ISBN-13: 9781439228050

Visit www.booksurge.com to order additional copies.

Dear Reader,

When I am conducting affairs in Saigon, known also by its more recent name, Ho Chi Minh City, I am often asked casually, "Where are you from?" The usual answer is, "I'm from America, but I grew up in Saigon." February 1970 was my first arrival in Saigon at the age of twenty during the Second Indochina War – the American War in Viet Nam. That significant event of my life was a milestone, particularly as a young man flying on intelligence combat missions.

Keep in mind this story is fiction, as are the characters, save several notable historical figures sprinkled throughout. The story is convened and wrapped within historical facts during the Second Indochina War. As a resident of Viet Nam, I have the pleasure to walk the same ground as the characters did; then and now. Except for a slight time modification of the camp at Thien Ngon to move the story along, all else is as it was during the time periods cited. Graham Greene once wrote regarding an historical fictional work of his, "I have no scruples about such small changes." Neither do I, and for a valid reason, as the reader will see. I did not write this as a piece of history, but history is a piece of the story.

Thomas A. Hutchings
Saigon, Viet Nam 2009

PREFACE

DEPARTMENT OF THE ARMY 1989

"Like the Iron Triangle, War Zone C was a major Viet Cong stronghold and had been a sanctuary for insurgents for over twenty years. It was also believed to be the location of headquarters of the Central Office of South Vietnam; however, owing to the remoteness of the area and the strict secrecy with which the enemy treated the headquarters, few facts were known about COSVN installations and units in the area. *Clandestine operations conducted in September of 1966 and during Operation ATTLEBORO in November had, however, developed significant intelligence on War Zone C.* [Emphasis added]

In discussing the genesis of Operation JUNCTION CITY, General Seaman, commanding general of II Field Force, Vietnam, stated:

'I've got to go back to Operation "Birmingham" which was conducted by the 1st Division in War Zone C, in May of 1966. It was conducted along the Cambodian Border as far north as Lo Go (about 30 kilometers northwest of Tay Ninh City) and the plan was to airlift a brigade into the then suspected location of COSVN headquarters. The 1st Division airlifted one battalion to the area, intending to get an entire brigade there within the day; but, unfortunately, the weather closed in and the rainy season started a couple of weeks earlier than anticipated. So, the decision was made by the division commander, MG DePuy, to withdraw that one battalion, feeling that he could not reinforce it if they got into any difficulty.

Following Operation "Birmingham," General Westmoreland said he wanted me to plan an operation in War Zone C to start as soon as possible after the Christmas and New Year's stand-downs of 1966-1967. He said, in effect, "to think big." This operation was to start about the 8th of January 1967, and would be a multi-division operation including an airborne drop. I (later) briefed General Westmoreland on the progress of our plans for "Junction City" and he approved my concept.'"

Excerpt from:
VIETNAM STUDIES
CEDAR FALLS-JUNCTION CITY:
A TURNING POINT
by
Lieutenant General Bernard William Rogers
DEPARTMENT OF THE ARMY WASHINGTON, D. C., 1989

CORRESPONDENCE

February 8, 1967

Dear Mr. President:

I am writing to you in the hope that the conflict in Vietnam can be brought to an end. That conflict has already taken a heavy toll in lives lost, in wounds inflicted, in property destroyed, and in simple human misery. If we fail to find a just and peaceful solution, history will judge us harshly.

Therefore, I believe that we both have a heavy obligation to seek earnestly the path to peace. It is in response to that obligation that I am writing directly to you. We have tried over the past several years, in a variety of ways and through a number of channels, to convey to you and your colleagues our desire to achieve a peaceful settlement. For whatever reasons, these efforts have not achieved any results.

In the past two weeks, I have noted public statements by representatives of your government suggesting that you would be prepared to enter into direct bilateral talks with representatives of the US Government, provided that we ceased "unconditionally" and permanently our bombing operations against your country and all military actions against it. In the last day, serious and responsible parties have assured us indirectly that this is in fact your proposal.

Let me frankly state that I see two great difficulties with this proposal. In view of your public position such action on our part would inevitably produce worldwide speculation that discussions were under way and would impair the privacy and secrecy of those discussions. Secondly, there would inevitably be grave concern on our part whether your government would make use of such action by us to improve its military position.

With these problems in mind, I am prepared to move even further towards an ending of hostilities than your Government has proposed in either public statements or through private diplomatic channels. I am prepared to order a cessation of bombing against your country and the stopping of further augmentation of US forces in South Viet-Nam as soon as I am assured that infiltration into South Viet-Nam by land and by sea has stopped. These acts of restraint on both sides would, I believe, make it possible for us to conduct serious and private discussions leading toward an early peace.

I make this proposal to you now with a specific sense of urgency arising from the imminent New Year holidays in Viet-Nam. If you are able to accept this proposal I see no reason why it could not take effect at the end of the New Year, or Tet, holidays. The proposal I have made would be greatly strengthened if your military authorities and those of the Government of South Viet-Nam could promptly negotiate an extension of the Tet truce.

As to the site of the bilateral discussions I propose, there are several possibilities. We could, for example, have our representatives meet in Moscow where contacts have already occurred. They could meet in some other country such as Burma. You may have other arrangements or sites in mind, and I would try to meet your suggestions.

The important thing is to end a conflict that has brought burdens to both our peoples, and above all to the people of South Viet-Nam. If you have any thoughts about the actions I propose, it would be most important that I receive them as soon as possible.

Sincerely,
Lyndon B. Johnson

February 15, 1967

Excellency, on February 10, 1967, I received your message. Here is my response.

Viet-Nam is situated thousands of miles from the United States. The Vietnamese people have never done any harm to the United States. But, contrary to the commitments made by its representative at the Geneva conference of 1954, the United States Government has constantly intervened in Viet-Nam, it has launched and intensified the war of aggression in South Viet-Nam for the purpose of prolonging the division of Viet-Nam and of transforming South Viet-Nam into an American neo-colony and an American military base. For more than two years now, the American Government, with its military aviation and its navy, has been waging war against the Democratic Republic of Viet-Nam, an independent and sovereign country.

The United States Government has committed war crimes, crimes against peace and against humanity. In South Viet-Nam a half-million American soldiers and soldiers from the satellite countries have resorted to the most inhumane arms and the most barbarous methods of warfare, such as napalm, chemicals, and poison gases in order to massacre our fellow countrymen, destroy the crops, and wipe out the villages. In North Viet-Nam thousands of American planes have rained down hundreds of thousands of tons of bombs, destroying cities, villages, mills, roads, bridges, dikes dams and even churches, pagodas, hospitals, and schools. In your message you appear to deplore the suffering and the destruction in Viet-Nam. Permit me to ask you: Who perpetrated these monstrous crimes? It was the American soldiers and the soldiers of the satellite countries. The United States Government is entirely responsible for the extremely grave situation in Viet-Nam.

The Vietnamese people deeply love independence, liberty, and peace. But in the face of the American aggression they have risen up as one man, without fearing the sacrifices and the privations. They are determined to continue their resistance until they have won real independence and liberty and true peace. Our just cause enjoys the approval and the powerful support of peoples throughout the world and of large segments of the American people.

The United States Government provoked the war of aggression in Viet-Nam. It must cease that aggression, it is the only road leading to the re-establishment of peace. The United States Government must halt definitively and unconditionally the bombings and all other acts of war against the Democratic Republic of Viet-Nam, withdraw from South Viet-Nam all American troops and all troops from the satellite countries recognize the National Front of the Liberation of South Viet-Nam and let the Vietnamese people settle their problems themselves. Such is the basic content of the four-point position of the Government of the Democratic Republic of Viet-Nam, such is the statement of the essential principles and essential arrangements of the Geneva agreements of 1954 on Viet-Nam. It is the basis for a correct political solution of the Vietnamese problem. In your message you suggested direct talks between the Democratic Republic of Viet-Nam and the United States. If the United States Government really wants talks, it must first halt unconditionally the bombings and all other acts of war against the Democratic Republic of Viet-Nam. It is only after the unconditional halting of the American bombings and of all other American acts of war against the Democratic Republic of Viet-Nam that the Democratic Republic of Viet-Nam and the United States could begin talks and discuss questions affecting the two parties.

The Vietnamese people will never give way to force, it will never accept conversation under the clear threat of bombs.

Our cause is absolutely just. It is desirable that the Government of the United States act in conformity to reason.

Sincerely,
Ho Chi Minh

———

Part 1

I

Someone was touching me in the dark. I felt a tired, but warm, hand on my shoulder; a calloused hand that was rough, but it didn't hurt my skin. I don't know who it was, but I wasn't afraid, no, I wasn't at all afraid. Somehow I knew – well, maybe 'sensed' is the better word for we are all sentient creatures, aren't we? – that everything would be alright. There was a familiar welcoming odor in the room, not unpleasant at all. It was an odor that triggered a fond memory. I really like that smell; it's the smell of comfort and love. The soothing aroma, like warm arms around me, seems to be coming from another room nearby, somewhere in this house, and I know that people are talking in there. They're telling stories, and I thought before they were folk tales. Who knows anymore? Who knows anything? But, they are talking. They're using words and sounds I've never heard before. What are those strange words?

Someone touched me again in the dark. Why is someone touching me through this long night? They touched my forehead, my cheeks, my lips, and stroked my long hair over my shoulders. They touched my eyes, but I kept them closed, but not from fear. I'm brave and haven't had to rely on fear for anything. I usually see images of strange things in the dark that could scare people, but they don't frighten me. There are still today the unusual dreams of mine, fantasies of flight that have been my companions for a long time. These nighttime imaginings sometimes trouble me, but I don't know how to figure them out. Someday, there will be an answer. Someday I'll find out who touched me.

II

The small, lithe, black-haired man sat in the old and broken wooden chair huddled against the cold, but it wasn't because of the September chill that he was shivering. He had some very personal reasons to be feeling the cold so intensely. The conscience of a man will have interesting effects on his person; chills, sweating, intestinal disorders, flatulence, quick, repeated cursory glances, and some men report suffering no ill-effects from the results of their ill-deeds. This man, though, shivered. His friend called out to him, "Brother, what is the matter with you? It's not that cold. Are you feeling alright, because if you're sick, you should go home or, better yet, go see the doctor at the hospital." He replied he was feeling alright, his jacket simply didn't have enough insulation for the sudden coolness this early autumn night. If he sat nearer the heater, perhaps he would be okay.

His positioning long ago among staff that evening wasn't by chance. Efforts had been arranged and directed years ago towards his high placement in a trusted position. That trust now provided information to him that needed to be relayed, to be divulged to the right party. The thoughts of his own ensured security began to warm him enough to subdue his trembling and shivering limbs, and he smiled, took his jacket off and tossed it aside to another antique, wooden chair adjacent to the tea pot, which rested on the well-worn table in the middle of the concrete-walled, black mold-encrusted room.

How his recent discovery, which he considered alarming, would be relayed to others was beyond what he was allowed to know, and he was satisfied that he wasn't privy to all the dimensions of the picture, which he played a small, but essential part. He was merely a small stroke of a brush in a much larger painting of a landscape. Elsewhere, he knew, there was another well-placed ally prepared to receive the message that needed to be delivered. After it went to his contact, he had no idea how it would travel, or where it would travel, and how it would be used. His only instructions were the guidelines given to him long ago over a hot cup of brewed tea in the chill of a winter afternoon over two years before by the old man, his thin beard trailing down his chest as he spoke.

"You have been placed here in a great position of trust," the older man told him a few years before, "and it is incumbent upon you to discern whether some information you hear may be critical to the cause. You alone have been chosen for this because you have shown to be a man from an honorable family and you have the trust of many others. In this, you cannot fail. You may deliver many goods, one good, or none at all. It is for you to decide."

Those were his simple instructions. He was simply to be trusted to use his own judgment. To use one's own discretion was the most difficult task of all, wasn't it? It's much easier if someone tells you exactly what they want, and then the other person can be responsible if some mishap occurs or something else goes wrong. But, how can anyone determine what is critical for another person without knowing the greater scheme? He would simply have to be aware of when, or if, the time arrived, as the old man whispered. When that did happen, his initiative and judgment would be recognized and he could live where there would not be a need to shiver anymore, for whatever reason. He simply needed to trust others to take care of him.

III

Six men sat quietly leaning back in leather backed chairs in pressed, expensive, Italian-tailored suits. The distinguished businessmen sat at the curved conference table made of dark, expensive hardwood quite possibly imported from Burma. Some men seemed a little ner⁊⁊. ⹂⹂d tapped their fingers on the table in anticipation, while some merely fidgeted and gripped the arms of the chairs as if they were about to experience their first chaotic ride at an amusement park, and for some it would be like that. Seldom were they ever summoned at a moment's notice. The dark, grained, leather chairs matched the table and the wood paneling blended with the table ensemble. This secluded room smelled of expensive wood. It was a very masculine room and testosterone clung to the walls of wood, mixed with the scents of aggression and deception. The men were identical in their dark suits, white shirts and conservative indigo ties, polished black shoes, and each sported a conservative haircut. Each of the men wore an expensive Rolex wristwatch partially hidden under folded French cuffs with diamond or emerald cufflinks. These were men who knew how to display their wealth in a befitting manner. They were hastily assembled at the last moment by their leader, one who exercised a natural dominance as the alpha male over each of them; that and the delicate information he possessed about each of their "proclivities for the exotic," as it would be called. Each man had been personally called and ordered to attend the meeting held at the lodge hidden deep in the forests of Connecticut. Mixed drinks were served by one person and one person only; the assistant to the principal of the group.

The men gathered after their arrivals at the regional airport and entered the limousines inside the security of a private hangar. Local flights had been diverted elsewhere by air traffic controllers who had orders to allow only seven specific private aircraft into the rural airport. The airport was effectively closed for over an hour to the dismay of local pilots, who had to divert to other airports and wait out the ground stop or keep flying around the sky simply poking holes in the clouds, as they liked to put it.

Security guards had already swept the house for listening devices and satisfied the premises were secure they retreated to their respective guard posts in and around the lodge built out of heavy, large logs from the forest.

Paranoia, whether real or imagined, was as loyal a companion to those invited men, as the dog was to a human. Each executive knew they didn't arrive at their status in life without having fears; the major fear being challenged and overtaken by someone else fighting their way to the top. They understood quite well the concept of being the alpha male within their own closed society and having to fight off any intruders into that territory. They would fight to the death to keep and maintain their status. They would betray family, if need be, and some of them had, to keep their status. Nothing would topple them. Nothing at all. They had no vulnerabilities, save their fear of loss of wealth, and more so the fear of losing power and control. Ruthlessness was the trademark for each and every one of them. It was a cold-blooded trait that bound them like brothers. Each of them had to trust the others, something that made them uncomfortable, but they had to live with that. The dominant male of the group who summoned them finally entered the room from a door that appeared concealed; it matched the wall paneling and the dark wood concealed the outline of the door. He also wore the attire of the elite. He spoke quietly, but with a grave sense of concern in his deep voice, something that caught the other men off guard, but none dared to look at the others while he spoke

"This could very well be troubling," the well-dressed man stated as he appeared to sweat in the cool, security protected room; it was also insulated from an unseasonable warm spell outside. The lodge where the men met was air-conditioned and sheltered from the sun, but he sweated nonetheless.

"I understand there may be hindrances that will affect us. There is word of non-productive and adverse information being transmitted by unconventional means and by an unconventional route. That delivery needs to be disrupted at all costs." He paused to let the meaning of his words be fully understood by the group convened for this one purpose. "Orders need to go out to terminate that transmission in whatever way possible." He then began to detail information he had learned and the serious consequences if the information was conveyed to its intended party.

After relaying his worries to the seated men, he turned to his personal aid and ordered, "Make the call and express my grave concerns to those who can affect such an order immediately."

He turned back to the quiet, gathered men once more, "I don't need to emphasize, gentlemen, this is a serious matter and I stress that it needs to be terminated by whatever means are necessary. I do not have to elaborate, do I? We all know what is at stake." Everyone nodded in assent.

The aid picked up the hard, black plastic handset of the dial-less telephone in the room and the connection was immediate. The handset was slippery from the aid's sweaty hand, and moisture from his perspiration adhered to the earpiece of the phone. He, too, knew the depth of their problem facing them, and even more so, the severe consequences if their deeds were discovered. A whispered and mostly muffled phone conversation ensued, lasting only a few moments. The men did not know who was at the other end. There were rumors, but no one dared speak them aloud. Even among this group, they abided by the long-standing rule of "on a need to know basis only." It was now that not only did they not need to know, they didn't want to know who was at the other end of that phone. One day, one of them may carry on the difficult and challenging undertaking of the group, but for now, not one member envied the position of the one who led them. Once the line disconnected, the young man confirmed that a remedy would be ordered immediately. "I'm to advise you that you will be apprised at every step," said the aid in an attempt to hide the slight twang in his voice. The aid was uncomfortable in his unique position; his black coat concealed the sweat soaking his shirt. Yet, the aid also knew he was experiencing an intense thrill for what he did. He felt the adrenaline coursing through his limbs. It felt like a rush from the drugs he took.

"Good." He turned to the men assembled, "You will only be given that information which you need to know. It is better that way." He wiped his brow in relief with an Italian silk handkerchief. There was no discussion counter to his intentions, not that he had expected any. The men understood quite completely the impending disaster they would endure if remedial measures were not taken. They could not suffer the risk. At the end of their meeting, the men retired to the dining room for a sumptuous meal of Argentinian steaks, Maine lobster and French champagne; silver candelabras accenting the dining table were unnecessarily lit for the occasion.

After enjoying the extravagant meal, they toasted each other's accomplishments in their respective, yet mutually beneficial, fields of expertise. Finally bidding each other good bye and hoping they would continue on their present courses, they were whisked away in their limousines back to the airport to board their planes for their respective flights home. Once again, a ground stop was ordered at the airport while the men departed under a moonless, black sky. Heavily-armed, roving security around the airport was recalled and the day's interruption was over.

IV

Hugh Campbell sat quietly at the old, dark and scarred wooden table; his hands folded and covering the indentations and scratches of interrogations past. The faded, green-tinged walls of the concrete room were cracked; cracked with age and v~ ikely cracked from the impact of human bodies. Many of the wall's fissures were shoulder height and some only waist high. A dark, brown-stained drain was set in the floor of the corner of the slightly sloping room when it was remodeled for its former use many years ago and it likely carried the memories of bloody wash-downs and cleanings. The lone, glassless, shuttered window in the room was open to let the air in and to let screams out that still echoed from the days of the old regime. The window's iron grate failed to keep the ghostly screams confined any longer. The ghastly shrieks, reminiscent of the old government, reverberated in the room and added to the deafening silence.

Hugh sweltered in the familiar, moist heat; sweat dripped from his armpits down the inside of his shirt and ran in rivulets on the inside of his arm to his elbows like downspouts of rain gutters. He waited for the questioner to arrive. Nobody ever departed a police building in Việt Nam without being questioned about something. Not even the heat or humidity ever left the buildings; not in Việt Nam, or anywhere else in Southeast Asia, they stick to the walls like a cold steak sticks to a hot frying pan.

The non-descript house looked like any other that were built by the Vietnamese for the French colonial upper-class a hundred years ago during their time in *Indochine,* or Indochina, if one preferred. This sad and tired building sat on a quiet alleyway in an old neighborhood just off Đường Nam Ký Khởi Nghĩa south of the wide, one-way boulevard, Đường Điện Biên Phủ in District One of Hồ Chí Minh City. It was like the other non-descript villas of the time; a faded, darkish, mustard yellow accented with black mold stains and the dirty discoloration from decades of heavy monsoons and neglect. The rust-red tiled roof was mostly intact, minus several tiles giving the roof a partially toothless grimace, mocking those who were severely questioned underneath in the past. The roof faded to a dull red and dark brown resembling the hue of a crab shell after cooking at a local restaurant. It was a shade of red completely devoid of life. The roof symbolized the former nature of this villa.

The chipped, plaster walls surrounding the villa were a dark, loquat color. The crown of the ten foot wall had glass and metal shards embedded in the concrete and fringed with sharp, rusty nails. To further discourage anyone of entry, or escape, there was a continuous, triple coil of razor-sharp concertina wire that stretched the entire length of the wall around the villa. The only quality of this villa that distinguished it from others in the silent neighborhood, besides the added protection on the wall's menacing decorations, was the contingent of uniformed police guards with automatic weapons at the ready. These police guards of the *Cảnh Sát* were the best trained. They were not only posted at the gateway, but they walked a patrol day and night, monsoon and glaring sun, around the inside and outside perimeter in their green uniforms and red-banded hats. Their guns were kept ready on automatic; never on safe.

Nobody dared possess a curiosity about the building, for to be inquisitive could lead to interrogation or worse. Vietnamese avoided the house at the end of the alley at all costs. Not even the street vendors selling fruits, vegetables and soups dared venture near the dwelling, nor did the recyclers or machine repairmen going through the neighborhoods plying their trades. The Vietnamese understood the tacit warning signs of the police and concrete quite clearly. Foreigners who didn't understand the cultural message and unwittingly stumbled into the alley out of curiosity and rumor were quickly stopped and their passports and visas heavily scrutinized; details of their mundane lives would be quickly jotted down and then they would be turned back, frightened for the moment, but with a thrilling story for friends and family when they returned to their home country. Some tourists were visited later at their hotels and "invited" to leave the country immediately, their visas quickly stamped "used" at the outbound immigration station of Tân Sơn Nhất Airport, north of town, which was the site of the large military airbase during the First and Second Indochina Wars. Future visa applications were customarily denied.

Accounts of the villa from the American war period that ended years before still persisted; tales of screams, of power declines and surges, of heavily guarded unmarked and unlicensed GMC Stepvans arriving and departing at odd hours driven by South Vietnamese and Americans alike in camouflaged uniforms – alike in so many ways and manners of interrogation and methods of gaining information from man or woman. It did not matter how. Information was the goal, it was the desired product and all that was needed, and human life, after all, was expendable during war. This particular villa was similar to another two dozen specially remodeled houses that were used around Saigon, the capitol city of the former Republic of Việt Nam; a city under siege by that regime and treated like a 'no-holds-barred' city by the Americans. This villa was kept as a reminder and as an enforcement mechanism for contemporary obstinate cases; murderers, drug smugglers, human traffickers or otherwise. Nobody even dared consider the "otherwise."

Hugh sat calmly keeping his thoughts subdued and showed no emotion as he tried to catch faint trace of air that would accidentally find its way through the grated window. Not even the wind wanted to venture inside; only the heat and the police were brave enough. The others were "invited."

A pea-green uniformed policeman appeared in the doorway. "Thank you for coming, Mr. Hugh. I am Inspector Nguyễn Văn Quỳ." Hugh saw the identification card hanging from button of the policeman's left breast shirt pocket revealing his name, rank and police employee number alongside the wreathed star of the Socialist Republic of Việt Nam in red and yellow. A round red imprint of an official government seal attested to the unquestioned validity and authority behind the card.

"I have only a few questions for you. I thank you for coming at my request," the young Inspector said with barely a trace of an Asian accent bleeding into his English.

"Your request, Inspector, was more like a demand. I still feel weak from my surgery and the stay in the hospital. Even though your policemen don't carry sidearms, it still felt more like an order than a request. You know, I remember hearing about this villa." Hugh felt no need to further embellish his statement about the house.

Inspector Quỳ, as he was known, kept his peculiar shade of pea green police uniform clean and neatly creased. In the oppressive Southeast Asian subtropical heat that makes everything sweat, even glasses of iced tea or coffee, Quỳ never sweated. Then again, the Vietnamese were used to the humidity and the climate, were they not? The inspector's jet black hair was closely trimmed, combed and neatly parted, and not a hair was out of place. He had apparently just returned from the outside because his forehead bore a horizontal mark, left by the sweatband of the policeman's hat, above his dark, almond-shaped eyes. He was average height for a Vietnamese, yet he carried his authority with dignity, which made him appear taller than he was. Quỳ's self-confidence was apparent, even when dealing with a foreigner. He remained standing while talking to the seated foreigner.

"Mr. Hugh, at times our requests have been refused by some foreigners and we wanted to ensure you would accept the gracious invitation to come and talk. We want to speak with you and you may certainly leave at any time. I trust you would like some tea and a cigarette?" Hugh wondered who the "we" were that he referenced. He let the question in his mind dissolve in the humidity.

"I'll have some tea with you, Inspector, but I no longer smoke. It became too much of a costly habit for me in the states and breathing became difficult. Thank you for the offer, but I must politely decline," Hugh replied in a typical Vietnamese manner so as not to sound as though he was refusing the kind offer outright. "Saving Face" meant everything in Asia.

"*Hai cốc trà nóng, em ơi,*" Quỳ said to the younger policeman standing outside the door in the airless hallway without turning his gaze away from Hugh, and within a moment two small, clear glasses and a tea pot in a red, silk-lined woven container arrived, neatly arranged on a bamboo tray. "You know my allegiance lies with my country, Mr. Hugh," addressing him in the traditional Vietnamese manner of using title with a first name. Hugh wondered about his careful choice of words. "But there are those in Hà Nội who wish to know more about the circumstances that, one might say, could be troubling if revealed, and may result in embarrassment of our country," Quỳ said with concern in his voice.

"I don't know what to say, Inspector. I am just as much in the dark as you and those in Hà Nội are. I came here only on a vacation, like so many other returning veterans of the war who want to have their souls and hearts cleansed from the sins of war. I want you to know, just as you wanted me to know, that young soldiers, airmen and sailors who served here in Việt Nam had not only a sense of duty and the requirement to follow orders, but there was also a commitment to their own homeland. I trust you can understand those sentiments, Inspector. I believe you have served in your country's military, haven't you?" Hugh noted the now dim black ink tracings of an amateur-drawn tattoo on Quỳ's forearm; a dragon alongside undecipherable Chinese characters.

"I am not the one to be questioned here, Mr. Hugh. We simply want to understand what has been happening. We only want an explanation for the strange incidences; incidences in our Tây Ninh Province that have been reported to us for which there are no explanations. Your friend who entered our country at Tân Sơn Nhất Airport with you has died under, what you would say in your own country, unusual circumstances. You, yourself, have been injured in a manner that is highly unusual for our peaceful country. You must owe a duty to your friend to help us determine who is responsible for these actions and bring those persons to justice."

What if there were people who can never be brought to justice, those who remain clean and innocent at a distance, Hugh pondered. What about those who, in the back rooms of their secret hiding places, conspire and develop their plots? Where was the justice for them? What was justice anyway; a death sentence, a prison term, parole or probation? Then again, all living beings are under a death sentence, even the innocent. And what about those whose entire careers emerged and rose from being adept at being so far removed from justice that they could not understand the idea of integrity and fairness, even vicariously?

"You must also know," Quỳ continued, "your friend's spirit won't rest here in a foreign land until we know the circumstances and can release the body to his family who will then want to return the remains to his homeland." Quỳ then quietly pulled out the old, scratched metal chair and sat without notepaper, which would not have been unusual in the horrible years past, and he simply looked at Hugh, almost with a look of compassion or understanding, Hugh thought.

"Have you notified his family yet? I am sure his father, who isn't in good health anymore, will want to see his son returned to him for a proper military burial at home."

Quỳ simply looked at Hugh and offered him a measured sigh of resignation with his offer of tea. "More tea?" he asked while raising the teapot.

"You haven't told the family yet or the Consulate, have you? You know you're supposed to notify them when a foreigner dies on your soil," Hugh reminded Quỳ.

"When we decide to call the proper authorities should not be a concern to you, although it may be conditioned on your talking to us, voluntarily, of course. Where should you begin, Mr. Hugh?" Quỳ stated more than asked. "Perhaps you could tell us what you know happened to your friend, Mr. Whitman Emerson. Or you could tell us about your familiarity with him. You were close friends weren't you?" Quỳ inquired.

"You could say that, Inspector, although friends may not be the appropriate word, but we could be considered friends because of a shared, unique experience so many years ago; something which so few men shared or dared talk about." Hugh then paused to collect his thoughts.

Before Quỳ arrived, Hugh had examined the room and could detect no wires or recording devices. Apparently, any conversation or information divulged would remain within the walls of the room and within the confines of their minds. Inspector Quỳ would have to share cursory details of the conversation with those who ordered him to do the questioning. This boyish-looking Inspector was the appropriate official to question the foreigner as he had been educated in the United States and understood quite well the native language and the idioms of his guest.

Hugh then spoke, "We trusted each other, so maybe confidants might be the better term than friend. You can tell secrets to a friend, but a confidant and a brother-in-arms is quite another person. No, Inspector, quite possibly we weren't best friends, after all, but we could never escape what we shared in the war.

"We met, as many did, during the initial buildup of President Johnson's war here. Like most other young men during that time, we were frightened and unsure of any future – maybe concerned is a better word. We met during Army Officer Candidate School at Fort Benning, Georgia. I can't go into detail about our jobs, as I trust you will understand, but they were unusual and unique. Whitman and I were selected for Special Forces training and assignments, and I would ask you respect my duty to my country, as I respect your duty."

"Yes, I can understand, Mr. Hugh. We are no longer enemies and we desire better trade with America. We are no longer interested in the work you may have done. We were at war with the Chinese for a thousand years and with the French for nearly one hundred years. America was our enemy for a much shorter time, so we forgive and we forget. But, if a crime has been committed in our country, we must make efforts to arrive at the truth and bring those to justice who are responsible."

"Inspector, your task may not be rewarded with positive results. In the world, I have discovered there is no justice; only the justice you find in the Buddhist beliefs in the gilded pagodas here in Việt Nam. Justice is only found in karma, Inspector."

"That may be so, Mr. Hugh. That may be so."

Inspector Quỳ sat facing Hugh with the confidence of an interrogator. "You know, Mr. Hugh, our government is quite concerned for your welfare because of events in Tây Ninh and would not want any further harm to come to you, given the sensitivity of the immediate situation. We are prepared to offer you better accommodations than what you presently have at the Continental Hotel. The Provincial Police have several private houses and we are happy to offer one of them to you during your stay. You are being invited by the Police to extend your stay here in our country. We will, of course, be arranging to have your suitcases removed to a house we think will be suitable for you. We have already brought your suitcases from the Anh Đào Hotel in Tây Ninh. In fact, we do not believe that you would want to decline our kind offer and have already transferred your belongings to a suitable house. I believe that you will accept our gracious invitation?"

"Inspector, it looks as though there is no choice in the matter, is there?"

"Mr. Hugh, you have a choice. I believe you have mentioned to others your great fondness for our country and I believe that this offer is, as Americans are fond to say, 'to your liking'."

"Inspector, I believe you are quite aware of my deep feelings and regard for Việt Nam and her people and they have been quite apparent, as you know. If you wish for me to remain indefinitely while you investigate, I will be honored to accept your invitation to stay. Quite frankly Inspector, there isn't much for me to return to in the States. I will be most pleased to accept your offer and I thank the government of the Socialist Republic of Việt Nam for the invitation and these generous arrangements. Perhaps with some rest, I can be of assistance, but for now, it is difficult for me, as you know. I am still recovering from my wounds and there are clouds in my mind that cover certain things."

The Inspector looked at Hugh. He was aware that he had some troubling times and difficulties with parts of his memory.

"Yes, Mr. Hugh, we know," Quỳ said. Perhaps the American was sincere about what he had related to him. "Mr. Hugh, we understand and we are prepared to wait. As you are staying in one of our safe locations, you will be allowed the freedom to travel around Hồ Chí Minh City, but you will also be aware that you will be escorted at a distance so as not to cause embarrassment to you, you understand. We want you to feel that you are a guest of the Police while you are helping us with this mysterious investigation. You may take any form of transportation that suits you. Do not be concerned about attempting to accommodate our needs. We have sufficient means to ensure your safety while in our care."

Hugh listened carefully to what Inspector Quỳ had to say and knew he meant that he could move freely around the city, but would be followed and watched at all times. Then again, Hugh thought, it wouldn't be an altogether uncomfortable arrangement. It would, in fact, be quite nice to be able to have the ability to move about the city and not feel the pressure of unwanted solicitations from taxi drivers, motorbike drivers, con artists, pimps, beggars, money changers and street children hawking everything from postcards to photocopied tour books selling at one-half or more off the copyright's original price. Hugh needn't worry about the pickpockets either. He welcomed the distant company to his movements.

Hugh glanced across the scarred table at Inspector Quỳ's wristwatch and saw it was already getting very late. The policeman wore an expensive Japanese watch, not one of those counterfeit knock-offs one usually finds in the over-priced tourist areas surrounding the Bến Thành Market or around the Phạm Ngũ Lão backpacker district. He was tired and wanted to lie down. In the past four days he had gone nowhere, but still he needed rest.

After Whitman's death – the incident that was the focus of Inspector Quỳ's interest – Hugh was taken immediately to Bệnh viện Đa Khoa Tây Ninh, the general hospital for the city and province of rural Tây Ninh, a hundred kilometers northwest of Hồ Chí Minh City. The open bay emergency room of the two-story hospital was more than adequate and prepared for handling emergencies such as Hugh's. Several of the experienced doctors on staff were young interns during the waning days of the American war and had seen enough traumas to know what to do when this large American came to them with a severe knife wound. His treatment at the hospital was more than adequate to save him from joining his partner in death and he was later transferred to the Franco-

Vietnamese Hospital in Hồ Chí Minh City's developing and affluent District Seven. It wasn't enough, though, for another patient.

The masked and white-hatted nurses punctured Hugh's skin with a needle and began to drip an intravenous solution with medicine into Hugh's veins in their attempt to wrest him away from death's reach. Barely conscious enough to watch the ceiling fan, he couldn't hear the diminishing, chortling breaths of the forty-five year old man dying in the bed nearest him, but he could hear his three young daughters. They pleaded for his life and were crying out in their native Vietnamese tongue. In the midnight sub-tropical heat even tears dry quickly. The dying man and his daughters had traveled earlier in the day to Việt Nam from their small village in Cambodia where they had a small farm near the border. They entered Việt Nam at the non-international border station at Xã Mát on Highway 22b used exclusively by Vietnamese and Cambodians; third country foreigners are chased away. They had come across the border to attend a festival in Tây Ninh. After the day's festivities and while he and his friends were drinking some *bia hôi*, a cheap lager brewed daily, he suffered a massive brain hemorrhage owing to his untreated, high blood pressure. The daughters pleaded desperately for their father to live and begged the doctors with as much passion to operate, or transfer him to another hospital in Hồ Chí Minh City where there could be a chance of survival. The doctors, with as much compassion as they could muster, explained to the grieving young country girls, still dressed in their peasant dress and headscarves, there was absolutely nothing at all they could do, except allow their father to die peacefully and painlessly there in the emergency room in the company of family and strangers, alike. In a country where there is nothing but hope for the future, at times there is also nothing but despair in the present.

Hugh had no one to cry for him. The one he loved was a specter in his dreams. If she were real, would she cry? If she were flesh, would she be there to hold his hand? He hoped she would.

"One further item, Mr. Hugh," Quỳ said, interrupting Hugh's thoughts. "I am directly aware that there is someone you seek from your dreams." Hugh, usually reserved, looked at Quỳ with a slight surprise, but kept his amazement as tepid as the heat and with about as much enthusiasm. "The police in Việt Nam know many things. We are not at all like the traffic police who stand at intersections and crossroads smoking cigarettes and watching traffic all day and we are very much unlike the parking wardens who seize motorbikes from sidewalks. We are a very efficient apparatus and we prefer to maintain a quiet nature about it, but we do know things."

Hugh knew he had talked while heavily medicated with pain-killing drugs, which made his delirious words flow smoothly, and now he wondered how much had been said about the pain of his blurred memories that could not be killed. Apparently not too much, or Inspector Quỳ wouldn't be asking questions about the incident in Tây Ninh Province or about Whitman. That much he knew, but his personal dreams, those were another matter. Had Quỳ, or his agents, been able to glean information from his ramblings and mutterings in the night and in the dusk of his drugged mind? Had the Inspector been able to learn that he is haunted by the same girl in the same dream every night and its usual conclusion in a sweat when she vanishes and he awakes? Hugh wondered these things and many other thoughts while he sorted out the information in his mind, like rustling through old files and folders in a vain attempt to organize one's household. Inspector Quỳ said nothing and was willing to let Hugh take his time. Silence was a currency in Asia and many were rich with it. Finally, Hugh said, "Inspector, you are quite adept at reading people, especially people from the West. Yes, there is something, and if you yourself have information, I would be grateful for your assistance," he said hopelessly.

"That, Mr. Hugh, can be up to you. Yes, it is up to you. We need to know about what happened in Tây Ninh Province. Perhaps as an incentive to each other, we can share some small bits of information with each other, no?" Inspector Quỳ inquired more than stated.

"I believe we can, Inspector."

V

Hugh met Whitman Emerson in early 1965, in the same way most young men strangers to each other met – they were thrown together into a forged-steel pot, brought to a quick boil and poured out into the uniformity of military parade grounds and barracks. America's involvement in Vietnam was beginning to build; it was a small country virtually unknown to many people. President Johnson's Gulf of Tonkin Resolution and Secretary of Defense Robert MacNamara saw to it that America would inject itself like heroin and become an addiction to those who handled the affairs of Southeast Asia. Many Army volunteers were young, eager, and very willing for a new adventure. Whitman and Hugh chanced to be assigned to the same Army Officer Candidate School at Fort Benning, Georgia. Whitman was well educated because of his good fortune of birth in a decent New England family. He had self-confidence, quite well earned, yet he possessed a dangerous vulnerability one couldn't define. Whitman's parents had named him after one of the great poets of America. There were other male relatives named after their very distant relative, Ralph Waldo Emerson, and they wanted to spare him an eponymous burden, thus they christened him Whitman. His parents had an affinity for early American poets.

Whitman was of medium height, fairly good looking with short, cropped blonde hair and he was in top physical condition, which caught the attention of recruiters for Special

Forces, besides the young girls with beehive boufants at his former university. His family connection in the Army had an influence in this choice assignment. His intelligence was measured above average by the Army. Being an only child, unlike Hugh thrown into the midst of six other children, Whitman had an unwavering streak of patriotism bordering on fervent jingoism. It was due in great part to his father, a career Army commissioned officer.

Hugh's own father served in the Marine Corps aviation unit as a corporal during the "Great World War." He raised Hugh with a sense of patriotism, but that patriotism imbued upon him developed into an enthusiasm tempered with judgment and the tendency to quietly question authority, when appropriate. In Army OCS, there was no questioning, though. In the Army there was no interest in the legality of orders. One only had to remember the incidents in My Son District where over five hundred civilians were massacred by US Army soldiers. The hamlet of Mỹ Lai bore that brunt of America's brutal savagery for a perverted democracy's sake. One obeyed commands or one died on the battle field, as soldiers were so often told, but where were the battlefields in Việt Nam? Certainly not in Mỹ Lai Hamlet, nor in that ditch that bore the massacred. One may never know the reasons for certain decisions, but as young soldiers, they were trained to accept missions that would be assigned seemingly without any rationale, just as individual dreams do not reveal in themselves their own pattern, except when pieced together over the course of time like an elaborate jigsaw puzzle – but follow orders they must. Such orders from the general ranks and above when trickled down the ranks would seem to the ordinary soldier isolated acts or incidences without rhyme or reason in the same vain a tree falling on a house during a storm is considered an "act of God." For those who have faith in the plans of an eternal deity, and Hugh certainly didn't and could never find a rationale for this myth, the Army and its deified leaders had a design for each mission. Whatever act of omission or commission attendant to any incident or mission, any aberration of moral behavior there may be, where were people who had the knowledge of the grander scope of battle plans and strategies during hostilities. These deities wore uniforms, insignias and had the medals to prove their sacred status. They alone saw the grander design from their pentagonal temple in the holy city.

From the time Hugh first met Whitman, Hugh saw that he read a lot. Most of his readings were military history because his family had a rich military background that was recounted in some history books documenting America's colonial days. Whitman's father, an active Army colonel, had distinguished himself during World War II and the Korean conflict and had served in the beginning days of the Việt Nam War as an advisor during Diệm's early and unfortunate days as President of the Republic of Việt Nam. Whitman came from a trustworthy family and several generations of loyalty guaranteed to help his career. Colonel Emerson had stalled becoming an officer and instead rose through the ranks as an enlisted man first. He had wanted Whitman to go through the enlisted ranks first, but retreated from his position because of the build up in Việt Nam and urged his son to attend OCS should the chance arise. Of course, it was later learned that a few properly placed phone calls brought Whitman to the attention of the Special Forces.

"Whitman, what are you reading now?" Hugh asked, lying on the top bunk in the open bay of the OCS barracks at Fort Benning, located just outside of "Sin City."

"I'm reading about Patton, the commanding general of the 3rd Army in Europe during the ending days of World War II. You know, he had this phrase, 'Don't tell people how to do things. Tell them what to do and let them surprise you with their ingenuity.' He was a hell of a commanding officer." Hugh recognized that Whitman was just as motivated by war and leadership as George Smith Patton, Jr. had been. Patton had a pedigree that included patriots in noble wars. Whitman had a similar derivation.

Yet, for all his motivation, Whitman was a quiet, thoughtful individual on the surface. He was nurtured in the shadow of an overbearing, career military father. However introspective he may have appeared, it concealed a terrifying lack of patience. Whitman wanted his commission as a second lieutenant immediately. If Whitman were an inanimate object, he could have been a precariously packed string of Chinese firecrackers, like the ones children used to set off in the days long before laws protecting people, in addition to their fingers and hands, came into being. There was one thing Hugh learned about Whitman and that was that his gunpowder would ignite with barely a spark. He was the unwatched kettle that boils over; a mixture of baking soda and vinegar in a student's elementary grade school science experiment spewing putrid foam out of a home-made volcano constructed of *papier-mâché* and chicken wire.

There was the incident following an endurance run during the early days of OCS. They had been a mere three weeks into officer training and Otis Rucker, a tall, quiet, but agonizingly slow boy from Palestine, Texas, had been holding the platoon back because of his lumbering gait. With all them looking the same in their green camouflaged fatigues and bare heads, the only trait that distinguished Rucker as an individual was his ability to be more viscous in the fluidity of his running than the rest of the company. Even his speech was slow. When asked where he hailed from, he would answer at a snail's pace, "Pal-uh-steeen-Tay-ksas," in his painfully slow drawl, and the other platoon members questioned how he had managed to enter OCS in the beginning. The tactical instructors reminded them about "encouraging" each other, even in the officer corps. Military encouragement, which many people didn't know, was the codeword for negative reinforcement of your fellow soldier after lights out. A discreet time of night, solid bars of soap and tins of black, Kiwi shoe wax in pillow cases and socks, and closed fists were the unwritten and unspoken encouragement given to one who needed to be taught a lesson – to be *motivated*. The night of the run, while some of his fellow OCS cadets were "encouraging" Rucker to speed up in the future, Whitman exploded, to the surprise of the others, and began beating the already dazed Rucker senselessly with his own black wool sock filled with soap bars; thuds of rock-hard soap struck against bone and flesh, and echoed off polished wood floors and walls. Whitman used all his energy to whip that sock around like a bolo gaining energy before launching towards its prey on the run and Whitman was ready to bring Rucker down like an animal. Maybe, that was what Whitman was thinking.

The platoon's tactical instructor, an old, weather-beaten staff sergeant, who had already survived his own military miseries during the Korean conflict and was nearing retirement, was rousted from a deep sleep by some more sensible officer cadets in the barracks. He didn't like being awakened, especially for something he didn't specifically authorize his recruits to do and certainly for something he didn't want to know about simply because ignorance can be an ally in the Army – "plausible denial," as it was called. A Jeep was quickly summoned and Rucker was taken to the infirmary. He never returned. The next day, two tactical instructors from another platoon came and packed Rucker's personal belongings and nothing of Rucker was ever mentioned again.

The platoon's tactical instructor met with Whitman, the first sergeant, and the company commander immediately following the beating. After that hushed meeting behind closed doors of the captain's office, there was nothing else of the matter of Rucker, the poor, slow boy from Palestine, Texas. It was as though he had faded into the rear view mirror of their collective memories and the incident never existed for anyone anymore, except in the quiet, hushed conversations and rumors in the latrine. They learned that just about anything in the Army can be whispered away, replaced with other truthful fictions, or eventually forgotten. Whitman kept his temper in check for the rest of his training, but one could see the anger festering behind his dark blue eyes.

The subdued, explosive temper that inhabited Whitman kept him motivated to complete OCS and goaded him during Special Forces training at Fort Bragg. Hugh recalled the motto of the Special Forces: "*De Opresso Liber*," – To free the oppressed. Whitman could never free himself of the oppression of his own rage.

There was nothing anyone could do to quell that rage in him. Whitman learned to take his anger out on inanimate objects. During bayonet practice he passionately jabbed the dummies, clad in black pajamas, with slanted eyes painted on the canvas faces, and conical hats, and he excelled at martial arts, which caused many compatriots wishing they had another partner to work with than Whitman. His anger took up residence in him like an unwanted house guest who had overstayed his welcome and the host wasn't sure how to expel him. That was Whitman's anger. That was his vulnerability. That was the ghost in his house. The anger and his father, the colonel, are what defined Whitman. He lived for his father and lived with his festering anger. He envied his father's military awards, which were proudly worn at every opportunity. Whitman enjoyed having his father tell him about each and every award and how they were earned. He lusted after the rainbow of colors and patterns of the ribbons and the badges on his father's uniform. Whitman was pleased the day he was told he was eligible to wear the predominantly red and yellow National Defense Ribbon and the expert marksmanship badge and eventually the gold bar of the rank of second lieutenant on his collars along with the crossed rifles that symbolized the Infantry Branch of the Army. But then, he could hardly wait to replace the crossed rifles with the crossed arrows that emblemized the Special Forces. They were short-haired, clean shaven young men wearing green uniforms. They were uniform. They resembled each other. They were almost like brothers, but not quite.

Whitman and Hugh ended up becoming closer as confidants than most others, he explained to Quỳ. They spent a period of time at the Defense Language Institute in Monterey, California, learning the northern and the southern dialects of the melodic Vietnamese language. One night, Whitman's companion-like anger returned for a long-overdue visit. Whitman seemed to be settling down but his quelled fury was slowly settling like flocculence in an undisturbed, home-made bottle of beer. The intensity of learning a foreign language that bore no resemblance to any Romance Language, however, swirled his anger up to the surface like squid drawn from the South China Sea by the fluorescent lights of fishing boats. That distant early spring evening of 1966 saw the Pacific Ocean bring a bone-chilling fog onto land that couldn't cool Whitman's emotional fires. That fog alone silently witnessed Hugh having to pull Whitman away from seriously injuring a local fisherman outside an Embarcadero bar before the patrons had a chance to call the police to save their friend and neighbor. Hugh's back was turned when Whitman attacked the fisherman, and it took all his training to get the fiery lieutenant out of that alley and to escape their pursuers. Isn't that what friends are for? Like Rucker, they never knew what happened to that fisherman. They didn't want to know. After language training, they were assigned several operations together in Europe and Central America before heading to Việt Nam.

They arrived in Việt Nam in late September of 1966 and stepped off the Boeing 707 at Tân Sơn Nhứt Airbase, as the airport was named during the war, and walked down the portable stairs into the heat. Tân Sơn Nhứt was located in the Gia Định area north of Saigon proper. The first assault of the war on them was a humid blast of hot air. The heat and the humidity became unforgettable and it was their first impression of Việt Nam. There was also a certain smell and a distinct scent to the country's air. The briquette fires of small kitchens and the steamy fogs of soup sold on the sidewalks swirled into the air mixing with the odors of urine, motorcycle exhausts, jet fuel, open latrine ditches, women's perfumes and cordite. They couldn't stop the sweat pouring off their skin when they arrived and Hugh couldn't stop Việt Nam from getting beneath his skin. Việt Nam pierced deep into Hugh's heart more intensely than any armor-piercing shell could ever do to a thick-skinned armored tank on the battlefield or an armored personnel carrier in the forest. The country had already passed midway through the wet season and the temperatures were still incessantly in the low to mid nineties Fahrenheit during the day and the low eighties during the night. After claiming their duffle bags the Special Forces lieutenants were escorted by two brutish and young looking Military Policemen and taken to the palm frond-framed base operations opposite the airport terminal where a Jeep was waiting for them. The driver explained he was detailed to take them to Personnel at MACV, the Army's Military Assistance Command, Việt Nam, for preliminary, in-country processing. They were provided special tropical camouflage uniforms, personal weapons and given immunizations to protect them against hepatitis and a host of other exotic tropical diseases. They were cautioned about syphilis and gonorrhea; sexual diseases that clung to the genitals and clung voraciously around the borders of military bases worldwide. After orientation, they met with Colonel Davidson who was assigned to the MACV-Studies and Observation Group, a highly classified organization and cover for Special Forces clandestine activities in Việt Nam. The commander had come from his air headquarters in Nha Trang solely to meet them. He explained to the young lieutenants they were under his command for administrative purposes only while they were in-country. The two lieutenants didn't know the impact their arrival had on commanders within MACV-SOG. Whitman and Hugh were low-level company grade officers, for all they knew and cared.

The colonel was a tall, lanky, handsome man from Florida who wore starched fatigues and never showed the telltale salt stains on his uniforms. He seemed impervious to the heat, like the Vietnamese themselves, and he never sweated. After a brief classified interview and briefing, the lieutenants were sent back to the driver and taken to an area of town that most civilians preferred not to go. That area of town had become the seedy part of the military buildup, where most of the camp followers gathered. Criminals, drug dealers, thieves on motorbikes – also called "cowboys" – prostitutes and pimps congregated in this area, because that was where the servicemen were. It was where they spent their money on the temporary means of escaping the war with booze, grass and women to blot out reality. That is where the Army decided to house Whitman and Hugh temporarily while it tried to get plans coordinated for an operation.

They were given separate non-descript rooms at the Montana, a hastily fortified Bachelor Enlisted Quarters on Nguyễn Văn Thoại Street, known affectionately as "Plantation Road," or even shorter yet, "P Road." They didn't know why they were housed with the enlisted men because they were newly promoted "First Lieutenants," but they knew never to question something so simple.

This area slightly northwest of downtown Saigon proper is where the enlisted soldiers, airmen and sailors assigned to nearby installations spent their days and evenings escaping the war. Some escaped for entire days along that sometimes brutal street of rough macadam pavement edged with dirt and shoulders lined with *mama-sans* selling marijuana cigarettes in factory-wrapped Winston and Marlboro packs. That street saw action like the Wild West back in America. That's where anyone could find bars aplenty playing the music defining that era; the rock and roll of the The Beatles, Rolling Stones, The Doors, Jimi Hendrix and with the Boxtops and Otis Redding thrown in for good measure along with many others. The petite Vietnamese bar girls were always waiting for some young soldier to buy them a drink. That's how one could find a young, slender, black-haired Vietnamese girl to keep their minds distracted from the war. It seemed as though these beautiful Vietnamese girls, mostly poor ones from the countryside, could say *"I love you beaucoup"* smack in the middle of all the hate and almost mean it. She could bring a promise of rest amidst the violence and a sense of life and creation apart from the death and destruction. She would be one whom a young man could share moments, for a price, of course, and she would passively offer her delicate body to satisfy the sexual needs of young men while frustration flourished in field and headquarters.

When a foreign soldier walked into a bar on P Road or anywhere else, the young girls, some aged by the war, and as young as 16 years and ofttimes less, would set upon the unsuspecting young man as he entered and would ask him to buy them a tea. That's how they earned their money with *"mama-san,"* the owner of the bar. *"Mama-san"* wasn't in the Vietnamese language, but the GIs who had spent time in Japan or Korea, brought the term with them and it was immediately adopted by the locals.

P Road was also home to the "cowboys;" young boys who rode tandem on Honda 50cc motorcycles and preyed on unsuspecting, foreign soldiers by stealing their watches, cameras and anything else they thought could have value. Hugh thought it peculiar, thinking back, how human life in war had no value, but a camera, watch or sunglasses could bring money to someone on the same street where lives were being summarily taken.

Street assassinations, Buddhist monk self-immolations, other acts of war and wholesale murder under the auspices of war became commonplace. Interrogation centers in Saigon were, in truth, torture prisons and were situated in about two dozen reconditioned French villas. They were operated first by the French, then by the Southern Vietnamese government with assistance from the Americans. Yet, tangible personal articles carried more value than life. Out on P Road, one could see Navy, Air Force, Army, Marines and even Australians drinking and carousing together. The women were something different, though. The men only saw the hookers; the girls who gathered around military bases around the world for as long as there have been occupation armies. Yet, in Việt Nam the women were quite different. Those girls were provocative, alluring, demure and passive. Their long, straight, black tresses were usually pulled tight at the back of their head into pony tails, or chicken tails as they were sometimes called, or the glistening hair was allowed to hang straight over their soft backs like shimmering black waterfalls in the moonlight. Their eyes were dark, penetrating, exotic and almond-shaped; eyes that were very striking and erotic. For Hugh, it was the eyes that attracted his attention. Some of the GIs he knew would appraise a woman by legs, breast or buttocks, but for the young lieutenant, it was their eyes. They expressed innocence even if they had committed the vilest crime; one could look into their eyes and thus be convinced of their virtue.

Some young girls retained the evidence of France's occupation in their blood, many of whom were born before and immediately after the French withdrawal in 1954. One could not imagine the ache reaching to the roots of a young pregnant Vietnamese girl's heart when she discovered her future destroyed and lost when she realized her French boyfriend has departed Việt Nam with the promise of his return; an unkept promise. She could not escape the pain of being left behind like a gift after the novelty has worn away and replaced with something newer; his return to France, and quite possibly to wife and family. One could only imagine the tears welling up behind the dam of the epicanthal folds, the delicate extensions of skin that gently melds into the inner corners of their mysterious eyes from the soft, low slant of the bridge of the nose. Those young Eurasian girls who carried the blood of Europeans in their veins were gorgeous. Many earned their pay in legitimate ways working for the government, private contractors or the allied military, and would never allow themselves to be tainted by the sexual activities of the common soldier or commissioned officer, for that matter. That was what their mothers had taught them. Many GIs, whether married in the States or not, would beg and sometimes fight like competing dogs to be with a Eurasian girl. They were willing to spend any amount of MPC, the military payment certificates used by servicemen as currency in those days. Some would smuggle US greenback dollars into the country – double the value of MPC – for the opportunity to show a girl they could provide for family and home, even if it was illegal. Other girls, mostly the illiterate from the countryside and lacking hope of a better life during war, needed to resort to using their beauty and their bodies to earn money. It was they who sometimes bore the burden of the American-backed regime's tendency to harass portions of South Vietnamese society; it was they who had to pay the bribes to keep working and surviving.

At the Montana Hotel on P Road, Whitman and Hugh survived, waited and trained. At night, using cover of darkness before and after the town's eleven o'clock curfew at the time because it usually fluctuated, they used unsuspecting Vietnamese as training equipment to keep their skills sharp; it was either that or drink while they waited. They didn't want to get weaker and as they learned later, it didn't matter. As Special Forces officers, they needed to keep the edges honed.

Everything in Saigon during the war was cheap; the booze, cigarettes, civilians and the women. The heat, humidity and frustration were free. For a mere few dollars, one could get anything they wanted in Saigon. At Hugh's suggestion and Whitman's reluctance, they visited an old lady street vendor who sold cellophane-wrapped and sealed Winston or Marlboro packages of cigarettes that actually contained twenty rolled marijuana cigarettes. The pack was only five-hundred piasters; the equivalent of about five US dollars in MPC scrip, and dispensed from the woman's secret compartment. The occasional marijuana cigarette smuggled in from across the border, and conveniently called "Cambodian Red," helped ease the pain of separation and the heat, and the young, exotic girls helped soothe the frustration and sexual tension that built their fires in the bodies of young men. And they waited; waited for a mission. Hugh thought they should have been careful because some wishes came with a heavy price.

VI

Hugh saw her in his dream again. He sees her every night. Her mollusk hat conceals most of her face in the darkness and her black pajamas conceal her lissom, slender body. The young woman's black and white checkered scarf is pulled up to cover her mouth and nose and he can only see her narrow eyes in the thin veil of light of the waning crescent moon reflected in the water of the paddy. It's her eyes that steal him away every night and keeps him captive in the dark. He sees her narrow, black eyes and the smooth skin on the inside of her eyes as it dips towards her nose and he once again becomes her prisoner. He slowly takes her in his arms and begins to unbutton her pajama's top. Softly, he touches her small breast, feeling for the dark brown nipple already erect under his touch and with his other hand he raises the woven scarf to kiss her. He suddenly wakes up in a profuse sweat and tries to get back to sleep. He wants to get past that moment to see her face, to see who she is. He knows her, but he simply cannot remember who she is or where it was. Something is blocking the memory like a locked iron gate for which there is no key.

Perhaps, he thinks, the far too many intervening years spent in the States wishing that he were back in Việt Nam has oxidized the locking mechanism and has rusted the gate shut. Maybe it was the many faces of nameless women who had meant something at one time, but then their love also faded like colors bleached in the sunlight. Maybe it was simply his imagination and his wishful thinking, a creation of his active mind; an apparition he only sees as a fantasy Vietnamese girl that comes to haunt him every night.

At the house belonging to the Special Investigative Police, Hugh slowly rose up from the bed, sheets sopping wet from his perspiration, and he turned the old black plastic knob on the floor fan in his room and focused its air current on the bed where he lay back down. The cooling breeze across his wet chest began to chill him and he finally started to relax and again closed his eyes. At the small pagoda nearby, the Buddhist nuns were beginning their morning prayers and chanting and he knew it is 4:00 in the morning without looking at the clock. The soft reverberation of the bell effused softly throughout the tightly housed neighborhood, streets and alleys like a large labyrinth twisting this way and that and the pagoda chimed and gonged in a measured rhythm, never having any edges to vibrations as they filtered through the sieve of home and street, and the tones simply "became." He barely heard the chanting; the softened whispers to the Buddha from the bare-headed *Ni Côs* – the nuns in grey tunics and their left shoulders covered with golden robes. Their shaved heads glistened and reflected the colored aural lights backlighting the huge image of their Blessed One, their Supremely Enlightened One, and their Wholly Perfected One, as he sits in perpetual ecstasy. 'If only I could find that peace,' he whispered to himself while staring at the ceiling's shadows. Lying in the dark on the firm bed, he tried to distract himself and imagined himself inside the pagoda kneeling before the three meter tall Buddha sitting in eternal contemplation on his pink, scarlet, and golden lotus throne.

He imagined the electrical lights mounted on the yellowing, aged wall flashing in arrays giving the impression of a lighted radiance emanating from Buddha's head when he attained Enlightenment, reminding devotees of the supreme sacrifice he made for all humanity, as the Buddhist's canonical literature relate.

The electric fan cooled his body finally, but his thoughts remained warm and they returned to the slender girl who keeps emerging from the paddy like a beautiful lotus growing from the underwater muck to send its beautiful, multi-petaled, pink bloom skyward. Even during waking hours, his thoughts always return to the girl. He has tried to remember who she is, but those memories are blocked. Specialists in the States tried to help him, but each and all failed. Doctors repeatedly told Hugh about representational imagery of dreams, but he thought the opinions of others were worthless. He knows her – she is real, he asserts. He simply cannot remember who she is. Sleep deprivation, street drugs, medications, therapy; he tried them all. None of them could keep the dream away or, at best, reveal her real identity. He closed his eyes and listened to the soft gong of the large, decorated, brass bell that wafted between the houses and alley ways. Each deep tone was struck by the bare-pated female bonze punctuating the end of a stanza of Buddhist prayer, and she bowed each time she thrusted the tethered wooden, cloth-tipped striker against the outside of the bell to produce the haunting tone. Each prayer asking forgiveness, asking for compassion, asking for happiness and a release from suffering for all beings. How could Hugh find release from his suffering? Hugh discovered Buddhism and found more solace in those ancient teachings; more solace than he ever found among the teachings of western professionals, practitioners, Christian religions and other hucksters and quasi-religious snake oil salesmen. Hugh surrendered his Christianity years ago when he realized the west used religion to suit political purposes. All those people attending churches, he believed, were being used as pawns by the obscene political parties, and the priests, ministers and pastors, alike, were unwitting pawns of political parties. Hugh believed Members of Congress were nothing more than pimps supplying the electorates for major business. He had more respect for the prostitutes of wartime Saigon than he had for the clergy. The clerics were, for the most part, procurers of bodies for a corrupt American political machine. So, Hugh turned to the teachings and wisdom of Eastern Asia. He realized all the healing techniques of therapy and drugs of the west could not match the tranquility he had found in Asian philosophy, but then again, Asian teachings could not help reveal her face or her name. Those teachings could calm him and he could trace his mind near to the root of the desire to find her. He knew she was real though others believed her to be a figment.

Hugh drifted back slowly to the gentle cusp that exists between waking and sleeping. There rests the tenuous region of the mind where some drugs do their best work – providing a person just enough reality while giving them enough enjoyment or suffering in the fantasy of the unconscious mind. In that region where one is neither asleep nor awake, but floating in that nether region of the mind, he saw her palm-woven conical hat again as she rose from the paddy in the dark of night. He froze the image to look at her eyes again. In the dream, she peers at him from above her scarf pulled tightly over her mouth and nose. Her dark eyes peering from behind her almond-slit eyelids. From this level of consciousness, he could direct his attention to her eyes, then on to her long, black, silky hair, pulled together at the back of her soft neck. He pulls her pony tail from around her neck and strokes and caresses the black strands, never wanting to let her go.

Suddenly, the image is shattered by bone and blood splattering over his face. Thick ooze covers her eyes, blotting them out forever. She becomes limp and lifeless and slumps in his arms, still wet from the paddy and from the blood. He cannot remain at this level anymore and once again wakes up in a sweat although the pouring rain outside sends its coolness inside and the fan stirs it like the dream stirs the fire of his imagination.

The old woman wore her mollusk hat tied firmly around her chin with a length of red ribbon and she grasped the straw and grass broom in hand. With her other hand, she opened the black, iron gate, which substituted for the front door of her mold-encrusted home. She at once saw him sitting on the short, wooden stool at the corner market that regularly served as an outdoor café and gossip center for the local men. Laborers, technicians, even *Việt Kiều* – the returning Vietnamese who fled years before for one reason or another – would come to sit and chat, drink tea or coffee, smoke a cigarette and then wander off to callings elsewhere, or they would sometimes stay and indulge in several animated games of Chinese chess. In this neighborhood, foreigners are seldom seen, if at all, and the locals clearly understood that he was staying at the house guarded by the police. The old lady saw the foreigner on recent mornings sitting on the small, wooden stool drinking the thick, black, drip coffee that filtered through the small aluminum container and, eventually, into the small glass. When she saw him, she often wondered what he was doing in this foreign land, what he was thinking, and although she was curious about police matters, she had other important things to concern herself with and now focused on sweeping her broom at the neighbor's yellow dog and yelling at it in Vietnamese trying to chase it away as it had just squatted and crapped near her door. It was her main frustration of the day; sweeping away the dry and sometimes wet dog droppings. In the war days, she had seen enough foreigners, mostly soldiers and airmen in Saigon and she quickly forgot about the foreigner who sat there as she watched the dog slowly saunter off, looking behind him the entire time to see if she would give chase. She didn't. She had washing to hang out to dry in the fetid, rising heat.

Hugh nodded to the broom-wielding woman unconsciously as he had done most mornings. Slowly he sipped his coffee, grasping the small cup in both of his large hands, as he tried to remember the dream that troubles him nightly. He's haunted by the images and can only remember pieces since he always wakes up in a sweat from the heat of his unconscious. Nearly every night, he would see her over and over again as she emerged from the dark rice field with barely enough moonlight to reveal her identity. It's been that way for years.

Orders finally came through. Hugh and Whitman were picked up in the morning when the soup vendors begin their early morning trade and before the subtropical sun heats the air. They were met by the brusque MPs who had delivered them to the Montana BEQ a few weeks earlier. The green Jeep wove its way past cowboys on motorcycles, students on bicycles and cyclos, the three wheeled open motor passenger vehicles with the driver seated behind. Driving towards Tân Sơn Nhứt Airbase, the driver dodged through pedestrians dangerously crossing the street and he honked his horn at the slow, small, yellow and blue Renault taxis, some with GIs sitting in the back and some with women from the night before on their way home from their amorous night's work.

Instead of going through the main gate of Tân Sơn Nhứt Airbase, the driver skirted the large tomb of the first bishop of Saigon, turned towards the triangular park, headed past 3rd Field Hospital and drove towards MACV headquarters. Hugh and Whitman reported to Colonel Davidson.

"You boys will be going to Tây Ninh this afternoon. A Huey from the 25th Aviation Battalion will be here to ferry you up to that area and you'll get further instructions from there," the tall colonel explained. "You won't need much with you. I understand you'll only be gone a few days, at the most, so you can leave your stuff at the Montana. We'll try to get you into the Bachelor Officers Quarters downtown by the time you get back. Sorry about having to have you live with the enlisted, but it's always good for junior officers to see how the enlisted live," he lied. Planners wanted to keep them separated from others assigned to MACV-SOG. He continued the briefing, "You'll be picked back up at 1400 hours and taken to Camp Alpha to meet your chopper."

Camp Alpha was the very active helicopter landing area on Tân Sơn Nhứt Airbase. At every hour and every day of that war, UH-1s, the Hueys as they were called and their younger brothers the Loaches, or Light Observation Helicopters, would be constantly arriving from or departing to their assigned tasks throughout the southern regions of Việt Nam. The Hueys had a distinctive sound to their rotor and anyone, even the novices of war, could identify them at once. Everyone knew the "whup, whup, whup" rhythm of the Hueys. The Loaches were the bumblebees of the war, highly maneuverable and small.

The two lieutenants had accustomed themselves to taking few things with them on operations. The less you carried the less you had to worry about. They were professional and elite. They could live off the land if they had to do so, and usually they did.

Whitman and Hugh saw the jagged lightning bolts painted on the side of the 25th Aviation Battalions chopper waiting for them at Camp Alpha. There were several of them there, some in the process of being loaded with other personnel, frightened, yet oddly eager young boys in clean uniforms, and others who had the battlefield appearance and would stare right through you when they turned in your direction. Already knowledge of this "thousand yard stare" was circulating around the troops in Việt Nam. Mail bags were thrown by soldiers in green t-shirts into a couple of the Hueys and at last they were loaded and away.

Hugh and Whitman sat in the passenger compartment – the term *passenger* was used for want of a better word. They watched Tân Sơn Nhứt Airbase fall away beneath them as they gained altitude and headed northwestward towards Tây Ninh and the newly reinstated airfield now owned and operated by the 196th Light Infantry Brigade. They briefed themselves with maps prior to their departure and knew intimately their intended route. They watched Route 1, the main highway, track below. Small motorcycles, 3-wheeled Lambrettas – beginning to be known as đồng carts because of the cheap fare – and military convoys dotted the roadway like ants in a line headed back to their underground chambers. As the rotors of the helicopter grabbed at more air and gained altitude to escape the risk of being shot at by small arms weapons, the beauty of Việt Nam began to unfold itself. At this altitude, a soldier could detach himself from the war and believe that only the lush, green countryside existed. The familiar "whup, whup, whup" of the Huey's rotors lulled them into a deceptive sense of peacefulness as they began to approach the village of Củ Chi where they saw the empty markets below, villagers, buyers and sellers had by now already returned to their homes. Just outside the village of Củ Chi and stretching out into the verdant distance, one saw the evidence of the bombs dropped by the B-52s. The deadly wrath of the United States was tracked on the ground by the all-too familiar craters lined up like an oversized cribbage board in the pockmarked earth, not marked with pegs but with the broken bones of the dead, the ones who have already seen the end of the war. Deadly seven hundred-fifty pound bombs rained down to the earth indiscriminately killing beast and human alike, for in war, weapons have no conscience; they don't discriminate; they cannot differentiate – they are pure killing mechanisms. One could not imagine the terror felt by those on the ground when the giant bombers of the United States began their bombing runs at a safe altitude over South Việt Nam. Pilots, navigators, bombadiers and tail gunners alike relaxed, flying by instruments, drinking their coffee, feeling the lightening of the plane as they dropped their burdens to become someone else's burden.

Flying beyond Củ Chi, the helicopter continued its course noting the passing of the small village of Tráng Bàng and the pilot checked his path over the highway to the Gô Dầu Ha bridge where Highway 1 pares itself to the left towards an area called the "Angel's Wing," so called because of the border's shape on the map reminded westerners of a peaceful icon of their religious proclivity. Nearly bisecting the Wing, Highway 1 continued to exotic Cambodia and its own mysteries and secrets in Phnom Penh, but the Huey continued north tracking QL22, the highway that connects Saigon and Tây Ninh and dotted with smaller settlements below. In the distance the sacred mountain had appeared almost as soon as they began to gain altitude after departing Tân Sơn Nhứt. Núi Bà Đen – Black Lady Mountain – was a landmark to fliers and people on the ground alike. Standing like a lone sentinel of peace against the madness of the war, she was drawn unwittingly into the deadly conflict by her own quiet exceptionality. Rising to nearly 3,000 feet above the plain, she is the only mountain within more than sixty miles and is considered holy to many living within her sight. She rises like a lone woman's breast to spiritually nurture her children, but she has been savagely mutilated by war. The Americans commanded the aureole and the nipple of the mountain while the Viet Cong controlled the tender sides that sloped towards the children she loves. The mountain loomed larger as they began their descent and approach into Tây Ninh. Already, they began to see the rows of tents dotting the encampment looming on the horizon.

Vast, verdant and luxuriant banana plantations, rice fields, taro fields and sweet potato farms passed beneath as the ground slowly began to rise to greet them. For the lieutenants, the dissonance of peaceful farm life and the war they became caught in were so far out of place with the realities they had so recently learned. During their brief stay in Saigon, the only inkling of the war they saw was the abundance of American troops in the bars and brothels. Occasional explosions or gunshots could be heard, but nothing else to betray the country was at war in the countryside. Here away from the tawdry night life was the war in its stark nakedness and its sheer brutality. Fire Support Bases, defoliated perimeters, large gun emplacements, steel helmeted soldiers carrying weapons became the standard and the viciousness of war became commonplace. The lieutenants were entering the area at the same time of the beginning of Operation Attleboro, a US offensive to clear War Zone C and retake it from the Việt Cộng. The weapon most apparent in the field was the "Matty Mattel" Colt M-16 rifle that was carried on the enlisted man's shoulder and young soldiers could have been mistaken for college students with backpacks casually slung over their shoulders. This was a hands-on college that taught about the barbarity of human existence and the effects of governments forgetting about allowing other countries the right of self-determination. The commissioned officers and the warrant officers, those few ranks between enlisted and commissioned officers, carried sidearms, generally the Colt .45 caliber semiautomatic pistol. Each soldier resembled each other in their haggard appearances.

The Chairman reflected on the meeting held in the forested seclusion of Connecticut and he sat alone in his office, idly staring at the world outside the 56th floor of his executive suite in New York. His furnishings neatly matched the appointments found in the Connecticut lodge where he had met his colleagues a few weeks earlier. He was still concerned about the focus of their discussion, but did not have time to dwell on the problem. He had already stated his concerns to his aide who had placed the call and received confirmation that the Chairman's request would be honored. He still could not reconcile the dichotomy of his actions and his own upbringing. Then again, each generation had to contend with its separate issues and redefine its own priorities. He lived by the rule that the end does justify the means.

Looking below he saw the city teeming with millions of lives, each with their own mix of sorrow and happiness. Yet for all the peace people wanted in their lives and to be left alone, they also relied on an economic system to keep them employed and allow them to exchange their time spent in labor for someone else's profit in order to have a day or two each week for themselves and the opportunity for recreation and the money to spend on whatever their choices would be for relaxation. To have an economy that allowed that mutual exchange was necessary and the only way to maintain that was to make difficult decisions. After all, it was for the greater good; to meliorate life; to progress, wasn't it?

The phone rang, which broke his musings and he turned towards it. The aid, who had placed the initial call for him from Connecticut, answered the phone. Like the phone at the lodge, this phone had no dial, and was a direct connection. The aid listened to the voice on the other end. He only nodded quietly and uttered the simple phrase, "I'll pass the message along."

The aid told the Chairman that the mission they had suggested was being carried out but there wouldn't be any word for at least two or three more weeks and additional fail-safe measures were being taken to ensure a successful operation. The Chairman nodded thoughtfully. He looked at his smartly dressed aid who appeared boyish and immature, but he took instructions quite well, and the Chairman owed the young man's father some favors, after all.

The aid continually considered his future and felt he was destined for greatness. He was a mere twenty-three years old with still a lot of little boy in him and he constantly exhibited a unique exuberance for his age. He had already expressed the desire to run his own companies, make money at any cost and to uphold the developing conservative thought of the day – anything and everything to support business to keep America strong. The Chairman didn't doubt his young assistant's motivation and fervor. Except for the aid's recreational drug use, they had similar ethics. The Chairman knew about the drug use and it could be overlooked as it had yet to become a problem. Nonetheless he would still keep a close eye on him; after all, he had been doing a stellar job.

The Chairman knew the aid's father, a United States Senator from a southern state, and they had been not only classmates at Harvard together, but they had remained social friends and usually helped each other in cases of need. They were connected to each other by a web of influential friends within and without the government of the United States and in several other countries. These strategically placed individuals were on the guard to ensure the safety of the Chairman and his colleagues' needs. Everyone would benefit from their mutual goals. That's all that was required. They had to operate, at times, outside the gates of their protected domains and outside sanctioned norms in order to protect the system. No matter the country the associates were in, it was their patriotic duty to do what they could to preserve systems.

VII

The tropical sun-faded, black "X" marking the heliport at Tây Ninh West begged the Huey, which hung mere feet above the cracked concrete pad, to land. The recently US Army-occupied base was established as a major camp for the area. After several moments of hovering like ⁓ ⁓ ang bird finding its nest after the first time out, the helicopter felt its footing and settled to the ground, rotors slowing to a stop in their revolutions. The solitary mountain still verdant from the last rains now seemed so much larger and took up the entire vista to the northeast of the base. They were amazed that this protrusion out of the earth was the only mountain for over sixty-two miles around. A young, blond second lieutenant looking as though he has never had combat experience approached Hugh and Whitman after they jumped out of the Huey with their gear. The second lieutenant's uniform had apparently just been washed and the black camouflaged crossed rifles sewn on his jungle fatigue shirt collar indicated he was in the Infantry Branch of the Army. He eagerly greeted the two newcomers and escorted them to officer's barracks, for want of a better description at the front lines; the buildings were elaborate canvas tents built on wooden platforms. The lieutenant simply told his senior officers politely to settle in as someone would be by later to talk to them – they were requested to standby until summoned. Still trying to get acclimatized to the heat and humidity, they gratefully complied. Two old Vietnamese women in white blouses, black silk trousers, and leathered faces sat in the afternoon shade quietly and watched the foreign soldiers speak, while fanning themselves with their palm frond conical hats. When the younger officer walked away and the two older ones walked into the billets, they resumed talking about husbands and children, barely caring about the unfamiliar faces. They had seen the French come and go, and now it would be the Americans. The Europeans and White governments could never last too long in their countryside. If the war didn't wear them down, then the heat and humidity would. After a quick, tepid shower, for there wasn't any hot water to speak of, the lieutenants took to their own bunks and slept the rest of the afternoon away.

Later that evening, a staff sergeant, who seemed in his early thirties and sported what may have been a bullet hole repair on the front of his shirt, arrived and knocked on their door. By now, Hugh and Whitman were feeling more refreshed and now that the sun had gone down, they anticipated a slight drop in the temperature as a slight breeze blew across the rice paddies and the Vàm Cỏ Đông River, just a little bit west of the camp. The sergeant led the officers to the camp's Commanding Officer, a lieutenant colonel. His quarters were a mobile home, heavily protected by barbed wire and sentries.

The colonel invited the young officers in and asked them to do away with the formalities. Sitting in a corner of the colonel's living room sat a civilian in tan cotton slacks and a white Cuban guayabera shirt open at the neck. The civilian was tanned and had leathered skin that showed years of experience beyond his age, which to Hugh seemed in the mid-forties, and he acted as though his work was routine. He seemed relaxed but gave an air of being in charge. It was quite possible that he held a civilian rank equal to the colonel.

The colonel spoke first, asking Whitman about his father. In the Army, officers tended to serve at assignments with others in their respective branches. Whitman's father and the colonel at Tây Ninh had served during the Korean War together in Seoul. After pleasantries, the colonel introduced Hugh and Whitman to the civilian simply called Morgan. The three men sat and maintained a semblance of small talk. They could not discuss anything confidential, as the colonel explained, because his housekeeper had stayed longer that night to prepare dinner for his three guests; the soldiers and the civilian. She emerged from the kitchen gliding barefoot across the polished wood floor bringing a bamboo tray filled with different-sized plates of spring rolls, chili peppers, small bowls of soy sauce, and drinks. She seemed to epitomize grace and Hugh straight away felt a pang of hunger, not from his stomach, but a hunger that only a man can feel who has loved before and aches for its return. He tried not to stare, but saw that she had also instantly noticed him. He detected a near indiscernible hesitation in her step when she looked at him and Hugh wondered if there was some forged connection predestined for them by whom, he wondered. Hugh had no religious upbringing though he found the Religious Studies class at the university very fascinating. After that class, he never questioned why he felt no connection to any religion. There was no need as he finally understood. Any god who may be kind or compassionate would not allow wars to happen, just as a father would not allow his children to murder each other out of anger.

While the men ate dinner comprised of a heavy mixture of vegetables, meat, fried shrimp, and noodles, the housekeeper busied herself sweeping the "house cum wheels;" cleaning the bathrooms and laying out new towels and linens for the new arrivals. It was her job, no, it was her traditional duty, to ensure the house was cleaned, the colonel content with his new surroundings and that all guests were made to feel welcome. There had been talk around the base that the colonel's housekeeper was his mistress, and those rumors had their genesis in the barracks, generally the locus of all rude, vulgar and cheap talk of sex and the attendant innuendoes. The rumors had been told to her by the other housekeepers of the officers' and enlisted men's barracks as they walked through the main gate in the morning each to their own jobs. When word had reached the colonel of this rumor, he saw to it that it was squelched. He was a married man – did that really matter? – and he was a faithful husband. He had actually employed the housekeeper because he knew her father, an Army of the Republic of Việt Nam Special Forces captain. The ARVN camp was slightly north of Tây Ninh. At the colonel's residence, she would be treated decently and paid a good salary. Rather than paying her in the customary Vietnamese piastres, which had a much lower value, he would pay her directly in the previous year's issued Series 641 Military Payment Certificates. Although it was considered preferential treatment, the colonel wanted to help her and her family as much as he could. It was, anyway, for good relations. He treated her more like a daughter and disciplined those who he felt treated her unkindly. He was her protector.

Võ Thị Thu Lan was a young eighteen year old and a captivatingly beautiful girl who was very meticulous about keeping a clean house for the colonel. He reminded her of her own father. Thu Lan's family had fled the north in 1954 along with about 850,000 northerners during that short nine months when Vietnamese were allowed to immigrate to the north or south unimpeded. Thu Lan's father had named her because she was his "Autumn Orchid" and he felt the name was justified by her beauty. But in the south of Việt Nam, there was no autumn and defoliants were beginning to work at destroying the forests and the orchids, save this precious one. Born in the fall of 1948, Thu Lan was only six years old when the family left their house in Nam Định, a city fifty-five miles south of the North's capital city Hà Nội. They left behind valued furniture from generations of the Võ family; there was only just enough room in their ancient Citroen Traction Avant for the family. They were able to take along some valued small treasures, photo albums and a couple old leather valises of clothing strapped to the top of the aging black automobile, but nothing else. In the south they didn't need much in the way of winter clothes, not in the heat and humidity. Sadly, but pragmatically, Thu Lan had to leave her pet dog, Trung Thành – which means 'faithful' – behind left in the care of neighbors who decided to stay. She could not foretell that after the borders closed and during land reform, her dog would become dinner to keep a family from starving for another day or so.

Thu Lan was loyal to the south and her father's cause for liberation. That is why the colonel trusted her to care for his house. At times, he became too comfortable around her and on a few occasions, while she busied herself cleaning, he had discussed confidential information during telephone calls over a secure landline – the phrase "Operation Gadsen" really wouldn't matter to her, anyway, without the details. He absent-mindedly thought she did not pay attention nor would she care about what he was discussing. He didn't worry. She was trusted.

After dinner, Thu Lan cleaned the table and busied herself in the kitchen and was instructed by the colonel not to disturb the men. He would tell her when they would be ready for after dinner desserts and hot Chinese tea poured from the hand-painted dragon motif pot, kept in the colonel's favorite red, silk-lined box; a gift from the Võ family for giving their daughter employment. Morgan took a slim manila folder from the coffee table in front of where he sat, opened it and invited the men to sit.

"Gentlemen," he uttered with as much enthusiasm as the heat and humidity of the countryside at night would allow. "You two were specifically chosen for this unique operation for several reasons that are evidenced by your personnel files, which, for obvious reasons, don't reflect everything you've accomplished. First, Lieutenant Emerson your father has not only an honorable career, but you have already demonstrated some unique individual qualities."

Hugh wondered if Morgan was alluding to the incidents with Rucker at OCS and the fisherman in Monterey.

"Lieutenant Campbell, you have also demonstrated a very adept common sense and the ability to creatively think on your feet. The fact you both are conversant in the southern and the northern dialects of Vietnamese enhances the likelihood for the successful accomplishment of this operation." The civilian spoke to them as though he were preparing the citation for the award of the Army Silver Star, an oft coveted military decoration for those who put stock into outward displays of their military plumage. He had yet to identify his official affiliation, but Hugh and Whitman could smell CIA. They let Morgan continue.

"There is a contact you will need to make with a certain North Vietnamese Army officer who is currently enroute to Tây Ninh Province. He is traveling down the Ho Chi Minh Trail," he said without adding the proper tones of the language that Hugh and Whitman had become used to pronouncing. Hugh lost himself in thought for a moment; "*The Hồ Chí Minh Trail*" was the famed, eponymous corridor of supplies, armaments and personnel dedicated to the nationalist leader of the North Vietnamese government, a trail that was just as enigmatic and unfathomable. It wasn't any one specific trail but a numberless amount of footpaths, narrow roads, bamboo bridges and submerged paths across streams that aided transport of matériel from the north; supplies of Chinese and Soviet manufacture alike, and distributed from caches in Cambodia and along the Vietnamese border to the Việt Cộng and the cause in the south. The Việt Cộng, or VC as everyone called them, were the enemy, yet the other side of the coin revealed that America was their enemy. The VC was the progeny of the Việt Minh but given the new name by the southern Vietnamese government that felt Việt Minh would be viewed in a positive way rather than negative. That much Hugh remembered from some readings he had found in the campus library before landing in OCS and from his later briefings.

The civilian continued, "We have information that Hà Nội is rethinking this war and is prepared for an all out effort in response to our buildup. They are sending an officer down here. This officer is bringing certain tactical and strategic documents that will prolong this war, which may result in the loss of thousands of American lives," he said as though Vietnamese lives were not as valued. "Inside this envelope is a map that entails War Zone C, of which Tây Ninh is part. You will proceed to Special Forces A-323 Trại Bí at grid coordinates X-Ray Tango one two zero five eight four. There, you will await further instructions and eventually make your way to Thiện Ngôn where there is a rudimentary Special Forces Camp at X-Ray Tango zero eight six eight one three and up to Xóm Mát. It is well known for not only smuggling but as one of the southernmost terminals of the Ho Chi Minh Trail coming out of Cambodia. North of Thiện Ngôn you will make contact with a South Vietnamese double agent who may be able to assist you. He has demonstrated his trust and reliability. Mr. Nguyễn Văn Hiền's information is contained in this folder along with the map, the UTM grid coordinates of a suspected meeting place between the northern officer and his southern counterpart. You men are to specifically terminate with extreme prejudice the mission of the NVA officer, the double agent and destroy the documents and return to Tây Ninh. You will not be able to remove this folder from the colonel's quarters. A couple of bunks have been set up in a back room so you can work from here. Your bags have already been brought over. You have about 10 days to completely review the materials and plan your operation. The NVA officer has already left Hà Nội and is expected here in a few weeks' time. This operation is of the uttermost importance to winning this war, gentlemen, and is necessary for the advancement of freedom in Southeast Asia and overcoming aggressor forces," Morgan again emphasized speaking more like a military award citation.

"Along Highway 22, between the areas of Trại Bí, Xóm Mát and where the meeting may take place, the area is heavy with VC and doubtless you will have to use every black op technique you know for your own survival. It was hoped the meeting place would be more convenient for us, but this is their home turf. You are aware that the North Vietnamese Army has a headquarters for all tactical and strategic operations in the south in that area. Central Office South Vietnam, or COSVN, operates from this region and is located a little northeast of Xóm Mát. It is believed that the rendezvous very well may be within spitting distance of COSVN. We know their general location and have requested an "Arc Light" blackout for the period of time you will be in the area." The lieutenants remembered during their initial in-country briefing that "Arc Light" was the operational name for the B-52 bombing runs in Southeast Asia. Morgan continued, "You men know the precautions to take and are aware that capture by the enemy is always a consideration. Memorize the contents of this folder and plan your operation. Again, you have, at the most, ten days to

give me a list of any equipment that you will require for the
successful accomplishment of the mission. It will only be the
two of you on this operation. Good luck." With that, Morgan
passed the unmarked folder across the cigarette burned and
water-stained table to Whitman. Morgan nodded to Hugh
with an awkward glance and the lieutenants rose, excused
themselves from the colonel and the CIA officer and went to
the back room to review and plan.

The "Top Secret" material explained that Captain Tô Văn
Huỳnh, a North Vietnamese Army intelligence officer, was
carrying tactical and strategic operation plans directly from
Hồ Chí Minh and General Võ Nguyên Giáp, the brilliant
commanding general of the NVA, to COSVN's command
element. Attempts to deliver the material by other means had
been foisted by military operations and there was a credible
source that provided the information contained in the folder.
There were detailed maps of the area surrounding Trại Bí,
Thiện Ngôn and Xóm Mát, and the area along the border of
Cambodia and Việt Nam between Xóm Mát and Kà Tum.
This area was known as the Mimot Plantation established by
the French in the late 1800s.

Whitman and Hugh examined the materials as though
they were studying for university final examinations. Not
one word was left unread and not one aerial photograph left
unexamined. Details of the aerial photographs provided by
an Air Force RF-4C, taken just a few days before, and their
interpretations were examined with magnifying glasses and
compared with the latest topographic map available dated
1965. They studied the photograph and the dossier of Captain
Tô Văn Huỳnh. Information about him was brief; his father

had been a charter member of the Indochina Communist Party, had been a fighter with the Việt Minh and was involved in the 1954 surrender of the French Forces at Điên Biên Phu in northwestern Việt Nam, near the Laotian border. Huỳnh, his son, had been groomed for a military career for the Fatherland. Huỳnh was an exceptional soldier and had been decorated once already as a Hero of Việt Nam by Hl Chí Minh. himself. This was the man the North trusted to carry the documents that would, hopefully, provide the strategy to win the war and end the hostilities and reunify the country. No mention was made of any security precautions being taken to ensure the success of Huỳnh's mission, as well. There was no mention of additional personnel assigned to Huỳnh, only a mere mention of Captain Huỳnh as a lone courier bringing top secret documents from the north and coming down the Trail unescorted and unprotected. Given the fact that the Trail was used by the NVA and the VC, it would make sense that any courier would be safe. But the possibility always existed of a rogue soldier who believed he could make more money from the sale of important documents or items than his usually unpaid military compensation provided. Everyone worked for the cause, but humanity has always demonstrated financial rewards sometimes overshadowed the greater good of the people.

Hugh was the first to pick up on this fact and spoke to Whitman about his concern. Did it make sense to trust the valuable documents such as the complete tactical and strategic running of the war to a lone courier? Hugh's cynicism started considering the possibilities. Captain Huỳnh was trusted by Uncle Hồ, as the Vietnamese called him, and had been given these documents to carry to the south on a journey over the Trail that would take him nearly a few weeks. He was unescorted and without protection from anyone who could seek personal gain or notoriety, if not death. If this were also true, Hugh argued, why were only two highly trained special operatives of the US Army dispatched to terminate the mission of Captain Huỳnh and destroy the documents? Wouldn't it be more prudent to send at least a half-dozen or more specially trained Special Forces personnel to not only terminate the mission but also to capture the documents and Captain Huỳnh himself? Why these two young lieutenants would be dispatched to destroy and not to retrieve was a question that began to irritate him like a mosquito's bite in an unreachable place for scratching.

Whitman took another approach. First, he argued, they were soldiers of the US Army and were not to question orders. They had been given a mission to accomplish and that what was they were to do without any equivocation. Second, it would make sense that dispatching a lone courier would not draw any attention to the importance of the secretive mission. Everyone along the Trail could be trusted as they were serving a cause greater than themselves and could sublimate their own goals and desires for the good of their country. Hadn't he and Hugh done the same also, forsaking completion of their university studies and the hopes of lucrative careers in corporate America to join the Army during its time of need during the Vietnam War? Whitman asked Hugh to translate that to the peasants who sincerely believed their lives would be better and their country would be better without foreign occupiers in their land. Whitman could argue that the VC was not a real intentional enemy of the United States but may actually be akin to Freedom Fighters or like the Minutemen, the early Americans who fought the British in order to gain independence. So, he argued, that it made perfect sense for an unescorted NVA captain to come down the trail by himself. Whitman's points seemed very credible to Hugh and he could accept the points, but still, the warning flags had been raised in his mind.

A subtle knock on the door by the housekeeper summoned the lieutenants back to the dining room. They arrived just as hot tea and small sweetened coconut cakes were being placed on the table by Thu Lan. During the near-ritualistic pouring of the tea, Hugh felt the slightest brush of her hand against his hand as they simultaneously reached for a small, hand-decorated tea cup. When she was across the table, pouring tea into Morgan's cup, Hugh saw her small, dark eyes glance towards him and they seemed to penetrate deep into his soul and his heart. Hugh was distracted from the talk about the weather and home town issues and began to wonder what Thu Lan was like outside of the colonel's residence; what her family was like; but mostly, he started dwelling on her beauty and suddenly his mind visualized the two of them joined together in lovemaking. Hugh caught his mind suddenly as he realized it was treading a bizarre and unfamiliar path. He had mused about strange women in the past, but not in this way. Although he had only met her this afternoon, he was surprised to feel something towards Thu Lan, something that was more than sexual. Hugh needed to question his mind, his rationale and his behavior. He wondered if it was merely her exotic appearance and her delicate but purposeful mannerisms that were drawing him towards the fantasy. He freed the trend of thought from his mind and focused on the conversation when Morgan had to ask him a second time about the football games leading up to the first ever Superbowl Championship game in January. Embarrassed, Hugh joined the conversation and begged forgiveness for not being a football fan. After dessert, the lieutenants again returned to their room locking themselves in for the night.

They spent the next several days reading through all the materials, reviewing each piece of information several times, quizzing each other on the contents and making a very short list of materiel that they required. Each day at 5:30AM, before it became too hot, the lieutenants would exercise and run at least five miles before returning for a shower and an American breakfast of bacon, eggs, toast, Vietnamese coffee and fresh orange juice squeezed by Thu Lan. They would then study the file until lunch and nap afterwards when the sun was glaring down upon Tây Ninh, seemingly cauterizing the wounds humanity inflicted on the earth. Another run and exercise before dinner at 6 PM and the remainder of the night found them finalizing their operation.

VIII

The following day, the colonel had his driver and a Vietnamese escort take the lieutenants to Tòa Thánh Tây Ninh, the large and impressive Cao Đài Temple, as part of their familiarization with the area. The temple sat on the eastern   of Tây Ninh, about five miles from the camp and like all else it was also in the shadow of the great Holy Mountain. The driver passed through the old, painted, iron gate and parked the jeep in the shade next to a small, enclosed, forested area across the main square from the temple. Here the lieutenants saw the small monkeys that were surviving the war in their protected habitat. They were cavorting around in the dense canopy of the tree cover, deftly moving about from branch to branch and tree to tree. Watching them, Hugh thought about his thoughts jumping around his mind when thinking aboutThu Lan. The Vietnamese escort interrupted Hugh's contemplation and began to explain how the Cao Đàist sect was founded in 1926 and was a blend of Catholicism, Confucianism, Taoism and Buddhism. The church had assumed for her saints the likes of Victor Hugo, Buddha and Christ. Ngô Văn Chiêu, its founder, was a civil servant and blessed with visions. The religion was founded on achieving peace, justice and harmony, yet found itself amidst the dissonant violence. An incongruity resulted from the Cao Đàists once having their own army, along with the Hòa Hảo, another religious sect, and the army of the Bình Xuyên criminal organization.

Hugh and Whitman were stunned at the splendor of the main temple itself; fantastic, dreamlike images carved in stone and impressed upon cement, plaster and iron work; a colorful kaleidoscope ever twirling back on itself as one walked through the main sanctuary and tried to digest the visual feast. Glossy yellow and black floor tiles, polished from years of bare feet and socks, reflected gaily painted three-dimensional dragons that wrapped themselves around the pillars separating the central worship hall from the north and south corridors. They were almost lifelike and threatened to disengage themselves from the pillars should the need arise. The light blue, starry, clouded ceiling bore more images of wispy dragons, saints and other entwined dragons of teal, dark green, blue and reddish-orange like the color of sunsets. Another section of ceiling depicted Ly Tai Pei – himself a legendary figure from the Tang dynasty of Việt Nam – and the planchette used in ceremonies to divine their sacred words and prophecies. Sitting atop the main altar of the temple was the huge globe – the Great Eye; the Divine Eye; the Cao Đàist's object of worship. This image, the lieutenants saw, was also found in the glassless barred windows along the sides of the temple, letting humid air inside to abide with the mysteries and divinations. The men walked around the temple, accompanied only by the escort because their driver was napping in the Jeep in the shade of trees while monkeys looked down at the differently dressed, slumbering human.

An elderly man entered the temple from the southern side door and approached the visitors to answer any questions they may have and Hugh mistakenly thought he was a priest.

He was wearing a white *áo dài*, the traditional long dress worn by both men and women of Việt Nam. Hugh and the old man, he simply called "Bác" which means uncle, became connected by the mysterious, unseen sinew of life and they became instant friends. It was one of those moments when people feel something indiscernible to human cognition that links them somehow. Hugh was taken aback that within a matter of a few weeks, he instantly felt connected with the Vietnamese. Hugh and Bác began to speak in the older man's southern dialect. Recognizing the lieutenants as visitors – for anyone who visits for the first time, their awe is apparent – Bác explained the history of the Cao Đàis and the mystery of the Divine Eye.

Whitman decided he wanted to wander on his own and walked off in the direction of the vestibule with the escort looking at the artwork, statues and scrolls. Hugh and Bác walked counter-clockwise down the corridors around the sanctuary. They ambled past the pulpits in the center of the Great Temple near the huge, wooden side doors now open for the late afternoon breeze, and they continued on without leaving sight of the large, greenish globe of the Divine Eye that sat upon an ornately carved eight-sided wooden table, which in turn rested on a twelve-step octagonal base. The Divine Eye was embodied against a field of gold-highlighted clouds surrounded by gold and silver stars. As they walked closer to the main altar, their view of the Divine Eye – and visitors are reminded it is the left eye of God – was briefly interrupted by pillared dragons looking down on them with tails wrapping skyward. They approached the wooden altar and the polished brass dragons stared at the duo as they protected the Divine Eye. In the rear corridor behind the Eye, where an artery and the optic nerve should have been, was a stone slab set into the floor with heavy padlocks protecting the inside from intrusion. Hugh, ever inquisitive, asked Bác what was concealed underneath the slab. Bác explained the heavy slab of stone was access to a room under the Giant Eye. No one was allowed and only he and one of the cardinals had keys. He did say that it was an excellent place for storage amongst the urns containing ash and bone of holy people.

After touring the interior, Hugh found Whitman and together they wandered around the luxuriant gardens and the psychedelic estate of the Cao Đàists for about an hour before deciding they should return to the base to continue their planning.

Each day, arriving in the coolness of the early morning, Thu Lan would come and prepare to serve Whitman and Hugh their meals, take their soiled linens and clothes to wash and tend to their needs. There was something about Thu Lan that caught Hugh's attention the first moment he saw her serving hors d'oeureves before dinner the night they arrived and the way she meticulously cleared the table without as much as a sound emanating from the silverware or plates against the table. In the morning, she would gently rap on their door announcing her arrival, but it was more like a soft patter of skin against wood and she would patiently wait at the door with their breakfast on the tray of bamboo with a small vase of sweet smelling, fresh-cut flowers. Hugh, fresh from his shower after jogging around the camp, opened the door to the room and allowed her to enter. She skillfully placed the tray at the edge of the small table in the center of the room and set the plates of eggs and bacon, hash browns, American coffee and orange juice along with the silverware and napkins. She placed the vase of flowers in the center of the table. As always, she placed a healthy serving of fresh papaya, mango, dragon fruit, or watermelon alongside their dishes. Hugh noted that not one clink, not one sound of tray, plate or glass against the wood of the table was ever made when Thu Lan served them. She placed the items down as if each were treated with padding so as not to risk breakage. Would it be ever so good if hearts and people were the same?

Hugh's memory revisited the moment when his former fiancée had broken off their engagement a little more than two years before and had married someone else since. The lack of cushioning around his heart had left a scar that oozed intermittently, even after the short time span. Odd, Hugh reflected how an event or incident as small as a tray placed on an old wooden table in the subtropics, thousands of miles from his home, could pick at a scab and irritate the wound in the heart. His thoughts returned to the enticing Thu Lan as she carefully arranged their breakfast and then quietly sat down nearby to wait. Whitman was still showering and Hugh took the opportunity to talk with Thu Lan in her native language, although she also spoke English. The English requirement was one of the colonel's who neither had the inclination nor the time to bother learning a foreign tongue, so characteristic of many foreigners in Việt Nam. His tour of duty would be only twelve months at most, shorter if he were seriously wounded, but he never left the safety of Tây Ninh West, except to go by helicopter to Saigon driven by "The Little Bears," the boys from the 25th Aviation Battalion.

Hugh was fascinated by Thu Lan's gentle appearance and he couldn't quite understand the feeling that she unknowingly awakened in him, nor the reason for the allure of her Asian features. She was a mix of Chinese and Annam, the name of the region that was the old protectorate of the French. Her ancestors, he learned, had their marriages arranged and distant cousins from the village of Vinh in Annam had married into the male Võ family line from Nam Định in the Tonkin north. Angst towards the French during the First Indochina War ran high in the Võ family as their homes had been destroyed during French bombings. Thu Lan explained America's help promised a better life in Việt Nam than that which was demonstrated under the French colonial rule, and she emphasized, it would be much better than what the communists had been promising.

Thu Lan, in a quiet, soft, reserved voice above a whisper, spoke to Hugh about the history of her immediate family; her father the loyal soldier, and her mother who had to quickly adapt with a family of six in the south after fleeing the north. Her mother was an elementary school teacher and brought with her to Tây Ninh the knowledge of French and English. Her grandfather made the journey with them and was still alive, though bedridden from gout and occasional bouts of malaria. Her grandfather, the patriarch of the family, was believed to be the only person in the Tây Ninh area who could speak the old Chinese language and write the ancient Vietnamese script. That writing system, based on Chinese pictograms, was later Romanized by the French Jesuit priest Alexandre de Rhodes in the seventeenth century. Thu Lan had learned English and French from her mother at an early age, thus providing her with linguistic skills that qualified her to be placed in the colonel's employ. Her mother and father's background provided the trust she needed.

Morgan called on the colonel and the lieutenants one evening. He told them that he had extended the deadline for the lieutenants as he had been called away on urgent conduct of the businesses of war elsewhere and their target would not arrive for some time, yet. With the extra days that she served them, Hugh had more of an occasion to learn about the history of Việt Nam, but he became distracted as the softness of her skin contrasted with the hardness of her life, her soft melodic voice lulled his heart to a soft state of serenity that was set diametrically opposite to the madness outside the house and without the camp's barbed and razor sharp, wire-topped chain link fences. Even Hugh no longer paid mind to the heat, though he would still be faintly aware of sweat trickling from his armpits down his sides to his stomach to be finally absorbed by his loose fitting green t-shirt at the waist. He ignored the heat while he gazed at Thu Lan and he felt the scars of the old love mending as he now began to experience a longing to be with Thu Lan. He surmised it simply wasn't the hormonal response of sexual needs and urges, but something more and something much deeper that was stirring within his heart. The way Thu Lan had looked at him gave him the impression that there may be something astir in her heart as well, for he found that she would usually, and with a little discretion, arrange her time to be near him, except when he and Whitman had the door closed and locked from the inside preventing her access while they digested the classified documents and the meals she prepared.

One Sunday at Tây Ninh was like any other day because they studied, planned and waited. The colonel always allowed Thu Lan time to attend Catholic church on Sunday. Instead of her usual change of dress into her black silk trousers and white blouse, after church she came to the lieutenants' room in her áo dài. She was dressed in white silk trousers that covered her diminutive feet. Her silk pants were thin enough to reveal just the slightest impression of her dainty underclothes. Her pink, silk dress embroidered with an intricate orchid pattern had a mandarin-style collar that lovingly embraced her neck and her soft, black hair played delicately over the collar in a breeze when she walked. The dress was split up both sides creating two long flaps, which joined together inches above her slim waist and it accentuated the curve of her hips and revealed a very light brown shade of her flat tummy skin, common in the Asian races. She was elegant and her walking appeared more like flowers floating in a dish of water at a dining table of a restaurant for lovers, or shaded candles gliding on the current of the river, launched by lovers sending their desires and hopes to the sea. This Sunday, her long, black hair was untied at the back and it fell over her shoulders and it cascaded down her back to nearly her waistline. Hugh focused on her eyes; the dark, small, narrow eyes that gently swept from the side of her face and flowed into the quiet extra fold of skin on the inside corner of her eyes. The black hair of her eyebrows emphasized the arch of her eyes. When she looked at him, Hugh could sense emotion. Thu Lan looked at him and saw that he had a high nose ridge and was larger framed than the average Vietnamese male. She liked his lighter "white" skin rather than the "yellow" skin so typical of Asians, and she felt conflicted over the preference.

Barefoot, she brought their breakfast on a tray. Carefully, she placed the silverware and plates and coffee cups just so with gentleness unmatched by any woman Hugh had ever known. Vietnamese women, Hugh thought, were unlike any others he had been familiar with around the world. They were not abrasive nor did they generally tend towards aggressivity like women in the west, did he think. And, except for many of the bar girls and taxi girls of downtown Saigon, they were not loud nor did they try to display their sexuality by baring skin or attempt to emphasize their breasts. Vietnamese women were not passive, he found, but respectful of their traditions; not serving, but helping with a respectful manner. There was refinement in the way the women conducted themselves. Their sexuality was hidden beneath their flowing silk robes and trousers and shaded by woven conical hats. Yet, for being nearly completely covered by clothing, their sensuality was displayed in a manner so vastly different than that of the west. Thu Lan stood at a mere four feet, eleven inches and weighed a only eighty-nine pounds, which Hugh estimated and she confirmed when he asked. But for her gentleness and kindness, there was an inner strength that placed table settings without hint of sound or disturbance. She was the respectful knock at the door, the soft padding of small, bare feet with delightfully elongated, straight toes on the newly swept wooden floor, the soft settling of a tray and the gentle movement of a woven reed broom sweeping dirt and dust to the dread of the war outside. Serenity was also in the way she would cleanse the wood floors with a washing rag while she squatted, resting her small, flat buttocks on her heels. To Hugh, she was becoming a refuge of calmness away from the chaos that echoed from artillery guns placed around the base camp and near the mountain. Her arrival in the early morning brought peace as the morning brought quiet from the nightly firing of artillery and mortars alike. The camp seemed immune from the ravages of war when she was there. Hugh didn't know how his thoughts were connected to the true state of things in the war around Tây Ninh.

Morgan re-appeared at the colonel's residence as quickly as he had disappeared a few days before. He acted as though not a moment had gone by since they last met and he asked if the two officers had prepared a list of equipment they would need and he told them where support would be located after the mission. They had indeed, the lieutenants replied, and they provided the list to Morgan who quickly perused it. Giving a nod, Morgan told the officers that they should be prepared to leave the following day, prior to dusk, for the journey to Trại Bí and thence to Thiện Ngôn near Xóm Mát.

The aid to the Chairman had been considering different aspects of the plan to maintain the status quo of their class. He also thought that, in order to secure a better relationship with the Chairman, he should take the initiative to present a safety measure to ensure success of the mission. He dwelt on the subject for several days and recalled several tactics his own father, the Senator, had used, not only in his political campaigns, but when he was also an overseer of certain foreign affairs of the United States.

Walking into the inner sanctum of the Chairman unannounced, the aid asked, "Sir?" He always called the Chairman "Sir" not only because he bore a likeness to his own father, but he could not grow accustomed to using first names with those in power. "Sir, I have been thinking seriously about the operation and quoting Shakespeare, 'Myself am one made privy to the plot,'" he inserted in a vain attempt to impress his superior, "I believe that we need an insurance policy to ensure the success of the plan. I understand through conversations with others in the Pentagon unrelated to our needs – uh, no Sir, no one knows of our connection nor do they know about our interests – and the area around the meeting site bears a heavy concentration of the Việt Cộng and North Vietnamese Army regulars. I have learned that the area is just now attempting to be cleared by a military operation called Attleboro. I believe in order to assure an even greater success for a satisfactory completion of the mission, we should have our contact in Hanoi provide limited information about the operation, only that two American Special Forces officers are there to protect the transference of documents and he should issue orders to the military and political leadership in the Tây Ninh area to ensure their safe passage through the area. That way, the officers are guaranteed to make contact with the courier. When they carry out their assigned mission, the Việt Cộng (he used the phrase eloquently for no one in the office used initials or colloquial phrases such as 'Charlie' or 'VC') may then terminate our mission. That way there will never be any revelation of their assigned task."

The Chairman thought for several moments in silence, a silence which disturbed the aid. He had never been so silent when contemplating a complicated business deal but this transcended the mere everyday business of gathering wealth. This, however, was to safeguard an entire economic ideal and it would affect millions upon millions of people. The aid took a seat as he was becoming to feel uncomfortable in the Chairman's long silence of contemplation.

At long last, the Chairman swiveled around from his view looking downward on the masses and stared at his aid. He thought to himself that, for someone who could not excel academically at university, he could exhibit malevolent traits that would do him well in the business or political realms. This was simply one of his better suggestions; simple, yet elegant in the fact that if the enemy unknowing of the intended mission, but believing there was another reason, no one would be the wiser, the documents would be destroyed, the officers would be a mere sacrifice for the millions who would be affected, and only a mere handful of select confidants would know only a few pieces of the the plan, their own conspiracy. The Chairman had long ago overcame his fear of using the word 'conspiracy' for he and his confederates had been required to plot and plan to maintain their economic interests on many occasions. Only the two of them, he and his aid, would know the complete arrangements along with the faceless contact at the other end of the direct telephone line. Only the Chairman knew it was a direct line to "The Farm," as it was known by some; "The Company" by others; he didn't know it had linked automatically overseas. Only he knew it connected corporate America with military and special intelligence resources that would be the assurance of capitalism surviving Marxism as an economic reality.

At long last, the Chairman instructed his young aid, "Go ahead. Make the call and tell them the basics. Make sure northern contacts are aware of only the basics. Provide them only with the fact that they need to send word to the south that our mission needs to be protected. Don't provide any other information. Get an update while you're at it."

"I will, sir," the aid replied excitedly. "Will there be anything else tonight, sir?"

"No, I think we've done quite enough for one day." The Chairman secretly thought that he had done quite enough for a lifetime.

Northeast and many miles from the small village of Xóm Mát, inside the border belt that runs between the Republic of Việt Nam and Cambodia, others had been also planning for Captain Tô Văn Huỳnh's arrival from North Việt Nam. A few select cadres had gathered in the leaf-roofed shelter to prepare plans for their special guests who would be meeting Captain Huỳnh. The briefing was conducted in a shelter covered with large, broad *trung quân* leaves, a leaf that acts as a natural fire retardant and is helpful in slowing fire damage in the aftermath of B-52 bomb strikes. The guests would be arriving at odd times and at odd places and were to be met by select members of the Việt Cộng 9th Division. On arrival, visitors would be blindfolded and led along the inches-wide paths through the thick undergrowth and would then congregate at a covered clearing in the thick forest and only then allowed to remove their blindfolds; only the route was secret. Everywhere inside the forest, everything looked the same, no matter where one stood. After all the guests arrived, they would be again blindfolded and led to a meeting hall deep within their secretive compound where they would meet the North Vietnamese agent. One of the cadre, dressed in a forest green uniform and still sporting a dark green pith helmet with a red star attached to the front, remarked that it had been strangely quiet for a few days, and the respite from the bombings was very relaxing. It was comforting because there was no need to quickly pack up and relocate operations across the border, which bisected the Mimot Plantation, into Cambodia and lose time in strategic planning. Under the protective canopy of trees towering more than sixty feet high, the four men sat around a simple wooden plank table and sipped Vietnamese green tea while they planned and waited.

The soldiers were aware that preparations were already made for Captain Huỳnh's arrival within the next several days. He would be arriving at a safe house outside of Xòm Mát village and from there he would meet with a counterpart from the southern regime. The men had instructions to allow the meeting to take place, but now they had been briefed of another facet of the meeting. Two American soldiers would also be present at the meeting. The men were astonished. American soldiers present in what was their highly-valued secret camps. Americans?! The enemy who had been aggressively pursuing their Việt Cộng 9th Division and 101st North Vietnamese Army Regiment and other units throughout Bình Dương and Tây Ninh Provinces for the past several months would also be meeting the men, and their reasons for joining the meeting were unclear. It sounded outrageous. However, those in Hà Nội had been specific in their instructions about Captain Tô Văn Huỳnh and Mr. Nguyễn Văn Hiền but those in the capitol did not earlier mention the inclusion of two American Special Forces officers. Perhaps they were simply being sent as protectors, as one man offered, to ensure the transfer of documents would be made. They wanted to radio Hà Nội and ask, but they feared provoking someone's anger. Previous radio transmissions in the past had either been leaked to the Americans by a spy among them, which they seriously doubted, or had been intercepted and their codes broken. No matter, they decided not to risk communications with Hà Nội and had to rely upon others to keep close surveillance. The men also thought that perhaps the American soldiers would attend in order to capture Captain Huỳnh, in which case, they would plan for their best trained soldiers to discreetly position themselves on the perimeter of the meeting place in the off-chance something may go wrong. Whatever the case, their instructions from Hà Nội were specific; allow the meeting between Huỳnh and Hiền to take place, regardless of whom else would be present.

IX

The tired and overcast sky just couldn't find the energy to rain, Hugh thought. Like returning war veterans from America who came to Việt Nam many years after their battles, both physical and psychological, the clouds also tried to find release and to purge themselves of their b. . . .a, in Asia, clouds release rain, rubber trees secrete latex from spiral-cut tree trunks, and the silent cries from veterans ooze from memories. With his two followers sitting at the next corner food vendor eating their noodle soup for breakfast, Hugh simply sat and drank his thick, brewed coffee, sitting with the old men who gathered to chain smoke, drink tea from aging aluminum pots and play Chinese chess. They found release in their tea and in their game. Hugh sat on a small wooden stool on the sidewalk near the faded yellow wall built during the French colonial time and listened to the men sing song with each other. They discussed chess strategy, woes with wives and girlfriends, or both. Hugh sat and tried to remember a name; tried to remember the face in a dream that escapes him every night.

It was already eight o'clock in the morning, four hours after waking, and he still couldn't shake the dream. A rivulet of water ran down the alley where he took his coffee; the water's source came from the old woman who watered her plants on the roof of her home nearby. A rivulet of memories began in his mind, but soon dried up before coming to the conscious level. There was no capillary action in his mind; nothing to bring the recollections to the surface. Remembrances and some memories wouldn't follow natural laws and rise to the top, but rather, they sank into a quagmire of forgetfulness. There could be something else to break those memories free, but what will it take? The smell of a cigarette after the act of love making? Polishing off a pint of Seagrams Seven at three o'clock in the morning? The flat, smooth stomach of a slim, young Annamite gradually rising to the prominence of soft hair on her pubic mound?

Hugh was temporarily brought back to the present when hit by shards of ice chipped from a larger solid block by Ông Tuận who owns the small store in the alley where Hugh took his coffee every morning. Ông Tuận's English improved a little everyday from conversations and Hugh's own Vietnamese linguistic skill returned to him in increments after years of non-use, but now both men were busy, one with running his store and the other with running his mind in reverse to find answers. Hugh sat alone thinking with his small glass of strongly brewed coffee in hand while Ông Tuận squatted with his sister who walks the neighborhoods all day long selling lottery tickets for two-thousand đồng each.

The ice delivery man on his decrepit Honda Cub motorcycle, powered by a too-small 70cc engine, coolly zig-zagged through a gaggle of children playing ball in the alley, their bicycles strewn about providing obstacles for others. He was returning from yet another ice delivery and the tailor women in the shop across the way zig-zagged on their ancient Singer sewing machines, apparently reconditioned in Hồ Chí Minh City or copied and produced in China.

At that time of the morning, it was still cool, by Indochina standards. With the clouds overhead, the ambient temperature was eighty degrees, but quite cool to those acclimatized. Taxi girls who lived nearby and dressed in loose fitting and lightly colored floral pajamas began to discharge their overnight guests. They won't show affection in public – to show affection in public is taboo – but have already shown their well-paid for affection through their long night behind locked doors and secure iron gates.

Hugh's memory sparked for a moment. A face appeared in the doorway of his mind and then as quickly, hid back inside the closet of recollection. Hugh wondered what sparked it so he could get it back again. He looked around the alley for clues. Was it the image of the taxi girls or the young girl at her sewing machine who took the time to look at Hugh and smile? Was it the mollusk-hatted woman who pushed her bicycle ladened with cardboard and other recycled items through the neighborhood; or the shy, young girl who daily peered at him from the doorway up the alley? Someday, he thought, he'd find the answer that will unlock the chamber revealing its secret contents like the pyramids did for Carter nearly eight decades ago. Hugh hoped his revelations won't come with a curse after opening the musty tombs of his memories.

A dog wandered out from its home, sniffed at doorposts and ground, looked at Hugh sitting with his coffee, and then was interrupted by motorbikes whizzing by above his eye level. The dog finally found the spot she was looking for and squatted to pee against a doorpost opposite the house she just exited, thus re-establishing her territory. Hugh, still squatting on the small wooden stool, recalled his own need to urinate after having downed three glasses of coffee, but like the dog, his urge was interrupted by a Caucasian who turned the corner from the main street 200 feet away and was walking towards him. He seemed oddly out of place because he was the only other foreigner Hugh has seen in this neighborhood. Only locals and the vendors and those who are familiar with the house where Hugh was residing, walked these back streets. With each step of the gargantuan, everyone stopped their activities to look at this odd foreigner, this "*người nước ngoài kỳ*." Although he ambled behind a cluster of high school girls in their white áo dàis and others returning from morning market carrying the plastic bags of fruit, produce, flowers and meat, he was more than a head or two taller than all of them. The stranger was strangely out of place in his walking shorts, tie-dyed t-shirt, white mid-calf socks and running shoes.

Walking up to Hugh, he announced, "I've been looking for you," his deep voice matching his hulk.

Hugh was taken aback. Here he had been sitting in a neighborhood away from the prying eyes of foreigners and completely surrounded by Vietnamese, and the only other foreigners to visit have been in his dreams of late, but this was no apparition, not the result of a night's drinking alone. This hulk was real.

"What do you mean 'you've been looking for me'?" Hugh asked guardedly.

"I heard there was another American living around this neighborhood. My girlfriend gets her hair cut and washed up the alley" – oh, yes, the shop where the shy young girl peers at me most mornings, Hugh thought – "all the women at the shop talk about you and say you sit here everyday and you look lonely" – I'm not, Hugh thinks to himself, I have my thoughts and need to remember things. There were a couple of drops from the sky that settled near Hugh for a moment, but then the clouds gave up trying. "They believe you're married, your wife goes to work every morning and leaves you alone. They thought you'd want a friend and another American to talk with," he finished.

The one-sided conversation was stopped by an invasion of eight young men with bright yellow golf shirts emblazoned with an American laundry detergent corporate logo. They were combing the neighborhoods in a house to house search operation to increase American corporate profits. The US military couldn't win their war of aggression by killing the Vietnamese, so the corporate armies returned for the profit-driven conquest to take prisoner their spendable income, what little of it there was. The Vietnamese still seemed innocently naive to the greedy environment of corporate America. Soon they'd succumb not to bombs, bullets, napalm, white phosphorous, defoliants, mortars or the mass killing of innocent civilians at a village ditch, but to the carpet bombing of home improvement products, appliances and other western "must haves and can't live withouts."

Americans, Hugh decided, had at long last removed the word "enough" from the English language and now wished to remove it from the remainder of the world's languages, deliberately attacking the developing world in their impoverishment and naïveté. Eventually, the beauty of the native language will disappear at the initial benign urgings of the corporations and replaced by the language of the economic enslavers. The yellow polo-shirted men with the American corporate logo were, in turn, interrupted in their own attack by the cauliflower and pineapple peddlers slowly bicycling down the alley, loudly hawking their products.

Checking his lingering thoughts, Hugh returned to the conversation with the large American as the clouds had completely given up and surrendered themselves to skies that were clearing.

"What makes you or others think I need someone to talk to?" Hugh stated emphatically. He didn't want the stranger to know he was staying in a house arranged by the police and continued, "If I wanted to talk to Americans, I could go down to District One, down to the Phạm Ngũ Lão area where the tourists and backpackers are, or, better yet, I could've stayed in America. Why in your arrogance do you think I need to be with or talk to other Americans? As a people, are we that insecure, paranoid or arrogant to think the only ones worthy of our presence or speech is another American? I'm actually very content here and don't need anyone to bother me." Hugh wanted to dissuade him in the simplest manner possible, but the stranger didn't understand the implications or the hint. Just then a cooling breeze came through the alleyway blowing out the spark of anger before it could ignite Hugh's resentment easily showed towards a country he likened to a herd of sheep led to slaughter by a political Judas Goat.

"I'm sorry," Hugh apologized, "for not showing manners. Please sit; I'll buy you a coffee. Iced or hot?"

"Iced coffee, but I can't take it strong, so I'll take some milk in it. Also, if you wouldn't mind ordering for me as I don't speak the language. I don't have an ear for it and the ladies said you do speak it pretty good for a foreigner."

Hugh ordered the coffee for both of them.

The coffee came, and except for the sounds of the motorbikes passing by them in the narrow alley and the children still at play, the men sat in silence. The stranger wanted to renew the conversation, but Hugh was tired even after four glasses of coffee and didn't feel like company.

Look, if you want conversation, you've come to the wrong guy. I'm here because I don't want to be around other foreigners," he said, again without giving the specific reason, "and especially Americans right now. I hope you'll understand. It's not personal. It's simply your national affiliation. You see, if I wanted conversation, and like I told you before, I'd go downtown, but right here it's quiet for me and I don't want the company. I'll pay for the coffees, don't worry. But, out of curiosity, where are you from in the States?" he inquired wanting to know just a bit more about this stranger.

"California; out in the desert near Barstow. It's quite hot like here, but at least it's dry and you don't feel sticky all the time from the humidity," the stranger said. "I used to play football but got injured and I'm here to get my wife back to the states."

"What brought you to Việt Nam in the first place?" Hugh asked, now somewhat more inquisitive, but also wary about the stranger.

"I have a disability from playing sports and decided to see part of the world. I landed here on my way back from Bangkok and decided to stay for awhile. I met this girl and we eventually got married. How about you?" The stranger seemed inquisitive himself.

"I was here for a bit during the war, up around the Tây Ninh area. Just a regular grunt, didn't see any combat," he lied. "I was just lucky to get back home after my tour."

"What's it like in Tây Ninh? I've never been there. Have you been to Dà Lạt, Nha Trang or Phan Thiết?" asking about three resort areas popular in Việt Nam.

Hugh was glad he had asked about other areas of Việt Nam as he didn't want to revisit Tây Ninh with the stranger, no matter how innocent he may appear to be, and he instantly dreaded mentioning it in the first place. Hugh looked around and felt safe after seeing the unobtrusive companions, who were still sitting hunched over their bowls of noodles and watching them, just as Inspector Quỳ had assured him. Hugh thought, 'at least if it gets too uncomfortable for me, they'll take care of him.' Hugh looked back to him and replied, "No, I haven't been, but I may get there at some point. I'll pay for the coffee now because I need to head home."

"Where are you staying? My wife thinks you live around here somewhere. You own or rent?" he asked.

"I live on another side alley several blocks away. See you around," Hugh excused himself leaving the questions unanswered and hoped the stranger would interpret the last phrase used for the silently stated, 'hope I don't see you again.'

Later back at the safe house, Inspector Quỳ had been waiting for Hugh to arrive. Hugh noticed his things had been discreetly searched, yet again, as insignificant indicators he left surrounding his luggage, black leather shaving bag and dresser drawers had moved from their original places ever so slightly.

Quỳ began the conversation, "Mr. Hugh, are you well today?"

"Yes, Inspector, thank you, as a matter of fact. If you'll excuse me, I've been drinking several cups of coffee and need to use the toilet."

"Yes, Mr. Hugh, please go ahead."

Hugh used the time to not only relieve himself, but to relive some moments in Tây Ninh in his mind that were sparked during the conversation with the American; Special Forces, Nũi Bà Đên, Cao Đài Temple. He remembered it all and wanted to rinse his face, hoping to wash away any tell-tale expressions. After using the toilet and refreshing himself, he returned to the living room where Quỳ was seated, uniform still meticulously pressed and black shoes shined.

"Mr. Hugh, we are still waiting for some more details, if you can help us. I have taken the liberty to make some unofficial contacts on your behalf recognizing that if I help you, you will help me. I do not want to be difficult, you see, but there are also questions still from superiors," the Inspector stated without divulging that he was being pressured from his managers. "Mr. Hugh, you also may want to know that we know that contact was made with you by an American intelligence source this morning. Your followers were not detected, but the man who spoke to you today is regularly seen entering and exiting your country's consulate on Lê Duẩn Boulevard, using an employee pass. You see, we also have special police on duty guarding your American presence here in Saigon. They have noticed this man and so have we. We can only wonder about why your own country's intelligence sources would have an interest in a tourist, as you call yourself. We also believe he is what your president has authorized as the Special Operations Command under your Defense Department. But we think about this question; why is America interested in you? We believe he is an agent of your government whose purpose is to look for terrorists," Quỳ stated matter-of-factly.

"Inspector, first, I had no idea ne may be an 'intelligence source' as you say. He gave a credible reason for being there and didn't pressure me for any information. What would make you think the CIA or SOCOM, for that matter, would have an interest in me," Hugh lied. "You know I'm not a terrorist and don't condone violence. I have no idea why 'my country,' as you say, has an interest in me. I'm a tourist and a returning veteran of the American war here, as you know. If anything, and I will be frank with you, with the current tenor of political and civil liberties, I feel more comfortable and at home here in Việt Nam than I do in America, and so I cannot imagine any reason for their interests in me."

"Mr. Hugh, that is what we are still trying to calculate, no that's not the word, figure out, yes, figure out. We have no reason to believe you are a terrorist, but your government has an interest in you that we cannot overlook. Also, Mr. Hugh, what were you and Mr. Whitman doing in Tây Ninh province? What was it you were intending to look for around Xã Mát and the border with Cambodia? There is nothing that would interest Americans there anymore, unless you found our culture historical monument of the Central Office of South Việt Nam, what you called COSVN during the war, interesting. Yes, it is interesting isn't it, our VC Center, as we Vietnamese like to call it. There are many sites there, but did you take the time to visit them? No, I think not. So, there is another reason for your interest in Tây Ninh; something very important to perhaps lead to the cause of Mr. Whitman's untimely and early departure from this life. I assure you again, Mr. Hugh, that what occurred during the war is the past. We are moving forward. Yet, I have my reports to complete," the Inspector emphasized looking at Hugh as though he was under pressure from his superiors and needed sympathy from him.

Hugh thought for a moment, looked at Quỳ and wondered how much he actually knew, and more so, how much he should tell him. Of all the people in the country who had contact with him, Quỳ seemed the most sincere even though he was a policeman.

"Inspector, you know my memory is still sketchy from those war days, and especially from the injuries I recently suffered in Tây Ninh. Perhaps if you can trust me for another day or so, I may start to recall events in my mind. You may tell your superiors that events are coming back to my memory, but the thoughts are still unconnected. I think those connections may just be another day or so, and if you can stall your managers, they may be more happy with a complete story in a few days rather than smaller pieces over a greater period of time if I am pressured," Hugh asserted.

"Mr. Hugh, I believe that will be satisfactory. In the meantime, I have some information that you may or may not wish to act upon. On this piece of paper is an address of a coffee shop on Hồ Văn Huê Street in the Phú Nhuận District.

It is not far, just a mere fifteen minute drive from here if you go by motorbike taxi," Quỳ said. "There is an Irish expatriate who owns the coffee shop with his Vietnamese wife. He has been quite helpful and has many contacts in the city, which is surprising for a foreigner, but it is his wife who has the important contacts. She is one you should see regarding your dreams. She may be able to help you. You understand that I myself am taking a risk, but I believe, Mr. Hugh there is much more to you than one can merely see. As your have been trained to keep certain facts to yourself, I trust this will be added to those things you will not divulge," Inspector Quỳ requested more than urged.

"Inspector, this is surprising, but I don't see how you can help me with my dreams. But, you have been very fair to me and I see no reason to turn down your assistance. I assure you no one will be aware of this information you gave me. As a courtesy, I will flush it down the toilet, as it is an easy address to memorize. I thank you, Inspector," Hugh said sincerely.

"I will leave you alone for a few days."

"Thank you, Inspector. Your trust is assured."

PART II

I

The morning of the lieutenants' departure began as usual, except for the nagging thoughts that Hugh fostered throughout the night. He and Whitman had stayed up late the night before reviewing each and every step, quizzing each other on every detail of the new reconnaissance photos they were provided, which were taken hours before and 'choppered up' by special courier from Headquarters Seventh Air Force at Tân Sơn Nhứt Airbase in Saigon. They received additional photographs of Captain Huỳnh and Mr Hiền, updates on the route in and out of Xóm Mát, the slight nuances of the Vietnamese dialect spoken in the Xóm Mát area and they questioned each other about the local favorite delicacies enjoyed by Vietnamese and Cambodian alike. The officers reviewed smuggler's trails, names and locations of safe houses reconfirmed within the past twenty-four hours by US and Vietnamese intelligence sources and prepared their equipment. The plan for them was to be dropped off at the camp at Trại Bí on Highway 22 and there meet another M113 Armored Personnel Carrier that would take them the rest of the way to a rudimentary camp at Thiện Ngọn, about four and a half kilometers south of Xóm Mát. Every contingency was planned for and they believed, no the word would be *hoped*, it may be a very easy mission. They would merely intercept a meeting between two men, terminate the mission of the one from the North, and destroy the documents and return. The only unknown factor was when the northerner would reach the Xóm Mát area and the location of the subsequent meeting point.

That morning, like a reliable chronometer that keeps time constant and accurate, came the expected soft rap on the door, marking the time for breakfast. Thu Lan stood there demurely at the door in her black silk trousers and white blouse, as she had on every other morning, save Sunday. Hugh calmly let her in. Betrayed by his own heart, and while Whitman was still showering after their run, Hugh had told Thu Lan he would be gone for a few days, but he would be returning to Tây Ninh and he wanted to see her again. He explained it may be easy to visit her because when he returned he would not be staying at the colonel's. He could not tell her any plans beyond his return because those plans were held in the hands of the "gods" in Washington, or wherever it was they resided on their stained thrones. Hugh added that something was stirring inside him and had been since he first saw her; a young, innocent and beautiful girl who waited on an American soldier. Perhaps they would be able to meet each other and exchange contact information once he returned from, what he called, personal business.

Thu Lan stood and listened to the American awkwardly reveal his feelings, something that was odd for a professional soldier, but she silently admitted she had begun feeling something towards this foreign soldier also. She had been trying to resolve the conflicts in her own heart. She was a traditional Vietnamese girl reared in the valued customs of her country, but once she first saw this soldier, this attractive stranger, she had also felt something but she could not betray her heart as he had done to his. There were other aspects of her that he could not know about, nor could she divulge her deeper secrets; secrets that even her own parents knew nothing about. Her conflicts suddenly began to overwhelm her, but her training and her upbringing had been perfected so that she did not display the emotion that was welling inside her demure, yet strong body. She could not do or say anything now. Perhaps there would be a time soon, but this could not be the time, nor could it ever be the place. She believed that circumstances often present themselves as tests for the individual and her Confucian traditions would save her and others from disasters. Yes, she admitted, there was a feeling for him, a feeling she had seen others act upon during war when people knew not whether they would survive another day or through another long night of the war and they had acted on those urges and their emotions and now she was feeling the same things. She also didn't know whether she would survive the next day in this war and often wondered whether there would ever be a future for her. She had seen her friends steal away to discrete places and heard them making love; the awkward groans, the squeaking of humidity-swollen, wooden beds held together by dowels; the rapid breathing and finally the muted gasps at the end. She wondered, the end of what? The conflict was between her traditions and her physical needs. Those physical needs began to manifest themselves about three years before. When she was alone in her bed, and heard her brother, sisters and parents sleeping, she would follow a natural urge and feel the moisture between her legs and begin to rub. The need would come back to her at times, and sometimes, late at night and alone, she would act on those sensations. Now, these feelings were coming back as the American told her of his interest in her. She could only reply to him simply, "We shall see what the future brings. This is war and everything is uncertain." She felt, though, another time may present itself, and if tragedy was the outcome, she would not question it, but clearly accept life as it was. That was how one treated everything during a war.

That night the lieutenants were treated to a special early dinner. Thu Lan had worked through her afternoon break to plan for the dinner. She prepared chả giò – spring rolls – on beds of lettuce, and thick, bright orange carrots were cut into the shapes of hearts, shells and stars that lined the rim of the plate. Next, she served the specially prepared chicken and fried rice. The main course was a traditional hot pot. It was placed on a burner in the center of the table, and when the broth came to a boil, meat, shrimp and vegetables were placed in the pot to cook. From a bowl kept off to the side of the table, she took white vermicelli noodles and placed the white, sticky noodles in individual bowls. When the soup came to a second boil, it was poured over the noodles for a sumptuous meal. While preparing their dinners at the table, Thu Lan told them all the food was grown locally so that its freshness was guaranteed. She added that each ingredient had been washed properly so as not to cause any discomfort later.

The colonel and the lieutenants finished their meal and Thu Lan cleared the dishes and went to retrieve the red silk box that contained the tea pot. Hugh realized this may be the last time he would see Thu Lan, unless there was some way he could ensure his return to Tây Ninh after the operation and get back to see her before other orders took him elsewhere. Everything, he thought, depended on the success of the operation – everything.

Just before it was time for Hugh and Whitman to depart, Thu Lan gently knocked on their door. "Please, take this with you." She placed a twenty piaster note folded origami-style of two swans facing each other, their graceful necks forming a heart, into the palm of his hand. "Remember me. Keep it for good luck, health and happiness," she ended. With that she shook his larger hand, using both of hers, and said good bye.

Hugh watched her walk down the short hall and she disappeared from view. He wanted to do all he could to get back to see her; all that he could.

An APC arrived shortly after five-thirty to pick up Whitman and Hugh. The officers took their packs and threw them into the armored vehicle next to a few special items they needed for the operation. The colonel didn't see them off as he had left the already residence, having the need to oversee some other matters near the Michellin Plantation to the east of Tây Ninh, near Dầu Tiếng. Without a word, the steel-plated vehicle took off with a discernible whirring up of the turbine engines and gathered speed as it left the colonel's compound. The semi-dirt road which served as Highway QL-22 was fairly flat, but then again, Hugh thought, everything was flat in this part of the country, except for the elephant grass, the huge termite mounds, and the mountain, which he could not see from inside the vehicle. Thirty minutes later the vehicle commander, a young sergeant from New Hampshire, announced they were approaching Trại Bí. They were in radio contact with the other APC that would take them to Thiện Ngôn, but it had hit a mine shortly after leaving the camp and there was no other equipment to pick them up and deliver them until tomorrow late morning, at the earliest. The lieutenants knew they had a rendezvous to keep and because the lieutenants were practiced in adapting quickly to rapidly changing situations, they decided to tell the sergeant to leave them there. They would make the remaining distance on foot and arrive at Thiện Ngôn much quicker than the Army could get them there. With a wish of good luck from the sergeant, the lieutenants took off on foot. They had completely briefed themselves about the area and knew every inch of it, including safe houses, people to contact, and the safest route to take. They estimated they would arrive at no later than eight-thirty or nine that night.

North of Trại Bí three people in black pajamas and palm-woven conical hats sat alongside a cratered and pock-marked paddy halfway into its growing season. They sat huddled together to keep the evening chill coming off the water from getting to their bones. They had already eaten a meager meal of rice and fish followed by some tea and a few cakes and they now waited for a rendezvous to occur. The leader told them it would be an unconventional meeting and though they might not understand; their leader needed to be trusted. They were waiting for two American soldiers their leader learned were now on foot towards them. Means had been taken ensure they would be walking this night. The Americans, they learned from others, were separated from each other by about twenty meters and walking in their direction. They were about one and a half kilometers away. At no point were they to be engaged as the enemy. Everyone had orders to allow the leader to make an undisturbed contact.

The crescent moon allowed the lieutenants just enough light to walk by and both were well trained to work in the dark and accustom their eyes to dim nights. They constantly scanned the horizon and used their peripheral vision to see for them without staring at a point, as it would "wash out" their vision if they looked intently in one direction. Occasional home fires of coal and wood were seen that assisted them and they were making fairly good progress on the highway towards Thien Ngon. Occasionally, they quietly passed small residential clusters of six or seven bamboo-framed huts, but not quite big enough to be a village. They each knew the several areas and had committed them to their memories. The lieutenants would now be reaching an area of rice paddies in their growing season and not harvestable for another two months. By then, their operation would be long over and they would be elsewhere. Quietly and without a sound coming from their footfall, they continued northward towards Thiên Ngôn. The skies were quiet except for a lone aircraft, what they believed sounded like a C-47, the ancient WWII workhorse of the Air Force. Because it was a cargo aircraft, they wondered what it was doing up there alone. They did not believe it was an AC-47, affectionately called "Puff the Magic Dragon," the famed two-engine gunship that could spray out its munitions of death with 7.62 millimeter Gatling guns that could cover every square inch of a football field in one minute. The lieutenants thought it could be a covering aircraft for them should they run into some unforeseen problems, but the aircraft seemed too high should they require help. If they did run into a situation that turned ugly, the lieutenants would use the one radio they had to call a mayday on the Guard channel, a channel that was monitored twenty-four hours a day, but mostly used unneccesarily for radio checks. Regardless, the lone aircraft droned on in a pattern known only to the pilots of the 360th Reconnaissance Squadron and the radio operators of the 6994th Security Squadron who crewed the back end.

II

Hugh was the point man on their journey north while Whitman followed at a safe distance behind. They had already passed a couple of rice paddies of rice stalks rising out of the water that reflected the crescent moon, and Hugh could make out a wood line separating two more sets of rice fields in the distance. He slowed his pace as a precaution to provide more reaction time should they need it. It was their training and it proved to be of value, but not for the surprise he experienced.

"Lieutenant Hugh," a voice called to him softly in the foreboding dark.

Hugh was dumbstruck. It could not be true. It cannot be her. His mind had been thinking of her and he knew his delusional wishful thinking was merely taking over. The voice from the darkness called again in a whisper.

"Lieutenant Hugh. Do not be alarmed. It is me, Miss Thu Lan."

Instantly, he called back in a voice above a whisper to Whitman who was 20 meters behind, "Hold up a moment." He returned to the direction of the voice ahead. "Thu Lan, where are you? What are you doing here?" he asked dumbfounded, confused and now feeling very alert for trouble.

Quietly and almost without sound, she climbed up the slope out of the paddy near the tree line. She was dressed in black pajamas with a canvas sling supporting a canteen on her waist. Around her neck, she wore a faded, black and white checkered scarf and a conical hat hung on her back with the attached strap of worn out cloth around the front of her neck. Hugh instantly recognized the typical, irregular uniform of the Việt Cộng. Mentally, he was shaken. Here was a beautiful Vietnamese girl, he had begun developing strong feelings for and she was the enemy. How she could betray him, he wondered. He wanted her, but she was, was… he could not gather words to describe what he was thinking or feeling. He was suddenly conflicted. Quickly, he aimed his rifle at her, relying on training rather than emotions. She saw him draw his weapon.

"Lieutenant Hugh, please no," she implored. "As you can now see, I have no gun or weapon. It is with great sadness I must betray myself in this manner and I know returning to the colonel at Tây Ninh is now and forever impossible. Yet, the things you told me this morning has given me cause to reveal myself to you and hope that for this one time, you may forget our different situations." She looked behind him to see the vague outline of Whitman Emerson who had taken a crouching position on the shoulder of the road. "Please tell Lieutenant Whitman not to worry. You both will not be harmed. You are actually ensured free passage to Thiện Ngôn tonight for there are others who make plans and you are also part of the plans; we are all pawns, never knowing when another piece will capture another, and we are in a game of chess. This is not unlike a game that we cannot control nor do we know all the rules. Any of us only know what we are told and when to do something.

"Like you, yes, I feel something, something for which I cannot explain and I have been giving it much thought all day," she added still speaking slightly above a whisper at the close distance. "If you can still trust me for some moments longer, I want you to accompany me over here. Please, Lieutenant Hugh, please trust me. We will never have a moment like this again. Please ask Lieutenant Whitman to wait for you. He will be watched over by my comrades. You have my promise he will not be harmed."

How would Whitman take the news that the girl Hugh had desired was VC and with him right now. The operation, he realized, was compromised as VC cadre also knew about part of their operation, but it was part of a plan. What insanity this was, he thought. What insanity, indeed! Hugh thought for a moment, his mind calculating hundreds of equations. Coming to a quick conclusion, he then whispered back to Whitman, "Wait, I've made friendly contact with information. Wait for me."

"Standing by," Whitman whispered back. Whitman could only see two silhouettes in the dark. The crescent moon could not provide enough light to accurately detail the scene that night, so he had to trust Hugh. Whitman quietly sat down in place, observing everything around his position.

Thu Lan took Hugh's unarmed left hand and led him several yards away to a reed-thatched hut. It was difficult for him to see in this minimal light. "Lieutenant, you expressed your feelings to me early this morning and it surprised me that a soldier could talk about the ways of his heart so easily. It is usually the woman who is able to talk so about feelings. You made me think much because I have also been thinking about you and having feelings since I met you. I have been on many tasks and assignments with many of my comrades; men and women. I know we feel that during war many values change. We Vietnamese women value children and our traditions and our heritage. We also know from the war with the French and now the Americans that our men are being lost and that will deprive us of a spouse or father for our children. What I am saying is that many of my comrades take free moments to hide themselves and to be with each other to express their feelings and release their physical needs.

"Lieutenant Hugh, I came here at great risk to my position. I have felt much distraction and also feel confused by the feelings that I have had. I have had to lead a secret life for a long time, working for the colonel, who I came to like and respect as he respected me, and my other secret life working for the cause of freedom for my country."

Hugh interrupted her, "You're VC. How could you betray your father, your parents? I can understand the colonel; he was your employer, a foreigner, but your parents?"

"Because of my father's rank and position, my leaders have spared me from any duties that would involve my father's company. But, working for the colonel, his residence and the base was always secure and safe when I was working there."

Hugh quickly realized why it was quiet when she was at the camp. They did not dare risk damaging a valued resource inside a secure compound. He reminded himself that "Arc Lights" have been temporarily suspended while he and Whitman are in the area. He understood that.

"But, Lieutenant Hugh, the reason I am here is different. I am here on a matter of the heart, for one, and on another matter, for two, I think you would say in English. You and Lieutenant Whitman are not the only ones aware of your mission. We have orders to ensure your safety through the area. My unit and I are here to make sure of your protection. We are aware of a meeting to take place. We are to stay away, but ensure the meeting takes place and you depart safely.

"I knew we would never be able to meet again after these actions. I have taken great risk to contact you, but it is for my own curiosity and needs. Lieutenant Hugh, I have begun to feel love for you. We don't know if there will ever be another chance again to be close to each other and feel love."

Inside, Thu Lan was feeling conflicted. She was thinking about the secret life she was leading that only her comrades, and now an 'enemy,' knew about. She was raised in a traditional home in a non-traditional time of war. She had seen many girls she knew going off secretly with men for whom they had feelings. They had wanted children, they had wanted to feel loved, to feel different, to feel…to feel like a woman for a change, not like a soldier. Yet, she had her traditions. She had been experiencing the absence of the feelings of yearning. She could only imagine what it would be like to be with a man. She didn't want to be indiscriminate like the others, she wanted someone special.

Thu Lan wished she could free herself of her conflicts: her secret life at night, the love for her parents and family and yet her loyalty to fight for independence for her country. She wanted freedom for her country, but also freedom from the conflict of maintaining traditions and her deep feelings for a man. She wanted to feel the arms of a man around her gently holding her and feeling love inside her. The conflict of being Việt Cộng and having overwhelming emotions for an enemy soldier troubled her. She wished the war was over, no matter the resolution, she simply wanted it over, though her wanting tended towards a reunified country free from foreigners like the Chinese, French and, yes, the Americans. She also felt her conflict grow between the tradition and custom of being a Vietnamese woman and only wanting for the husband to be the first man to see her naked and to experience him inside her, and the need to be with this man standing in front of her now. She alone war in the position of deciding when to lose her precious status and she desired…, she hesitated in her thoughts. What was her desire? She wanted the American. The conflicts trapped her in a conundrum, which was her present life coupled with a woman's physical need. She began to reason that this situation was not an ordinary matter and the constant discord inside her underscored the conflict that was taking place between the superpowers Soviet Union, China and the United States, all using Việt Nam to assert their global positions towards dominance of a certain economic and political system. Rather than fighting between themselves, they used and exploited the Vietnamese who simply wanted a reunified country. Each nation had fought for those same goals. Thu Lan decided she should fight for her own independence against her sometimes better judgment. That was when she realized she wanted the lieutenant who walked into the colonel's quarters and into her life, for whatever reasons there were. She had now crossed the threshold where she could no longer return to the employ of the colonel and she could not withdraw from the decision to be with Lieutenant Hugh. It was her decision to end the conflict in her once and for all and to achieve some modicum of peace and independence within herself even if it could not be found in the world without.

She motioned for him to undress as she wanted him to have her. "Please lay your guns on the other side. I assure you the safety of Lieutenant Whitman and yourself is completely guaranteed. Please be soft with me. I am afraid, I am shy but I am also curious. I am afraid there will be much pain, but there is already much pain in life and how much more can there be when people love each other?" she asked rhetorically.

Hugh was completely stunned by her revelations and wanted to take her somewhere else far away from Tây Ninh Province, far away from Việt Nam and completely far away from all war and her own conflicts. He simply told her, "Thu Lan," and then stopped. Hugh realized words were absolutely inadequate at this point. She took off her hat and laid it aside. He took off his weapons and laid them inside the upturned mollusk hat that she put in the corner. It was dark inside the hut. The barest illumination came from a homefire in a kitchen not far away; indiscernible mutterings inside the home were as dim as the firelight and carried far at night.

Thu Lan drew closer to Hugh and his long arms surrounded her waist, captivating her and she drew her hands up to his chest and unbuttoned his utility shirt. Slowly, and with more caution he would muster within an enemy's reach, he softly moved his hands around her sides and inside her black shirt. Gradually and carefully, he moved them up to find her firm, petite, rounded breasts and taut nipples. He sensed her breathing becoming a little more rapid and with one hand, removed it from her blouse to her neck. He felt the soft hairs and concealed the checking of her carotid artery for her rising pulse by gently stroking the soft skin of her throat and neck. Hugh became acutely aware of her changing physical state. He recalled the first time he had been with his former fiancée and quickly damning the memory, diverted it from the moment. Hugh now only wanted to focus on Thu Lan, the peaceful foe in his arms.

They both slowly found the wooden bed in the corner of the small room and sat down together. Undressing each other, they were now vulnerable to each other and to the forces they each represented, but the only force they now engaged was their feelings for each other.

Thu Lan was surprised at herself and her feelings. She was allowing this act to happen and felt as though she had finally stepped out of her body. The abundance of the colonel's house, although not quite much, but more than the typical Vietnamese, and the privative nature of her guerilla lifestyle were in stark contrast as were the traditions of her culture with her physical and emotional needs at the moment. Here, in this illogical hut alongside the road that runs from Tây Ninh to Xóm Mát and beyond, she was illogically yielding herself to satisfy her own needs before war took them away permanently. She wanted her conflicts to end. By yielding to Hugh, the conflict between her duty as a Việt Cộng and her duty to the colonel would end – she was now compromised and would have to devote her life now to the cause. The need for love in a world of hate was being sated, and as she bared her body and she also revealed the femininity she so much desired to give to someone she loved. Not with any man, but her love would be given to someone memorable and special. Perhaps, she thought, there may be a future with a home and children in a peaceful country. She felt she was building a bridge with her body as she arched backwards in his arms. She was forging a connection between enemies out of love and a desire for a peaceful world, she believed. As Hugh was stroking her neck, she felt her own heartbeat and her breathing increasing, as well. She was becoming more afraid, afraid of the possible pain, the embarrassment of her naked body that no man, not even a doctor, had seen before. Here in the dim light of the hut, there would not be much to see, but in a sense, she wanted Hugh to be pleased with her young body. Thu Lan was also very curious about the act of love. Would it be similar to the way she secretly rubbed herself? The breathing and heartbeat felt the same, but this would be something different, she knew. What am I supposed to do, what am I supposed to feel, she questioned herself; doubts, fears, embarrassment, shyness, curiosity, desire, anticipation? All these inquisitive emotions stirred within her heart and body and she realized she had been slowly reaching towards Hugh's pants and feeling for him while he touched her.

Slowly, cautiously and with tenderness at odds with the outside world, they undressed each other. Hugh was being mindful of warnings, whether truthful or not, about women who had booby-trapped themselves with explosives or other devices to permanently injure or kill allied soldiers. He was cautious in two manners and he cursed himself for thinking that Thu Lan would do such a thing, but he damned his training and tried to shake the idea out of his mind, but could not. Yet, slowly he began to yield to her, and his cautionary thoughts shifted to concern for the pain she may feel when he would enter her small, young body.

Slowly, he glided on top of her, both of them now completely naked to the world, bare to the stark hostilities that surrounded them in the still of the black night. There in the darkness where hardly any light penetrated the windows, Hugh slowly and carefully penetrated Thu Lan, ever mindful to be slow for her, not to force everything at once, but to let their love be slow, advancing ever so slightly with each movement in, pausing and slowly advancing; a pause, a moment of breath in the dark, a look at her beautiful face accented by her eyes in the dimness and shadowed areas melded with his memory of her standing in the doorway in Tây Ninh in her áo dài and in her fragility. Slowly, carefully, slowly.

Thu Lan felt Hugh finally putting himself in her very slowly. It was not as painful as the other girls had talked about after their first time at making love with fellow comrades in a clearing smoothed out of the jungle or forest. That love making, she was told, had been rapid, but she felt that Hugh was purposely taking his time and being slow for her. She thought the war in her country had lasted for a long time, so why shouldn't love also endure to balance it out? Ticklish and sensitive types of feelings began to emerge from her private area, from that spot she liked to massage in the quiet of her solitary bed. Now that spot was beginning to swell with enjoyment as the American soldier lay on top of her, inside her, moving ever so slowly. She discovered her own body was naturally reacting to the penetration. Her back was arching and her pelvis was rising as if wanting to consume more of him inside her. Her buttocks tensed rhythmically, her pelvis began to move more towards him, meekly demanding more. She had never seen a man naked before and wondered for a moment what he looked like, but she could only imagine as he would move ahead deep inside her with each slow movement forward, which she accepted and responded with the natural rhythm of her body that surprised her. There, in the hut alongside a paddy, the darkness filtered their emotions.

Each was aware of the other's rising anticipation. Thu Lan was feeling the pleasure she had only wondered about and became lost in a wave of ticklish, sensitive pleasure that began to overwhelm her body in a rising, spasmodic feeling. She moved her body against his to place him in special areas where she felt the most pleasure and she kissed him on the mouth, tasting the coolness of his breath. Hugh had also felt the rising tide inside him and still, he was slow in his motions so as not to cause her any pain but to maximize her delight, as much as he could. He didn't want all this for himself, he decided, he wanted this for her, mostly; to create something that could endure the war and create a love that could outlast the hate. He wanted moments of peace that would overcome the hostilities raging in the paddies, villages, countryside and towns. Slowly, a heaviness began to well up inside her, and deep within him as Thu Lan's body began to rise ever so rapidly and her respirations increased. He was no longer aware of his military caution; that evaporated with each measured and cautious push inside her. He felt safe with her now, he trusted her and no longer thought of her as the enemy, but a woman he wanted to be with, that together they could do what generals and politicians had failed to do to in order to create a better world. Here, deep in the core of hate and in the eye of the tempest, they were finding love. A spark that began as dim as the home fire burning against the dark of night began to rage inside the confines of their bodies. Her body rose with a quicker tempo and he felt the gathering of his seed swelling within him to a point that he could no longer restrain it. Each of them knew the point at which the ultimate pleasure was now coming to fruition for the other. They each believed the moment lasted for a lifetime. For that long moment, all war ceased and there was no enmity in the world.

In the still of that autumn night, alongside the dirt road to Xóm Mát from Tây Ninh, and in that ramshackle hut lit only by stars, a home fire and the paleness of a crescent moon, two people silently exploded in rapture and pitched themselves headlong into a different world from which they could never return. Here is where they acted out of love and creation against a world of destruction and animosity. They had changed life for themselves and they could never withdraw from a position they created with each other. They were no longer on opposite sides of an imaginary line, but were now together, lying on that wooden bed, naked in their innocence like children.

Thu Lan began to weep softly. Hugh saw the slight glistening of a tear in the corners of her dark and innocent eyes that were turned towards the moon. He suddenly remembered another autumn night in his hometown in California when he and his high school sweetheart first made love in the back seat of his father's Buick in the hills above their hometown. That had also been a night of a crescent moon. After their first time at making love, Hugh saw a tear of that remote fall season pooling in the corner of her eye. But now, this was an Autumn Tear from an Autumn Orchid. Hugh felt his masculine façade fade as he yielded to emotions and feelings he had been burying since he entered the Army and was commissioned an officer and trained in Special Forces. In his position, no one had feelings and no one expressed feelings, unless it was a jingoistic display of patriotism. Those were the only feelings allowed; love for god and country, but not usually in that order. No attachment, no feelings, no connection to anything to divert attention away from your operation, your mission, your duty or your country. Yet, here in the beautiful Vietnamese countryside, in this hut next to bomb-scarred paddies, he now felt emotion and tears welled in his eyes, as well. These two newly initiated lovers now wept silently without moving, without speaking. He was still inside her and she lay there holding him around the waist, not wanting him to withdraw away from her.

Tears dropped from his face onto her cheeks and the moistness gathered and collected in the inner corner of her soft, dark, penetrating eyes. Leaning down towards her face, he delicately kissed her eyes, forehead, nose and cheeks and then gently blotted the tears from her eyes with her scarf that was nearby. There were no words they could find to say to the other. They were both proficient in each other's language, but they lay silently in each other's arms forgetting their allegiances, blocking the unreal world without the hut. The sweat of their bodies mingled on stomachs and chest against breast. He could feel her delicate nipples against the hair on his chest, and he was acutely aware of how fragile, yet strong, she was, how small and how beautiful. A soft wind plied through the palms, giving rise to a song among the palm fronds and crickets outside, and the song of wind found its way inside the hut; a tender movement of air came between them, cooling their heat, but not the passion. Time was lost in that hut. Time no longer existed. Slowly and with hesitation, Hugh began to delicately withdraw from inside Thu Lan. She resisted for an instant, wanting to feel him inside her just one moment longer then, with a sense of regret, released him from her hold around him.

With the stillness of his training, he slowly rose and began to dress, trying not to think about the implications of their act, but simply absorbing everything that had taken place and the sense of amazement that it even took place at all. They were both standing now, dressing each other; he pulling her black shirt around her and buttoning the front and holding her black pants as she slipped each leg into them. She helped him with his uniform which she had hand-washed the day before and helped with his equipment. They were no longer enemies. They had completed the passage from the dichotomy of friend or foe and were now standing as fellow citizens on the same shore of an unknown and foreign land only known to them.

She, at long last, said to him in her slightly-accented English, "Lieutenant Hugh, I do not know exactly the words to say what is in my heart. I only hope that we will keep this night always for ourselves and please do not ever forget me or be angry at me. I cannot change who I am, but I have changed what I feel. Please do not think less of me for what I have allowed to happen. We have both violated the rules of our different sides. I do not think now we will ever have the chance to be with each other again. I hope we could because of the feelings I have for you, but it is hopeless while our countries fight each other.

"Please remember that you and Lieutenant Whitman will have a protected journey this night as we have our orders not to attack or try to harm or stop you. As I told you before, we are to see that you complete your mission, whatever it is," she reassured him. "Please keep this moment in your mind to remember me."

It was as though Hugh didn't need the reassurance. He did not even know how long they had been together, but their time had been undisturbed as she had promised. Looking at his watch revealed that they had been together approximately thirty-five minutes, though paradoxically it seemed much longer and yet much shorter.

"Thu Lan ơi." Hugh had begun using the more personal manner of calling her and adding the word 'ơi' while at the Colonel's, as it did make sense; something that Whitman refused to do. Whitman preferred pejorative terms towards the Vietnamese. After all, he was the son of a career Army officer, wasn't he, who had served in Korea and in the earlier years of the American War in Việt Nam against the Communists. When he saw her looking up at him Hugh continued, "What we have done here tonight is something that will never be divulged to anyone else. If there were some way I could make this craziness go away and maybe have the possibility of a life here with you, I would. But, for now, we are on different sides. I understand your commitment to your cause may very well be much stronger than mine. It's your country you are fighting for, your homes and culture. I'm a foreigner who has sometimes questioned quietly why America is here in the first place. It may not make sense to me, but I have an obligation to my country, a duty to see through and orders to follow. I wish everything could change because I have very strong feelings for you and hope that tonight you felt and understood them. We are two strangers here in the dark. At some point, possibly years from now, we just may be able to get together and try to have some semblance of a normal life, but, sadly, this is not normal.

"Thu Lan, you and I will always have this night together. Even if we are unable to see each other at all for the rest of our lives, you will never be forgotten, you will never be unloved. Look outside and somewhere in the sky there are stars that have watched our love tonight and they will remember. Anytime we look into the night sky we will be reminded of our night of love. I wish to heaven we could simply walk away from all of this and try to make a life for ourselves, but we both know it's impossible," he finished with a slight tremble in his voice.

She quietly raised her hand and pressed her fingertips against his lips. She knew what she was feeling and knew instinctively he was feeling the same, but right now she didn't want talk. She wanted him to hold her one last time, once more before they had to return to the ugliness in the world and the violence outside the doorless shack. She knew that someday they will face the ghosts in their past and remember this night. For now, she wanted quiet against the backdrop of sporadic, automatic gunfire and the impact of mortar rounds somewhere in the distance, punctuating the stillness of the night. She wanted to remember not the words, but the feeling of this man she now loved. She began to weep again without a sound and Hugh felt her trembling slightly as he held her in his arms against the world. With a final kiss, they each returned to resume the routine abnormalities of their lives, once again as enemies, but now with different rules of engagement. Could either of them ever fire a shot at the other or allow another to do so? Could they ever follow orders to kill an enemy?

Thu Lan returned to her comrades. She told them that she had orders to make contact with the enemy soldier and that there was difficulty in some of the translation, she half-way lied.

Hugh returned to Whitman, who had been sitting on his pack for the past nearly three-quarters of an hour. Hugh simply advised him a partisan initiated contact, provided information that there were no enemy movements in the area, and their passage would be safe and unmolested all the way to Thi□n Ngôn. With that, they would be able to hasten their step and arrive much sooner than expected. He told Whitman that some regional nuances of translation had been difficult and that took most of the time, he also partially lied.

Decisions unknown to Hugh and Thu Lan made so far away had woven their paths together, though the weavers would never know the subtle design created out of their warp and weft. This night and their lovemaking was an unintended consequence of an intricate pattern set upon the loom. These two threads woven together would never be known to the designers; only to the two of them. Hugh could not divulge to Whitman that he had made love to a Việt Cộng without severe repercussions, and he believed that Thu Lan could never reveal their love to her own comrades and still maintain her position amongst the cadres. Of all the military secrets kept by countries and armies, this was one that would never be known.

III

Hugh woke up in a drenching sweat again at four in the morning and immediately knew the correct time, as the chanting had begun at the small pagoda nearby. He lay there, like most mornings, contemplating the prayers of the nuns being lifted up to the heavens to whoever it was that intentionally ignored the plight and the worries of the human world. As a child, Hugh had been ignored many times by the gods of his people, the occidental god. That is the reason he gave up on the gods at an early age when others still believed in the legends and myths. Shaking himself free from the disturbance of the forgotten memory, he paused a moment and tried to get back to the dream but felt some thing more pressing that required his attention. At the cusp of wake and sleep, he tried to recall the information Inspector Quỳ gave him. He had destroyed the paper as promised and was now trying to remember the address of the coffee shop run by the expatriate Irishman and his Vietnamese wife.

Later that morning, finding a motorbike driver was easy and finding the coffee shop was easier still. As long as Hugh remembered the street and the district, locating the coffee shop was a certainty as there were not many, in fact there were none, coffee shops run by a couple described the way Inspector Quỳ had. Hugh and the motorbike driver found the coffee shop on Hồ Văn Huê Street in the shadow of an large, concrete water tower in Phú Nhuận District in about fifteen minutes, as the Inspector had said. The coffee shop looked practically like any others on the street; several motorbikes parked in front, a young man to keep a watchful eye over them and girls in revealing dresses who sat at a table in front as lures for unsuspecting and knowledgable coffee drinkers alike. Even though it was morning, there were flashing lights on the façade of the building in the middle of a city block that was owned by the Vietnamese Army. Hugh paid the driver the agreed-upon amount. The motorbike driver, a young man of thirty-five was average height for a Vietnamese, had the usual black hair, tobacco-stained, twisted teeth, sweaty clothing and the ever-present loyalty of a possible return fare. The driver offered to wait for Hugh and he assented, finding it easier to have him wait rather than find someone else later, and not really knowing when he would be through talking. The driver parked his Honda Dream nearby, squatted and lit a cigarette and talked to the boy who safeguarded the other motorbikes. The followers sat at the coffee shop across the busy street.

Hugh walked into the darkened coffee shop. A young, thin girl in a black mini-skirt and white tank top quietly followed him in. After passing through the water-misted entry, Hugh took off his dark glasses, hat and cotton face mask, as nearly all commuters in Saigon wear masks to protect their respiratory systems from pollutants, and took a moment for his eyes to get accustomed to the dark interior. He looked around and saw this coffee shop was similar to the many others. The music was blaring out into the street, the television was playing a Thai kickboxing match on a cable channel from Bangkok, and a few tables were occupied by men sitting with the girls who had their bare feet up on vacant chairs chatting with each other while the men watched the pugilism. Just below the bar's counter at the back was the red-lighted Buddhist family shrine. Spent ashes from the incense sticks dropped onto the plate of fruit set in offering to the ancestors and Buddhist deities.

Hugh walked to the back and asked the young Asian man behind the counter if he knew where the Irishman was who ran the place. With a brogue as deep as the River Shannon, Daniel replied, "You're looking at him, mate."

Hugh was taken aback. He had long ago learned to keep his nerves settled when surprised, but this caught him off-guard. Sitting behind the counter sat the most unlikely Irishman one could expect. Daniel Williams had been sitting on a high stool behind the bar watching the strange foreigner walk in. Daniel was not, what one could say, the stereotyped Irishman. He was of Chinese descent, with very light Caucasian features. His Irish grandfather, while serving as a merchant marine, had married a Chinese woman before the 1949 revolution and they fled south to Hong Kong, to the British protectorate. There, the family maintained the Irish heritage while incorporating a few of the British mannerisms and speech. After his wife died, the grandfather sent his natural son to live with relatives in the Republic of Ireland, away from the troubles in the north. The son, who resembled his father, also developed an affinity for Asian women and married a Chinese woman while on a trip to Hong Kong. They eventually returned to Ireland to raise their son, Daniel, in his motherland. Hugh settling himself then asked cautiously, "Is there someplace we can talk privately?"

"There's no place more private than here. Music's too loud for any eavesdropping equipment or bugs, even with unidirectional, line of sight, hearing devices. Just won't work when the music's on. What can I help you with?"

"I've got a friend who gave me your address and said you and your wife may be able to help me with something that's been bothering me. From the looks of it though, I really wonder if you can."

"If you want to go around insultin' me and me place, you can just well turn your arse around and walk out the feckin' door and don'na come back," he said with a hint of ire.

Hugh thought for a moment. Like one of the Thai boys on the cable channel, he had been knocked against the ropes with the unexpected kick. He took a moment to collect himself. It had already been a long morning since waking after the dream, and now all he wanted was to talk to someone, have some coffee and seek answers. "Alright, I'm sorry. It wasn't intentional and I do need help." Turning to the girl who was waiting for his order, Hugh simply looked at her and said, "*Cà phê sữa đá.*" He wanted his regular iced coffee with sweetened condensed milk.

"H'alright then, set your feckin' ass on the seat and tell me what's the help you'll be needin'," Daniel offered.

Hugh told him parts of the story, as long as the music was playing. Other men had come into the coffee shop and sat around with their drinks and talking to the girls Daniel hired for that exact reason. None of them paid any attention to the foreigner at the bar talking to Daniel. As a native English speaker, he had other western expats visiting the bar from time to time to talk in their mother tongue and tell old, stale jokes. For many, it was refreshing to hear an Irish brogue coming from an Asian man who practically looked

Vietnamese himself. Hugh finished his iced milk coffee and sipped the iced green tea when it was refilled by the young girl. Every so often, on her way to the back to fill an order, she'd pinch Hugh's waist. "Don't be worryin' about Kim there. She's got a bit of a taste for western men."

"Doesn't it matter that I'm more than thirty years older than her?" Hugh wondered.

"This ain't the west, lad. This is Asia. This is Việt Nam. Age doesn't matter much when it comes to a physical attraction with a westerner. An' it ain't the money, neither."

Hugh finished the sanitized version of his story and sat quietly. He spoke briefly of the dreams and the woman in the dreams he believes is real. He left out some of the details of the operation but did include that it happened in the autumn of 1966 in Tây Ninh Province near the border village of Xóm Mát with Cambodia.

"Ain't no such place as I recall. I've seen some maps, what maps ya can find, an' I don'na recall any Xóm Mát in that area. Write it down, if ya don'na mind and I'll do some checkin', but it'll be me wife ya'll be wantin' to talk to. She knows everythin'. Sumthin' like an oral tradition with her family after the war was over. That I won't talk about, but I think I'll be rememberin' an interestin' story from those days. Me wife's at the market. Ya'll be welcome to stay here for awhile my friend. Now, what about that motorbike driver. Ya may be wantin' to send him off. Ya'll be here awhile if it's answers ya'r lookin' for," Daniel suggested.

Hugh sat for awhile weighing his options. Which was more important, he questioned himself, the opportunity to find out who the girl is in the dream or the need to do something else? But what else would he do? It didn't take long for Hugh to decide.

"Daniel," he said at long last, "I'll take you up on the offer and wait." At Daniel's suggestion, Hugh paid the waiting driver extra for his time and sent him off. Hugh looked outside around the street and saw his followers across the street idly smoking cigarettes and drinking iced coffees while seated on their new Honda Neo 125cc motorbikes. He smiled at them and returned to his seat inside the noisy coffee shop.

"Fine, now that's settled, I've got Tullamore Dew whiskey. It's me private stock that family brings from Ireland, if ya be wantin' some," Daniel offered while already pouring two glasses without waiting for an answer.

"I'd rather not in this heat, but since you've already poured, I'll take you up on your kind offer." Daniel sipped at the smooth, malty flavored whiskey and he detected the slightest hint of charred wood that made the drink very pleasant. Hugh, who had given up drinking alcohol years before, thought he could get used to this drink, in small amounts.

Daniel switched the cable channel and they both watched the football matches – soccer to the Americans, mostly – and talked about many things from origins of languages to human development to world events and weather. Theirs was an animated conversation and Hugh ended up drinking two more iced milk coffees after his whiskey before Daniel's wife finally returned from the market. She was a beautiful, young Vietnamese woman; thin, long straight black hair that hung down to her waist and very Asian eyes. She seemed to be near the same age as Daniel, but guessing the age of a Vietnamese woman was very difficult. A girl may look fifteen and will indeed be well into her mid to late twenties – sometimes older. The young man charged with watching the motorbikes in front helped her with the plastic sacks of fruits and vegetables and cans of condensed milk for the coffee shop. After all was settled, Daniel followed her into the back and was gone for a long time.

A duration of time that seemed nearly a half hour passed and Daniel finally returned and fetched Hugh upstairs to the private residence. Walking through the kitchen in the back where some of the girls squatted on their heels while preparing food, and past the French toilet in the corner with only a pull screen for privacy, he followed his host up the narrow concrete stairs that led to a door that had apparently been in use somewhere else before being hung here above the coffee shop. Daniel opened the door and allowed his guest to enter first. It was a simple front room, the rest of the residence hid from view with screens in the doorways. A fan was turned on, a seat was offered, and Hugh sat down on the still-fading, green fabric sofa. Hugh met Daniel's wife, this time formally. Mai was a very pleasant woman, a little older than the mid-twenties Hugh estimated, but she was still young and very beautiful. Her soft voice did not betray any disaffection towards him, but rather more of a sincere interest.

"Mr. Hugh, my husband has told me briefly about you. You seem to be an interesting man," she noted in near perfect English. "Before you tell me about your dream, tell me who it was who sent you. I have my suspicions, but it would help me greatly if I am to assist you with answers," she said testing him very slightly. "There are still those who harbor ill feelings from many years ago. They still feel betrayed from the time before 1975 when assurances were made and broken. As a result, many people suffered needlessly during the change. Please tell me," she requested politely as only a Vietnamese woman can do.

"Miss Mai, I cannot. It has been my custom to keep the confidences of many people over the years and I cannot violate those even now. Perhaps at some point some secrets may be known because, as you say, many were affected and suffered needlessly, but that time will come much later. I trust you will respect my confidence."

"Yes, I can. From what you have just said, I do believe I know who it was who sent you. My cousin, who is a very capable man and suitable for his position from his studies in America may be the one who has sent you. I believe he alluded to this when we met for lunch about two days ago. If it was, and by the slight change in your expression I can tell it was, please do not worry. I can help. First, tell me about the dream, in your own words. I have only heard a brief mention of it from my cousin Quỳ."

If Hugh had not been sitting on the lumpy couch, he would have staggered over Mai's revelation that the inspector was her cousin. Yet, for all his training and distrust in life, Hugh felt oddly trusting of this couple. He retold his nightly vision; while walking on a dirt road at night, a woman emerges from the paddies. He approaches and then she disappears into the recesses of his neural pathways. Some nights, he awakes to the image of bone and blood splattering over his face. It's always the same, he explains to Mai.

Mai sat there expressionless. While Hugh was reliving his nightmare, she poured him some green tea from the pot in her own red, silk-lined box. Hugh remembered seeing the same box before; somewhere recently or in the past? Yes! It's the same patterned box that Inspector Quỳ used, he remembered. Perhaps it was a coincidence, for aren't there many of these boxes sold throughout the markets in Hồ Chí Minh City? Tourists can buy them at Bến Thành Market, the more famous covered market in downtown's District One, or further out in District Five's Chợ Lớn, which translates to "Big Market," or any of the other markets. It must be a common one, but these are the only two alike he's seen. He then thought he had seen another but dismissed it from thought.

"Miss Mai, your silk tea box is quite beautiful and exquisitely embroidered."

"Yes, it is. I trust you may have seen another one recently, haven't you, otherwise you would not have commented about it. These are special and were made long ago especially for our family. My cousin uses one at work. It gives him a sense of comfort when having to speak, so to say, to different people about many different things. Mr. Hugh, I will be honest with you. I believe many answers to your dreams lie right here in Hồ Chí Minh City and elsewhere, but to help you, we need to trust each other. I should tell you that my cousin is one person to be trusted, as well. You may find out that, even though he is a police inspector, he needs to uncover facts about incidences in his realm; he can still be an ally. He did send you here."

"Yes, he did, but this almost appears to be too coincidental. The very police inspector who questions me sends me to his cousin to help me. Miss Mai, you must admit this is quite unusual," Hugh explained, still trying to place all the pieces into a puzzle that would hopefully present him with a larger picture when finally pieced together.

"Mr. Hugh. I have no ulterior motives for helping you. It is simply helping another human being who appears to be suffering. It is my religion to help others who suffer. Everyday I go to the pagoda to offer incense and pray in order to be a better person. Mr. Hugh, this is all about trust. I cannot imagine how it looks to you, a foreigner who has not been raised in this culture and these times. Although I am married myself to a foreigner, there are some things I do not understand and he does not understand. Please know, at least, that much."

Hugh needed to be cautious, yet he was now being presented with an opportunity to end years of his own nightly suffering. Like a schoolboy who is about to cheat for the first time and weighs the benefits of the deception with the harm of being caught by the teacher, Hugh was overwhelmed with a hesitancy. Cautiously, he only said, "Please give me a moment."

They sat for a lengthy amount of time while Hugh put different pieces of the incomplete puzzle together trying to make them fit into something that was intelligible; something that could make sense to him. A white cat with its tail pointed upwards and slowly whipping back and forth, came out of the back room, stared at Hugh, and went over to the stranger's legs and rubbed its face and hips on the fabric. The cat then sat on its haunches in the sunlight to bath itself with sandpaper tongue and paws. Hugh watched the cat as it licked its paw and rubbed its face over and over again. Hugh's mind went over the facts, as he knew them, over and over again with the same methodical motions as the cat washing its face.

Finally, Hugh said, "Miss Mai, I want to know. At my age, distrust mixed with an equal amount of what some people have called paranoia has become a way of life for me. It has been to my advantage, though on occasions it has also been to my own detriment. I am now tired of searching and I want to know the truth."

"Mr. Hugh, I believe that from your past, and what I know about it, the answers can be made known, but your utmost trust is also required. I do not help you for money or to gain anything, but only to help you," she stated again with sincerity that was confirmed in her eyes.

Saying thus, Mai began to tell Hugh about the waning days of the American War in Việt Nam and certain details that were kept from the history books. During the war, she related, her mother had worked on Thống Nhứt Street at the American Embassy, which many came to know from the photographs of Vietnamese trying to climb over the gates to escape the advancing North Vietnamese Army poised on the outskirts of town in their drive to reunify the country. Vietnamese piled up against the gates and walls. A few blocks to the south, at 22 Gia Long Street, known as the Pittman Apartments, a helicopter took off from the rooftop with only some American civilians and a few Vietnamese escaping aboard the helicopter. She added the photo of that building is famous, but sadly mislabeled as the US embassy. She told Hugh this apartment building housed the CIA officers. In Saigon, there was mass panic because the Americans were leaving the innocent and guilty behind. Promises were left behind, as well. During the war years, because of her English proficiency, Mai's mother assisted the different CIA station chiefs at the embassy. Her father had helped her obtain the position because of his contacts in the South Vietnamese Regime's secret police that often cooperated with the CIA to root out suspected Việt Cộng agents in Saigon and elsewhere. Circumstances at home prevented her from being able to get out in those last days of April 1975 before the fall of the American-backed government. She also knew that many files were not being destroyed and would harm many who had worked with or for the Americans. So she took it upon herself, after the station chief had left with his own equipment and documents, to enter the office and open the file cabinet in order to keep them from being obtained by the advancing army. She took as many files with her as possible, but she could not be indiscriminate about which ones she would take. She had to ensure her own family was protected and took the files from a certain time frame of the war. These files, as she continued to explain to Hugh, were from the years when her mother began working for the American intelligence in early 1965. Her name and her family had been in specific files, but she knew there were no other files after 1968 that could possibly have her name in them. She already knew that from experience because she would look at files when the station chief was in the field. She only took those three or four years of folders and tried to destroy the others, but could not successfully destroy them all. There wasn't time and she needed to get as far away as possible with the files she had. She scooped up the armload of files and fled the embassy.

The files were kept as a family secret; they were the skeletons in the closet, known only to a few trusted family members during that time. When things began to settle, the family moved to another district, her father had a secure job and a good salary. Unbeknownst to the new government of his former ties, her father was spared time in the re-education camps.

When she was a young girl, and possessing a curiosity like her mother's, Mai had the chance to look at the files and learned many things about her family and about many of the friends they had kept for the past three decades. Mai explained to Hugh that she found an interesting story. It was only a piece of a convoluted tale that could only have been woven by the CIA. It wasn't a complete file and the scribbled notes were at times hard to decipher and to understand. As typical of the other files, western names and Vietnamese names were used in the same sentences, meetings, handoffs, suspects, and contacts. Mai told Hugh that she remembered his name, Hugh Campbell, an Army Special Forces Lieutenant. She and her cousin, Quỳ, were close and would secretly look at the files out of natural curiosity and also to help with the knowledge of American colloquialisms because they studied English in school, and the files were rife with slang. The files, she remembers and could obtain in due time, had scribbled notes about meetings in northern Tây Ninh Province, American fire support bases, two Army Lieutentants and suspected Việt Cộng agents, one of whom was a woman who had worked for a colonel in Tây Ninh and vanished about the same time of this operation. Discretely, Mai had made inquiries when she visited Tây Ninh to see extended family who lived in the area. She knew about Thu Lan who was mentioned in the reports and her family.

The floor fan was aimed directly at Hugh to ease the discomfort of the heat trapped in the upper rooms of the house, and by now, perspiration dripped from his forehead and collected on his chin and jowls. Sweat poured from his underarms, wetting his shirt and it collected on his waist at the beltline where gravity and age had given him a little extra paunch, not much, but enough to allow the sweat to collect before spilling over onto the front of his cotton pants. Hugh's mind was racing with thoughts, now reeling and he was recalling the past, recalling the operation in detail.

"Mr. Hugh, I can see this is very troubling for you. There were many notes in the file about your operation. They have been kept, along with many others, not for financial rewards, but to reveal the truth about many events someday. As a gesture of trust, I will allow you to look at the file. You can never discuss where you saw it or how you obtained it, but it may provide the answers to your nightmares and they may answer questions that I have had about those mysterious days and what followed through those long years. Your story, Mr. Hugh, is quite interesting and has given me and cousin Quỳ much to think about. He told me when he studied in America he tried to find out certain things. He was always met with the answer that nothing is known, but strangely, just immediately before his graduation from university, his student visa was cancelled and he had to leave America. Quỳ always felt he had stumbled onto something that was beyond his experiences and may have set off warnings. Perhaps your knowledge of what happened will be able to solve the mystery for many," she finished.

IV

The lieutenants approached within literal shouting distance of the camp sentry post at Thiện Ngôn. They had been walking unimpeded for the past two and a half hours after Hugh's assignation with Thu Lan. The sentries knew two Special Forces lieutenants would be arriv̶i̶.̶.̶.̶ ̶ ̶ ̶u̶t̶ knowing that a sane person would not be out after dark, and given this was "Charlie Country," they diminished the likelihood of their arriving until the following day. They were surprised when Whitman made the first contact by offering the appropriate challenge for recognition as he stood in the lights focused outward from the perimeter wire of the base camp. Minimizing the danger of the sentries' being startled and shooting first and asking questions later was foremost in his mind, After receiving the correct reply, the lieutenants were allowed into the darkened camp.

The lieutenants settled into a make-shift tin roofed, canvas-sided building that substituted for barracks, while others in the camp shared cargo shipping containers modified for sleeping quarters. Hugh and Whitman showered adjacent to the outdoor latrine to rid themselves of the stickiness of their forced march and the humidity from their skin. It had been a long trek for the two of them and just before showering, Hugh detected Thu Lan's delicate scent on himself. As he stepped into the shower, he felt his pubic hairs, now caked with flakes of semi-dried and co-mingled body fluids from their lovemaking. His mind raced back to those moments in that frond-covered hut alongside the rice paddy and his heart ached for her and it pained him that their situations made a future together highly untenable. After quickly showering in the tepid water, Hugh lay down on the bare mattress of a bunk, and allowed a breeze to flow over his body and cool him down before dressing again; it also helped him cool the passion for Thu Lan. Hugh wanted her again and, in his mind, he relived the moments of their love. He wanted her more than anything, yet they were enemies, an impossible situation no matter how anyone viewed the relationship. He remembered a scriptural verse often quoted in his own culture; "Love Thine Enemies." He wondered how many would accept the truest sense of that phrase. He mused; enemy and friend were simply relative terms. What transpired that night was something that he could never confide to Whitman, who determined to be like his father, would do anything to secure advancements in the Army. He would not keep silent about a betrayal. Hugh knew he would likely spend the remainder of his natural life in Fort Leavenworth, Kansas, the infamous federal prison in America's heartland reserved for the most heinous criminals who committed crimes against their homeland. Odd, he suddenly considered about America's placement of her 'unwanted.' She kept some of her most dangerous close to her heart amongst the 'amber waves of grain,' while her unfavorable and disaffected lived in their unwalled prisons of Hell's Kitchen, Watts, or the poor backroads of Alabama, Georgia or Mississippi. These were the places where American society consigned the impoverished; out of sight and not desiring to be reminded of their existence. Hugh dismissed the thoughts and allowed his body to rest and find sleep.

Hugh was dreaming of a Fourth of July picnic with his family and his deceased father had come alive in the nighttime fantasy. He dreamt they were in the backyard of their house in the cool of a summer evening and they were lighting firecrackers. Bits of paper flew away in puffs of smoke from the small explosions, and his father kept telling his children to stay away from the firecrackers to keep them safe. He tended to watch over his children, but himself he could not save from the cancer that ravaged his body years later. The family laughed and screamed at the firecrackers, his brothers and sisters bumped into him as they ran about. Hugh suddenly was shaken awake by Whitman; real explosions in the background, someone screaming in pain.

"Take cover. It's a mortar attack!" Whitman advised, not yielding to the fear that was in his own body. They were soldiers and knew what to do. "You were really out. I'd been yelling at you, but you were really out asleep. You okay?" he asked. Special Forces soldiers were usually light sleepers.

"Yeah, fine," he said from underneath his bunk, the three-inch thick, cotton mattress and the corrugated roof that was his only protection from the rockets. The attack lasted only moments as it was answered by friendly mortars and the sound of automatic weapons. Small secondary explosions were heard in the distance, a product of luck and guesswork, perhaps, rather than precision.

Whitman said, "It's not as quiet as Tây Ninh West was." Hugh had learned this night why Tây Ninh West had been quiet. It was always quiet when Thu Lan was working at the colonel's and nobody connected her work schedule with the silence of the guns; not until now. Only Hugh knew her deeper secret, but she knew other secrets as confirmed by her relating his operation that was to be carried out and the promise that no harm would come to the two American soldiers transiting their area.

This troubled Hugh. Why was his mission, apparently planned by the CIA and the Pentagon, known to the Việt Cộng? Morgan had briefed the two of them regarding the contents of the courier's packet due to arrive anytime. If it bore the North's tactical and strategic plan to end the war in the South, then why was the VC helping protect the very ones who were ordered to terminate the mission and destroy the documents? Perhaps this was an expected double-cross against the VC that possibly believed it may be something else. Hugh began to question every detail of their operation. They had orders to follow, but something kept nagging at him. He realized that no one would have considered the remostest possibility that two enemy soldiers would know of the other and unwittingly divulge a few more pieces of the puzzle as to cause the increasing doubt in Lieutenant Hugh Campbell. That was it. Whoever was behind this entire operation and scheme was playing both sides, but why? Why use people as pawns? Yes, it was war and people do crazy things in war; people spy, encampments infiltrated, documents stolen, copied or destroyed, lives lost, mostly innocent civilian bystanders to the horrors of battle that overtake their villages and towns. But, why the game?

In the silence following the rocket attach, Hugh began to sort out the data he knew: A courier traveling from the north with documents related to the military victory in the South by the VC and NVA was to be met by a trusted South Vietnamese double agent. Perhaps the courier believed the agent to be a trusted COSVN cadre member. Next, he and Whitman were tasked by the CIA to infiltrate the area, identify the courier and kill him and destroy any and all documents he may have. And earlier tonight, he learned the VC was ordered to protect his mission, and they also questioned why they would protect the Americans. Hugh could not envisage the piece that was missing; the piece out of place. He wondered who was controlling this whole game. He had long ago realized that money was always at the bottom of almost all decisions that were made anywhere. Bullets, guns, aircraft, personnel and so many other things required money, cash and currency. And there were people who would profit handsomely; the war profiteers posted gains while soldiers and civilians were posted on the loss side of the balance sheet. Hugh's mind was reeling inside a fog of ignorance and doubt. He knew something was wrong with the entire mission, but he had his orders. Follow orders or Fort Leavenworth. Do or die. *Potius mori quam foedare –* Death before dishonor. Confusion leaked in through the steaming mist in his mind. There were pieces still missing, he knew. The mortars were silent, but the reverberations of his upcoming operation echoed loudly in his mind as he tried to comprehend what was happening. Hugh believed he didn't have to know the entire story, but knowing more would certainly protect his life and that of Whitman. Events of the last several hours had placed his mind on guard like a faithful dog's muzzle sniffing danger on the wind would protect a family and the larder from attack. Hugh's defenses were heightened now, believing something was wrong with the operation and they weren't being told everything about it. Perhaps he and Whitman were expendable, that they were assets which could be crossed off the balance sheet and transferred to another column of figures and then archived into a cardboard box, never to be seen again in some forgotten storage warehouse; consigned as another statistic. Hugh's instinct for survival suddenly became more heightened. This wasn't like any other operation he and Whitman had been involved in. This was a high stakes game with big players using them and many others as pawns for whatever reasons that Hugh could not decipher.

"Whitman," Hugh called, "I'm still bothered by all of this. Like I told you at the colonel's, I've got this gut feeling there's something wrong with this op and I don't feel right about it. You know I was told by a contact that we were practically guaranteed safe passage through the area. There was nothing until those mortars awhile ago. So, tell me, why were we allowed to proceed safely when elements of the 271st and the 272nd Regiments of the VC 9th Division are in the area? There's something that's raising a bunch of red flags."

"Hugh, settle down. There's nothing mysterious about this. People in the background are simply lying and setting the scenario for our operation to be successful. They're using deception. They do it all the time. This just might be easier than it seems and you may be making too much of it,"

Whitman explained trying to mollify Hugh and get him back focused on simply following military orders as they were commissioned to do.

Hugh could only surrender to Whitman's simplistic answers with "Yeah, okay, I guess you're right. I'm making too much of this, I know." Hugh was only conceding to his team mate verbally. He knew that they would have to be more cautious than usual on this operation.

The next day was quiet. Work to repair the minimal damage to the latrines and the camp's supply was already being undertaken by the privates and corporals when the lieutenants were eating breakfast in the tented mess hall. After breakfast, they were met by the commander of Thiền Ngôn Camp, a meeting that only took a couple of minutes and they never saw the commander again, nor would they even bother to remember his name. That day was mostly quiet. Soldiers sat around, shirtless, listening to radios and a tape recorder playing music of The Doors, The Beatles, Rolling Stones and The Animals. A famous hit of the Animals from the previous year, "We Gotta Get Outa This Place," soon became a favored song by nearly all the troops in Viềt Nam. Certainly, the enemy wished the Americans would get out of "their" place. The lieutenants' day was spent relaxing and waiting. Relaxing was the easy part of the day, but the wait was exhausting. Waiting for others which one had no control over was the worst part of any operation. They would usually spend that time training, reviewing, planning, but the day was hot, steamy, and they were tired and they had little sleep last night. The rest was welcomed.

The call came the early morning of their second day at Thiện Ngôn. Nguyễn Văn Hiền, the southern agent, was contacted by Captain Tô Văn Huỳnh, who had arrived after his long trip down the Hồ Chí Minh Trail. The two were to meet later that night a few kilometers northeast of Xóm Mát. Mr. Hiền gave the grid coordinates to the lieutenants. They were to be in place prior to the meeting scheduled for two hours before midnight; 2200 hours military time. Hugh wanted to ask him questions, but didn't, fearing problems from Whitman who could no more question an order than he could ever disobey his father or control his temper.

Shortly after lunch, the lieutenants re-checked their equipment and set off towards the location, guided by compass and maps they had stored in their memories. The location was within a hundred meters of a road and located inside the ever-changing border belt with Cambodia. They were venturing where no other Americans had trod before, yet Hugh was assured they would be safe. Thu Lan told Hugh that was their orders; the Americans were not to be harmed. Suddenly, Hugh began to ponder why the enemy would protect them, unless they knew it was in their best interests. What lie was told to them, what subterfuges were hatched that would make soldiers protect their enemies. They must have believed that whatever was in that courier's packet was extremely important for the South and the North Vietnamese, or why else would there be a meeting by an agent from both sides with Special Forces protection? Hugh knew the answer lay in the packet. He would follow orders, do what he could to survive, but Hugh wanted to know why and was determined to see those documents before they were destroyed.

They walked along unmarked footpaths, barely discernible to the laymen, but they could see them with their trained eyes as easily as a person driving to their neighborhood market. They were cautious of booby traps along the way, guarding against trip wires and small pieces of wire from landmines protruding from the forest's floor. They looked for signs of disturbance in the vegetation and near-dead or dried foliage where everything else was green. By seven-thirty that night, they were in place; safely in their own harbor. It was alarmingly quiet in the forest, save the drone of a lone twin-engine, propeller-driven airplane. It seemed the entire forest, usually rebellious in its sounds, had come to a halt. With the little ambient light he had, Hugh sat and played with the column of ants that crawled on the their own well-worn path nearby. He watched Whitman who sat with his back to a tree and scanned back and forth. Darkness settled heavily at night in the forest. One moment it was light, then quickly the darkness descended and brought with it strange and ominous sounds of clicking, buzzing, rustling and slithering sounds. Lacking were the sounds of city or rural life like radios, televisions, conversations or traffic. The natural sounds that were present that night had been there long before humans arose as a dominant species on earth. They were the ancient sounds of earth, her real life, not the artificial life fashioned by the two-legged creatures. Suddenly, there was an eerie silence and just as Hugh was thinking these thoughts, there was a snap, a click and the night went blacker than expected without another sound.

As he regained his bearings shortly after being struck, Hugh heard some slight rustling noises and thought Whitman must have resisted his abductors. Hugh had nothing to gain by fighting and resisting, not while it was still their game. He would have his moment, he had the assurance they were needed still in the game. He knew no harm would come to them.

They were led blindfolded silently through the forest, their abductors said nothing. Hugh thought he could detect the subtle trace of a familiar scent carried on the heavy mist of the forest. For Hugh, their quiet surrender was temporary. He was stopped and a stick against his shin cautioned him to move slowly. There was a step. Trusting the game he seemingly was caught in, he stepped up and was pushed down onto a wooden bench. He heard other footsteps and faintly smelt Whitman's soap. Had that given them away or was it simply the VC knew all along where they were and watched them at a close proximity that allowed the quick seizure of the trained soldiers by other equally well-trained soldiers on their home turf.

Their blindfolds remained on and they were kept silent for the next hour. Quietly, someone approached them and the black and white checkered scarves that substituted as blindfolds were removed. Their eyes were already accustomed to the dark and Hugh could now survey the surroundings and match images with sounds he already heard and impressed on his mind. They were in a canopied shelter in the forest. Plain, short, wooden benches were against two walls that were only a few feet high. There was nothing else he could note, except that Whitman was sitting on the other bench, their weapons were in the corner and perhaps a dozen VC stood around watching the American soldiers with a very distinct curiosity. Hugh thought they had probably never seen the enemy up close, especially ones they had orders to leave alone by capturing them. At the end of the other bench sat a Vietnamese in civilian clothes. He wasn't sure, but in the dark he looked like the southern agent, Mr. Hiền.

Hugh whispered, "*Anh Hiền ời.*"

"*Ưng rồi,*" was the affirmative response from Hiền.

"*Im đi!*" the black pajama-clad boy, who looked no older than fifteen years old, told the men, literally telling them to shut up. The others merely stood around and watched. The boy who commanded them to be quiet glanced quickly outside the shelter. Hugh tracked the boy's eyes in the general direction of his fleeting look and saw the outline of Thu Lan in the darkness. He knew her for her size, her hair, her scarf and he now knew her body and craved to have her again. He glanced back at the boy, fearful of not being observed, but frightened of his own yearnings for this enemy whom he loved and wanted.

At least another thirty minutes passed before they were blindfolded again and led along another path, sometimes crossing over a log, sometimes stepping over a ditch, but being led adroitly through the forest, nonetheless. Hugh counted his steps to gauge the distance from where they had just been to where they were headed. He tried to orient the compass in his mind but had to give up after many twists and turns along their route. Hugh estimated they had walked a little over an hour, maybe an hour and a half, before they stopped again. Through the black and white checkered blindfold, Hugh could detect the faint glow of a light, shimmering on the threads near his eyes. The way it flickered and glimmered through the weave suggested it was a candle. There were no sounds of generators or other forms of electrical generating power equipment and he deduced they were indeed deep within the forest, deep within enemy terrain and, quite possibly, deep within the confines of the Mimot Plantation and COSVN itself.

There were several muffled voices. Most were speaking the southern dialect and Hugh heard traces of the northern dialect among a few of them. One of the voices must be the NVA Captain Tô Văn Huỳnh, he deduced. The voices were in the middle of a conversation when the trio arrived blindfolded. There were sudden footsteps, some cautious, some hurried, and the blindfolds were removed. Two candles rested on the wooden desk in the center of the shelter. It was much like the one they had been held at earlier, and near the candles were a brown pottery tea pot and several stained and chipped tea cups. Hugh had no idea whether he was still in Việt Nam or in Cambodia at the moment. He looked up to find familiar stars, but the canopy of foliage above them obscured the entire sky; even the bare light of the crescent moon could not penetrate the dense cover overhead. They were still being forced to stand along the narrow path immediately outside the shelter. Several men stood inside. One, he could tell was the northerner by his accent and his uniform. He was standing next to the desk and holding a well-worn, brown, leather pouch, much like the ones couriers use. It had the appearance of resting on the table, but Captain Tô Văn Huỳnh had his hand still firmly holding on to it, apparently not quite trusting the local cadre or perhaps he was very much attached to that which he had traveled with and protected for so long; he seemed unwilling to part with his companion. Hugh and Whitman exchanged glances. The moment had not yet arrived; the moment when they would take action and complete the mission they were assigned. Glances out of the corners of his eyes revealed three local southern cadres, the northerner, themselves and Mr. Hiền and five VC escorts. Hugh wondered, where was Thu Lan? The muted conversation in the shelter continued. At long last, one of the southerners, who spoke with a northern accent, identified himself as Colonel Nguyễn Văn Minh, aid to General Trân Văn Tra, Chair of the Military Affairs Committee of B-2 Front Theater. The aid to General Tra was most curious about the meeting taking place, but he had his orders. On behalf of General Tra, he was to personally oversee transfer of the pouch from Captain Huỳnh to Mr. Hiền. Whitman looked quizzically at Hugh. Hugh could not tell if he was still puzzled or if he now believed that everyone there was being used like puppets unable to control their own movements, but dependent on those unseen behind the stage sets and props. Whitman looked as though he were frozen.

The gentlemen inside the shelter invited all, even the two Americans to join them for a cup of tea, as is the custom in all of Asia, whether you are an enemy or a friend. Some customs, Hugh was relieved to see, transcended the hostilities and the killing. Everyone drank tea very slowly and cautiously. The lieutenants took the opportunity to confirm their initial assessment of the total number of people in the surrounding area. Hugh surmised there was no one else around. It dawned on Hugh that this place was very secret, thus only a few escorts and the top cadre knew its location and the means to get there. Even the northern captain had a black and white checkered bandana around his neck from also being led to the meeting place while blindfolded. Hugh thought quickly; there must be more to this operation that would allow two Americans to be this deep inside COSVN, Hugh pondered, and thought they must be under the impression they were simply guards for Mr. Hiền.

After tea was finished, Mr. Hiền was called forward by Captain Huỳnh. Private words were exchanged between the two men. Suddenly the silence of the dark night erupted as the two American lieutenants jumped forward; Hugh grabbed the pouch and bare-handedly terminated Huỳnh and Hiền, as planned, then quickly joined Whitman to fight the escorts, who were unable to match the strength, speed, and the martial art skills of two larger well-trained American officers. It only took a matter of seconds before the fighting was over. With their training, the odds were with Hugh and Whitman and it appeared much easier than they had expected. The hardest part was to follow. How in the hell would they get back to Xóm Mát and the protection of the Fire Support Base? All the men, except for Captain Huỳnh and Mr. Hiền who were "terminated" in compliance with their orders, were quickly bound and gagged before consciousness returned. They would safely remain unconscious for hours. More than likely it wouldn't be until morning when someone would realize that the late night meeting should have been over long before and would find other escorts to go in following their own security precautions. By their reckoning, the lieutenants estimated they may have at least a five to six hour head start. But getting out of the unfamiliar surroundings could take that much time. They had no idea where they were. The two of them paused for a moment. Whitman demanded the pouch and its documents be destroyed immediately. Hugh argued against it stating that the pouch was so well secure that they would have to use stronger means to destroy it and it would take too much time and too much noise. They simply couldn't take the time to rip everything apart even if they wanted to as the pouch was made of a very durable canvas and leather with elaborate locking devices. Trying to destroy it then and there could shorten the lead they would have. Hugh argued that they could blow it up securely back at Thiện Ngôn. Whitman agreed with Hugh's points. They drank a quick cup of tea to replenish their fluids, extinguished the candles, and set off in the direction they believed they had traveled. The two men were experts at orienteering, traveling over lengths of terrain at night, besides the daytime, and each compared their mental notes of how many steps between each log, each ditch, where the turns were, what the ground felt like, and where they brushed against trees.

They had timed their journey and their training paid for itself many times over because within two hours they arrived within sight of the initial shelter where they were brought after their first capture. Four young men in black pants and matching shirts, each carrying an AK-47 and ammunition belts across their chests, sat idly smoking cigarettes and boasting about their more recent sexual conquests, eager to take advantage of the younger girls who desired some permanency in the impermanence of war. Hugh immediately felt disgusted by their talk. It reminded himself of what he was when emotions and thoughts were stripped away. He was just like them, just another male of the human species with the need to procreate, though it was filtered through physical attraction, emotional needs and much more at a deeper level of understanding. The four men were obviously oblivious to the presence of the enemy soldiers eavesdropping nearby along the narrow, quiet, dirt path. The thick forest and the dark night seem to swallow all that was within it, with the exception of these four young soldiers. The men were animated in their conversation and never heard the two outsiders silently passing their position. There was one soldier who did watch them leave.

The lieutenants eventually made it back to the original point where they had waited, the point where they had been taken. The weapons they had secreted away in their harbor had not been found. Hugh still had the pouch with him, carrying it in a sling under his arm, close to his body. The entire time on the way back he wanted to stop and read its contents and try to understand why everything had gone the way it was. Whitman found the radio that had been hidden. It would still take them hours to return to the FSB from their location and they needed to file an urgent sit-rep; a situation report.

"Dusty Hopper, Dusty Hopper, this is Lefty Timber with traffic, over," Whitman called on the radio in more of a whisper than his normal voice, and using the randomly selected radio call signs difficult for Asian speakers and designated for this special op. He waited through a long moment before the reply was heard.

"Lefty Timber, this is Dusty Hopper. Go ahead with traffic, over," replied the anonymous voice through the static.

"Dusty Hopper, number was called; telephone line is no longer busy. I say again, telephone line is no longer busy. Over." Whitman had been using a prearranged code to mean that there operation had been completed.

"Lefty Timber, copy and understand telephone line is no longer busy. Confirm final message delivered." The anonymous voice asked without knowing the concealed meaning of the coded message. If he did know, he was asking about the destruction of the documents that were in the pouch Hugh was carrying.

"Dusty Hopper, negative, I say again, negative. Recipient unable to receive message until later,"

"Lefty Timber this is Dusty Hopper, confirming recipient unable to receive message. Dusty Hopper out."

After the short radio conversation, the message was coded and forwarded to a higher command. Later, the message was decoded in a windowless room and confirmed the courier was terminated, but the pouch had yet to be destroyed.

Thirty thousand feet over the South China Sea, a half dozen B-52Ds carrying war loads of 60,000 pounds each and capable of high density bombing flew in a racetrack pattern for the past few hours, burning fuel and waiting. They had been flying that pattern since leaving Andersen Air Force Base on Guam earlier that night. Their mission was to simply hold off the coast of Southern South Vietnam, maintain a holding pattern and await further instructions, which were sealed in an envelope carried in the flight case of the navigator on the lead plane. The crew had been idly chattering about life in their hometowns, sports and activities around Andersen while monitoring radio channels and the heavy bomber's gauges. The tail gunner, out of boredom, crawled up through a maze from his position in the rear of the plane and had coffee with the navigator. In the middle of their third cup of coffee, the crackled message came over the radio from their squadron's operations advising them in code to continue the mission.

The navigator in the lead bomber opened the envelope. The orders were to proceed to specific grid coordinates and conduct a saturation bombing of the area. 'Finally, we can give Charlie a gift from America,' said the navigator and relayed the information to the pilot and the crews of the five other heavy bombers. Their mission was simple. It was a saturation bombing and each plane would drop their complete loads of 108 seven hundred-fifty pound bombs and then fly to U Tapao in Thailand. The navigator gave the pilots the information, the bearing to the target and provided the Radar Navigator, as the Bombardier was called, the target coordinates. They then waited until they were over the target.

Elsewhere on the guard radio frequencies used for emergencies only, a deep, anonymous and unemotional voice broke the silence; "Attention all aircraft, this is Tây Ninh Arty on guard with an advisory. An Arc Light is scheduled to commence at eighteen forty-five Zulu at grid coordinates X-Ray Tango one two zero niner two five. I say again, an Arc Light is schedule to commence at eighteen forty-five Zulu at grid coordinates X-Ray Tango one two zero niner two five. All aircraft are advised to maintain a twenty-five nautical miles stand off range. Tây Ninh Arty out."

"Tây Ninh Arty" was responsible for advising friendly military units when artillery or other forms of 'fire' was being used. In this case, they were advising units in the field and aircraft aloft of a B-52 carpet bombing strike to take place in the general vicinity of the suspected site of the headquarters for the Central Office South Việt Nam. This bombing raid, however, was just directed slightly southwest of the suspected main location for COSVN and west of the Suối May River. The two lieutenants had already shut their radio off when the warning was broadcast in the blind over the guard channel.

Radio operators at COSVN's communications center were undisturbed by the warning. They also monitored America's guard channel over radio equipment taken from Americans themselves, or sometimes inadvertently left in the forest. They also had the same maps which served to pinpoint the focus of the bombing raids. It helped, especially when the warning was given at least thirty minutes or more ahead of time. This gave the cadre and others time to flee laterally from the intended coordinates, or across the border into Cambodia, though they knew that line was not a bar to the Americans. They had been bombing Cambodia for the past year or more. Tonight, they wouldn't have to flee. They would be safe as the bombing was slightly southwest of their location. Some decided to leave as a precaution, though.

Over the Michellin Plantation near Dầu Tiếng, a lone aircraft appeared to fly aimlessly in the near-black sky. They, too, had been monitoring radio frequencies and the guard channel. It was another boring night of few radio signals to intercept and plot for the radio operators. After the "Arc Light" warning had been broadcast, the pilot asked the navigator to find out where it would take place as he knew the map letter designator, X-ray Tango, was in their target area. After plotting the coordinates, the navigator advised the pilot where it was in relation to their position. The pilot replied, "Good, let's drive there and watch." It was another diversion for them from the mundane. Watching the saturation bombing from their position at a few thousand feet above ground level gave the back-end crew an exciting experience. They felt fortunate to be in the sky at a decent stand off range rather than under that rain of hell.

At three fifteen on a blustery East Coast afternoon, the aid walked in on the Chairman who was talking with a congressman on the telephone. Motioning to the Chairman he needed to speak with him, the reply was a finger in the air signaling a moment to wait.

"Yes, Congressman, I believe that will be suitable legislation for us and I thank you for the extra work you did in attaching the amendment to an uncontroversial spending bill." The Chairman replaced the receiver in its cradle and asked the aid what he needed, knowing that only very urgent matters were the cause of an intrusion during his legislative call time.

"Sir, I received an update a few moments ago. The operation has, as you know, been set into motion. A couple hours ago, by estimates, the courier's mission was terminated. There are no other details, but a radio transmission was received advising it was terminated but the documents have yet to be destroyed," the enthusiastic aid told his superior.

Without surprise or concern in his voice, a trademark of all his business dealings, even those without principle, the Chairman asked nonchalantly, "And what is being done?"

"Sir, in about another fifteen minutes or so, which is the middle of the night over there, six B-52 bombers will cover the entire area with their full loads of bombs. It will literally destroy everything in the area. The planes were an extra insurance policy and had been flying off the coast in a holding pattern for the past few hours. It will soon be over."

"Thank you. I trust it will, but we still have to ensure everything is destroyed. We cannot take chances. Make a call and suggest that someone evaluate the situation on the ground. I am sure there is already someone in place. I want this whole affair over within the next twenty-four hours," the Chairman demanded rather than insisted.

"I will make it so."

V

There it is again. Someone is taking my hand, but what are they doing? Where are they taking me? This blindfold is detestable, why can't it be taken off? The smells from the kitchen area are gone now and I haven't smelled anything for a long time. I keep seeing these images, these visions. They are amusing and now I'm remembering something else. What was it called, though? Well, it doesn't matter anyway, what matters is that I remembered it. There are too many things to forget nowadays, so forgetting what something's called is not a great deal to me.

Who's that? Why am I being led to another room? Did I do something wrong? I question them, but they don't reply. They're quiet now. There's another smell, something is burning. It smells sweet; they burn it all the time. The sweet burning, the sweet burning of wanting to know, yes, that's what it is, the sweet burning of wanting to know, the yearning for learning. The burning yearning for learning. Yes, I'm now being silly, but I have to play the games to keep from going insane in this situation. Where are they taking me? I need to know.

VI

Daniel and Mai allowed Hugh to sit on their green couch for as long as he needed. They understood he required some time to relax and, much more, needed time to think. From the coffee shop downstairs, a tall glass of iced green tea was brought up,   ...g Hugh's thirst for the first time of the day. The information Mai gave him was too much to consider for quick responses. He sat quietly watching the white cat sleeping on top of their television set in the corner of the small room. The cat was lying on its side, its paws hanging over the edge, and it would twitch every so often as the cat dreamed, quite possibly of catching the large rats that haunted some of the back alleys of the district. Hugh wanted to look at the files that had been preserved for these many years, files that should not have been kept as he was told the mission wasn't to be recorded by anyone. To have information written by someone violated all rules of secrecy, but then again, everyone was practicing "CYA"– Cover Your Ass – at the time. Sensitive information about the operation had been compromised. Someone had written details about the mission to cover themselves later. It was a common insurance policy many used to save ruined or failed careers. He understood that.

Finally, he said to Mai, "There's too much that I want to know. What happened is something I already remember major parts of. Some things have become foggy after these many years, but I need to know. Mostly, I need to know the face and who it belonged to. Help me with that and I'll be indebted to you and Daniel."

"You may think I have ulterior motives, Mr. Hugh, but there is also the matter of my cousin. He has questions and he has an interest in your case. You may find that he is a very capable questioner, or is that interrogator? I sometimes can't remember the correct English word. I will help you. You see, we are interconnected with each other. You, Mr. Hugh, help my cousin Quỳ and I help you. Quỳ has his own natural curiosity because of what happened to him in the United States. He is not angry, but the curiosity of a policeman is unquenchable until they know the entire story. We have spoken to each other and know you have had many problems and he understands. Help him, Mr. Hugh. I will help you. If you come back the day after tomorrow, then you will be able to see the file. Please come at the same time as I will have finished going to market by the time you arrive."

"I'll come back," Hugh acknowledged.

Daniel found a motorbike driver for Hugh to return to the police house. Daniel, as an added courtesy, bargained for the one-way fare on Hugh's behalf. He knew Hugh had a rough morning "what with all that ya've been told, ya should be drinkin' sumthin' stronger than coffee, mind ya'," Daniel advised as Hugh mounted the Honda behind the driver.

Zipping through traffic on the back of the Chinese-made 110cc motorbike was an experience that kept Hugh's attention on survival rather than the file. At traffic signals, though, he could not keep from dwelling on the folder and what it could possibly contain. Suddenly, he remembered that CIA agent who had briefed them in Tây Ninh back in 1966; Morgan, yes, that's right, Morgan. He repeated the name again so it could be recalled quicker if he had to do so. Morgan. Maybe that was how he had survived "The Company" for so long. Writing notes to himself, saving names as currency like a kid keeping loose change in a bottle hidden under a bed and saving it for a rainy day. That's how Morgan earned his leathered skin. He was tough and knew which pieces of information were valuable and which weren't. Hugh also wondered what happened to him. He'd be into his late seventies or older by his reckoning. Or he just might be dead, an end-product of his own work, or retired in Cebu City, Philippines, still wearing his Guyabara shirt and watching life go by.

Hugh arrived back at the house. He liked the amenities. He didn't care if it had listening devices. He never talked to himself nor did he have any guests over. He only had himself and his recurring dream as a constant companion. Maybe he'd be rid of them if he found the right solution. Maybe he'd be rid of the sweat if he took a bath, he thought.

Hugh's body felt sticky from the humidity on this warm, subtropical afternoon. It rained briefly that morning, but the air quickly returned to its usual heat and clammy air, the way it's been for the innumerable eons. Nothing changes here, he thought. The Vietnamese have worn the same clothes, harvested the same rice, beets, yams, manioc and sugar cane, worshiped the same ancestors and deities and all in the same sultry atmosphere that made clothing stick to the body, encouraged the black mold on the houses, and hung in the air waiting for anyone to breathe it in. Like everything else, the air just waited in Việt Nam. When it couldn't wait longer, it simply drifted over to the Philippines, Cambodia, Laos or

China, depending on the winds that pushed them forward, and would wait elsewhere. Hugh stepped into the bath, took the shower head off its bracket and played the cool water over his body. The thoughts of standing in the shower in Tây Ninh West so many years back came pouring into his brain as though it had been brought there by the water lines in the house the police owned. Cool, refreshing thoughts were loosened as the water streamed over his scalp and face and brought back a memory that could be closely linked to the dream. His eyes were closed. A quick image of a face raced across the inside of his eyelids; a quick face, a blur of clothing and it was gone. He directed the spray at his eyelids hoping the cool water would lure the image back to his mind and back to the coolness, but it simply washed away like so many memories that ended up down the drain. He directed the shower over his back, under his arms, across his groin and down his legs. He began to feel a chill as air from the outside began to pour into the bathroom passing over the water like a swamp cooler, bringing Hugh's inner temperature down, but still not enough to pull up the memories.

He began to anticipate the next couple of days when he would be able to find out more information about the specter in his dreams, the girl who taunts and haunts him every night, soaking his aging body in sweat. Some things in his older body have dried; his tears and his seed as he had left no progeny for rights of primogeniture. It was a regret he had, but Hugh had no assets to pass on. Life had taken care of that. Life in the United Fucking States of America, as Hugh preferred to refer to the land of his birth, had seen to it that Hugh would not gain from any of the fruits of his work. Snap decisions deemed wrong by supervisors at a later time, corporate mergers, downsizing, layoffs during recessions, dismissals for no reasons; each and all worked towards Hugh's lack of savings or resources to fall back on except for a small annuity, a grateful gift from a patriotic, wealthy relative. It wasn't much, but he knew it would be enough to be comfortable in Việt Nam, if he had to. Hugh wasn't one to say life was out to get him; he simply relegated the unfortunate set of circumstances to his being out of step with the rest of America after his return from Việt Nam. Nothing, not even life itself, had been the same since he went home. He dabbled in alcoholism for awhile, but didn't like it and quit drinking on his own and never went back; not back like he used to, but just enough to dull the senses when times got rough for him. Street drugs, and recreational drugs like marijuana were okay, but he didn't smoke that much and really never know anyone to buy it from. Anything he ever smoked was usually a gift from a benign acquaintance. Harder drugs never appealed to him. Sometimes, he would simply self-medicate using cheap beer and whatever prescription meds he had around the house for depression and pain management. He lived fast on his motorcycle until he sold it out of necessity when he had lost a job. He had overdue rent, credit card payments and bill collectors were hounding him constantly. He was frugal, yet he could never get ahead to save money anymore. It seems his life was on the right track before the war, but afterwards everything had changed. It was that operation that changed everything. Hugh would resignedly tell people, "Shit didn't matter anyway."

Hugh brought his itinerant thoughts back to the moment as he rinsed the shampoo and soap off his body, gave himself another cooling rinse, then walked over to the bed and fell onto it naked. He wondered if surveillance cameras had been installed in the bedroom, but he didn't care. It was too hot for caring. He simply wanted to feel the cool rush of air from the floor fan across his wet body. He wanted the cool refreshing feeling of his own natural air conditioning. He wanted his memory refreshed so he could cleanse himself of the spirits that disturbed his sleep. They were the spirits that should have been rinsed down the drain or blown away by the fan to leave him in a calm state of mind. That's all he wanted.

Hugh had fallen asleep naked on the bed. The feeling of final relaxation overwhelmed him and when he awoke he saw the room was darkening. Glancing at the clock on the bureau he saw it was nearing five-thirty. He had slept for about two and a half hours unknowing how tired he had become. The humidity sapped the strength from his body; the dreams sapped the strength from his mind. He mustered the energy to rise on one elbow and started to wonder what his next plan would be. He was hungry and thirsty.

Finding the same motorbike driver as before, and looking as though he was mesmerized by the traffic, Hugh said he wanted to go across town to the Phú Nhuận District where he had seen a restaurant that looked interesting. In a little corner of the district, a block from Bình Thạnh District, on Nguyễn Văn Đậu Street near Phan Đăng Lưu Street, was a vegetarian restaurant. Thuyền Viên appeared interesting from the outside. He knew it was vegetarian because of the 'Cơm Chay' sign, denoting vegetarian food. He had seen several Buddhist nuns walking in one morning; the product of a quick glance from the back of a motorbike, but a place to remember. He considered it would be a good place for dinner. He'd even treat the driver to a free meal just for the company.

Approaching the restaurant, the driver pulled into oncoming traffic, a very common driving maneuver in the city, and dropped Hugh off at the counter that opened out to the street. Hugh walked into the restaurant, gathered his bearings and found a vacant, stainless steel-topped table in the main aisle and to the left. A prisoner of his habits, he sat next to the mirrored wall with his back facing the rear. From this seat, he could practically command a full view of the restaurant and all who came in. The first to come in were his "followers," the police assigned to watch over him. They had regular shifts and he now recognized each of them. They all appeared to work everyday. Hugh felt generous enough to offer them seats at his table, but they shrugged him off and chose to sit across the room adjacent to a cross aisle in case they had to move quickly for any reason. Although he didn't feel he needed it, their presence was still reassuring. They were very unobtrusive when he was at the coffee shop earlier in the day. Had the adroit inspector briefed them, had he given them instructions to be unwatched while he spoke to Mai upstairs? Hugh could not second-guess the Inspector anymore and felt he should simply trust him. Tomorrow, he would call him and begin to tell him the story about what happened in Tây Ninh Province. He couldn't divulge everything, but he also needed to return to Tây Ninh as he had unfinished work remaining. To go back, he first had to shake his followers. He was still weak from the injury, but was feeling better as each day progressed. Perhaps the natural sauna of the Mekong region of Southeast Asia was accelerating the recovery process. He had had injuries before in the States, and they seemed to take ages to heal. When he knew it was time, he would make it back to Tây Ninh. Back to his recovery.

He and the driver shared several plates of what any human carnivore could have mistaken for ham, beef, and chicken, except that they were made of soya, tofu and grain products. The waitress wearing a cobalt blue shirt brought a scratched-up pitcher of the standard Vietnamese green tea; very popular and served everywhere in the country. It was even served as an accompanying drink in the many coffee shops. Hugh and the driver shared the fried rice, egg noodles, lotus salad and the vegetarian "meats." The driver, who Hugh learned was named Thiên, ate voraciously. He thought Thiên quite possibly earned less than three or four US dollars a day, and that would be on a good twelve or fourteen hour workday. Hugh was happy to treat him to a meal. Even though he wasn't wealthy himself, Hugh had always had a feeling of beneficence and good feelings towards the Vietnamese. After the war, when veterans would get together, Hugh was quick to admonish anyone who referred to them as "gooks," "zipperheads," or "slopeheads." He felt terms like that were undeserving and offensive. He recalls once getting into a fight with another veteran in the 1970s after he resigned his commission as a captain. He had been on the list for promotion to major, but something in Hugh began to continually question military leadership. He understood and appreciated the reasons for the military to maintain a country's defense, but perhaps it was the abuse and manipulation of the people in uniform by the politicians and corporate business concerns. It was their senseless caring that would send young lives to their deaths to protect what he believed were primarily American business interests overseas. If not, why didn't the US involve itself in the crisis in Tibet in 1959 or in Cambodia during the 1975 genocide or in East Timor, where American munitions companies made gigantic profits by selling arms and ammunition to the Indonesian government to kill tens of thousands of their own people. Hugh had later discovered that then-President Ronald Reagan refused to ban the use of American ammunitions in the killing of Timorese by Indonesia, a US ally. No, Hugh had had enough and tried his hand at civilian life.

In 1975, after the Reunification of Việt Nam, or the Fall of Saigon – for one termed it from whichever side they supported – Hugh had been living in Orange County, California, and assisted the Vietnamese refugees when they temporarily lived in the tent cities on Camp Pendleton, the Marine Corps base inland from Oceanside. Hugh spent many hours assisting in the processing of Vietnamese because of his fluency in the northern and southern dialects, and at times Hugh housed some refugees at his house temporarily while they waited for sponsors or transportation by bus, train or plane to other parts of the country. Often, Hugh would glance at the women; petite, frightened, vulnerable and worried about their futures. He thought back to one young woman in particular he began a friendship with, a young girl of twenty-two years old. Her name was Miss Duyên. Her family originated in the north but had been living in Saigon until April 1975. She was four feet ten inches tall and she weighed seventy-nine pounds. Her short black hair fell to her shoulders and glistened brightly in the sunlight. She was the epitome of the meaning of her name, grace. She possessed a natural beauty and never once betrayed her own vulnerability. She spoke very little English and her university education had been cut short by the rapid deterioration of the political and military situation in the south. She had preferred to stay to help her country but her parents swept her up into the sea of change and into a helicopter and now she found herself and family as foundlings in a new country. She spent her days busying herself helping parents with young children who were taken from familiar surroundings and living in communal tents on dirt roads, inside a chain link fenced area, in the cool mountainous region of coastal Southern California. The refugees had been cut off from the rest of the world. Hugh brought her small gifts to help alleviate the fears and helped dispel the rumors that typically floated around refugee camps. Eventually, Miss Duyên and her family found sponsors in the distant reaches of Minnesota in the cold northern US, far from the subtropical regions that had been their home. She was tearful when she told Hugh goodbye. The day her family had to leave "Tent City," she wished Hugh a good bye, then turned and walked away, wearing the only áo dài she had brought with her; yellow hydrangeas set against a soft, orchid-lavender, silk dress. Hugh felt a deep pang of regret and sorrow he didn't do more for her and, worse, he didn't find out where her permanent address would be so she would have someone else in America who cared for her.

She glided back to her tent to collect what little belongings she had; clothes, childhood jewelry, a photo album. The morning sun had risen over the Santa Ana Mountains and as she walked away, the morning sun backlit her and Hugh saw the slim outline of her body underneath the silk of her robe and pants. Suddenly he felt a wrenching heartache and a figure surfaced for air and satisfied, settled back down into the lost depths of his mind. Struck suddenly by a gossamer image within himself, Hugh excused himself and returned home to cry. Cry for what, he wasn't sure and it distressed him even more.

Hugh caught his mind wandering like it was prone to do and brought himself back to the present when the waitress brought the plates of food. Thiên, the driver, took chopsticks from the holder, which also contained forks and spoons, tapped them on the table to ensure the lengths matched, grabbed at some tissue paper from the dispenser and wiped the chopsticks vigorously and handed the pair to Hugh. He then took another pair and followed the same procedure for himself. The two spoke of many things over their dinner, each dipping food into the small bowls with sliced chili peppers and seeds floating in soy sauce or vegetarian *nước mắm*, the fish seasoning sauce.

Hugh paid the bill, which did not amount to much, but it could have been a huge portion of Thiên's earnings for the day. Hugh was happy to pay and found he was a very interesting man and had a lot of common sense but, sadly and like so many others, his family lacked the resources for him to complete his education. Thus, he saved what little money he could to buy a used motorbike. Everyday, he would sit at an entrance to the *hẻm*, the alley where Hugh had been staying, waiting for anyone who needed a ride somewhere. That was Thiên's place in Vietnamese society, along with thousands of other men, young and old, who sat near the entrances to the alleys, schools or markets waiting for fares like fishermen who would sit on the bank waiting for their poles to jerk with yet another meal for the family.

After dinner, Hugh asked Thiên to drop him off at some distance away from the police house so he could walk. He enjoyed walking and finding coffee shops, much like Daniel and Mai's, and sitting in the front he would watch the lives of the Vietnamese pass him by, all unknowing of the foreigner and the secrets he bore deep within.

He found one such coffee shop on Trần Quốc Thảo Street. The young girl brought the coffee to him in a tall glass filled with ice and sweetened, condensed milk and thick coffee from the Buôn Ma Thuột coffee growing region. She held the straw and stirred the mixture for Hugh, herself wondering what had brought this foreigner to her coffee shop. Shunning her company politely, he simply wanted to be alone with his thoughts. Hugh was aware this neighborhood wasn't a tourist area and he was just as out of place as Miss Duyên had been in Minnesota many years before

He seemed apart from, yet somehow connected to, others sitting in that coffee shop. Vietnamese love songs were blaring from the speaker system while Tom and Jerry cartoons, favorite characters among the young and old, surrealistically played on the television set high in the corner. There weren't many customers; just a few businessmen on their way home to their wives and the girls who served the coffees, teas and beer. The humidity filtered into the coffee shop and was stirred by oscillating fans hanging on the two side walls. A young girl of twelve sat idly on the tan, PVC-covered couch that had been delivered that morning and was taking a break from selling lottery tickets throughout the neighborhood and trying to capture a little bit of her childhood. Small and demure, she watched the cartoons laughing at the pratfalls and misbehavings of the cat and mouse. She held her purse, which contained the tickets and cash, tight to her body, though no one was within reach of her to take her life's only means of income. The girls in their blue and red striped tank tops and short black skirts sat lazily in a couple of clusters chatting, reading newspapers and waiting with their feet up on other chairs and a few examined the polish on their toenails. They were all waiting, for what, they didn't really know. Maybe in a poor developing country, the only thing people can afford is to wait for a chance to leave in only one of two ways – an airplane or death. It seems in Việt Nam, everyone and everything waits constantly and patience is a pervasive virtue.

Forgetting the operation, the police, and the dream, Hugh was lulled into a sense of quiet amidst the background din of the music and traffic. There were thousands upon thousands of motorbikes shrieking by at a rapid pace, each one inches from the other, all going to who-knows-where. Hugh looked out into the street and saw what appeared to be an eddy in the flow of traffic around something in the road, and the eye of the whirlpool was moving. Straining his eyes into the flow of traffic, he finally saw a legless man inching his way diagonally across the street using the alternating forward motion of his hips and his hands to keep going. Keenly aware of the danger swirling around and above him, he paid traffic little heed and continued on his way, having done so too often to care anymore. Painfully, Hugh watched as the man finally gained the opposite side of the four-lane street and continued down a side alley. To what destination? Soon after Whitman's and his return to Việt Nam, Hugh saw a legless man on a piece of plywood with casters plying his way across the street and wondered if anyone could ever be envious of him. Quite possibly, here in this land where nothing goes to waste or is discarded, even its own humanity, the legless man without the plywood may be envious. His mind then raced to the man he had seen the week before with twisted legs laboriously meandering down the sidewalk and having to rest every eight to ten store fronts to rest. He would carefully sit down and contort his legs in such a manner that did not seem humanly possible. Another young man he saw, probably about twenty years old, was painstakingly making his way down the street selling lottery tickets. His legs were also twisted and he had to rely on crutches to maintain some semblance of balance in his imbalanced world. What Hugh found remarkable was the incredible smile on the face of each of the men. Hugh thought of the human misery, beneficiaries of a war long over, ever collecting their monthly entitlements in the form of twisted limbs for simply being born in a country used as a pawn between the superpowers of the day. Presidents, Prime Ministers, Commissars each and all oblivious to the horrors they would unleash; Johnson's Christmas bombing of Hanoi, Nixon's incursion into Cambodia and the secret war in Laos. The Soviet Union's invasion of Afghanistan, another pawn country, saw the US support a Saudi who would later become termed a terrorist by the US government. Friend one day, enemy the next. When did the international policies of countries become governed by the flawed rule of "the enemy of my enemy is my friend?" That was the true and sad state of foreign policy of the United States and it troubled Hugh to a great degree.

Hugh returned his thought to people's suffering. His mind also returned momentarily to napalm, Agent Orange and Agent Blue, white phosphorous and eventually to suspected enemy agents being pushed out of helicopters at fatal altitudes. Hugh returned to the remembrances of his own operation, which he swore would be the last.

PART III

I

After the lieutenants made the radio call reporting their situation, they began to collect their equipment for the trek back towards Thiện Ngôn. Earlier that night as a precaution, they had buried extra weapons and ammunition should they lose their others. They picked up their Colt .45 automatics, extra magazines and their rifles that were left under a canvas and camouflaged with debris from the forest floor. They had already started the long trek back and didn't hear the B-52s overhead nor did they hear the bombing until it was too late. Suddenly, the world exploded around them and rampant fire scorched the earth in their direction, tearing their world apart; fire, steam, smoke, flying debris everywhere amidst the confusion. They were running to save their lives and the concussion of the bombs was striking their bodies with an increasing intensity as the bombing pattern approached them. Hugh and Whitman usually kept a distance of about twenty meters between them and Whitman was point man this time on the return to Thiện Ngôn, still many kilometers away. Amidst the fire, the concussions, and the devastation, the two officers were separated. In the terror, they were lost. An arm quickly seized Hugh, pulling him along through the forest, hands forcefully grabbing him; delicate, forceful hands. Hugh realized they were a woman's hands and knew it was Thu Lan. Heated debris, burning wood, molten dirt and stones and heat continued to fly in all directions at them and away from them. Their bodies were pummeled by the concussions of the explosions and it hurt. They had never conceived of the horror that befell others on the ground during the American carpet bombing. Thousands of feet above, manicured fingers pressed buttons to release their death and below, legs ran to stay alive and seek safety. Thu Lan kept tugging Hugh, urging him forward. He wanted to let go and find his partner, but survival and the need to live begged him to follow her lead and trust her. If he could survive, then he could deal with anything else that came along.

They stumbled into an old crater. Thu Lan, as part of the Việt Cộng Tây Ninh Armed Forces, knew every inch of forest and where the ideal places to wait out the bombs, and more importantly, how to survive the bombings. Lesser known than the famed tunnels of Củ Chi, were the few tunnels in their locale. They had been dug during the French occupation, the First Indochina War, and were again maintained at the beginning of the Second Indochina War, the war with the Americans. Thu Lan threw herself into the ground and seemed to disappear, causing Hugh to think she had been blown away, but instead, she dove headlong into a tunnel entrance. This posed a problem for Hugh, not only because of the equipment he was carrying, including the pouch, but mainly because of his size. Tunnels had been dug to conserve energy and tunnel sizes were, at times, tight even for the smaller Vietnamese and never made for the larger foreigners. They realized the trouble immediately, and she pulled him instead towards another area and the world kept flying at them in a blistering heat. They fell into another B-52 bomb crater from a previous bomb run and tried to cover themselves with whatever they could find for protection from flying debris and the deadly shocks of horror. The terror rained around them and Hugh lost all sense of time. The two enemy soldiers held each other for protection, each silent as the noise was too loud to even hear something yelled directly into the ear, which started to bleed. Hugh experienced the terror that many Vietnamese who had lived, and mostly died underneath those huge bombers, could feel. The bombing seemed to go on forever, and then it decreased and finally tapered off to stillness in the distance leaving the stench of explosives, burning vegetation and death all around them. They could still hear the bombings in their ears, which bled slightly, but miraculously they were still alive. A little more than six feet below ground level, the customary depth where the dead reside – the ones who no longer know war – these two held each other for comfort, for protection against the horrors. The din and explosions were remembered by their ears and in their minds, though the huge lumbering aircraft were headed towards U Tapoa, Thailand, their thirst for death once again slaked and their mission accomplished. With no light to guide them in the crater, they instinctively knew each other's bodies already. They wanted to feel creation in the midst of destruction; produce love where hatred reigned and rained. That crater provided them the protection, like the womb of the earth, from the outside and from a merciless world above. Silently, they undressed each other. He moved his hand slowly up the

flat of her stomach to her small rounded breasts, his fingers
remembering the small brown nipples and again becoming
rigid under the touch of his fingers. She in turn, placed her
small, child-like delicate hands inside his trousers. Slowly
and methodically, they undressed each other and placed their
clothes on the slope of the crater upon which they lay down,
laying next to each other as they explored and then slowly,
Hugh placed himself atop her slight, but able, body. She had
been watching out for him and had saved his life. If anyone
knew, she would be deemed a traitor and probably executed.
He would be court-martialed and sent away to prison for life.
The thought of the operation's near-conclusion in the shelter
back in COSVN passed through his mind and he realized
that she did not know what took place. Perhaps she was still
following orders to ensure the American soldiers' safety. He
didn't want to question motives, but still he had to stay alert
for all possibilities, but he knew this was love and they made
love passionately, knowing this may very well be their last
time together.

It had been a long and busy day for Thu Lan, because
she fell asleep exhausted from traipsing through the forest,
for what must have been a couple of days as they awaited
the arrival of Captain Huỳnh from the north and acting as
overseer of the enemy soldiers. The fear of death, the joy
of love and the release of sexual tension combined together
in her to give her a much needed rest. Hugh had no idea of
Whitman's fate and realized he had the opportunity to open
the pouch and see the contents, the alleged strategic and
tactical plans for the winning of the war by the Communists.
Perhaps they would be too valuable as intelligence to destroy

and he would attempt to get the documents back to MACV-SOG at Tân Sơn Nhứt Airbase in Saigon. If it was worth risking so much and the ruse to even employ the VC to help, then it was worth a look and an evaluation. Hugh believed he had nearly paid with his life for the privilege to see the product.

Hugh found the olive-drab green flashlight in his equipment bag at the bottom of the crater. He flipped on the light revealing a soft red glow of the plastic lens used for night operations. He then began to work at opening the pouch. The covering was difficult at first, but then his knife made headway. It seemed to take him forever, but finally, the opening revealed the papers inside. Against a backdrop of sizzling and crackling forest, he quietly released the papers from the protective pouch. At first he was mystified that there were only papers and envelopes. He had expected booklets and maps. Setting the damaged pouch to the side, Hugh drew his knees to his chest, placed the flashlight between his knees and began to read the papers, holding the documents with both hands.

The experienced American Special Forces officer could not believe what he had seen and thoroughly examined them a few more times to confirm the meaning of the documents. Hugh was dumbfounded by the revelation. His world was suddenly shaken again, not by returning B-52s, but by the documents. He realized his suspicions and his innate instincts were vindicated. Someone, somewhere, did not want these documents falling into the right hands. Someone desperately needed to have these intercepted, but who? He realized he needed to secure the documents someplace where they would be safe for the time being. Realizing they must not be destroyed, and while Thu Lan was still asleep, he took out a waterproof pouch out of his bag, placed the documents inside, then taped them to his back, and replaced his camouflage shirt that Thu Lan had taken off him earlier. Checking his watch, he had about three more hours until daylight. He needed to move and get back towards the FSB. He wanted to stay next to Thu Lan and hold her as she slept, but his new found knowledge demanded that his movement was a priority. Softly and very tenderly, Hugh replaced Thu Lan's clothing. There wasn't much in the way of covering; her feminine undergarments must have been her way to maintain her femininity while being clad in the back uniform of the Việt Cộng. She moved ever so slightly while he dressed her, as though assisting him. Hugh then climbed out of the crater, and regretfully climbed out of Thu Lan's life at the same time.

Hugh's mind was on high alert as he made his way back to the base. He was trying to find Whitman, completely unaware of whether he was dead, alive, or vaporized while at the same time trying to piece the puzzle together now that he had the main piece, but so many others were missing. He recalled Morgan, the career spy, telling them all "Arc Lights" were suspended while they were in the area. Other people at ranks above them obviously knew they were still in the area. They knew how far they would have to go on foot, how long it would take them and knew the two lieutenants would be within a certain radius after they had made their radio call. It finally exploded in him like a delayed fuse on a bomb. Someone knew the documents had not been destroyed because that was part of their situation report. Someone ordered the bombing raid on them. Someone high up had wanted the B-52s to destroy the papers and kill them at the same time. Hugh suddenly wondered who the real enemy was. Was it really Thu Lan and her comrades in the VC and NVA or was the real enemy concealed within the borders of America? Who would be high enough or powerful enough to order the strike? Hugh realized his life was not worth much now if he made it back with the documents and he needed to either destroy them and swear he never knew what they contained, or he would somehow find a safe place for them until he could decide what to do with them – and still lie about it. Hugh's anger was beginning to well up inside him, rising like a body's temperature infected with a virus. Just like a virus for which there is no cure, there was nothing that could diminish the anger he now had realizing that it's one thing to be an enemy and try to kill the other soldier, but to have someone on your own side want you dead?! The documents would have to be hidden, but where? Where would they be safe for the time being? Hugh thought there was one place and one person he could trust and he had to make it back to him as soon as he could. The problem was that he needed to return to Thiện Ngôn, report in and tell them the pouch had been destroyed during the bombing raid while he was going in and out of craters. Hugh suddenly thought about his choice of words, smiled a moment, and then returned to the serious survival side of his brain. He would report in, try to rendezvous with Whitman or ascertain his status, all the while trying to keep the documents hidden on his body until he could get to the best place to conceal them. He now wondered if Whitman could be trusted. He was a friend and confidant, but a trusted friend? He wondered. His father was a career man who had taught his son to follow orders and it was also Whitman who was, more or less, resigned to trust superior officers and their judgment in giving orders, no matter how insane they seemed. Hugh now trusted no one, save one person whom he knew slightly, but felt the trust anyway. Hugh made it back to the FSB after spending hours looking for Whitman, without success. For all he knew, whoever ordered the bombing run had inadvertently killed the wrong soldier.

Hugh used a secure FM radio, a recent addition to the FSB, to report to the colonel at Tây Ninh West. He only told him what he needed to know, which would be passed on to Morgan. He reported that the intended person's mission was terminated, and a bombing raid caused loss and destruction of the pouch. Hugh regretfully said the other officer was now MIA, missing in action, and Hugh had nothing further to report. Most of his report to the colonel was truth, and it was true the pouch was destroyed, so it wasn't a complete lie as far as Hugh was concerned. The colonel expressed regrets at Whitman's current MIA status and prayed his remains would be recovered. Hugh didn't want to betray his concern about the timing of the B-52s so he simply let the colonel do the talking. Hugh would be ferried back to Tây Ninh West in the afternoon and would await further orders.

Hugh needed to shower but feared someone would see the concealed pouch taped to his back, which was now becoming uncomfortable. It was his sole reminder of the anger and now a need for revenge that was building inside him. He gathered what few belongings he had left behind at the hut and went to the chowhall for something to eat. Filling up a tray of eggs, bacon, toast, hash browns and coffee, he sat down and realized his anger had replaced his desire to eat. He picked at the food slowly. He used the food to feed his indignation at some faceless person who had wanted the two lieutenants dead for the sake of what he had read and now carried like a monkey on his back. The weight of the pouch was negligible compared to the weight of the implications of everything going through his mind. Hugh's concentration was so intense he didn't hear the warrant officer Huey pilot who had come in and told him his ride was waiting to take him back to Tây Ninh West as soon as he finished eating. Hugh shoved the tray away, gathered his belongings, and without saying a word, followed the chopper pilot to the pad where the Huey sat with its rotor slowly turning in the mid-morning heat like a child on a swing twirling the supporting chains in the sun to while away the time. Fifteen minutes later, Hugh found himself back at Tây Ninh West, where he was greeted by the colonel and Morgan. He was painfully aware he would never see Thu Lan again and she began to slowly fade somewhere.

"Lieutenant, it's so good to see you. Congratulations on a successful operation. I am saddened, as is the Army, on the possible loss of Lieutenant Emerson. We all pray for his safe return, but realize this is war," the colonel said as Morgan looked on quietly staring at him and his reactions. "You'll stay the night in the officer's quarters and transfer back to Saigon tomorrow morning after breakfast. If there's anything I can get you, let me know. I'd be happy to have you as a guest at my quarters, but I lost my housekeeper. I've got no idea what happened to her. She just didn't show up after you two left. You know, that happens around here, sometimes. Her family thinks she may have been kidnapped by the VC and killed because she worked for me. Damn, but it's hard to get good cheap help nowadays," he seriously and selfishly lamented.

Morgan interrupted them, "Lieutenant, after you've had a chance to settle, I'd like to meet with you. I believe the colonel can afford to allow us to meet at his residence for a quick de-briefing, won't you, sir?" Morgan instructed rather than requested.

"Of course, take as much time as you want. I have to return to headquarters and get some more work done. Here's the key," said the colonel handing the key to Morgan.

Each of the men went in different directions. Hugh realized he needed to hide the documents temporarily until he could get to the other place he knew would be safe. He was shown to the temporary officer's quarters by a bored sergeant. Once inside, he found an area that was vacant, then found another area and threw his things on the bed. He paused to think about what he was going to do. He didn't want the documents out of his sight, yet he didn't want them on his as a reminder when he would debrief later with Morgan. He looked outside his room and saw that things were quiet as it was nearing noon. Walking quietly into the next room, he looked down and noticed the floor had not been entirely secured with nails and it was easy to pull a corner of plywood up. With a pain from the bombing that he could ignore, Hugh pulled the taped waterproof pouch from his back and applied it to the back of the flooring where it would be further secured on a joist. He replaced the flooring and added a negligible piece of thread to the corner. He repositioned the chair, left the vacant area and then took a shower to get the leaves, the dirt, the sweat and the filth of betrayal off his body and temporarily off his mind.

A corporal arrived later to request the lieutenant to report to the colonel's residence at his leisure. This translated to "please report to the colonel's residence as soon as possible," while allowing for courtesies to be maintained during hostilities. Hugh grabbed his beret and walked over to the mobile home where he had first met Thu Lan. The veiled memory of her standing in the doorway to the bedroom on that Sunday in her áo dài floated across his mind like leaves on a stream and spilled over the causeway of his consciousness and into the reservoir of his feelings. He recalled the first time he saw her; small, tender, bare feet and dressed in a plain white blouse and black pants. His mind raced to find the last time he saw her in the subdued light of his red flashlight, asleep in a bomb crater where they had made love, for what just may ever be, the last time. Now she was fading in the subued light of his mind. Hugh walked to the residence at a deliberate and steady pace, not wanting to exhibit nonchalance, hesitation or haste. He was professional, after all. He signed in with the sentry at the gate and went to the door and knocked.

Morgan left the window where he had been watching the lieutenant from behind the curtains and saw him walk towards the house, showing no emotion. A professional soldier, he thought. Morgan opened the door and greeted him somewhat coldly.

"Thank you, lieutenant, for coming here today. I am sorry about the MIA status of your fellow officer, but as the colonel explained, this is a war and we must all be soldiers and prepared to experience losses from time to time. It's all for the greater good. Please come in and have a seat."

Without replying, Hugh walked over to the table where someone had set out some cold cut sandwiches, potato chips, fruit and a pitcher of iced tea. It looked like it was prepared in the Army's dining hall. Morgan started the conversation.

"Lieutenant, this is an official debriefing that only you and I will know about. As you recall our earlier discussion, this operation never existed and after this meeting, you will not discuss it nor will you ever acknowledge that it ever occurred, no matter what, and if anyone does ask you directly about it, your reply should simply be that if ever a mission like this in fact did occur, you would never be at liberty to discuss it. Do I make myself clear?" Hugh nodded in assent. "I don't need to know every little detail of your journey to and from, but I do need to know the details of the operation that night. I need to know everything from when you left Thiện Ngôn to the time you returned the following morning. Do not leave out any details, however slight. We are trying to develop and assess intellignce regarding COSVN. Every detail you can provide will lend towards to the successful completion of future operations in the area," Morgan stated.

Hugh then described everything in detail, how they were taken captive by stealth by an element of the Việt Cộng Tây Ninh Armed Forces, blindfolded and led to a shelter where they were allowed to take their blindfolds off. He described the VC, their uniforms and their equipment, omitting any references about Thu Lan, and he reported how they were again blindfolded and the subsequent meeting in, yet, another shelter about over an hours walk along an inches-width path. He described in detail the meeting, including the instantaneous deaths of Captain Huỳnh and Mr. Hiền and the capturing of the pouch.

Morgan was particularly interested in the status of the pouch. He was under the understanding it had not been destroyed and if he or Lieutenant Emerson knew what it contained.

Hugh described the discussion between himself and Whitman and that the destruction of the pouch would have to be accomplished later due to the nature of the fabric of the pouch, the time involved and the necessity to spirit the pouch away and destroy it with a grenade or some other device at a safer location. He couldn't leave any portions out in case Whitman returned. If Whitman did return and gave a differing report, then Hugh felt there might be too many questions. He spoke about how they were separated during the bombing and that one of his packs and the pouch had been destroyed and nothing remained. It was a different version of the truth than what Morgan, or possibly others wanted, but it was the truth as it happened. Hugh refused to let his mind imagine the flooring in the vacant area of the billets. After ninety minutes of questioning, Morgan was satisfied with Hugh's statements and answers and bade the lieutenant good bye and led him to the front door. Before walking out, he said to Hugh, "Remember the highly sensitive nature of this operation. When you walk out this door, nothing will be said by you to any others about it. It is now a forgotten operation and there will be no record of it. Do you fully understand, lieutenant?"

"Yes, sir," came the terse reply.

Concerned about arousing suspicion with a quick return to the BOQ, Hugh walked casually to the post exchange, which was simply a small trailer with wooden steps for access, where he could get a few things that had been lost or misplaced over the last few weeks of moving around. He purchased a pack of double-edge razors, a small can of shaving cream, toothpaste, deodorant and a few snacks. He bought a small box of the plastic resealable bags that were becoming popular to keep personal possessions dry in the humidity of Southeast Asia. He nodded courteously to the Vietnamese clerk, overseen by an overweight sergeant – Hugh wondered what his thoughts were about the petite checkout girl – and paid for his purchases and walked back to the barracks.

He entered the billets and paused by the vacant area to see if the piece of thread had been disturbed. His doubts and concerns about his fellow Americans were now becoming stronger. Morgan had been very careful in his wording and his tacit warning about disclosure. He wondered if Morgan suspected he had read the documents, but reading him during the debriefing gave him an indication that he may have believed his story. Hugh did not believe it would be out of place for him to now try and take the pouch to a secure place where it would be safe and he could retrieve it later. He couldn't take it with him back to Saigon nor out of the country should anyone become suspicious. Whoever it was that had ordered the "Arc Light" right on top of them after learning the pouch had not been destroyed would certainly take any measures to ensure whatever conspiracy they had plotted would be safely concealed and their tracks covered. Hugh knew he was expendable, like a simple twenty-three cent bullet in an M-16 rifle. The Army could do without him. He knew that he was simply another warm body in a uniform, but he did have more expensive training that the regular "grunt" who carried a rifle and pounded the dirt in forest, or in this case, the muck in Việt Nam. A lengthy idle glance out the window, with forearms on the side jambs, would give anyone the impression he was bored, when in fact, he was ensuring that no one would be coming near the billeting area. He would need at least thirty seconds to retrieve the pouch, another ten seconds to sweep any debris away and get back out. It took him less time than that.

Hugh showered, re-taped the pouch to his lower back and got dressed. He went out the gate and found a cyclo driver to take him to the Cao Đài Temple, about five miles from the post. He paid the driver two hundred piasters and calmly walked around ensuring that he hadn't been followed or anyone had been watching from a distance. He walked down the main road to the smaller Temple of the Divine Mother and walked around as though he was simply a tourist. He meandered past the topiary gardens, directly south of the main temple, and looked at the exquisite shapes of dragons, turtles, bonsais trees and shrubberies, twisted into Oriental designs and shapes. Hugh felt uncommonly comfortable walking around the grounds, but had hoped "Bác," the older man he called "uncle" in Vietnamese, would be around the gardens and find him. Slowly he made his way to the temple when he was confident he had not been followed. He removed his boots, as he did on his first visit, and entered the southwest door and set his boots inside as he walked in his stocking feet. There would be another Mass celebrated at six in the evening and Hugh had only a little more than an hour to do what he needed, but he needed Bác to help him. He had to trust someone and the old man was the only one completely unconnected to the operation. But, where was he? Certainly, someone would have noticed the American soldier walking around unescorted and word would have spread around the Cao Đài Temple grounds that would encourage somebody to approach him. He walked slowly along the south aisle of the main chamber, looking out the lotus embellished grates that filled the window space in lieu of glass. In the ever-changing shadows of day, the brightly painted dragons began to turn grey, going through their daily aging process to be reborn when the lights were switched on or when daybreak returned. As he neared the center south door, adjacent to the dragon supported pulpit, Bác entered the temple.

"*Chào*, Bác," Hugh greeted the old man with a subdued delight.

"*Chào*, Cậu," said the old man using the more personal term in his greeting. He was pleased to see the American officer coming back to visit the temple. "It is unusual for Americans to come here so late in the afternoon. As you know we do not support the Việt Cộng, but they are still around and Americans do not feel comfortable, especially if they are by themselves. I think there may be another reason for your coming to visit us here, no?"

"Bác, the first time I was here, you and I seemed to have a connection, something that made me feel very comfortable with you," Hugh told the older man dressed in white shirt and pants.

"The Divine Eye knows all that is in the hearts of mankind. It is the only truth that binds us together. We can find the harmony and peace of our lives through The Divine Eye as our founders, ancestors and saints have told us. Here, one can find solitude and peace and a safe place during time of war. Although, we no longer are allowed to keep our own Army as in the older times, we do maintain a sense of security to ensure safety. Under The Divine Eye, all is safe," Bác explained.

"That is why I am here. There is something that needs to be hidden safely away, never to be opened or revealed to any other person. I have no one to trust and this something needs a secure location where it will never be found. I may come back some day to get it, but I have no idea when. Bác, I find it unusual to trust someone I have only met once, but would you be willing to help me?" implored Hugh.

"Cậu, your trust is well placed and it is an honor that you would believe I will help you with your secrets. I do not need to know what it is, but how large it is."

"It is an envelope, a waterproof pouch. I have it with me."

"If it is as small as you say, there is one place where it will be safe from all for a day, for a hundred years or more if you like." Bác led him to the floor at the rear of the base of the octagonal altar upon which The Divine Eye rested, watching out for all of humanity. Hugh remembered the slab of stone. "I have a key. Maybe I told you before, only I and the chief cardinal have the keys to the lock. Even the chief cardinal thinks he has lost his key. We must use caution as others will be coming soon. Do you prefer to wait, or wish to hide it now?"

"It has to be done now. If I wait, others may have the opportunity or curiosity to see what it is I intend. This needs to be done right away," Hugh explained.

Silently nodding, Bác removed a chain from his neck that bore a single key. While Hugh kept watch, he disengaged the two locks securing the huge stone slab in place. It took the both of them a few moments of straining to pry the slab from its resting place. The old man invited Hugh to step down inside and conceal whatever it was he needed to keep safe for however long.

Hugh stepped down into the pitch dark and switched his flashlight on, the subdued red light softly swept across musical instruments and the dust on top of urns and old wooden boxes, some locked and some not. This was a chamber of human detritus under the watchful Eye. In the back of the dank, dusty room, Hugh found several crevices, some which were large enough to hold the pouch without betraying its location. "Hurry up," Bác whispered. Hugh placed the pouch in its hiding place and climbed out. They set the heavy block of stone back in place and it was again locked. Moments later, two other Cao Đái priests walked around the corner of the altar in early preparation for the six o'clock Mass. Candles needed to be lit and offerings set in place. Hugh and his confidant walked around to the north side of the temple and back towards the entrance to the holy chambers. Hugh remembered then what the old man had told him earlier, "Under The Divine Eye, all is safe."

"I wish someday you will know how much you have helped me today. I do not know when I will return, but return I shall. Someday all this will be over and the truth will be known about many things. For now, The Divine Eye must keep a safe watch over the envelope, yes?" Hugh asked for reassurance.

"Cậu, your secret is safe. I wish you good fortune and health in your life and that someday all truth will be known by all men. I do hope to see you again." With that, Hugh turned to the south entrance to reclaim his boots. Finding a cyclo outside the north gate of the compound, Hugh returned to the camp. He thought, one more night in Tây Ninh and he'd be back in Saigon at MACV-SOG to wait for another operation. Already he doubted whether he'd be able to accept another operation, especially now fully understanding that forces operated completely shielded from view, from responsibility and from any basis of morality. He had been given a very rude, for want of another appropriate word, awakening to the world of betrayal and deception, without regard to the cost in money or lives. He tried to estimate the cost of the B-52s and the ordnance they dropped and the damage to the environment and, quite possibly, the loss of human life in an apparent attempt to destroy the documents, and he found the sums to be very promiscuous. Hugh found himself dwelling on the arrogance of the planning that went into the entire plot and allowed it to feed a growing anger inside him. Hugh knew it involved people in Hà Nội, the US Army, US Air Force, CIA and, most certainly, high levels of the Pentagon in order to target a bomb strike pending one radio transmission. Or, Hugh wondered, if everyone and all were mere pawns just as he and Whitman were. Hugh wondered if he'd ever be able to invest himself any more in military or clandestine operations, especially in Việt Nam. His doubts were now a risk to himself and others should he decide to continue.

Arriving back at Tây Ninh West, he decided to get something for dinner. He had lightly picked at breakfast, barely ate the food offered by Morgan at the colonel's and now his stomach was demanding his attention once more. He was stunned when he walked into the Mess Hall and saw Whitman sitting at a table by himself, and perhaps stunned was not the right feeling for what he felt was a feeling of relief and of concern; relief that his friend had made it through the bombing, but concern because he could cast doubts on his own story about the pouch and cause others to question its destruction. It was difficult for him to conceal the concern, as best he could, and Whitman caught it.

"One would have thought a more joyous hello would be appropriate instead of a surprised look. Aren't you at the least bit glad to see me, Hugh? After all, we've been through one hell of a bombing together."

"Hell no, I am glad to see you. The colonel and Morgan had given you up for dead and when I couldn't find you hours later, I thought you had been killed. I'm looking at you like this because I'm amazed. Where the hell were you? What happened?" Hugh inquired, while looking at his friend's bruised face.

"Where were you, would be more appropriate. When the bombs started dropping, you disappeared. I didn't see you behind me and I tried to locate you, but thought you also had been killed. I made it maybe a couple, three hundred feet away, trying to run perpendicular to what I thought was the line of the bomb run and was knocked out either by the concussion of the ordnance or something hit me. I woke up a little banged up and practically wrapped around a tree stump in the middle of a crater. I made it back to camp and I guess it was at least most of a day that I had lain there, most of it blacked out. I spent some trying to get my senses and bearing back. I think it's a miracle and thank God I'm still alive," Whitman emphasized knowing Hugh's proclivity for being an unbeliever.

"It is really good to see you, partner. I wasn't about to leave you behind, but after searching for several hours at daybreak, I couldn't find you anywhere, so I headed back back to Thiện Ngôn. Shit, you're lucky the VC didn't find you." Hugh's mind stumbled for a moment, realizing what he had said and how he thought he had been helped by a Việt Cộng. "I already had a debriefing with Morgan and went into town to look around and kill some time. Did you see him, yet?" he asked, looking for an indication in his eyes and speech for doubts about Hugh that Whitman could relate to Morgan during his debrief.

"No, he must've figured I was dead. The colonel said he already hitched a ride on a late afternoon chopper headed to Saigon. I caught up to him by telephone not too long ago, in fact, before I came to eat – Christ, I'm starved – and I've gotta debrief with him tomorrow back at MACV-SOG. We're both headed back to Saigon in the morning. Me to see Morgan, and we both will have to await further orders from

SOG. I think they're gonna keep us in-country because of knowing Vietnamese. What do you think?"

"It doesn't matter to me," Hugh said after a hesitated moment. "We've got a commitment; we've done only one mission in-country. Hell, they may keep us here for the entire year tour-of-duty, just like everyone else, Bud." Hugh sometimes liked to call Whitman 'Bud,' a shortened form of buddy. He can't recall where he picked up that idiosyncrasy but Whitman never objected. He continued, "You know, it really doesn't matter."

Hugh tried to think of Thu Lan for a moment and found it difficult to dredge up that memory. He could be court-martialed and lose his commission and any benefits if anyone learned and reported that he had consorted with the enemy, though she provided more aid and comfort to him than he her. He knew it was risky. He asked himself the question everyman in his situation would probably ask; "Does it really matter? Does it really fucking matter?"

Relaxed even more now with some food in his stomach, Whitman was animated as he ate and Hugh thought it had been awhile since he's been like this. Experiences like theirs, and more particularly Whitman's, had a lasting effect on a person after they've realized they've met with Death but it was not quite their time. The two lieutenants walked back to the BOQ in a mist of humidity eerily glowing from the lights illuminating the post and one of them was awash in a mist of doubt about the other. They both retired to their billets, Whitman never asking about the pouch or its contents or how Hugh had survived the bombing.

II

Hugh woke up early again. It was The Dream, but he was feeling a bit better about the nightly haunting because he knew that he may be able to find the answer or a clue within a few days. His mind mulled what he would tell Inspector Quỳ and how much. The adept policeman had a side to himself that Hugh now discovered and realized that he had quite possibly more of a personal interest in his story than those in Hà Nội. He thought the reserved policeman may possibly be his most valued ally in Việt Nam. He realized the personal investment of the policeman was the rationale for willing to take the heat from his superiors for taking longer than usual in the investigation. It seemed to Hugh that he was willing to put his career on the line by housing the foreigner in a police owned house for as long as it was convenient, but which still had a time-sensitive nature to it. Quỳ's close family connection with Mai, the Irishman's wife, could cause a problem. That is why he possibly had Mai reveal that they were cousins. That way, Hugh may be sensitive to reveal certain facts and yet keep his knowledge of their own history confidential. They were taking a risk with him in order to satisfy their own curiosity regarding remnants of their childhoods and carried with them to adulthood as an insatiable hunger for truth and clarity. For Quỳ, it would also be a vindication of his instinct that he had stumbled on something that resulted in his surprise removal from the US before his graduation from university. He realized, to some degree, he had a responsibility to them for their trust but also because they were married to truth and its discovery. Hugh recalled his long ago marriage vow of one of his marriages that almost became a success, when one promise to his wife was to be also married to the truth. What was truth for one was merely a different perspective for another. Truth became relative. Soon enough Hugh would see the file and know more of the truth. If he did discover the truth, he could also help Quỳ and Mai.

Hugh went down the cement stairs of the house to the ground floor and told the sentry outside he would see Quỳ today, if the Inspector was available. Hugh spoke to him in Vietnamese, as his language skills were quickly returning absent the more current Saigon slang phrases. The sentry said he would get the word to Inspector Quỳ.

Hugh returned inside to the kitchen and prepared some thick drip coffee. Since returning to Việt Nam he developed a taste for the sweetened milk coffee. Hugh took the can of condensed milk and the ground coffee from the refrigerator. While the purified water heated – for nobody uses tapwater for drinking purposes – he spooned the thick, viscous, sweet milk into a glass then covered it with the small, aluminum filter. He very carefully measured three teaspoons of coffee into the filter and waited for the water to boil. Hugh took comfort in his coffee ceremony. It allowed him the time to pause at the beginning of the day and return to practicing mindfulness and restraint. It served as a time for him to consider his dream and to try and understand not only the meaning, but to discover who the girl was.

Inspector Quỳ's quick arrival was a surprise to Hugh and he believed that if the Inspector was not residing in a nearby house, then he had been practically waiting around the corner. As he would learn later, Quỳ did in fact live around the corner in a house also owned by the police but rented to officials only. As such, the Inspector enjoyed lower water and electricity rates as an augment for his low government salary.

"Mr. Hugh, I see you are already. I hope you had a peaceful sleep last night. You look healthy today. Did you go to bed early?" Hugh knew that Quỳ was not prying, but being courteous in the Vietnamese manner.

"Inspector, you are quite quick, and yes, thank you, I did have a peaceful night's sleep," he lied, but then what good would it do to be truthful as the Inspector already knew he was troubled by the nightly specter.

"Mr. Hugh, if you wish, we can talk here instead of driving downtown. I believe these surroundings are more suitable for us to talk together, may I say, quite frankly." Hugh felt the Inspector wanted to talk about something personal with Hugh, which would account for his wanting to interview Hugh at the house, which Hugh also took to mean that the house was not bugged, as he believed.

"Yes, Inspector, in fact, it is more comfortable here. Please, in fact. I take no offense at your choice."

"Also for me, no offense is taken, Mr. Hugh. Please, you should know your cooperation is greatly appreciated. You should also know that others feel that you may be trusted with other revelations that could not be discussed. I trust you understand what I am speaking about, no?" the Inspector asked.

"Inspector, yes, I completely understand and those who have confidence in my ability to remain quiet can be assured they have trusted the right person," Hugh explained sincerely. Hugh thought back to the various confidences he kept over the years, but even now felt he would be betraying one confidence, that of the United States. But another conundrum arose in Hugh's mind: were his actions betraying the United States or were his actions reinforcing an ethical standard the government should have been holding itself to, but had been corrupted by the powerful, the rich and the schemers. He became lost in thought as he considered quickly the thought that there was now an inconsistency in his "secrets of the confessional" and the effects of what he may do. Hugh damned himself for living his life believing the good of many took precedence over the detriment of a few. Quỳ's question brought him back to the moment.

"I am pleased, as others are, to hear that. We may talk anywhere it will please you."

Hugh led him to the kitchen and made their glasses of iced milk coffee. "Inspector, you know that some things I tell you are not a complete story, that just as this water is filtered through the coffee, leaving the grounds behind, I, too, shall give you the story flavored with my version of what happened in Tây Ninh, but will leave the some of the grounds behind. I am sure you will understand."

"Your version will suffice. Perhaps, another story, which you are aware that portions have already been revealed, may not be filtered. That is a story for which only very few have a need or interest in knowing. For now, only recent events concern me, Mr. Hugh. I believe your filtering process is complete," Quỳ pointed to the coffee glasses, now full, on the kitchen counter. "May we begin?" the Inspector requested politely.

Hugh had wanted to tell him the full story of what had happened. Before their return to the United States after their short tour of duty in Việt Nam, Hugh applied to be an instructor for Special Forces. He knew in that position he would still retain his talents and teach others knowing the ability to be used as a pawn would be minimized. He did not resign his commission, but he resigned himself to not wanting to work in the field again. He explained to his commanding officer that he needed a break from special operations for awhile. It was a surprise to Hugh that Whitman was assigned to the same Special Forces training unit after Việt Nam. Whitman had wanted to return to the war after duty in the States, but those orders were never approved. Whitman felt his father had influenced personnel in charge of assignments and had called in some IOUs to have his only son kept safely in America, far and away from the dangers of jungle warfare. Even though Whitman had not told his father about being under the B-52 carpet bombing, he felt his father may have discovered it somehow.

Hugh resigned his commission when his six-year Army obligation was concluded. Having attained the rank of Captain in a short amount of time pleased him, but he did not want to remain with the Army and decided he would return to the civilian sector.

Hugh's decision was met with, not only trepidation, but uncertainty as he discovered he had joined the mob of unemployed veterans returning from the war in Việt Nam who were also seeking work across the country. The vets he met were disenchanted with the government and with society and the culture of America after their experiences in the war. They appeared to want to return to Việt Nam, although it was, by then, the waning days of President Nixon's "Vietnamization" of the war – the turning over of the war to the Vietnamese to fight their own battles. The returning US service personnel came back to the states to face their own battles of unemployment and many carried with them deep psychological scars. Some vets Hugh knew became suicide statistics, others returned to the uniformed life, though it was a prison blue; sentenced for their inability to assimilate in American society once more. Hugh felt that after a year of being ordered to kill people, military or civilian, the guys who returned were simply fucked up in their minds. They were returned to a culture they had no more emotional contact with; a culture, they thought, had wanted them to do those horrible things but did not support them upon their return. They were taught to be killing machines, but were never told how to turn those switches off by the trainers. Their fathers were welcomed as heroes after World War II and even Korea. But the vets who served in Việt Nam were spit upon and called names, such as "Baby Killer" and other epithets that Hugh had since pushed out of his mind like the face in the dream. He could not believe the misery and suffering those war veterans endured. Hugh would invariably get angry when he thought about the absolute lack of psychological support from the US government and the military that sent them to Southeast Asia. "Mother fuckers," Hugh was fond of calling the nameless and faceless cowards in Washington, D.C. Cowards with the courage to order others to kill and be killed while safely eleven thousand miles away. Their practice was ordering deaths one moment and ordering martinis for themselves and their mistresses the next. "Mother fuckers," he thought again with disgust.

It wasn't so much that, Hugh thought. He felt his own life had become disoriented and desynchronized from the west. He believed the opportunity to finish his university degree, find a steady girl to get married and have a house with the white picket fence had been interrupted by the war – a war he believed, and later discovered, was absolutely senseless. Everyday he damned the need to keep his personal freedom by maintaining the secrets of others.

Hugh and Whitman had kept in touch through the intervening years. Whitman had stayed in the Army to become a career man, eventually retiring after a mere twenty years, but only at the rank of colonel. Whitman weighed a decision to retire early, but it was his Special Forces training that would only allow him to rise to the rank of full colonel and no further. Without a West Point degree, there wouldn't be any opportunity in the generals ranks. He couldn't be groomed any longer and he had begun to receive offers from the private sector for, not only corporate board positions, but also for leadership in corporate security. Those offers were more lucrative than his pay at the grade of O-6 and the chance to improve his salary with bonuses and incentives and a better retirement plan confirmed the decision that he would retire and find his future in corporate America – a Colonel with the Captains of Industry. Whitman thought it had a ring to it. Whitman could never maintain a relationship long enough to have a wife and left many women in many places in his wake. Thus, being unimpeded, he moved on to the business world.

Hugh spent the intervening years in and out of love. The woman who stayed long enough with him tolerated the nightmares until they, too, were consumed by the pain. Giving up on helping him, they each in turn left him and sought their own counseling. Civilian life did afford more freedom but he felt as though he had to look over his shoulder too many times. The cynicism and the instinct for survival were strong. His borderline mistrust annoyed his employers, one by one, and just as Hugh could not maintain a regular relationship, his working career nearly mirrored a similar pattern. He migrated from job to job and worked at his academic degrees piecemeal because going to college and the university provided him with a modicum of consistency in an unconventional life. Hugh became a jack-of-all-trades, yet, he could not keep any one job longer than a few years or so; most averaged less than two years before he finally resigned or was somehow terminated.

Hugh became a heavy drinker during the last two years in the military. His drinking, the military's personnel excess towards the end of the war in Việt Nam and his expanding need for privacy combined to result in his decision to leave. Hugh's favorite job, and one he thought would be a career for him and employment with a long-term prospectus, was in law enforcement. The sole qualifier that gave him a boost amongst the other candidates was his Special Forces background. Hugh was still in very good physical condition, could easily pass written tests and interviews because he knew the tricks of the trade from his days as an instructor. He landed a job with a police department in Northern California, not too far from where he and Whitman had attended the language school, the place where Whitman nearly killed a fisherman because of his temper. Hugh found early on at the police academy, where he was sent in Southern California, that law enforcement personnel did not have the same sense of camaraderie as the military. He quickly became an enemy of a former Marine who had also served in Việt Nam and boasted about it to the other police cadets who had no prior military experience, except for Hugh. Hugh could not talk about what he did and this became the brunt of jokes by his fellow cadet, the former Marine. One night during night exercises, the Marine had been taunting Hugh. He confronted the Marine in the dark and instantly remembered Whitman at officer's training. Hugh quickly applied a carotid sleeper hold while quietly whispering in his ear, and left the former Marine police cadet semi-conscious in the dark. The Marine later came back to the lighted assembly area, dirty and shaken but for the most part unhurt. Hugh was never taunted again, but the class knew something had happened and the remaining six weeks of training were uncomfortable for many. Hugh was glad to graduate and get back to his department.

Hugh developed not only a good reputation in the town as a cop, but he developed a relationship with a police dispatcher in an adjoining city. Some nights, they would go for long rides on his motorcycle after finishing their shifts at midnight. During spring, long moonlit rides in the sweetly-scented orange orchards outside of town refreshed their spirits and the sweet blossoms' perfume aroused their passions. They would make love very slowly, enjoying the building tension and the eventual release, then fall asleep in each other's arms. Laurel became Hugh's second wife; he never talked to other people about his first wife who had left him. Laurel lasted until she tired of the morning mothering after his nightmares. He never spoke about them to her or related what they were about, but she knew they were related to his war experiences, as she sometimes heard him cry out in his troubled sleep.

Hugh had been on the job for a few years when he shot a suspect wanted for burglaries and parole violations. He was fleeing and had drawn a gun on Hugh. Although he was an expert marksman, the dark, tree-lined street mixed with thoughts of Laurel and her recent talk of leaving him distracted a fatal shot. The suspect got up and ran into the dark, discarding the gun while Hugh was calling on his radio for assistance – assistance that took ten minutes to arrive. A cursory sweep of the area for the gun didn't turn up any weapon and the suspect refused to talk about possessing a gun because he was a parolee and a gun charge would add time to his guaranteed return to prison. The District Attorney's Office didn't file criminal charges against Hugh and determined the shooting was in self-defense. However, a department shooting review board, tilted heavy with administrative officers, split their decision on the shooting justification and Hugh was again jobless. A day later, Laurel left. Within a day of that, Hugh's friend, Dennis who worked for the Marshal's office, presented him with the divorce papers Laurel had filed.

All the while, Hugh and Whitman stayed in touch. It was always Whitman who would initiate contact to check up on his friend, whom he worried about. At times, usually every year or so, they would get together for a few days to visit, play golf and head into the mountains to go camping and fishing, something that provided comfort to Hugh. It reminded him of being in Special Forces once again. They would practice their skills, knowing that someday time would begin to work against them and deprive them of their energy and quick responses. They swore to stave off old age as long as they could. Hugh had quit drinking years before and enjoyed the times when he and Whitman were together. Occasionally on a trip, Whitman would broach the operation they conducted in Tây Ninh Province. Hugh's mind would flashback to a few of those moments, but the times with Thu Lan was nothing more than blank spots in his memory. His mind, though, did not forget the document he put away in a safe place as an insurance policy later. What he would use it for, he didn't know. Each time Whitman asked him about the operation, Hugh would keep the conversation to their skills in the forest and their surviving the B-52 bombing raid. Hugh felt pangs of anxiety when North Việt Nam finally liberated South Việt Nam and concluded the war in 1975. Even though he took comfort in helping the refugees at Camp Pendleton, he was very nervous about the documents. At times, Whitman would ask him out of curiosity about the pouch and if Hugh knew what they contained. Each time, Hugh told him it was vaporized in the bombing with its contents known only to the earth and air. Hugh didn't mind the lie as it did have some element of truth, but it disturbed him that Whitman would ask each time they were together.

During the spring of 2003, Hugh and Whitman were eating dinner together at a Vietnamese restaurant in an area known as "Little Saigon" in Southern California. Over a bowl of p^{h_i} a meat flavored noodle soup, Whitman asked, "Hugh, have you ever thought about going back to 'Nam'?"

Hugh hesitated as he never wanted to leave Việt Nam in the first place, and now that relations were improving and the Vietnamese were welcoming Americans back, Hugh had thought about going back often. He knew Việt Nam had never left him.

"As a matter of fact, I've wanted to go back ever since we left," he said. "When I lost that one job in the mid-nineties, I nearly went back if it hadn't been for the divorce I was going through and got cleaned out financially. But that country is never far from my mind. I want to go back, but I don't have enough money and have too many bills. How about you?" Hugh asked his friend.

"Yes, I'd like to. I think it would be good to go back, see some of the places we were before and see how things have changed. You know, we're not getting any younger and our dollars would go a long distance in Việt Nam since it's a poor country. We'd pick up some good deals on souvenirs, you know. Come on; let's try to get a trip together. We'll have a good time. If you need help, I can help with some of the trip," Whitman offered.

"Well, my bills are coming down. I've refinanced some of my debt and accelerated payments on the balances, so if I work hard at it, I could be in a better place financially in about another six months and we could go then." Quickly, Hugh's mind shot back to the Cao Đài Temple. "Yeah, let's do it. About six months from now. That'll give us time to outline a general plan of where we'd like to go, check on hotels and, you know, I'd like to stay at the Continental Hotel in Saigon this time. I think Saigon in the autumn would be good," and suddenly a memory ignited something in his mind for a moment and a girl's face appeared as quickly as the bill for the dinner and left again.

Whitman noticed how Hugh's reply was very animated and he detected a slight pause in Hugh's concentration, but shook it off as reactions to the war, much like his own.

Hugh began thinking about his usual opined dissatisfaction with the government of the United States and how the political parties had seemed to merge when it came to political campaign contributions and their voting in Congress. He was extremely dissatisfied with the current administration under President Paul H. Taylor, a popular southerner who could only see things in black and white, but who reveled in the prosecution of senseless wars and idiotic and repetitive rhetoric. When people ridiculed Hugh for his conspiracy theories, Hugh simply told them not to trust government. He would tell them he had the experience in Special Forces but could never go into detail to prove his point. Religious conservatives called him paranoid and a threat to America. Others would simply dismiss him as a follower of conspiracy theorists. Most felt sorry for him and didn't take him seriously. Something in Whitman's statement planted the seed of his need to return; not to vindicate himself but to give voice to the truth. Truth needed to be served and Hugh believed he had the vehicle for that. He believed. The year before, he requested old files from the government concerning him under the Freedom of Information Act, somehow under a belief that the truth would lie there, as well.

After that dinner in "Little Saigon" the two veterans kept in closer touch. They compared notes on which guide books to buy, what clothes to take, what personal items would be necessary, how much money was needed, which credit cards, and maybe hone their Vietnamese language skills that had become dull over the years. They looked for the most inexpensive flights to Saigon, now called Hồ Chí Minh City. To both men, though, the "Paris of the Orient" would always be "Saigon." Hugh also felt there may be answers to his dreams. Whitman felt there would simply be answers.

III

Whitman and Hugh caught a ride, once again, with the 25th Aviation Little Bears from Tây Ninh West and arrived at Camp Alpha at Tân Sơn Nhứt Airbase in Saigon. They discovered a Jeep waiting for them that transported them to MACV-SOG headquarters, where they ha...... before the operation in Tây Ninh Province. They noticed their bags left at the Montana Hotel a couple weeks before were placed in the corner awaiting them. They reported again to Colonel Davidson. Morgan entered from an adjacent office carrying a ceramic mug with a flag of the US emblazoned on the side and hot, black coffee steaming like the Mekong delta at noon in April. The Colonel spoke first.

"Gentlemen, please be seated. We know you've been under some harrowing circumstances and I am glad to say the US Army is proud to have you men serving our Country and more glad that you have returned safe from a successful operation. I want to present you both with the US Army Bronze Star," and Colonel Davidson began to read a sanitized citation about the "skillful performance of an operation in the III Corps Area, War Zone C, of the Republic of Việt Nam during the time period indicated (the citation listed a nebulous two month period of time), and the individual superbly accomplished this highly intricate and hazardous operation in support of free world forces combating aggression. Through his personal bravery and energetic application of his knowledge and skill, he significantly furthered the goal of the United States in Southeast Asia."

No specifics, no details; everything veiled in standardized verse, covering broad lengths of time, which ensured the confidentiality of the operation. Hugh thought the military award wasn't sufficient for what the two men had gone through and wondered what benefits the men who had ordered the unsuccessful attempt at killing them would gain. The men had Bronze Stars to place on their chests with the other awards they had already received. What really mattered to Lieutenant Hugh Campbell, newly-decorated officer in the United States Army Special Forces, was the document he had read and buried deep within the bowels of Tây Ninh's Cao Đài Great Temple.

After the quick award ceremony, Morgan took each man separately into the next room. Hugh was first. He was with Morgan for an hour. He felt uncomfortable with the CIA agent, but when grilled about the details of Captain Huỳnh's death and the documents repeatedly, he was becoming more and more uncomfortable. Hugh lost his temper.

"This feels more like an interrogation. What's the purpose of the repeated questioning?" he demanded at one point.

"It's not an interrogation, lieutenant. This is merely an extended de-briefing. When you reported details to me a couple of days ago, I didn't have all the information I do now; now that Lieutenant Emerson reported back. It's simply for my final report and then we can close this affair permanently."

"If you were professional, you wouldn't have to repeat all the questions. We did that a couple of days ago. Look, I don't really know who you're with or what your pay grade is or what your connection is to this, but I'm a commissioned officer of the Unites States Army Special Forces. My partner and I successfully completed a clandestine operation, as ordered, and I resent the continued questioning. You've got what you need from me." And Lieutenant Hugh Campbell walked out of the office.

"Wait a minute, I have a few more questions," Morgan said rising out of his chair and nearly knocking his coffee cup over.

"I terminate this de-briefing and you can go fuck yourself," Hugh replied as he walked out the door.

Morgan was already used to walkouts with some SOG and other Special Forces operatives in the past and thought about how close he was to retiring from it all. He sat back down and waited for Emerson.

Whitman, on the other hand, spent more than two hours in the office with Morgan, which discomforted Hugh. What could they be talking about that would take so much time, he wondered. Hugh felt they were going over the incident inside COSVN and their argument about the destruction of the pouch. Hugh discovered later he was right. Whitman assured Morgan he believed Hugh, but he never saw the pouch after they had become separated at the onset of the bombing.

"So, Lieutenant, as far as your know, the pouch may still be in existence, correct?" Morgan asked simply.

"Sir, if you put it that way, I can only say that we argued about the immediate destruction of the pouch and its contents and Lieutenant Campbell presented a good argument for destroying the pouch later after we could escape from COSVN and get back to where we could destroy it with some explosives or incinerate it according to Army regulations. I can only say that when we left COSVN, Lieutenant Campbell had the pouch in his possession and I never saw it again. As you know, I spent nearly a day unconscious in the forest as a result of the bombing; a bombing that I question because of your assurance the "Arc Lights" were on hold while we were in the targeted area of operation," Whitman said accusatorily.

"Lieutenant, I can assure you that someone had made a simple miscalculation between local time and Zulu time and the dates. I want you to know I personally looked into it, and discovered someone in targeting and planning made the near-fatal mistake," he lied unreassuringly. "Yes, it almost cost you your life and Lieutenant Campbell's, but you both are safe. That's the point. I congratulate you on a successful operation, but there are some more questions I'd like to ask you, just for clarification." Morgan then began to question him again about the meeting at COSVN and the argument about the pouch again.

After Whitman completed his debrief, both men picked up their baggage and were driven downtown to stay temporarily at the Rex Hotel. After checking in, the men went to the rooftop bar to relax and drink a beer. They were also given a free week of leave, a vacation of sorts that would not be deducted from their generous leave balances each man had been accruing. They spent some time shopping at Bến Thành Market and walking along Lê Lợi Street from the railroad station to the National Assembly building at the end of Lê Lợi, in the plaza that intersects with Tự Do Street. One of the habitués of the lobby at the Rex, a bearded young man and part of the Saigon Press Corps, had given them a brief history of Saigon, which included a background of the National Assembly Building. He told them it was the old opera house built by the French around 1897, was a beautiful centerpiece in its day, but now looking quite rundown with barricades around the building. The lieutenants spent time getting custom shirts and suits made by the Indian tailors who had their shops on Lê Lợi, around the corner from the elaborately decorated Sri Thenday Litthapani Hindu Temple on Tôn Thất Thiệp Street, just behind Lê Lợi Street. Acting more like tourists than purveyors for death, both men took many photos of the downtown Saigon area. Hugh focused his Nikon, a gift from his father, on the huge traffic circle and the outdoor advertising outside and opposite the Bến Thành Market. One outdoor advertisement seemed rather oddly out of place in Việt Nam because the black and white Hynos Toothpaste logo depicted a very black man with a bright, white smile. Hugh's favorite photo subjects were the girls with long, flowing, black hair who floated by in their silk áo dàis, young girls gliding along without hardly evidence of walking and seemingly ignorant of the war in the outer districts and provinces. When he saw the girls, his mind would return to Tây Ninh and he knew some things were getting murcky in his mind.

Troubled by what he perceived as blank spots, Hugh went to the 3rd Field Hospital on Võ Tánh Boulevard near Tân Sơn Nhứt Airbase to see a doctor under the pretense of having a severe cold. He asked the doctor privately, and off the record, what could cause recent memory to become blurred and faded. The doctor, a recent medical school graduate, explained how traumatic situations in an individual's life may be blocked in order to protect the fragile mind from having to bear too much pain and gave the bombing survival as an example. The boyish doctor gave Hugh some examples, which he could extrapolate to his own experiences. Hugh, though showing a half-hearted interest by now, no longer had enthusiasm to listen to the doctor. He politely refused a referral to the Army's psychiatrist. Hugh knew some *thing* had happened, but now his mind was blocking that *something* out. "What was it" would be the question growing in his mind and continuing for decades later.

Their stay at the Rex was somewhat relaxing, except for the noise of the reporters, the personnel with the Public Affairs Office and knowledge that death was raining down from huge American bombers just outside the city. During the first two days, the two lieutenants spent restful afternoons and early evenings in the shade of the rooftop bar and restaurant and would stay well until after dinner watching the war in the distance that looked more like a disjointed fireworks display. From their vantage point, they looked towards the east, across the Saigon River, and watched the explosions and the tracers – red-tipped bullets – arcing through the air speeding in bright, red streaks towards their targets. At times, they would see Spookys, the AC-47s of the 4th ACS, spewing out red hot lead from their three General Electric-designed 7.62 mm miniguns pointed out the back left windows of the aircraft. The fire from the guns looked like a red-hot funnel piercing the ground as the aircraft flew in circles. For the most part, it was quiet on the roof of the Rex. Whitman felt a dissonant and surrealistic calm and peace as he sat and watched the war from afar – a war in which he wanted to return. Hugh sat deep in thought, which bothered Whitman. He shrugged it off to the rain of death they endured in the forested area of Tây Ninh Province several days before. He also saw that Hugh was developing, what was called "The Look," or "The Thousand Yard Stare." It began to trouble Whitman and he wondered what Hugh could be hiding behind that distant gaze. The maitre d', a young Vietnamese man dressed in smartly pressed black slacks and white shirt and tie, came over and said to the officers, "Beautiful, isn't it; all the bullets traveling through the air. Nowhere else can people sit, drink beer, and watch the war happening over someone else's home. Someday, it will end. Someday, Saigon will be thriving without a war to keep it going." He turned to call the waiter to bring two more beers for the thirsty lieutenants.

Whitman and Hugh avoided the topic of their recent operation, but they both began to talk about the future of Việt Nam. Whitman felt the south's government, with America's help, will eventually win the war. Whitman based his conclusions on the historic record of World War I and World War II, and went as far back as the Civil War. Whitman, again paraphrasing his idol General Patton, always referred to the indeterminable spirit of the American soldier, and America itself, to always be the winner in any war.

Hugh felt otherwise, but for the first time hesitated to express his beliefs because of the interrogation with Morgan and Whitman's lengthy time in his debriefing and avoiding any talk about what was said. Hugh began to lessen the trust he had in his partner of the past couple of years, one whom he shared the planning, execution and their own close calls with death in Tây Ninh Province that took them straight into the headquarters of COSVN. They would never be able to talk about it. He could no longer confide in Whitman, no matter what. Now he was hoping they would be assigned to separate operations or duty stations once they completed their leave. Hugh didn't want his partner's company; at least for the immediate future.

Leaving Whitman at the Rex, Hugh walked by himself down Lê Lợi a block to Tư Do Street, formerly known as Rue Catinat during the French colonial period, the infamous street where one, as it was truthfully rumored, one could find anything to take their mind off the war; a beautiful, black-haired, petite Vietnamese woman who would love you, a pipe of opium, a pack of marijuana cigarettes or even heroin. Hugh had heard that, nowadays, much of the opium and heroin was being smuggled in with the help of the CIA, a rumor he had difficulty disbelieving. Strolling down Tư Do Street, away from the Continental Palace Hotel and towards the Saigon River, Hugh was nearly accosted by every young girl offering sex and men soliciting other women, or even their own services. Hugh found a quiet bar remotely named "The Manhattan Club" and walked in. He found an empty stool at the end of the long wooden bar; a seat furthest away from the front door, and he looked around and saw other officers, a smattering of men in civilian clothes and a few enlisted men, though being called "boys" would be more appropriate. Many of them had young, scantily-clad girls seated next to them or sitting in their laps. This was a new experience for Hugh and a moment after sitting down, a young girl wearing a short skirt and a see-through white, satin blouse, exposing dark, brown, erect nipples underneath sat next to him.

"Hey, GI. You buy me Saigon Tea, GI?" she asked with a Pidgin English accent that made Hugh want to laugh and cry at the same time.

"She wants you to buy her a drink. That's how *mama-san* pays them. You buy them drinks and it keeps *mama-san* happy," another young lieutenant explained to him. Hugh noticed the crossed rifles insignia on his collar, an indication he was in the Infantry branch of the Army.

"Yeah, honey, you buy me tea? No tea, no talk; no money, no honey," this time changing her tactic. Hugh believed she must have parroted the phrase from her co-workers.

"I've never seen you in here before, but you have that look that you've been in some shit the rest of us want to stay away from," the officer said. "Look, guy, if you want her to sit with you, you have to buy her a drink. It's only green tea, but it's expensive. If you want to screw her, that'll cost you about five dollars MPC, or about six-hundred piasters," he explained.

"What if I don't want her, but want someone else?" Hugh asked his fellow Army officer.

"Then tell her to '*Đi đi mau*,' afterwards you can have your pick. She'll just wait for the next guy to walk in. Me, I like sitting here watching the world. The girls leave me alone because my girlfriend would kill them if she found out they were trying to take me away from her. When my girl's not here, it's a good place to sit without the hassle of anyone begging a tea or money from me. Besides, mama-san and I are on good terms, the beer's good, the drinks are watered down though, and they'll get me food if I want it and the music is okay," the lieutenant explained.

"So, where's your girl?"

"Well, you know, that's the downside of having a girlfriend who works in a place like this. She's gotta pay mama-san a fee for working here and for the protection she gets from the White Mice.

"White Mice?"

"Yeah, the local Saigon cops. With their white shirts and sometimes-white service hats, well, they look like little white mice. Some people call them "rats." They're almost all crooked as hell and nearly all of them on the take, taking bribes and collecting money from unsuspecting GIs who don't know any better, shop owners, bar girls, you name it. If it has two legs, the White Mice will squeeze them for money. Almost all of them are assholes, completely inadequate and poorly trained. But then again, everything down here is nothing but corruption. Seems like they've had corruption before, but now that we're here, the Americans with a lot of money to spend, everyone wants a piece of it. Me? I don't think the south will survive by itself if America ever pulls out."

"So, you didn't answer me, where's your girl?" Hugh asked again.

"Oh yeah, like I said, that's one of the problems you have to accept for the good times with her. She's gotta work for a living and she's with some guy in the back room who's paying big bucks to be with her right now. I can't complain. Just as long as my wife back home doesn't know and as long as she isn't fucking anyone, I'm content. I like it here. The women take good care of you. If you're with one, they won't become emotionally involved with anyone else. For them, they're just renting their bodies out for fifteen, twenty, thirty minutes. They put their minds someplace else and think of what they need to buy at the market, or think about the last movie they saw; anything, but what they're doing, especially, if they came from any sort of traditional Vietnamese family."

"So, how long have you been in-country?"

"I've got eight and a half months in, already. Only a few more months until my my return from overseas, my DEROS, and I'm trying to stay as safe as I can. I've actually been thinking about staying longer, but my wife'd kill me if Charlie or some asshole sapper doesn't," he said. "So, what'd you do in the States before Uncle Sam got you?" he asked with a barroom curiosity, more out of boredom than interest.

"I was going to the university and I decided to join the officer corps before I got drafted. That way, I'd have more of a say over my future than if I became some infantryman, no offense, out in the boonies," which, Hugh thought, was exactly what he had become, except he had to think for himself. Or did he? Hugh thought again for a moment about how he believed that Whitman and he had been nothing more than mere pawns in a perverted game of chess, in a small part of the world, in a small part of Việt Nam. Who would care about what they had done anyway? Who'd care if they died in the cause of "freedom:" freedom for whom, he wondered.

"You ever read? You know, I mean read good books, not the smut trash guys leave behind in the barracks." Hugh shook his head up and down, muttering 'yeah.' "There's a book I read awhile back when I was in college. Our English professor had us read the book "The Quiet American" by an English author, Graham Greene. In fact, during his time here, Tư Do Street outside used to be called Rue Catinat when the French governed Indochina. Very interesting book. Much of the story, except for places like Tây Ninh, Phát Diệm and Hà Nội, took place right here in Saigon. Greene had a place just down the street from here and sometimes stayed at the Majestic; good old 'Number 1, Tu Do Street,'" he said pronouncing the Majestic's address as "too doe," rather than the proper "tu yuh". He picked up his drink to feel the condensation on his hands and again turned to Hugh and said, "I read another couple of his books, don't remember the titles, but the one he wrote here was excellent. The guy was like a fortune teller. He just about predicted the mess that our country is getting itself into here. I've got a paperback copy back in my room, somewhere. If you want it, I'll be glad to give it to you. Worth reading, if you've got the time," he finished saying as he picked up his drink, looked around the semi-darkened bar briefly, then back to Hugh for an answer.

"You know, I've got a few more days to relax, maybe I'll take you up on the offer."

"Sure, and I don't know if you're into it or not, but I know a couple good opium houses around, that is if you want to. Greene's book kinda sparked an interest for me. You know, the whole Oriental way of doing things and relaxing, smoking opium, having a beautiful girl lying beside you. If you're interested, I'll take you to a good place. It's not too far from here. In fact, it's near 74 Hai Bà Tr□ng, where the French government operated an opium factory for years. Gotta hand it to the French to take advantage of everything they can," he informed Hugh.

Hugh cleared his mind for several moments and considered his immediate future. He needed to have some distance from Whitman and could get along without him for a bit. It would keep Whitman from asking him questions, and besides, Hugh didn't exactly relish the idea of Whitman possibly reporting to Morgan about his leave activities. As far as Hugh was concerned, it was no one's business, save his own. With that in mind and another few days of rest, what harm would there be in spending a few hours in an opium house? That just might keep him out of trouble, get Tây Ninh out of his system and relax his mind and escape the war; a war for which his sense of patriotic duty had been vaporized along with the earth and trees in the B-52 bombing; a bombing he believed its full focus was to eliminate Whitman and himself. Hugh quietly sipped his beer, a local "33" brand served warm with ice added to the glass to cool it down. Iced beer in a glass – he admitted beer with ice was something he could grow accustomed to drinking.

Hugh finally spoke in a relaxed tone of voice, "I think I'll take you up on the offer of the book. I'll think about the other offer and let you know. For now, I think just drinking some beer and listening to music, without a bar girl, is a good way for me to relax. How can I get the book from you?" Hugh asked.

"I'm billeted at the Rex and we can meet there or somewhere else. Actually, I should say, I keep a room at the Rex and try to stay there a few days a week, that's where the book is."

"I'm also at the Rex. I'm going back for dinner a bit later."

"How about I'll say goodbye to my girl when she's done and I'll go with you. She'll be pissed for awhile, but fuck her," he said disparagingly. "You know what? We'll head back now if you want. I'll show you some of the interesting places between here and the Rex."

"Sounds good enough."

Later that night after the brief walking tour of downtown, Hugh had dinner with the other lieutenant then went to his room to relax and read Greene's "The Quiet American." Hugh was captivated by the book and read until the small hours of the morning when he finally put it down, exhausted and consumed by the story. Hugh had actually felt sorry for the elderly newsman and his love for the Vietnamese girl, whom he did not want to lose to a much younger man. Hugh also developed an extreme dislike later in the book for the American character, Alden Pyle. Hugh reflected at length after finishing the book and decided to accept the officer's invitation to spend some time in an opium house.

IV

The next day, after lunch, Hugh and the other lieutenant walked the two long blocks down Lê Lợi past the antiquated Opera House, now the National Assembly building, and they turned left on Hai Bà Trưng Street, walking away from the Saigon River. They walked past the old opium factory, its archway festooned with a poppy flower motif and yellowed with age and mold. When they reached Gia Long Street, named for a former Emperor of Việt Nam, the two officers turned down the street and ducked into a narrow alley, which was more like the eye of a needle. The hungry, dark alley consumed the two Army officers as they threaded their way through the narrow passages weaving an unimaginable route with their thoughts. They became silent as they made yet another turn into a darker alley and Hugh thought it could not get darker than what they were experiencing. Even though it was mid-morning, the darkness compelled the residents to light small oil lamps that burned cautiously in the tenement-like quarter. Occasionally, Hugh looked inside someone's quarters respectfully to see the same scenery, as though set in some surreal stage production; small wooden beds, simple table and chairs, little cooking stoves, some pots and pans, faded black and white photographs on a small family altar with incense burning. Frail, withered people sat like dried sticks in chairs, on stools or on the floor; living memories who may not have been under nor seen the sun since the French occupied the area; toothless and feeble old men with bones protruding from yellowed skin in shorts

and graying, sweat-stained athletic t-shirts sat alongside
toothless old women in tattered, patterned clothing. They
sat in their homes looking at each other quietly or at the
occasional passer-by. They were very poor and hadn't any
conversation to share with each other. Their words had long
since been spent. Here in the bleakness of the labyrinthine
passages no one had anything of value to share; poverty
and their humanity were the only assets that bound them
all together. Hugh felt the bleakness of the scene draw him
deeper into the soul of Việt Nam and her people. This alley
drew him closer to the heart of the country and it closed in
around him and held on to him and nearly smothered him.
Hugh sensed something that he couldn't identify but it was
akin to a feeling of sorrow and belonging at the same time.
It was a longing to stay, but a need to leave with what he
knew that belonged to him. His thoughts went back to the
darkness of the night when the bombs began to drop, and
in his mind the bombs exploded into different feelings of
betrayal and deception and they raped his patrial loyalty in
a forested place. A retching feeling and the seed of distrust
for America was nourished by the smoke of the small oil
lamps and the vapors of the incense, kerosene, urine, and
the fetid smell of the water running in a sluice underfoot
and it reached in through his breast and grasped his soul to
shake his confidence. He felt trapped in the country now,
yet oddly it was completely voluntary. He slowly begun
to understand the feeling that he belonged to the people of
Vi☐t Nam without regard for North or South. Here in this
darkened forest of buildings and treeless, narrow passages,
the lamps reminded him of the small, crackling fires quietly
dimming themselves after the bombing. Hugh followed the

other lieutenant deeper into the bowels of the neighborhood until they approached, what could have been in years gone, an orange door. To Hugh, it appeared orange in the dim light but it could have been grey for all that mattered about it. A smell of stale urine mixed with the fumes of kerosene and purloined JP4 jet fuel in the darkness and it continued to scent the air in spite of his thoughts. Another sweet, foreign smell issued forth from somewhere adding to the scented mixture in the air and underfoot the pavement had changed slightly. He realized they had arrived at their destination.

The lieutenant knocked quietly on the door, in no particular pattern that Hugh could discern, and moments later, after listening only to their heartbeats and the whimpering and licking of nearby fuel-soaked cotton wicks, the door creaked open and revealed what Hugh believed was a human skeleton in dark, threadbare clothing silhouetted against a soft glow of small oil lamps and a steamy heaviness in the air. The old man creaked like the door and wheezed. The lieutenant confided to Hugh, "They say this man smokes about fifty pipes a day. We won't do that, but I believe you will have a very pleasant experience. I forgot to tell you, don't worry about the cost. It won't cost much and I'll take care of it. To be honest with you, guy, I really think this is what you need. Looks like you've had a tough time out there. This is my treat for what you've probably been through, and I could never imagine. But you have that look. It's not that thousand yard stare of someone who's been in some firefights with Charlie or sat in the bush scared shitless someone will shoot at him, but you've got a different look. Can't quite place my finger on it, but you've got it. I studied psychology before I decided to join. I was very interested in combat experiences.

You look like something or someone's betrayed you," he said in a nonchalant manner that evoked a little compassion. "Don't worry, this place is safe."

The dim house was narrow. They took their boots off near the door and placed them alongside well-worn sandals and a couple other pair of spit-shined Army issue boots. The house swallowed them into a vacuum devoid of most noise. The only sound evident were people inhaling, pulling in a long draw on decorated china or bamoou-stemmed opium pipes, and tended by expressionless, young girls in loose flowered robes; their long, black hair hanging straight down alongside their gentle faces, amber-colored by the lamps and opium. They held the bowls of the long pipes over the open flames of the lamps while the opium beads bubbled and smoked. Old, gaunt Vietnamese men lay on their sides, heads resting on sweat-stained cotton bolsters that looked like bandages from a war; the stigmata of previous users purging themselves of their conscious sins in the semi-conscious dreams of the opium. Here, men were held in the sweet arms of Morpheus, their only true love. Hugh remembered the words of Greene, how the opium *dries the spit and the seed of men.* Something flashed across his mind, a darkened scene, a dark like the passageway they had just left on the other side of the orange door, but this seemed elsewhere. Hugh again realized that something had happened to his memory. Something was evading him. Like a soldier pursuing the enemy through the forest, Hugh began chasing the memory down the dark alleys of dendritic connections trying to find where that memory was concealing itself. It evaded Hugh by turning down any of tens of thousands of routes past the ganglion intersection.

A thin arm reached for Hugh's elbow, bringing him back to the present. The other lieutenant was standing behind the old man who had opened the door and nodded an "okay" to Hugh, a non-verbal approval of his initiation into the cult of those who smoked the opium pipe.

Hugh was led further back into the maw of the dimly lit house, now getting quieter with each stockinged footfall. Further on, the darkness of the house and a young girl welcomed him with a mere gesture of her hand, and she delicately offered him the padded pallet to rest upon. The girl, like the others, was clad only in a silk flowered robe and not wearing trousers. She spoke to him in Pidgin English, a few phrases softly said in the sing-song tone of her Vietnamese voice asking how he was. She was only slightly stunned when Hugh responded back in her own language. He took his shirt off and she hung it on the bent, rusting nail on the pole attached to the foot of the bed in the cubicle separated from the others by shoji screens that depicted dragons and divers phoenix. She motioned for Hugh to lie down and she sat alongside him on the wooden bed, her robe now opened to reveal soft, petite breasts with dark brown, Asian areolas and small nipples. Hugh also noticed the soft, black, tuft of hair of her pubic area. Perhaps she was also for his enjoyment. Hugh estimated her age to be near sixteen or seventeen, but it no longer mattered. He didn't know if he would want her after he had smoked.

The girl took a needle and began to warm the bead of opium over the flame. When it began to bubble, she thrust it into the bowl of the long bamboo pipe and motioned for Hugh to inhale. He gasped and coughed several times, but her gentle patience and silence calmed him. After a few short draws of air, Hugh was able to finally take in a long inhalation. He stomach felt nauseous, but it too soon became as quiet as the house. She prepared another pipe for him as he rested his head, adding the stain of his sweat-soaked sins to those of the previous penitents at the bolster.

Hugh began to realize the opium provided him some clarity of mind. He had begun to experience a quickening of thought that covered the time from Whitman's and his helicopter ferry flight to Tây Ninh and culminated in their final debrief with Morgan at MACV-SOG a few days earlier. Hugh was sensitive to gaps developing in his memory. Most instances were acute, but there were some key lapses; the trip enroute to Thiện Ngôn and following the B-52 bombing. Hugh felt something was missing, but he was unable to pinpoint or now even develop the yearning to understand it, and so he settled back into settling the conspiracy that was against him and Whitman, summing up all the numbers of the players. He knew soldiers like him were merely intricate marionettes with strings pulled, perhaps by those in Washington D.C., just as the current southern regime's strings were very likely pulled by the same people.

After smoking three pipes, Hugh told the girl he did not wish to smoke anymore, but only desired to lie there and if she was available, he would like her to lie with him and comfort him. When she pressed her soft, experienced fingers against his cheek, she knew at once he had been crying. The release of the opium in his mind had also released the sorrow for things that had happened to Whitman, the Vietnamese and himself. He wondered if he was meant to bear the sins of others. With the young beautiful girl next to him, Hugh realized that Việt Nam had become an integral part of him. She was a bond that could never be severed. He now knew he never wanted to go home. He didn't want to be part of the intrigues that captivated the players. Hugh only wanted a simple life. A life here in Southeast Asia; here in the city known as "The Paris of the Orient."

The half-nude, young girl interrupted his thought again by pressing her palm against his chest, his green t-shirt moistened with sweat. She found a fan and passed it slowly over his chest, bringing a cooling sensation to Hugh as he lay there on the bed. She sat up and continued to fan him and then maneuvered her fingers carefully into his loosened pants to feel what the tall foreigner felt like in the grasp of her small, hands and slender fingers. Compared to Vietnamese men she had known about, he was larger and she wondered for a moment what it would feel like to have the foreigner inside her. The effects of the opium in the house combined to dim the thought and she removed her hand and continued to fan him until he fell asleep.

Hugh imagined he was walking in the dark on an elevated dirt road illuminated only by stars and a crescent moon. A dark figure, clad in black and wearing a *nón lá*, the limpet-shaped hat made of palm fronds, rose silently from the vaporous paddy, slowly rising with the mist to meet him. Her face was concealed by a black and white checkered scarf and just as suddenly as she appeared, a voice was calling him, but in a voice that was quite different.

"Hey guy, you alright? Hey, guy, wake up. The White Mice and some MPs are at the front door asking about you and me. What the fuck are you, man? What'd you do, murder someone? The old man is holding them off, but you gotta get your stuff and follow me," the Lieutenant said.

Hugh's training assured him he was alert. In a moment, he had his shirt on and the other officer handed him his boots which the old man had given him before opening the door. The man may smoke fifty pipes a day, but he recognized the footfalls outside his door and he knew these were too heavy and bore the anger of a country. Without thought, he picked up the boots, gave them to the officer and told him to go out the safe way. The den had a safe exit that was known only to a few clients and to the permanent residents. It was only revealed in special cases when the need arose. This was a time for the officer to show Hugh. They had to climb out a window that appeared to open to nothing but another brick wall, an abutting building, but there was enough space for the two officers to walk sideways between the buildings until about seventy-five feet later, they intersected a dark passageway, similar to the one they used to enter the opium house. This passageway led them through many twists and turns, some narrowing then widening when it intersected another passage. About ten minutes later, or an hour as it seemed to Hugh, they arrived within visual distance of Hai Bà Trưng Street. The officers collected themselves, resting for several minutes and decided it was better if they had separated at this moment.

"You know guy, I don't know what's happening. I'm just trying to keep alive until I leave here," the young lieutenant offered. "You've got the look that I've never seen before and I've seen many Special Forces guys after they'd come out of the bush, but you're different. Whatever it was you did or didn't do, just remember; this is a fucking war and nothing fucking counts anymore. I feel you've already paid your dues. Fuck the phony Army press information briefings back at the Rex, fuck the guys in Washington and fuck this stupid ass war. We had better separate here. You know, guy, there's reasons why I didn't ask your name and there's reasons why many guys never learn the names of friends. Life can end only too quickly here. You be safe and get home. Hey, you can keep the book," he ordered his fellow officer.

With that, the officer picked up his step, cautiously looked up and down the street, gave an "okay" sign to Hugh and he was gone. Hugh waited several moments to collect his thoughts. He wasn't that familiar with Saigon, but he knew he wasn't far from the Rex and his sense of direction aided him when he emerged through that birth canal called "an alley." He checked himself in the fading daylight and then slowly walked back to the Rex, completely lucid, but with a lingering tinge of paranoia, like a child who is afraid his or her parents will discover the thing he or she has done wrong.

The clerk at the Rex noticed Hugh returning and curtly said, "Sir, you have a message." He handed him a slip of paper with a phone number on it. Hugh phoned and the line connected to Morgan. He simply stated, "This is not a secure line. I've been looking for you and want to talk to you. Tomorrow morning, nine o'clock good for you?" which sounded more like an order than suggestion.

"Sure, but I don't know what we can talk about. You said it a few days ago, things in the past are dead."

"Lieutenant, let's talk tomorrow, this line is not secure. I'll send a car for you. It'll pick you up at nine o'clock." Morgan hung up.

V

The Chairman expressed a deep frustration to his aid. "You assured me every measure had been thought out, planned for and arranged. Now you tell me there may have been a compromise?"

"It's only a possibility. It seems that the two Special Forces officers somehow managed to survive the carpet bombing. It's almost as though they had help from God, but survive it they did," he drawled. "It's my understanding that they were leaving with the pouch intact because they couldn't destroy it when they were supposed to without attracting too much attention, so they decided to take it out and destroy it when they returned to a fire support camp, or some kind of military place. But, they both survived the bombing. Our contact is not completely satisfied the pouch was destroyed. He's a thorough agent and I understand something is nagging him," the aid advised.

"I don't give a damn if his wife or girlfriend is nagging him. I want to know whether it was destroyed or not. Don't waste my fucking precious time telling me bad news. I only want to hear good news, and if you can't do it, then I'll get someone else, do you understand?" the Chairman stated emphatically. He was not prone to profanity, but he wanted to ensure the point that what he demanded is what he expecteded to receive. He wanted his message driven home with no lingering doubts in the mind of the aid.

"Sir, our contact, excuse me, my contact says that one of the officers is trustworthy and the other officer is now questionable in the opinion of my contact and the other Special Forces soldier," the aid said again in his drawl that was beginning to irritate the Chairman. Realizing the southern inflection came out only when he was nervous, he cursed himself and tried to be calm. He continued, "I'll make sure this is resolved as soon as possible and I'll not bother you until there is undeniable word the documents are destroyed." Without the customary dismissal, the aid turned and walked out of the office. His own anger growing, not with the Chairman, because he was his idol, but at the officer who was now in doubt. He thought to himself, "how in the hell can an Army officer go against orders?" With other urgent needs, he dismissed the thoughts from his mind and would let the "Chairman's contact" take care of the details. He then checked his pocket to make sure his recreational drugs were still there. They'd help take the edge of his twang.

PART IV

I

The dream returned to me, as it always does. But then it evaporated like the tea in my cup. It's terribly quiet outside. There are no noises, there are no smells, and the darkness of night covers everything. No one has come by for awhile to touch me, talk to me or be with me. All I have is the dream. It is my only companion through the long nights of being alone. I'm tired of being alone; I'm tired of not having anyone or anything to keep me company, so I have to keep my dream.

The days are kind to me. That's when the smells and noises keep me occupied and my mind is reeling with so many new things. The food is brought to me and it tastes good. I don't know what it is; it is simply "food" to me. I've learned to use the implements by myself and to hold the bowl and nobody has to help with that part. But, I am not allowed to handle the food or see it before it's prepared for me and everyone else.

The sensations of the day are pleasant; the warmth on my face, the intermittent cool of water being splashed, a new change of clothing. That's what I like most about the day is the change of clothing in the morning. Sometimes, though, I wish the change were at night. It would be better that way. Maybe it would be.

II

The two men sat silently at the table in the kitchen, simply looking at their iced milk coffee. Hugh noticed the iced glasses sweating again like everything else. Inspector Quỳ broke the ice first, "Mr. Hugh, you called me here today. You may feel much better if you can begin to tell me. You must also know that we have completed the autopsy on your friend. A bullet went straight into his brain. The bullet also, as you say, bounced around inside his skull that caused more damage. The doctors do not believe he suffered as death was immediate. I believe that your talking to me and the repatriation of his body to his homeland will be about at the same time, do you agree with me, Mr. Hugh?" the Inspector asked.

"Yes, Inspector."

"To assure you, we have already begun making arrangements with your American Consulate."

Carefully, Hugh related the incident at Tây Ninh. He only mentioned that he and Whitman had gone out for a walk late at night and were mugged. That was all the information he could trust the Inspector with for now.

The two elder civilians emerged from their rooms on the second floor of the Continental Hotel overlooking Đồng Khởi Street and went downstairs for the complimentary breakfast. They had arranged with the hotel for a car to take them to Tây Ninh, as many tourists are fond of doing. It was usually recommended by many to combine a tour of the Củ Chi Tunnels in the morning, with an arrival at the Cao Đài Temple for the noon mass and then to Tây Ninh Mountain in the early afternoon. The officers also wanted to take a quick side trip to Thiện Ngôn. Sometimes visitors would stay the night at the Hoà Bình or the An Đào Hotel, a mere half mile from the other in Tây Ninh if they believed there would be the fear of getting back to Hồ Chí Minh City too late at night. It was the traveling on the sometimes slow, two-laned highway QL22 that took most of the time. Whitman and Hugh decided to stay the night at the An Đào Hotel since it was nearer the center of town. Their visit to the Củ Chi Tunnels was longer than expected because Hugh was having some problems with the heat and the size of the tunnels. They arrived too late for the highly touted noon mass at the Great Temple in Tây Ninh, so they decided to stay another day in the city.

During the trip to Củ Chi, the men sat quietly in the sedan driven by an employee of the hotel; each man was lost in his own thoughts and didn't reveal anything to the other. The visit to the Tunnels, the heat and discomfort notwithstanding, and the War Memorial at the nearby pagoda were found to be very interesting to the two war veterans. Hugh took time from the pagoda to go down to the bank of the Saigon River that flowed nearby. He watched the large clusters of water hyacinth that floated lazily by the banks and thought it would provide a soothing photograph for later viewing. Sometimes a large clump of hyacinth would get caught on something submerged, free itself and continue on. Hugh felt his life had also snagged on something submerged and he also wanted to be free. He took numerous photographs of the hyacinth clumps and nearby fishermen working their nets in the current. Nearby foreign and Vietnamese tourists alike were gathered around a caged area that held alligators captive, a plain metal sign warning, "Caution, Wild Beasts." Hugh customarily used an SLR film camera, but for this trip he was using the latest in camera technology; a new digital camera that loaded images straight to a card then eventually to a small disc. He could also edit images with a zoom and crop function.

He liked the new camera as it was comfortable in the hand and he had become accustomed to the several features it offered. He liked to tell others that with his new camera, he could take a thousand pictures and he could delete nine hundred and ninety-nine of them without costing him a penny. While he sat quietly on the bank with his camera in hand, Hugh brought up the photos in his camera. Hugh noticed that in several photos around the tunnels and the pagoda, the same individual appeared occasionally. It did not disturb Hugh much, as it is bound to happen in small areas with tour groups, some people innocently keep reappearing in different photos. Hugh, though, with his mind already in an alert state for the past thirty-nine years decided not to discard the photos nor ignore the caution flags in his mind. Already at sixty-one, he had been trying to keep fit mentally and physically, trying to adhere to a strict regimen of diet and exercise, but those years of self-treatment with alcohol and street drugs to ward off the emotions when the dreams returned had taken a slight toll. Yet, he was still better fit than most sixty-one year olds.

Hugh left the bank of the river and found Whitman on the upper terrace and front steps of the pagoda taking photographs of the war memorial that transected the walkway from the car park to the pagoda. The two men walked over to Xuân, the driver. He had been patiently waiting for the men, completely unconcerned about the two respectful and silent Americans who had returned for whatever reason it was that American veterans returned. The Vietnamese had forgiven America and had been working hard to rebuild their country; even after America reneged on the 3.3 billion dollars in war reparation promised by President Nixon. After the United States used its money and its influence to bully the world to economically embargo Việt Nam for the next nearly twenty years, the country suffered thousands upon thousands of deaths due to starvation from drought, yet, Việt Nam still told America "don't worry, you're forgiven." Hugh admired and loved the Vietnamese.

Hugh related to Quỳ that they then drove up towards Thiện Ngôn, but couldn't recognize what they had experienced before. Quỳ mentioned it would not be unusual because some names of places had changed in the past thirty years after 1975. Hugh said they next visited Tây Ninh Mountain, as some called Núi Bà Đen. They took the cable tram to the half way point up the breast-shaped mountain, and not desiring to walk to the top, they decided to rest near the mountainside pagoda and they quietly spoke to the people and took photographs. Hugh, feeling tired from the traveling and heat decided to walk over to an adjacent building, set aside especially for those who need to take an afternoon rest. In the cool of the large open building, Hugh was lulled to a sleep by the gong of the bell struck by devotees at the nearby pagoda. A while later, Whitman came in to wake him and told him it was beginning to darken and they should start back down the mountain.

The two men took the tram back down the mountainside and met their patient driver, Xuân. He asked the men what their wishes were, as it was getting late; did they want to return to the Continental Hotel in Hồ Chí Minh City or stay the night in Tây Ninh. They told him to take them to the An Đào Hotel. Arriving twenty minutes later, they were given two separate rooms and tickets for the complimentary breakfast at the small restaurant next door. Xuân, as a driver, had his own arrangements in town. As a driver of foreign tourists for a hotel, he had arrangements in every town. After showering they joined each other in the lobby and set out with Xuân, on foot, to find dinner.

Hugh did not tell Quỳ about the nagging urge to return to the Cao Đài Temple immediately because he didn't want to betray his intentions after so many years. He often wondered if Bác were still alive and if so, would he even remember. Hugh thought the old man must be at least in his early eighties by now and after 1975, who knows who had survived. All Hugh could consider in his mind was that he needed to get back to the Great Temple east of Tây Ninh and he needed to do it without being noticed by Whitman. It was better that they had separate rooms. Hugh decided that later he would be able to leave his room, get downstairs, and exit out the back employee door while the desk clerk slept. The hotels of Tây Ninh didn't get many visitors late at night. The only nightly visitors in Tây Ninh were the police who inspected the registration cards nightly and the hourly users of the rooms at the Hoà Bình Hotel.

Around twelve thirty, armed only with a lock picking set and dressed in dark clothing, Hugh left his street-facing room, and as was his paranoiac habit that never left, he left behind tiny threads in specific places to determine if anyone had entered his room while he was away. Silently, he stole away down the back concrete stairs and made it safely out the door without being seen or heard. He caught a passing motorbike driver who was happy to make an extra twenty thousand đồng by taking the foreigner to the area of the Cao Đài Temple. Hugh had the driver drop him off outside the northernmost yellowed, metal gates and he quietly walked passed the vacant white shack and towards the temple building that anchored the long mall.

Hugh slowly walked around the back of the temple without noticing any other persons in the area. He wasn't aware of the other motorbike that had been following him with its headlight off, and it had stopped at a discrete distance from the temple on the back road from Trảng Bàng. He walked around the temple underneath dark clouds that still clung to the humid, night air and hovered in the warmth of the night. The humidity added an uncomfortable wetness to the mounting sweat from his nervousness and the darkness lent an eerie experience for Hugh as he begun to sweat more. He perspired not from the anxiety he was feeling from this anticipated mission, nor from the heat. He sweated from the culmination of years of anger that he hoped would soon be divested; anger that had been festering and underlying his life for thirty-nine years.

Hugh walked as quietly as possible and his follower was just as quiet. A third man also joined them on the grounds, unknown to the two foreigners. Hugh was hesitant to make any moves towards the resting place of the documents in case he was followed. He didn't want to reveal his intentions should anyone be nearby and question what a foreigner was doing at the Great Temple at this late hour of night. Hugh continued to reconnoiter the area trying to decide how he was going to get into the temple without making noise. The darkness of Tây Ninh would keep him concealed, as the darkness of the temple's vault kept his secret concealed. Large, dark wooden doors and their locks appeared formidable. The Cao Đàists were quite protective of their Divine Eye. Hugh slowly walked around the building, then sensed something was wrong and began to walk south from the main temple, walking under the sleepy gaze of the monkeys in the close by trees. He continued walking towards the smaller Mother temple across from the topiary garden that was located another 100 meters down the desolate road. Nearing a small, yellowed building he remembered from years before, but now grey in the dark, Hugh paused to look around, and sensed the presence of another person. Was it the monkeys in the trees, generations after the ones he remembered seeing in 1966? Hugh couldn't tell, but he knew shadows in the dark played tricks on the minds of people. At 61 years old, quite possibly time and age were beginning to take their effects and displaying illusions that only a mind seduced by paranoia could imagine.

He waited several moments for his ears and eyes to once again accustom themselves to the changing darkness of the night and his mind. Satisfied that he may still be alone, he continued his careful walk down the rough dirt-packed road. He quickly crossed the street at the small traffic circle that also functioned as a flagpole and stopped at the corner just north of the Temple of the Divine Mother, catty-corner from the garden that contained the many trees and bushes sculpted into magical and whimsical shapes and contours of dragons, turtles, phoenixes and other creatures that cavorted in the minds of the gardener-sculptors.

Hugh took his water bottle out, felt his ankle to ensure the lock pick set was still taped there and sat quietly against the wall; the overhanging branches of the tree provided even more concealment on this dark, overcast night. Hugh rested in order to still his heart and his breathing so he could hear the ambient sounds of the night and to distinguish any possible human sounds apart from the natural sounds he had become familiar with over the years. For as long as humans walked the earth, their footfalls were always different than those from the animal world; heavier and measured. Even while attempting stealth, humans still had a distinctive gait. Hugh sat at the corner without seeing or hearing anything else. What he'd give for a pair of night vision goggles, he thought, and went back to concentrating on listening to the sounds once his respiration and heart beat slowed and became part of the night's quiet noise.

Whitman had anticipated Hugh would quite possibly make a move tonight. He had always wanted to believe his friend had destroyed the documents, but he and others had lingering doubts and needed confirmation. Whitman was doing this out of a sense of commitment. He was still unsure what he would do, although his instructions in the past had been quite clear. His orders, he felt, had never changed from those in 1966. Terminate the mission with extreme prejudice and destroy the documents. Even now, as a retired colonel, he still felt obliged to follow his orders and was reminded of that obligation several times over the years, even though his reminders began to decline and seemed to evaporate in the last several years. Following orders was what his father had ingrained in him. That was what the Army and his government had ordered him to do and expected him to follow those orders, no matter how long it took. Even now, he still wanted to err in favor of his friend of all these years; a friend who had for those years had been consistent in disavowing any knowledge of the continued existence of the documents. Yet, even now, Whitman was feeling a new emotion – a hurt that he had been betrayed and lied to by his friend and had deceived the US government. Whitman was sorrowful because Hugh's quiet departure from the hotel had also meant that he had never trusted Whitman. Just that thought may have been the biggest blow to the retired military man's ego more than anything else.

Whitman always adhered to the words so eloquently spoken by General Douglas Mac Arthur's at the Army's West Point Academy in the early 1960s – "Duty, Honor, Country." For Whitman, these words were inviolable for the officer corps and especially for those in the Special Forces. Whitman tried to sort out his feelings as he asked the motorbike driver to keep his lights off while they followed the other motorbike. When he was dropped off a short distance from the main north gate of the temple grounds, he paid the driver handsomely, not quite sure of the mix of cotton-based and the new polymer currency, and told the driver he would be paid better if he waited for him. Having no other chances for a paying fare this late at night, the driver was content to wheel his Honda Dream up to the wall and reclined on the handlebars and seat as he watched the foreigner disappear through the entrance. Then he fell asleep.

Whitman was wearing his old soft-soled shoes and quietly followed Hugh at a distance that would muffle his steps and provide him time to conceal or stand quietly in shadows without being counter-observed. He watched Hugh walk around the temple area, checking some of the doors and using his body to cover the doors, not knowing that he was using lock picks. As Hugh made his way across the north side of the temple, Whitman positioned himself in the dark across the square from the temple and concealed himself in the cover of night. Whitman felt it was a calculated guess that Hugh would walk around the temple and make his way to the south side. If he didn't, Whitman would conclude that Hugh had somehow gained entry to the main temple and a confrontation could be made much easier. Whitman didn't want to consider what would happen, what his orders entailed, but he only needed to confirm first the betrayal and then carry out the unfulfilled orders; terminate the mission and destroy the documents. He began to feel that betrayal was becoming more certain; he almost relished the idea of solely satisfying the thirty-nine year old order they were charged with. He watched as Hugh turned the corner of the temple, came back into sight and very slowly walked south along the divided boulevard that bisected the temple grounds. He watched as Hugh stopped to pause and look around. Whitman was huddled against the ground in the dark, still against the wall near the covered, concrete bleachers. In the dark, he could never be seen as a human figure. To the night, he was a rock, an inanimate object out of place, but still unseen. He crept to the corner and observed Hugh walking across the street further down from his location and Whitman quietly damned himself for not being more observant or aware of the surrounding areas, but then, he was told the Great Temple of Cao Đài in Tây Ninh was only a possibility, should the documents still exist. There were other possibilities, even in old Saigon, in some darkened alleys and passageways, but Hugh hadn't gone there or seemed to have any interest in those neighborhoods. The area around Thiện Ngôn had also been considered, but on the maps that Whitman had reviewed, he couldn't find where the old camp had been located. As many other place names had changed to reflect the reunification of Việt Nam, the old village had been renamed. Finding it difficult to locate, the men had Xuân drive back to Tây Ninh. So, here he was now at the Temple, the most logical site of the documents and he still had no idea of what they contained that was so important.

As Whitman huddled against the darkness, he began to consider the importance of the documents, even now, and he suddenly had misgivings. He had been so intent on following orders all these years that he had forgotten what had been explained to them in the first place; the documents were the strategic and tactical battle plans for the Việt Cộng and elements of the North Vietnamese Army in the south to successfully drive the Americans out of Việt Nam and win the war. That's what they were told. Whitman realized his focus was on his military orders and facts became obscured by his fidelity to the Army and the government, both he believed would never lie. Whitman sat consumed in the dark while a light of understanding wished to dawn on him. If he were still under orders, at least from the last government contact he had, to terminate his friend and finally destroy the documents believed to yet exist, why were they still so important? Việt Nam had been reunified for thirty years, which would have made those plans ineffective even during 1973 when the last US troops were going home during President Nixon's term. Whitman cursed himself for never questioning and was suddenly beginning to feel like a pawn. He had never felt this feeling during his military career, but now that he had to work in the private sector and think on his own, a flood of doubt washed across his mind as his eyes and his consciousness went dark. Whitman only felt a sudden, hard rap against his skull before slumping to the ground unconscious.

The short man had been stalking the stalker and was concerned that the friend of forty years may freeze if any action was needed. The operative knew Whitman would be in the way and perhaps ruin the surveillance. He didn't want to follow two men, but only the main target, Hugh Campbell, the suspected traitor. He had been following him for most of the day. His Vietnamese heritage allowed him to blend in with the rest of the unseen villagers, motorbike drivers, street vendors and the unemployed. Hugh and Whitman wouldn't have noticed him, although at a few times during the day, he had unintentionally been in the background with other people when Hugh had swung his camera around to take photographs around Củ Chi and the mountain. Even though this CIA operative working for the US on Vietnamese soil was Vietnamese-American, it was his western largesse, due to the higher fat diet in America that had made him seem just slightly different to Hugh in some of the photographs. With Whitman safely unconscious for awhile, Anh, as he was called, took up surveillance of Hugh and wondered why he was sitting for so long at the corner. Anh wondered if he was waiting for a contact to arrive, if he was asleep, or had his aging body simply tired out and he was resting. Anh even considered that he could be dead because he wasn't moving at all. The agent was looking at him through a night vision monocular. He couldn't quite see each detail of Hugh, but he did see that his target was in a sitting position against the wall. What the fuck is he waiting for? Anh thought. He heard Whitman quietly breathing behind him.

Satisfied that he wasn't being followed, Hugh stretched his legs, massaged the blood back into the calves, ankles and feet and finally rid them of the numbness. As blood began to recirculate and pinched nerves revitalized, his legs started to tingle as punishment for the uncomfortable position he had made them suffer. Hugh softly pounded his legs with the butt of his fists to get them active and alive and to stop the stinging sensation. With his legs finally settled as circulation returned, he scanned the empty boulevard in both directions. He was content that he was alone and thought he may have dozed for a moment and dreamt of noises down the street.

He checked his watch and noticed he had been in the same position for nearly half an hour and suddenly feared that he did fall asleep. The exertion on the mountain must have drained his energy, he thought.

Hugh rose quietly, stretched his legs like a cat and satisfied that he was alone began to walk up the street quietly, on the same side of the street where Anh was sitting next to Whitman in a supine position and still unconscious. Hugh walked slowly towards Anh's position then crossed the street mid-block to the relief of Anh, who was ready to incapacitate the older, former Special Forces lieutenant. Hugh walked past the greyish building at the car park and crossed back to the temple concealing himself in the darkness of the overhangs of the huge trees and the walkway around the temple. Anh watched Hugh as he approached the temple and hoped he wouldn't disappear behind the rear of the building. But he did.

Whitman dove behind some still-standing trees as the B-52s dropped their lethal burdens to the earth. The air burst apart in a super-heated mixture of explosives, hot air, fire, smoke, splinters, stones and dirt. Whitman picked himself up and ran and was again knocked down by something hitting his head. His mind flashed a brilliant white and the bomb exploded in his brain and it went dark. Afraid, Whitman opened his eyes cautiously worried where the next bomb would hit and saw a Vietnamese squatting next to him with something to his eyes. There was a slight green glow emanating from corner of his eye and the realization of the situation struck him, so he struck back. While still lying there, Whitman raised his arm and struck the Vietnamese with a force on the back of the head that knocked the night vision monocular from his eyes as he slumped to the ground. Whitman had a throbbing headache and checked his watch to see how long he had been unconscious. Twenty-five minutes. Jesus Christ, my head hurts, he thought, hoping Jesus would take away the pain of his head and his sins. Striking the Vietnamese was a reaction that Whitman didn't have time to think about. Years with the Special Forces and conducting covert operations kept his mind attuned to the outside and he swore at himself for being stalked and taken out without knowing it. At least the time he was unconscious was minimized by his years of training. Whitman checked the pockets of the Vietnamese to find his identity. He only found seven-million Vietnamese đồng in brand new bluish five-hundred thousand đồng notes and a handful of smaller denomination bills and coins. He stuffed the money into his own pocket then looked for any semblance of identification and couldn't find any. He stripped the Vietnamese of his belt and wrapped it around his hands and legs tightly so he couldn't free himself too soon after he recovered. He checked the buckle and finally did another search of the man for concealed weapons. Secured to his ankle were a small .22 caliber pistol and a polished ceramic-blade knife in a scabbard around his other ankle. Whitman was surprised to find the gun as they are illegal and very rare in the country, and not even all the police carried them. He quickly stripped the man of his weapons and put them into his own pocket. Whitman forgot any doubts about his orders. The rap from behind and the flashing of bombs in his head thrust him back into his military survival mode and the need to successfully accomplish his mission. He picked up the monocular night vision and examined it. Using ambient light and the faded green glow from the eyepiece he saw it was US made. What surprised him further was that he knew it was issue for CIA field use. Whitman had spent too much time with them not to recognize the tell-tale signs of a Company man. He remembered the last suspected Company Man he met had met in Việt Nam, coincidentally in Tây Ninh, was Morgan. He was all business, all mystery and a very effective interrogator. He remembered the interrogation after he returned from being missing in action during the bombing near Thiện Ngôn and how Morgan had him fidgeting and believing that Hugh may be a traitor and asked him leading questions to suit what Morgan wanted to hear. He looked at the Vietnamese lying nearby, rose and kicked the unconscious man in the head to ensure he would remain a non-threat, and more so because of spite.

Whitman looked through the monocular at the corner where he last saw Hugh and saw he was missing. He scanned the street, the car park and surrounding areas and still could not see his former Special Forces partner. He remembered that the operative had been looking in the general direction of the Great Temple and deduced Hugh must be in that area. Whitman returned to an earlier thought about the documents and realized that if the CIA was involved, those documents were simply not VC and NVA battle plans but something much more important, something that could potentially still be harmful to powerful people in the US What the hell have I been used for, he thought to himself, but again could not dwell on that issue. To have the CIA following him as extra insurance provided genesis for the next thought; was the B-52 bombing raid extra insurance that the documents and the guardians of those documents would be eliminated? All traces of it gone and only two flag draped, log-filled coffins would be reminders to the parents of the Special Forces lieutenants who died honorably for their country fighting third world aggressor forces, as the nationalists were known.

Whitman suddenly felt disconnected from the real world he had known, a world of regulations, of following orders of never questioning the government of the United States of America because it always had the best interests of its people at heart, always fighting injustice, always fighting in support of democracy and freedom everywhere in the world. He fondly remembered his father, a retired colonel, once telling him that his undying duty was always to country, but he should leave just a little room for doubt. His father told him that when he was passed over for promotion to brigadier general. He never knew why, but the disappointment of not getting the promotion to one star prompted the off-the-cuff remark to his son, at the time a captain – a veteran of the American War in Việt Nam.

Whitman took the initiative and stole softly across the darkened street to see if he could find Hugh. He looked above at the Great Temple and saw the dragons casting down castigating glances at him for the foul deed he was contemplating on their peaceful grounds. He cursed himself for being back in the hot and steamy climate and he cursed Hugh for getting him re-involved in this god-forsaken country. He wanted to return to the States and he wanted to sit in his air-conditioned office and meet with friends for drinks in the afternoon at the golf club. The thought of meeting fellow retirees at the Officer's Club at the nearby fort, one of the few in his area that had been saved from base closures resulting from "peace dividends," crossed his mind, and he wanted that, too. He just wanted out of Việt Nam and to stop baby-sitting another adult. He looked up again at the strange dragons and never could understand the Asian mind, the Asian way of doing things. He knew Hugh had a deep love for this country, but *he* loved America and all it stood for, even if some parts of it were wrong – even if it wanted the two of them killed. Whitman began to feel more anger welling up inside him and knew his emotions at a time like this accentuated with a pounding headache were dangerous and he felt himself losing focus for a moment. Shuddering to himself, he stopped and listened. He heard slight chattering in the trees, muffled sounds of leaves and branches rubbing against each other as the monkeys shifted themselves in their nests high above the ground away from night predators; shifting around to watch the sad comedy of the humans out at night.

Slowly, Whitman inched his way around the side of the temple and paused at the corner before looking around the curved back of the building. He kept the gun ready in hand and pocketed the monocular in his pocket, cushioned by the large amount of cash. He listened for sounds and only heard his own rhythmic in and out breathing as he was trained to do. It would calm his heart and calm his mind for several moments so he could assess the environment, which was now one that he detested. He still heard nothing more than branches moving and a slight breeze stirring the leaves in the nearby trees buffering the temple from the other buildings. At a corner door, Whitman finally saw Hugh cowering, hunched over, and doing something in the dark. Wanting a more distinct view, he drew the monocular goggle from his pocket, which also caught the hilt of the ceramic-blade knife in his pocket and it fell to the ground with a clang. Hugh looked up, frightened by the sound and Whitman cursed himself, angered at his inability to take back that moment, and he picked up the knife. The men confronted each other.

"What the fuck are you doing here?" demanded Hugh, angered at Whitman's presence and angered by the muffling of his own hearing senses not to detect his former military partner sneak up on him.

"Even more so, what the fuck are *you* doing here?" Whitman emphasized with a sarcasm that reflected his own distaste for Việt Nam.

"Whit, you still don't get it do you? I don't have to ask you why you're following me, 'cause it's apparent. You're still attached to them, you still believe that those documents were strategic plans for the VC. They're not."

"You fucking shit! You opened the pouch and read it, didn't you?" Whitman accused Hugh realizing he had read the contents of the pouch.

"Didn't you wonder about all the different players involved in the operation? You didn't know the VC was ordered to protect us. Why do you think we were allowed right into the lion's den at COSVN? Someone high up in both places knew what was going on and they wanted to ensure we would safely make it to the rendezvous site, kill the courier and the double-agent and destroy the documents. Remember how we had the conversation here in Tây Ninh at the colonel's house about why they wanted battle plans destroyed rather than retained for intelligence purposes? Remember? Remember after we got out we told them we hadn't destroyed the pouch yet and the fucking Air Force started dropping bombs right on top of our fucking heads? You know, Whit, you never could question orders; you always followed orders like you're doing now. Don't you know they don't give a shit about you or me?" Hugh said passionately.

"Who is 'they' you keep referring to? Who is it that's out to get you, Hugh? You're so fucking paranoid. Who is 'they'?" demanded Whitman.

"Christ, Whit, it's the assholes that keep making the insane decisions, the ones that got the US involved in Việt Nam in the first place. It's the same assholes who set up Diệm and others like Manuel Noriega in Panama then pulled his plug. It's the same assholes who established and financed bin Laden in Afghanistan then turned on him and look what he did with our training. It's the same assholes that helped Saddam Hussein get to power, gave him all the weapons to fight the Iranians who deposed the Shah we supported. It's the same assholes who then sold our fucking weapons to the Iranians and took the profits to give to the Contras. It's the same fucking assholes, Whit, that are fucking around with you and me right now and I think they've been doing it for the past thirty-some odd years since we've left Tây Ninh. Come on, Whit, don't you get it?" Hugh's voice rose at the end, and then dropped in exasperation.

Whitman thought for a moment and his mind went to his own thoughts and to the unconscious Vietnamese, whom he was convinced was CIA, but decided not to tell Hugh about him. Whitman looked at Hugh for a long moment while he processed information.

Finally, he asked, "What was in the pouch?"

"You know, Whit, at this point, I'm not going to tell you. You've been their fucking errand boy for years, running around doing what you're told. If I tell you, you wouldn't believe me, and you'd make sure it was destroyed and you'd fucking destroy me too, wouldn't you? I can see it in your eyes. Why else would you have weapons with you?" All the while, Hugh was walking slowly towards his former partner, not in a threatening manner, but more as a comforting friend, trying to help him see the light of day in the dark. Whitman, kept deep in considering the facts, was distracted and unaware of the natural appearing and casual movement of his once-trusted friend and was suddenly caught off guard by the quick thrust of Hugh's fist into his stomach. Whitman doubled over while Hugh tried to grab the knife. The men struggled for the gun and fought each other at the wall of the temple that also struggled to maintain its peace, harmony and tranquility.

Not far from struggle, an old man had been awakened by loud talking and scuffling and the sound of metal striking stones. He was too old to work any longer, but still ardent enough to volunteer at the temple and took it upon himself to oversee and be the watchman at night. He put the pants of his áo dài on, ignored getting his shirt and walked quickly out his unlocked door to the temple where the foreign sounds were coming from. The old, white haired man turned the corner and in the dark of the night he could make out two large foreigners fighting each other. He had witnessed strange occurrences over the years working and volunteering at the temple. Normally, it was a tourist center and an object of curiosity rather than devotion for many. But this strange fighting at night between foreigners surprised him and then he suddenly recognized one of them was whom he had beeen waiting for.

The old man had taken his position as a watchman, a volunteer at the temple because he knew the promise made so many years ago would be fulfilled by the young man he trusted. Now here he was and he was thrilled, but also pained to see the suffering that was going on. The old man also knew that the documents contained in the pouch buried so long ago underneath the watchful gaze of the Diving Eye were still there and only one other person had ever looked at it – himself. He also knew the secret but could never reveal what he knew because it was not his duty, but that of the man who had charge of it. It was his chosen task to take proper actions with it, but in the immediate case, there was a possibility that the task may not be accomplished unless the old man intervened. It was his karmic duty. He picked up the gun that had been knocked away in the fight, pointed it at the back of Whitman's head and pulled the trigger firing a single bullet. Traveling at over one thousand feet per second in that short space, the small grained bullet penetrated Whitman's skull at the lambdoid suture, pushing splintered bone fragments into the buttery brain. Then the bullet, losing only a portion of its momentum in the boney structure and the grey matter, began to ricochet around the inside of his skull, boring holes and severing ganglion, neurons, axons and dendrites, destroying thoughts, hopes, wishes and plans and eliminating all doubt from the world. Whitman died instantly from a brain now a porous mush and never to ponder ever again how he had been manipulated by those he trusted.

Hugh shocked by the sound of the gun glided away on the polished stones lubricated by blood and pushed himself away from Whitman's corpse with his feet, not realizing that most of the blood was his own. In the scuffle, he did not see what the old man saw. He had been severely cut by the scalpel-like ceramic blade and was beginning to bleed profusely from the opened wound made larger by the fight and from the increased pumping of his heart in the excitement. He looked up to see his old friend who he called "Bác." Barely a moment later, the siren of the local police was heard. Bác quickly and assuringly told him, "Say nothing. They will take you to the hospital for treatment. I am here. The gun is no longer, and your secret is still safe with me. I have waited all these years, but you have another problem. I will wait, but remember to say nothing," and into the black of night, he ran away very quickly for a man of eighty years.

III

The pea soup green uniformed police arrived and drove through the narrow opening of the gate. Their white Jeep, marked with "*Cảnh Sát*" inside a blue stripe on the sides, barely made it through the opening without scraping the mirrors. The driver shone the spot ___ ___ ___n the northern side of the temple and saw the two bodies laying on the cold stones in the dark. They jumped out of the Jeep, ran over to the men and saw one was dead and the other was close to dying. They argued with each other for a minute about who would stay with the dead one and immediately the junior officer lost. Sensing the urgency of the foreigner's wounds, they hefted Hugh into the back of the open air Jeep with great difficulty and the senior policeman drove to the hospital while the other one stayed with the body to examine it. He turned his flashlight on and after turning Whitman's head to the side, saw blood and a pinkish fluid coming from a small wound in the back of the man's skull. It was a wound easy to see through the blondish-white crew cut. He looked at the pupils, saw they were fixed and dilated, and he checked the breathing and pulse. Both were absent. The officer simply said to the temple and the dragons as his witnesses, "*Chết rồi.*" This man is dead, already.

The other officer driving with Hugh belted in the front seat arrived at Bệnh viện Đa Khoa Tây Ninh, Tây Ninh General Hospital, in about three minutes. After shutting off the siren, he had to honk his horn twice for the night guard to open the gate so he could drive in and up the ramp to the entrance of the emergency room. The doctor and two nurses on duty came out immediately. They knew when the police arrived at the Emergency Room with its siren blaring in the dead of the night that it would be something they would need to be very attentive to as the police would usually not bother with a routine case. The officer simply told them the foreigner was found lying in blood at the Cao Đài Temple along with another foreigner who was already dead and would be brought in later for them to examine.

Another doctor came out from the back of the open bay ER and they worked together to lift Hugh out of the Jeep and place him on a rust-stained gurney and then wheeled him in for examination. Washing him down they took his vital information; blood pressure was falling and they found the source of bleeding and went to work immediately to treat the severe wound caused by the knife. Hugh had already lost quite a bit of blood and the policeman was upset at now having to clean the mess in his police Jeep before it dried – he'd have his subordinate do it. Hugh was nearing unconsciousness and the doctors felt it was necessary to send him to surgery as the wound was deeper than they thought. The policeman quickly searched Hugh's pockets and found nothing. Hugh had sanitized himself, having learned from training to leave identification behind during an operation and not to give the enemy, or in this case the police, too much information. He believed they had to work for it.

The old man returned safely to his little sleeping room a moment before the police arrived. He looked at the small gun in his hand in the dim light of the oil lamp. It glistened in his hand and it smelt like the war again. It almost smelt comforting to him. Unsure of what should be done about the small pistol, he opened the cover of his cotton mattress and tucked it inside and underneath as far as he could. He then looked at the leather case that had various metal prongs protruding and shining in the dark. They were an odd assortment of small toothpick implements with hooks and bends. He felt it may have something to do with locks, but wasn't sure and placed it inside the mattress cover along with the gun. The old man turned the wheel of the small oil lamp that lowered the wick and extinguished the flame, just as he extinguished the flame of Whitman's life and thought for a moment of what he had done. It was his karma, but he didn't give it a good or bad value. It was an action and it was also Whitman's karma to be in Tây Ninh and to die that night. They all were pawns in a strange game played by the gods. He arose from his quick contemplations and looked outside. From his vantage point, he could barely see the light of the returning police Jeep and its glow illuminated a portion of the area. The old man saw movement out of the corner of his eye, near the monkey park, and knew that something was out of place. The old man has been here for so many years and knew every inch of the grounds in the light and the dark. The 'something' he saw did not fit into the picture in his mind. With the police on the other side of the building, the old white-haired man quietly stole outside his room and walked silently across the street south of the square to see what it was that was not only out of place but now squirming. He saw it was a young Vietnamese man.

He said to him, "Who are you, what are you doing here this late?"

"Free me, Bác," and the old man's mind froze for a moment with a recollection. He looked for the buckle, urged the post out from the leather hole and freed the man. Without as much as a "thank you" or a "goodbye" the small man ran south along the wall of the monkey park towards the Mother Temple and was quickly devoured by the maw of darkness.

Hugh lay on his back in the emergency room of the Tây Ninh General Hospital after he arrived barely conscious, just at the cusp of death. The hospital could be considered primitive by western medical standards, but Hugh did not care. When the policeman brought him in, he was placed on a gurney and wheeled into the open-bay emergency room. He just may have been the first foreigner ever to seek treatment there and he became the focus of everyone's curiosity, conversation and concern. Concerns over a foreigner having an emergency and being close to death is an event the hospital doctors never forsaw. It was only too easy for a Vietnamese to die in their hospital, which they did often enough. It was difficult if a foreigner died in their care and questions by other foreigners and their government would be asked. Westerners didn't understand the rural medical practices. When something went wrong, they tended to blame others than those responsible and the ones being treated for their misfortune. Hugh was fortunate to have three doctors and four nurses attending him. He was still in pain from the wound and heard them talking about surgery. Hugh locked his eyes on the water-stained ceiling, watched the fans slowly stirring the tepid, midnight air and listened to the sounds of the emergency room and its occupants.

Odd, Hugh thought, that an open bay emergency room does a lot for one needing treatment as everyone suddenly becomes family and he felt comforted by several people who were there for other patients. He knew the Vietnamese tended to help not just family but each other. As Hugh stood at the cusp of unconsciousness, his mind found the connection with the image from his dreams, his fantasy lover. The voices in the background dissipated his thoughts and he focused again on the fans whirling above his head. And like the fans, Hugh now had strangers hovering over him fanning him and helping move the gurney at the nurse's or doctor's insistence. In his vulnerable and fragile state of health, Hugh didn't feel insecure or frightened. Quite the opposite, he drifted into a very safe and sheltered emotional state of mind, a sort of quiet acceptance of assignment of responsibility and caring to others. He knew, for all that it was worth, he was in very good hands of professionals and families alike. Hugh finally allowed himself to drift off to a dreamless sleep. He wasn't aware that the pain-reducing medication was taking effect in preparation of his surgery.

When the dream returned, she slowly rose from the paddy again as she has done on so many nights for so many years. Her mollusk hat tilted slightly back, face concealed, and she was wearing her black pajamas. He again put his hand inside her blouse and felt a nipple becoming taut under the touch of his fingertips. She stood for a moment, and then brushed his hand away, black fading to white, the color of the nurse's uniform, and the nurse who was wearing a surgical mask was trying to rouse him from his medicated stupor after his surgery. The medical staff in post-op wanted to ensure he regained consciousness easily after the operation to mend the vein that had been cut during the fight. The doctors and nurses didn't care how the wound occurred; their only concern was to mend the foreigner. In the background, slowly coming into focus was a uniformed policeman, his red-banded, green service hat in hand. He stood watching the foreigner regaining awareness and surprised that he replied in Vietnamese when questioned by the nurse about how he was feeling. Hugh caught himself and spoke in rudimentary phrases, not wanting the police to take advantage of his fluency. They'd have to work for that also. Except for two nurses and a doctor who sat at a low table preparing reports, all left the room, including the policeman. Hugh glanced at the rusty analog clock hanging above the doorway and saw it was two-thirty. In the post-op room, he didn't know if it was day or night, or which day it was. Hugh had no idea how long he had been unconscious, either. He asked the nearest nurse which day it was and how long he had been sleeping. She told him he arrived around two forty-five in the morning, went into surgery around five in the morning and had been asleep for quite some time. They were concerned that he wasn't waking quickly. Hugh only wondered how long they would keep him there. Now that he was conscious, two nurses wheeled the gurney to another ward, also open like the emergency room and which had many beds occupied by the infirm. One patient's bed was moved from his position near the nurses' station and the foreigner wheeled into his place. Two other nurses came to him, took his temperature, blood pressure, oxygen levels and pulse rate. The masked nurses' eyes showed kindness and concern for the patient. Hugh looked into their eyes and saw the eyes in his dream, the soft curving eyelids blending into the fold of skin on the inside of the eye, the narrow, dark eyes burrowing themselves into this own, seeking his soul in return for his love and his faithfulness. In a soft, respectful voice, one of the nurses with a clipboard began to ask some information, because he had arrived in the middle of the night without identification. The police wouldn't know who he was until later when the hotel registration records would be reviewed and the hotel staff would report to the police that the foreigners who had checked in the evening before were missing. The driver from the Continental Hotel in Hồ Chí Minh City was also concerned and together with An Đào Hotel staff, reported their worries to the police. Nobody in Việt Nam liked unaccounted-for foreigners.

Hugh politely cooperated with the nurse, provided his full name, birthdate, hotel information in Tây Ninh and in Hồ Chí Minh City. Hugh also provided information, when asked, about his medical history, which there wasn't much to report; cholesterol reducing medication and a non-steroidal inflammatory drug to keep the waxing effects of arthritis in check. The nurses giggled to each other about how their foreign patient was handsome and still fit for one who was sixty-one. They spoke to each other and commented on his brown-grey hair, light skin, blue eyes and his high nose ridge, unlike their own noses, which were mostly flat and lacked the ridge. They simply never had much cause for contact with foreigners and thus, it was a matter of great curiosity for them. The nurses caringly gave him a sponge bath. They washed his face, opened the back of his hospital gown and washed his back with soap and water. They asked him to turn on his side so they could wash the back of his legs. Moving him onto his back again, they washed his neck, chest, stomach and the front of his legs. Both helped in washing Hugh's groin area, one holding his member while the other washed and rinsed underneath. Hugh reflected how there wasn't any sense of embarrassment on his or their part. The nurses' touch was compassionate. They replaced Hugh's gown with a clean one, brought him some drinking water and let him rest.

Later, the policeman came back in with his clipboard in hand and a magazine. He must have won the draw to interview the foreigner and he seemed quite pleased. Today, he wouldn't have to walk around his ward checking store tax receipts or house registration booklets. He could relax and spend the day in the hospital and be treated kindly, not having to pay for his food or drink for the day. He was glad the foreigner was now awake because it was nearing the end of his shift. When he was done questioning and writing his report, he could go home and have stories to tell his children and wife.

"*Anh nói tiếng Việt được, không?*" the policeman asked Hugh.

"*Anh nói một ít tiếng Việt. Anh biết tiếng Anh được, không?*" Hugh replied saying that he only spoke a little Vietnamese, but wondering if the policeman understood English.

Hesitatingly, the policeman said in a broken Pidgin-like English, "I only talk little Englitsch. You talk me what happen. You friend dead."

The news of Whitman's death struck him. He didn't know what had happened to him and he caught himself not thinking about Whitman after arriving at the hospital or even after surgery. Not until now. The police, he thought, don't have much of a bedside manner, but then again, they wouldn't be police if they did.

"How did he die?"

"Gun kill you friend. Gun where?" he asked while using his hand to imitate a gun.

"I don't know anything about a gun. I don't have one, I don't own one, and it's illegal to have one. I am only a tourist. I think my friend and I were attacked by a thieves or robbers. I can't remember," Hugh lied.

"Why you at *toà thánh* in night time? Why you at temple Cao Đài?" the small policeman demanded more than asked.

Hugh felt at a loss of words in English and in Vietnamese to explain what had happened or why he and Whitman were out late at night. He could only offer, "My head was hit. I don't remember; I don't understand what you're saying."

"Why you at Cao Đài? Gun where?" he insisted.

"Sir, my head and my side hurts a lot. Excuse me, nurse, I need you," Hugh moaned for release from questioning.

The policeman was angered at the foreigner's inability to cooperate and also felt the language barrier added to this frustration. He asked once more, "Why you friend dead? Gun where? Why you at temple at night?"

The nurse arrived and Hugh heard her tell the annoyed policeman that the patient mustn't be disturbed. She explained carefully to him that it wouldn't do any good if the patient's condition worsened because of the questioning and there would be too many questions asked by consulate officers and government ministry officials. She told him that he will be getting transferred to a hospital in Hồ Chí Minh City in a day or so and maybe it was better for the police there to be burdened with the foreigner and his problems. She assured him the hospital, and a certain policeman, didn't want the attention of ministry officials poking around their territory. The policeman considered her position and the extra money he earned on the side by helping people keep their paperwork legal and he didn't want that to be disrupted with outside eyes looking in. He looked at the patient and said, "Xin chào tạm biệt, Ông. I hope you better someday."

"Thank you, officer," Hugh quietly replied. The policeman walked away without knowing anything about what happened and Hugh then fell asleep; returning to the dream; returning to the arms of his lover in the black pajamas.

Hugh spent two more nights at Tây Ninh General Hospital. The medical staff, still concerned about a foreigner in their care, had done everything to stabilize him and wanted the sutures to be set in place before transferring him to Hồ Chí Minh City, a drive over roads still rough that would certainly do damage and undo the sutures if he traveled too soon after the surgery. A nurse made the phone calls and prepared the paperwork for Hugh's transfer to Franco-Vietnamese Hospital in Hồ Chí Minh City's District Seven – Saigon South. It was a fairly new hospital, which, Hugh had heard, enjoyed a much respected reputation. Late afternoon of the third day after Whitman's death and Hugh's retrieval from near death, and at a time just before a moisture-laden dusk settled heavily over the Vietnamese countryside, he was transferred to a stretcher by five Vietnamese men and put onto a gurney and wheeled to the sally port of the emergency room where the ambulance waited for him.

The ambulance was an antiquated fifteen passenger van that had its rear seats removed and an inexpensive, stainless steel platform installed behind the driver. Several men had to work to lift Hugh into the back of the vehicle and then onto the platform, which didn't have any restraints to hold the stretcher. Hugh's medical records were carried by an accompanying nurse with a white hat set properly atop her black hair, and wearing a mask to keep from breathing the dust of the road, and the trio set out for Hồ Chí Minh City. The driver used the siren unnecessarily for most of the two and a half hour trip. While the ambulance bounced along the road, the nurse would occasionally take his blood pressure and check the dressing covering his wound to ensure there wasn't any new bleeding or oozing caused by the jerks of the van and the pitching over pot holes in the road. Hugh's wound ached and he tried to keep his attention diverted by watching the stars, which started to appear intermittently through the clouds.

The driver behind the wheel was an old man in a stained t-shirt and fingertips yellowed from years of smoking "555" brand cigarettes. He coughed and wheezed in unison with the motor of the old van and, at times, Hugh almost couldn't distinguish between the van's motor and the driver. The nurse, a young lady whose age Hugh could not estimate, looked at him during the trip. He couldn't tell if her interest was medical or simply a curiosity of attending a foreigner. She spoke to him in English.

"How do you feel, Mr. Hugh?"

"The ride is bumpy, and the wound hurts, but otherwise, not bad. I've had things worse than this."

"I never have a chance to talk with foreigners, with native English speakers. I only learn English in school from Vietnamese teacher, never foreigner. My mother taught me a little. May I talk with you?" she said, although she felt *e dè*, a little reserved and self – conscious.

"Sure, yes. I would be happy to talk with you. What is your name?"

"My name is Phạm Thị Thu Hương. I am from Tây Ninh City." Hugh thought for a moment, translating her name into English: *The Scent of Autumn*. He added, *The Scent of* Tây Ninh".

"There are five people in my family; my father, mother and two younger sisters. Oh, yes (she giggled under the mask) and me," she recited, apparently a rote introduction learned in English class.

"You seem quite young to be a nurse," he said truthfully. "How old are you?"

"I am twenty-nine years old. I am not married yet. Do you have a wife?"

Hugh pained at the question as it picked at wounds that never healed and couldn't be fixed in any hospital. He had had two wives and regretted losing both of them, but accepted the loss. They were a result of his mistakes, the pain of his errors in love. The question also picked at an emotional wound he thought had finally closed, but instead it still oozed with sorrow. No skilled surgeon could mend that scar. "No, I do not have a wife. Before I was married, but now divorced." She looked at him quizzically as the word was absent from her vocabulary. "*Ly dị*," he clarified for her. "*Bây giờ, Tôi không có vợ.*" Hugh explained in Vietnamese he was divorced and did not have a wife.

"Will you to get married someday again," she asked, confusing use of the infinitive, which was quite common among Vietnamese English speakers.

"I really don't know," was his regretful reply.

"Are you sad?" she asked

"No, my dear, I am not sad. I have made mistakes in life. I am not sad now because you are taking care of me," he said with a melancholic truthfulness, which made her feel embarrassed.

"You make me shy, Mr. Hugh. Maybe you will stay in Việt Nam and find a wife here. Vietnamese wives are very good," she offered while glancing at him sideways.

"Miss Hương, I assure you that it is quite possible I might. I wouldn't mind staying here, but I have to return to America when I am better," he said regretfully.

"Mr. Hugh, you do not have to return to America if you do not want to," she offered very innocently. It saddened Hugh to think that someday soon he would have to return stateside. Already, the mere thought of leaving Việt Nam again made him pine on the metal stretcher.

"Miss Hương, tell me about your family. What does your father do?" Hugh wanted to change to another subject, one that didn't chafe the wounds in his heart.

"My father is a tailor. He has his own machine to sew pants, shirts, jeans and khaki. One sister works for the post office in Tây Ninh, and the other sister stays home with my mother, *bởi vì bé không có con mắt* – she doesn't have eyes when she was born. Doctors say it is because '*chát độc màu da cam*.' I don't know how to say it in English. I am sorry my English is not good, Mr. Hugh," she offered apologetically from behind the mask.

"Don't be worried about your English, my dear. It is quite good. '*Chát độc màu da cam*' is called 'Agent Orange' in English. It was a very nasty chemical that the American government knew was very toxic and hazardous before they started to spray it here. It was made by several American chemical companies. Dow and Monsanto are the two largest that come to mind, but I also remember Hercules and Thompson Hayward Chemical. They didn't care about causing harm to people, Vietnamese *or* American. What's more sad is the American government stood behind the chemical companies like cowards when Vietnamese people sued the companies claiming it was chemical warfare. I believe it is still somewhere in the United States court system. I am sorry, Miss Hương, for your sister's suffering and everyone else's. It seemed that America knew it couldn't win the war so it did everything to destroy your country – undiluted Agents Orange and Blue used at full strength; bombing raids on Hà Nội and civilian cities in the north and the illegal bombings in Cambodia and Laos." Hugh sagged in the gurney under the weight of the regrets that his own country's political and military leadership and her agents failed to act with any moral or ethical reserve in war and then hid behind the cowardice of its military strength. He also realized that he was starting to negatively pontificate and didn't want her to become infected with his jaundiced attitude. It was something he was acutely aware of but lacked the governor to retard his opinion.

"It is no bother, Mr. Hugh. *Không sao đâu.* Life does continue. Life in Việt Nam does get better. You must forget the war," she instructed.

Hugh thought about her remark "*Không sao đâu*" – translated to "it doesn't matter," but it was also a play on words meaning, "no star where." He looked back out the window and now couldn't see the stars for the clouds and because of the lights of Hồ Chí Minh City, which they were now approaching and the abundance of neon and fluorescent lights brutalized the evening sky.

From where he was laying down, Hugh looked outside the dirt-stained window to get his bearings. They had driven down QL 22 to Highway 1 and had now turned onto Công Hoà Boulevard, the former Republic Street of the American Tan Son Nhut Airbase. Past the huge Maxi-Mark shopping center was the large traffic circle that was once home to the large military base's main gate. After passing Công Viện Hoàng Văn Thụ, the large triangular park, the make-shift ambulance passed the old 3rd Field Hospital, now a museum, and turned down Nguyễn Văn Trỗi Street heading through town to the hospital on the south side of the city. The driver kept his siren on as traffic was very congested even at night; the streets clogged with workers going home and young couples riding their motorbikes in the cool evening air. Many young lovers were headed towards public parks to sit and talk about romance and their burgeoning love and future plans. Some young couples slipped away to places where they could be alone for a night away from watchful parental eyes or sibling intrusion; girls armed with an innocent precociousness, charm and shyness, and boys protected with condoms. Hugh couldn't be envious of their youth as he tried to focus on other things besides love, and the pain at his surgical site. Finally after negotiating the congested and clogged streets of the city, the rickety van finally pulled into the Franco-Vietnamese Hospital's emergency room receiving bay, the van's collection of metal and joints creaking at the prospect of a much deserved rest. The driver exited the vehicle and immediately stretched his creaking joints and lit another cigarette.

"Mr. Hugh, I wish we could have met before. You are very handsome and very nice. Chúc ông sức khoẻ, may mắn và hành phúc," she said wishing him health, luck and happiness.

"Miss Hương, if only I were very much younger." Hugh said regretfully and returned her good wishes and bade her good bye as he was taken into an examination room for pre-admission processing. He regretted not being able to see her back to Tây Ninh and he regretted not seeing her face that was hidden behind the mask. He didn't feel sorry for her having to make the trek back home, at a slower pace. She wouldn't worry with the wheezing driver, who now was smoking a second cigarette near the front of the ambulance because it was simply part of her job – a job she was thoroughly content with. He was wheeled into the new hospital thinking and remembering the impact of her penetrating dark eyes.

IV

The non-descript, olive-green Ford sedan pulled up to the sandbags and barricade in front of the Rex Hotel promptly at nine o'clock as Morgan had assured Lieutenant Campbell it would. However, Hugh was not at the door and the driver had to wait another ten ..tes before his charge came downstairs. After getting into the military sedan, the driver pulled out into traffic, turned the corner and turned again onto Pasteur Street, named for Louis Pasteur who established medical research institutes in Việt Nam. As they approached Hiền Vương Street, the driver, a young staff sergeant who showed apprehension about his passenger, attempted to engage the officer in conversation. However, the lieutenant was in no mood for conversation and simply told the driver, "Save it. I don't feel like talking." They turned onto Công Lý Street, which became Cách Mạng Boulevard on the other side of the small black canal of smelly sludge that bisects part of the city. Arriving at MACV-SOG, the driver proceeded through the gates and deposited his charge at the entrance to the building. Hugh knew better and instead walked around to the rear and to another adjacent building where Morgan had his office, separate from inquisitive eyes.

The door was open. Morgan was waiting without showing his irritation at the lieutenant who, he believed, purposely arrived late for the appointment. Morgan didn't wait for convivial engagement, but went straight to the heart of the matter.

"Sit down, Lieutenant. I want to discuss certain things with you about the recent operation…"

Hugh interrupted him, "Sir, I have no knowledge of any recent operation. I cannot confirm or deny any operation existed and if one did, I would not be at liberty to discuss it."

"Goddamn it, Lieutenant, you were taking orders from me, so cut the crap!" Morgan's temper slipped through. "This room is secure and I need to know about certain things because I now know that there had been a compromise of your operation before you arrived at Thiện Ngôn. Don't fuck with me, Lieutenant. I want you to tell me exactly what happened to that goddamn pouch you and Lieutenant Emerson were supposed to destroy," Morgan emphasized, his face turning red, not from the heat of the morning, but from the heat of his own rising temper.

"Sir, I have told you everything already. I don't believe this is necessary. Think what you want, but when we came out of COSVN, we made our radio contact, as directed by you. We reported the termination of the mission, as directed by you. We advised the state of the pouch, as directed by you. Lieutenant Emerson and I felt it was prudent to destroy the pouch where it would be more secure rather than in the forest where our position could be compromised and the pouch possibly repatriated to the enemy, sir. It was moments later that an "Arc Light" targeted our area, quite possibly," and Hugh then pointed an accusatory finger at Morgan, "directed by you."

"Sir, some of my equipment and the pouch were destroyed, I should say 'vaporized', in the bombing. I could not reclaim any of my equipment. A thorough search of the area for the pouch, Lieutenant Emerson, and my equipment, in that order, was made and I only found a few fragments of green canvas, quite possibly from my equipment bag. I ran for my life and dropped my bag when I tripped. The pouch was in the bag. That area is a fucking bomb crater now, sir, and if you want to go look for it, I will show you the area the B-52s were not to bomb, but did, while Lieutenant Emerson and I were in the area, as directed by you. I think your fucking, happy, horse-shit game fucked with our lives and I do not like my life being fucked with," he exclaimed. "With all due respect, sir," Hugh quickly added.

Morgan looked long and hard at the lieutenant. His deep, blue eyes had nearly turned black with his rage. He remained silent looking at Hugh, waiting for Hugh to speak next. Hugh, on the other hand, knew that an interrogation technique called for the interrogator to remain silent, causing an uncomfortable quiet that a suspect would feel the need to break by further conversation and admissions. Hugh felt he had already said what he wanted to say and stared at Morgan. Morgan, after a very long five minutes of silence broke the stillness.

"Lieutenant, I have information that you were contacted by a Việt Cộng agent enroute to Thiện Ngôn. Would you like to comment?" he asked.

Hugh did not show emotion. Hugh did not know what he was talking about. This was something that had blocked itself from his memory. That branch of memories extending out from a crystallized, arborescent knot in his brain had been vibrated loose during the bombing leaving mere molecular fragments barely touching with small gaps only providing the pieces of anguishing images. He really didn't know or remember.

"I don't know what you're talking about, sir," he honestly replied.

"Again, Lieutenant, I am telling *you* not to fuck with me. Lieutenant Emerson said you were contacted, as he reported, by a friendly contact enroute to Thiện Ngôn. We believe that person was VC, and quite possibly the girl who worked for the colonel at Tây Ninh West. What do you have to say?" he demanded.

With a look of sincerity and his voice to match, Hugh simply said, "We had no contact with any VC. There may have been a contact we were already told about, but I don't recall any specific contact, sir, and if there was a contact, I would have already reported it. As it was, Lieutenant Emerson and I successfully performed our operation, one which I now wish to forget and get on with my military duties, sir. I do not believe my sitting here will add any additional useful information that has not been covered already."

Morgan sat considering his options. Morgan thought that either Lieutenant Campbell is very skilled in interrogation techniques or he is simply telling the truth. Then, Morgan wondered, why would Lieutenant Emerson report things that Campbell didn't know anything about? Morgan didn't know who to believe and now to be on the safe side he believed neither. That's what kept him alive for so long in this special field. However, one thing that had been disturbing Morgan was the "Arc Light" that was not to have occurred when the men were in their area of operations. There was a complete blackout for the entire area over and around COSVN. Then how did the bombing get ordered? That fact did keep him awake and he was not able to access the information. Usually, Morgan had no problems with access to higher military officers who had the 'need to know' and would share some information. This was something his contacts in the upper echelons could not answer. It was directed from elsewhere. Morgan thought it had the smell of the special assistant for counterinsurgency and special activities in Washington.

"Lieutenant, you're excused," he offered calmly. "I'm sure you and Lieutenant Emerson will be receiving orders shortly as there is always a need for your skills. Dismissed," the CIA operative concluded.

"Thank you, sir," and Hugh walked out of the office and went to find the driver to take him back downtown to the Rex.

Morgan sat and stared at his brown, coffee-stained cup emblazoned with the MACV insignia on the side. Somehow in the last couple days he had lost his new cup with the American flag on it. He opened a folder and jotted notes. His notes mentioned the Colonel's housekeeper by name and her suspected role with the Việt Cộng Tây Ninh Armed Forces as part of the 9th VC Division and included a complete list of sources and his synopsis on Lieutenants Campbell and Emerson. He omitted information about the pouch, but included information about terminating the mission of the North Vietnamese Army Captain Nguyễn Văn Hiền, the southern agent, and Paul, his contact in America; a young, arrogant and snotty voice at the end of his telephone.

Morgan felt exasperated. He was closing this specific office at MACV-SOG that had been on loan to him and was returning what he had to the CIA Station Chief at the US Embassy. Morgan was happy to be finally retiring and living anywhere he wanted. He felt he had enough of this crap and now wanted to simply head into the mountains of his native South Carolina and lose himself in fishing and hunting while he pondered what he'd do with the rest of his life, but not until he transferred the files downtown.

He picked up the phone and pressed a button to the right of the rotary dial. He waited the two or three minutes as secure connections were established along circuits extending across the Pacific Ocean to, what he believed, was some office in the eastern United States. He looked at the clock and calculated it was already ten forty-five in the evening, the night before. He had no compunction about disturbing anyone. His life had been about disturbing others and he had become quite fond of being an annoyance to others when it amused him. He would have preferred to have had the time be much later to disturb the other party even more, but he timed things for his convenience as a priority. The line was answered.

"Paul," announced the familiar young voice.

"Paul, this is Morgan. I met with the questionable officer again, just moments ago. By the way, what time is it there?" Morgan enjoyed the ability to irritate a wound.

"It's already ten thirty-eight p.m." This confirmed Morgan's suspicions the contact was on the East Coast of the United States. He continued, "And it's been a long day. What d'ya have?" the Chairman's aid drawled.

"I spoke to him at length. I've had him followed and we've searched his room. We've found nothing. There are possibilities that he's hidden the documents in Tây Ninh

Province somewhere, but then again, his story has been consistent and he's been truthful, as far as I can tell," Morgan confided.

"But you said that there are possibilities, so you are not quite absolutely sure, are you?"

"Listen, kid, I don't know who you are, but in this business there are no absolutes. The only absolute is that if you fuck up, you're dead; beyond that, no. You can waste the resources if you want. You can have him followed here, you can toss his stuff when he returns to the States and, in fact, you can have him transferred to the States. That way if he does have it with him, he'll take it with him rather than leaving it here for someone else to find," Morgan paused. He himself did not know what was in the pouch apart from what he was also told.

"He's waiting for orders now for his next operation. You can make special arrangements and it would be easy for some special trained soldier to follow him in uniform. He wouldn't be noticed," Morgan said.

Paul thought for a few moments. He'd already stuck his neck out with the B-52 bombing, so why not continue to make this officer's life miserable and force his hand. He said quietly, "Thank you. I believe your services will no longer be needed. We, er, I thank you for your help. Your assessment will be taken into consideration. Again, thank you for the work at your end." Paul disconnected.

Morgan replaced the telephone in the cradle. "Prick," was his only comment spoken to the lifeless phone. He continued writing some notes down, including the name at the other end of the line. He should have known you don't ever use your first and last name. He let it slip in a previous conversation and Morgan thought it best to include the full name in his notes. Morgan finished the report, marked it confidential and put *"DESSERT"* in small lettering on the file, remembering the desserts the Colonel's housekeeper fed them. They were a sweet ending for the wonderful meals she prepared. Marking the file that way wouldn't arouse anyone's interests. He looked at the file one more time before tossing it into a box to be taken to the embassy and said once again, looking at the phone, "Prick." He waited for the technician to arrive and disconnect the line forever.

Gosh, it's still dark. When will they free me and let me out. I want to feel the warmth on my body, to feel those other sensations that only come to me once in awhile. Okay, they're talking now, let me listen. Yes, they're talking about the meal, I think….the dishes…the glasses…and me, but I can't hear it all. Okay, alright now, I'm starting to feel that image returning to me and it's always dark when it comes to me here in the night. I know the night and it is much warmer for me and friendlier that the daytime. I don't like the daytime. It's too hot, too crowded with things, too many people walking around and I don't like getting bumped into. I like it right here, right where I belong. I will always belong to the night, no matter what anyone says or anyone does. The night owns me. The nights in Tây Ninh own me, too.

V

Inspector Quỳ needed to take a day off from his investigation into the death of the American Whitman Emerson in Tây Ninh and had to begin another inquiry in the nearby Thủ Đức District. He had obtained from Hugh most of the information he needed in or͟ ͟make a preliminary report to keep his supervisors temporarily contented, though there were still gaps needing to be filled. 'They can wait,' he thought. 'Besides, we have an old bureaucratic system bequeathed to us from the French, so waiting will be acceptable.' Quỳ suspected why the two foreigners were at the temple late at night because he remembered little bits of information from the file. Hugh had told him that he could not sleep and had gone for a long walk. He only supposed that Whitman Emerson had trailed behind in case his friend needed any help. Quỳ thought that the two of them would have walked together, but they didn't. The men had been fighting with each other. Why? What about the gun and the knife wound? The knife was found underneath the dead man's body, but the gun remained a mystery. Certainly, they would not have brought a gun with them to Việt Nam as it would be discovered by the very thorough Customs Police officials at the airport who scan all baggage coming into the country. The gun must have come from somewhere else, Quỳ concluded, but where?

The telephone call he received from Hà Nội was unexpected. His supervisors had started to become insistent that he conclude the report and ascertain what the foreigners were doing out late at night and was there something they were looking for? Quỳ wondered why Hà Nội would ask that question. He knew they were looking for something, something that possibly Mr. Hugh had hid so many years before. How would Hà Nội know something that Qu☐ thought only his cousin, Mai, and Hugh would know about? Now it began to get complicated for the Inspector who only wanted to satisfy his and his cousin's childhood curiosity, but now the capital city people were becoming inquisitive. Perhaps the hidden information had something to do with them, as well? Quỳ didn't like mysteries that involved too many people. It added to the complexity of an investigation, yet it made it more challenging. Well, he thought, he would have a day off to do something else and not worry about this case. Quỳ placed a call to Hugh telling him he was needed out of town for a day and not to worry about any questioning.

Hugh was relieved to hear he wouldn't have to talk about the past or recent incidents in Tây Ninh. Hugh had, by now, befriended some of the police that were "guarding" him at the residence. He came to know several by name and some were happy to practice their English with him when he passed through the gate. Việt Nam worked towards equal opportunity for women and Hugh came to like one of the front gate guards, whose name is Thảo, meaning an "herb plant." She looked a bit depressed that morning and told Hugh about her grandmother passing away during the night. She had to do half her shift and asked if Hugh would be interested in accompanying her to the funeral. She felt there were no improprieties in asking Hugh since she was

not involved in the case, and besides, the Inspector had set a
tone of friendliness with the foreigner that everybody came
to appreciate. Hugh didn't have to think twice and quickly
accepted the invitation.

The hot dust in the outlying, rural District Twelve north
of Hồ Chí Minh City parched Hugh's throat as he sat on
a small, red plastic stool. An older lady, bent with age and
missing most of her teeth, beckoned to him to move his small
chair to the protection of the shade provided by a blue tarp
that stretched across the small front yard of the old house
where the grandmother had died. Temporary round tables
on rusted metal frames were set up for visitors and family.
Husband, sons, daughters and grandchildren wore white
headbands and white mourning clothes, some of gauze,
some made from paper. The large, heavy, wooden casket,
painted a glossy brown and fringed with gold paint and
red dragons, sat atop bright red saw horses. Adjacent to the
funeral bier, the grandmother's son sat cross-legged to the
left and nearly underneath the gilt-trimmed coffin, and he
burned the papers to mark the memories of Nguyễn Thị Gái,
grandmother of Hugh's host and guard. He also burned the
worthless paper money she could use in the afterlife. She
died at the age of sixty-three barely twelve hours before.
Her casket was decorated with the marks and symbols of
her Buddhist upbringing. A gaily painted, ceramic Buddha
sat in contemplation off to the side, and a bowl filled with
many years' worth of incense ashes, and dishes filled with
fruit and glasses of drink offerings surrounded the Buddha
in his solitude. In front of her casket was another table with

a photograph, freezing her younger years on paper mounted behind glass. She is at rest as is the rest of the family. They sat around lazily and occasionally paying obeisance and greeting friends and neighbors as they arrived to pay their respect, drink some tea, leave behind a donation to help with the cost of dying and leave the family to their grief.

Three musicians sat on a nearby raised pallet that was once used for her bed and had since been pulled out into the yard to make room for the coffin and visitors. One musician, a darker-skinned Khmer, played mournful tunes on electric piano with an accompanying electronic rhythm. The second musician, the guitar player, sat idly nearby in the shade of a flowering vine that stretched overhead bearing *giàn mướp*, a long loufa-type vegetable that hung downwards from the trellis. He also sat cross-legged playing a slide guitar and accompanied the piano player. The both of them were synchronized note for note. Flies gathered around the musicians, friends and family gathered around glasses of tea and swatted flies away. The flies, taking their cues from the family who gathered around the casket, gathered around Hugh's glass of Mirinda root beer, sat on the rim and rubbed their front legs together as though they also prayed for the deceased. As each guest arrived, the musicians gently put down their instruments and the Khmer musician would pick up a horn and spit into the tarnished mouthpiece to test his lips against the instrument. The third musician was barefoot and his t-shirt and striped pants were faded. He had been sitting for the past half hour idly swatting at flies. He now stood, collected his drum sticks and began noisily drumming a rhythm along with the Khmer's horn. Mourners walked slowly to the oil lamp to light long red-stemmed joss sticks and bowed before the Buddha's picture, adding more smoke to the room and more ash to the bowl; burned and exhausted stems, rising up like tree trunks after a forest fire, remained after the scented powder had long consumed itself. Mourners then turned and faced the coffin where Mrs. Gái was peacefully resting inside; a few coins and some grains of rice inside her mouth to help her on the journey to the Western Heavens. They bowed respecually with burning joss sticks in hand as they raised their joined palms to their foreheads three times and then placed the sticks in the other bowl on the table at the foot of the coffin. The table was home for the offerings to Mrs. Gái's spirit with old chipped bowls, plates and glasses, brought from the kitchen and filled with fruit, vegetables, meat and whiskey; more nourishment for the journey to Western Realms. Just as quick as the *agitato* horn and drum tune began, it ended just as quickly as the mourners left the front room of the home; a room which had been converted to a temporary shrine, mortuary and visitation room. Everyone then awaited the monk to preside over the prayers and chants.

Hugh sat among the old women who had been friends, confidants and neighbors of Mrs. Gái. Just as quickly as they spoke quietly out of respect for their deceased friend, the next moment they shrieked at a child in the street who was misbehaving for the moment and showing disrespect of the dead. Admonishments subsided and the quiet returned; two musicians returned to the slide guitar and the electric piano again. A bare footed and shabbily clothed young boy of about ten picked up a small stick and kept up the beat on an old, chipped ceramic rice bowl and looked around in boredom more than curiosity. More than likely, the indolent boy has attended many funerals for his young age and death was just as much a companion for him as childhood friends were. Thảo, Hugh's friend-cum-guard, came over to Hugh and offered him another root beer and replenished the melting ice in the glass. Hugh couldn't help but notice the graceful movements of her body when she was not in uniform and her hands betrayed the informality of her upbringing and the traditional mannerisms typical of a young Vietnamese woman. The twist of her hand from downward to upward reflected the quiet offer of another drink and the reflection of the blue tarp on the lightly colored palm of her hand looked a light pale green, blending with the soft yellow of her skin. Thin fingers gracefully pointed to the scratched glass as an offer for more. Hugh nodded his head in a "yes" gesture, keeping quiet out of respect for the family and for Gái who was sleeping peacefully. Quietly, Hugh sat and listened to the old women in conversation, each singing to one another in their melodic language. Hugh closed his eyes and imagined them like small, brown chickadees in a tree telling each other the news of the day. His drink and ice were replenished.

A slightly overweight monk eventually arrived on his Chinese-manufactured motorbike. Pausing outside, he nodded a hello to the men who followed Hugh; he then lit a cigarette, for even the dead are no longer waiting. Hugh thought the smoking was out of place for one who should be a model of giving up attachments. The monk's bright saffron bag, in stark contrast to his dirt-brown robes, was slung over the right shoulder as he arrived and he placed it on the wooden bed, next to the guitar player and withdrew the more formal saffron overrobe for the ceremony. Giving his cigarette to the guitar player to finish, he slipped his arms into the sleeves of the robe, tied it on the right side, kicked the red dust-covered sandals off his calloused feet and entered the front room of the home.

Consoling words were said to the grieving husband, and more words to the son who continued to sit cross-legged to the left of the elevated casket. People began to gather and sat on several of the short blue or red plastic stools that have been the main preference for sitting in countryside and town, alike, for many years. Incense mingled like invited guests, wafting across shoulders and around arms, and gathered mourners closer together. The family assembled cross-legged on the floor in front of the casket, wearing white, sheer linen or paper gowns now red from the dirt in the yard and road. Mrs. Gái's grandchildren wore white headbands with a blue dot signifying a female relative of the deceased or a red dot for the males – a symbol of family status among those still living.

The monk slowly picked up a microphone, someone switched on a cassette tape recorder with music and the ceremony began. The Khmer tuned his traditional violin and the slide guitar player replaced his instrument with a *đàn nguyệt*, the Vietnamese moon-shaped lute-like instrument. Both were in perfect tune with the other and the musicians struck the exact same notes together with the recorded music. They have done this before, countless times. The goateed monk, a smattering of chin hairs dangling, begun his chant; music, monk and musicians became one. Everyone in the home was barefoot, even the flies on the foreheads, arms and feet. The guests in the yard provided additional resting spaces for the flies, fatigued from the heat and non-stop buzzing and flying around the salty-sweaty mourners and the sweetened soft drinks.

Hugh sat with the old women as the chanting went on, the monk lit a few joss sticks, poured whiskey into a glass, and took up a portion of meat with chopsticks and put it into a bowl and handed it yet to another son, all the while, continuing the chant and balancing the microphone. He glanced at Hugh for a moment, the only foreigner for kilometers around; the only white face in the group. Hugh sat respectfully quiet. The old women at the table were also quiet. For a moment, Hugh felt that he had become part of the scene with everyone else, and remembered that in a few more months it would be Tết, the Lunar New Year. He recalled that the grieving period must be over so no one is sad when the New Year arrives, otherwise the home will have bad luck for the New Year. No one cried for Mrs. Gái now. It wasn't time. It was almost as though this was business as usual, and for Vietnamese it was, having spent the last thousand years fighting, suffering and dying for their country. The Vietnamese knew death and have had a very close relationship with it. To them, death has become very much a part of life like birth. The body may finally exhaust itself of the life energy force, but the spirit will continue, living in the house and needing to be occasionally fed. Only the body becomes lifeless. The Spirit doesn't.

Finally, the chanting came to an end and Hugh rose for a moment and stretched his legs. The heat of the day infiltrated the house and the candles bowed over, like old men bent over from age. The subtropical heat even seemed to bend time, as Hugh lost all sense of it under the blue tarp. The monk straightened the candles, and they at once began to sag again; it was like raking leaves in the wind. With the ceremony finally concluded, the family dispersed to different areas of the home and some congregated in the small front yard. Neighbors who had watched from ᵗʰᵉ berry-vined fence, red with the years of dust from the road and sagging from the weight of the years, went home. They had to return to their own lives and their own worries.

Thảo again came to Hugh and sat next to him. He noticed that without her uniform, she was slender and barely weighed 90 pounds. Her dark almond eyes captivated Hugh as she took her seat and the old women paused from their conversation to watch his reaction. She asked if he was alright and Hugh responded that he was, 'thank you.' Her grandfather took the seat on the other side of him. He smiled at Hugh with a gold front tooth, punctuating his yellowing teeth and a drooping mustache that looked more like whale baleen. He whispered something to Thảo, which Hugh did not hear.

She said to Hugh, "Today, the first ceremony is over and we will have dinner now. My grandfather invites you to stay for dinner."

"Thank you, Miss Thảo, I would be happy to stay for dinner," he said.

They ate a dinner of white, steamed rice, vegetables, pork, and sodas washed the mixture down. Miss Thảo ensured her colleagues were also fed as they were invited inside the patio area of the house, but politely ate at a separate table from the family and Hugh. After dinner, the plates were cleared by the women of the family who immediately set about the task of cleaning up and readying everything for the night's vigil and the next day's funeral service at the house and cemetery.

"It is getting late and you must go back to the city. I will take you by motorbike," she whispered in a voice very soft and very clear.

"Thank you," replied Hugh, anxious to sit behind this young beautiful woman on her motorbike for the nearly one hour ride back to Hồ Chí Minh City.

"Grandfather invites you to return tomorrow at three o'clock in the afternoon. It is for the burial and he would feel honored if you attend," she requested.

Hugh could not refuse the sincere offer of acceptance and inclusion. "Yes, I shall come back," and Hugh told the grandfather, in his native tongue. "Thank you for the honor of inviting me. The grandfather was pleased and extended to Hugh his withered hand in gratitude for attending his wife's funeral service.

She wheeled her Honda motorbike from the front yard across the street where it had been parked to make room for the tables for the funeral service, started the engine and motioned to Hugh to sit behind her. She offered him a spare mask to keep out the pollution from the road, which he politely refused. She looked at him with a glance that was as warm as the day. They glided through the cooler air of the countryside, trailed at a discrete distance by the followers. They traveled at length on dusty roads, but muddy in some areas where people watered the road to keep the dirt settled and from entering their homes and shops. After some distance of about two kilometers, they eventually reached the paved road that marked the leading edge of the urban area. To feel more secure in riding on the back of her motorbike, Hugh boldly, but naturally, slipped his hands into the front pockets of her trousers and felt her hip bones underneath the thin material. He asked if it was alright to hold on to her as they rode ride back to the police house in the city. She simply said "Sure." He sensed the smile underneath the mask; a mask she wore to keep out dust and exhaust, yet betrayed the expression of her eyes. They whisked through narrow streets, passed open-air markets with several fluorescent-lit stalls offering for sale various decorations for the approaching Christmas-*Giáng Sinh* season; plums, watermelons with golden, triangular, good luck seals, gigantic grapefruit-like pomellos, bright red dragon fruit, and many other exotic, tropical fruits indigenous to Việt Nam. They motored past shoppers buying beef, chicken and pork for the night's meal and the shoppers took no notice of the young woman with the foreigner on the back. Her long, black, soft hair lightly whipped Hugh's face as they slipped through traffic. He wasn't bothered in the least bit by the lashing and felt that sitting behind her had started to excite him. Hugh earnestly believed he needed the flagellation to remind him of the sins committed in this country so many years ago and the sins of his own mind in the present. He sat holding her and looked around the front to see her face and rested his chin on her shoulder. She glanced back at him and smiled with her eyes. They seemed to ride as one. She purposely took the long way back to the house, to the dismay of the followers who merely wanted to go home and relax after a day of sitting. After arriving at the house, Hugh wished he could have invited her in to remove the chill of the loneliness of the house, but knew it could not be allowed. Hugh had not only surprised himself at his actions, but he realized he suddenly ached for the love of a Vietnamese woman; a familiar, yet a somewhat foreign feeling for him.

The following morning, he placed a call to Inspector Quỳ and asked him to delay any more questioning until the next day. The policeman was eager to grant Hugh's request as he still needed to write his final report from the other case in Thủ Đức.

The following afternoon, Hugh had Thiên, the motorbike driver, take him back to Thảo's grandfather's house. Thiên was quick and cut the ride by fifteen minutes and arrived in only forty-five minutes, rather than the hour that it took Thảo. The only time he slowed was when they passed through the crowded *Chợ Xóm Mới* market, north of the city. When they arrived at the grandfather's house, Hugh quickly dismounted, as he had already paid Thiên the agreed-upon fare before leaving the police house to forestall the necessity of taking his wallet out in front of the grieving family and mourners. Thảo also arrived at the same time. A large, white, windowed van was parked nearby. Sixteen men in white uniforms with gold trim and matching military style service hats, some carrying trumpets under their arms and others carrying trombones or drums, stood idly about near the bent fence, and each smoked cigarettes of varying lengths. They paused from conversation and everyone's eyes tracked the foreigner who came among them to grieve. Hugh arrived at 3:00 PM, but the ceremony had already begun moments before. Once again, the family sat cross-legged on the floor in front of the raised casket. Mrs. Gài's son still sat in his place under the brown-hued coffin and continued to burn fake paper money for her journey. Hugh believed he hadn't moved since he saw him the day before. The only evidence of his moving had been the white gauze mourning clothes appearing more soiled than the day before. Hugh watched as Thảo walked to the back of the family grouped in front of the casket, her white head band back in place. She sat down at the edge of the step that marked the entry into the home and her small, slender, delicate feet drooped naturally over that first step. Hugh once again took his seat near the same old women when they beckoned to him. He had been standing in the hot sun again and wasn't aware of it. They must think all foreigners like the sun since their skin seemed darker than theirs. Hugh remembered his life in the States near the thirty-fifth parallel. This part of Việt Nam was slightly above the 10th parallel, much closer to the equator and, it seemed, much closer to the sun. He again took his seat on a plastic stool at the round table under the blue canvas cover and the *giàn mướp* trellised-vine that trapped some of the humidity inside for it to thrive upon. Thảo turned to Hugh and smiled. A moment later, she softly and slowly waved a delicate hand in his direction. Hugh nodded with a smile and the old women clacked and whispered to each other in their musical language that Hugh couldn't hear.

After the ceremony at home where the deceased is allowed to finally "say goodbye," the casket was carried by eight of the white-uniformed men and placed in the white van; hefty, wooden poles supported the casket on the men's shoulders.

Mrs. Gài began the last crossing to where her earthly remains would lie in wait for an eternity. Only the dead have great skills at waiting for an eternity. Hugh suddenly discovered he couldn't wait to finish providing what he could tell Inspector Quỳ and had pangs of emotion about what he should tell him. At the cemetery, he watched the coffin slowly lowered by ropes into the open scar of the ground by the pallbearers. He considered telling Quỳ the contents of the documents, but he couldn't quite yet. He didn't know if he should and how Hà Nội would take the information knowing that extremely sensitive information was conveyed to others. He wondered who would still be alive to remember and now, thirty-nine years later, what retribution would there be for those who had divulged their contents abroad. Hugh thought these concerns were beyond him. He could tell Quỳ there were documents hidden, but he had forgotten the essence of the contents over the past four decades. That was understandable, as the Inspector knew that segments of his memory had somehow been erased or were painted over by time. He wanted to put Quỳ off for one more day, if possible, and talk to Mai in that time. She had the file and quite possibly it was already at the coffee shop that she and her husband owned. Perhaps Quỳ could give him one more day conditioned on full disclosure when they met again.

PART V

I

In the early morning following the burial, just before the lethargic air could arouse itself to heat the day, Hugh found Thiên sitting sidesaddle on the seat of his Honda peering intently into the motorbike's mirror tweezing out what few hairs protruded from his chin. Hugh called to him and saw, not too far away, his followers sitting on their motorbikes, their attention now on Hugh. He didn't have to call Quỳ to tell him where he was going. His followers would do that for him. He told Thiên he wanted to return to the coffee shop on Hồ Văn Huê Street in Phú Nhuận District. That's all he had to say and they were rumbling down the street heading north towards their destination. It was already rush hour in Hồ Chí Minh City and they fought their way through the tangles that clotted the crossroads. Hugh didn't bother to count the vehicles on the road. He could only estimate by the clogged streets and boulevards, motorbikes mirror to mirror like little sausages in a tin, that he was only one of hundreds of thousands of people motoring to work, or some other place, that morning. The traffic jams were heavy at this time of day, and also beginning at five o'clock in the evening, and it took nearly thirty minutes to make their way to the coffee shop.

The girls in their tight tank tops and skirts immediately recognized the foreigner from his last visit several days before. Two of them rose from their chairs and took him by each arm and led him to the bar at the back where Daniel sat idly watching yet another kick-boxing match broadcast from Thailand; seemingly young boys with armbands on their biceps punched and kicked each other to an aroused, cheering crowd in Bangkok and in the coffee shop. Hugh had no interest and instead looked at one of the girls and ordered an iced milk coffee. He turned to Daniel and made some small talk while he waited for his drink. He didn't care to reveal too much about his activities over the past several days, but eventually asked if Mai was in. Daniel said she was and went to get her.

Mai was dressed in a grey tank top with the word "FCUK" emblazoned in chartreuse and underscored in magenta on the front, and low, hip-hugging black jeans that accentuated her sensual figure and slim legs. Hugh, unaware of the fashion design world, thought was an apparent misspelling of an English epithet.

"Mr. Hugh, I wondered when I would see you again. You have been well, I hope?" she asked.

"Mai, I've had some interesting days. You may or may not know that I've been cooperating with your cousin and I'm now wondering when I could look at the file you mentioned."

"Mr. Hugh, it is here. Last night, my cousin came to visit and we looked at the file again. It was like we were little children sneaking our looks at it for the first time. We had the most fun again and giggled. I would like to say we are getting excited at maybe knowing answers to some of the mysteries, but my cousin must remain professional. He and I would like to know things," she said.

"Mai, I, too, would like to know things. When may I see the file?" he asked.

"Follow me. Honey ơi," she said calling her husband, "have Mr. Hugh's coffee brought upstairs."

She pulled a concealed box from under the metal-framed bed and drew the file from it. She closed the curtains, switched on some lights and a fan and handed the file folder to Hugh. Hugh felt his breathing and his pulse quicken as she placed the folder in his hands. It was marked, oddly enough in someone's handprinting, "*DESSERT.*" Hugh couldn't imagine why, unless it was to camouflage the contents by naming it something very innocuous; a sweet treat after dinner. Hugh thought that would guarantee no one would have an interest once it was filed.

There was a faint knock on the door of the upstairs residence and Hugh saw it was one of the girls, Châu, delivering his iced milk coffee. Once she left, he picked up the file again. His hands trembled slightly and he felt light-headed at holding the heavy past in his lap. He feared opening the file, afraid of the demons that lurked inside, but knew he had to muster the courage to face what Quỳ and Mai already knew. Only he could sew the story together with the tattered and split threads of thought in his mind. He opened the file and began to read.

After he read the file completely, Hugh felt his emotions range from awareness to disgust. Each revealing note and observation after another flooded into his mind, re-igniting synaptic connections and reawakening distant memories. Names he saw jumped out from the page, some names he couldn't remember, some of them Vietnamese names, and one in particular that excited him but he didn't know why. He wondered why only a name would arouse his deepest interest. But there was one name mentioned several times in the file that was unmistakable – one name that shouldn't have been there, but it was there as Hugh read the file a second, third and a fourth time to confirm his immediate misgivings. The readings combined to help his recall of the actions that took place and confirmed his suspicions of long ago.

Hugh asked Mai, "There's one name in particular that somehow interests me; a Vietnamese name. Do you know anything about this person? It is possible to meet this one person? There are some things missing in my mind and I think this person may help."

Mai replied, "Mr. Hugh, I and my cousin are here to help solve the mystery and you have become a person we can trust. You should know this file no longer belongs to us, but we have agreed you should possess the file as it is *your* history." Mai emphasized the word, 'your' for Hugh. "This person you ask about we do know, yes. My cousin and I already believed you would find this name special and, yesterday, we made a contact for you. We are sorry for doing things without your approval, but you are to meet someone tonight, if you want. My cousin told me you are vegetarian and we have arranged a meeting at a restaurant you may find suitable. The food is good, inexpensive and there you may have privacy. Is this suitable for you, Mr. Hugh?" she asked quite respectfully, knowing the work it took to arrange the meeting, but more so, she was very concerned about his welfare, though she found it difficult to express in English.

"Miss Mai, there is a lot for me to take in right now, you understand. Everything that is in this file is directly related to a certain event in Tây Ninh Province in 1966. It is something that I directly participated in, and oddly, was never to have been known by anyone afterwards. The fact that your mother worked for the CIA at the time and managed to flee with certain files is amazing. I am simply amazed that this file is related exactly to the Tây Ninh operation. That I will admit. It must be my memory, but some names are not familiar, but you say you have someone for me to meet. Can you tell me who it is?" Hugh wondered.

'Mr. Hugh, some mysteries are better understood when revealed by those involved. You are to meet a young girl at the vegetarian restaurant at number 40 Cách Mạng Tháng Tám. She will meet you at five o'clock tonight. She will be wearing a yellow hat. You do not need to worry about your followers. I have been assured they will be instructed to watch you from afar and not from inside the restaurant. Is that suitable for you?" Mai was hoping that her extra care in arranging the meeting would meet with Hugh's approval.

"Certainly. *Cảm ơn, em,*" he said, thanking her.

"*Không có gì.*"

II

Hugh sat inside the nearly hard-to-find, hole-in-the-wall, vegetarian restaurant on Cách Mạng Tháng Tám and waited for the girl in the yellow hat to arrive. The restaurant was wedged in between two other stores and a tree was offset in front of the building obscuring the door for entry. ˉ ⸗ ⸗· dropped him off a little before five o'clock as the afternoon sun was slowly slinking away from its day's work of bearing down on the city. He was greeted by a waiter and shown to a private table towards the back of the restaurant. He immediately requested the owner to direct the wall fan towards him so the circulating air could provide some comfort for his body. Buddhist chants from a Chinese CD player filled the room and circulated in his mind.

While Hugh waited, he idly watched the bustling traffic during rush hour through the narrow, front glass. The chants and his mindless gaze focused on traffic outside helped calm the nerves. Hugh found it oddly comforting to watch the harrowing hoards of motorbikes and their passengers whooshing by in either direction, just mere inches apart, on the four-lane street. Hugh knew not where they were all headed or their reasons; only that they passed each other non-stop like molecules in a stream of water. He recalled the phrase that one can never step into the same river twice for the same reason one could never step into the same street twice in Hồ Chí Minh City. He knew one can never step back into their past again. Drivers maneuvered their motorbikes, mostly powered by 110 or 125cc engines, and ceaselessly jockeyed for position in a race that had no beginning and would never end. An old man with long chin whiskers and reminiscent of Uncle Hồ slowly passed by the restaurant, his tattered t-shirt hanging from bony shoulders. He was completely oblivious to the whirling traffic just feet away from his tired legs that propelled him down the street.

Hugh patiently waited for the one person who could possibly help unlock the key to his dreams. He didn't know if she would meet with him or not, but he was assured by Mai that she would arrive. Hugh looked for the clock on a wall and found it hanging over the doorway to the kitchen. Ten after five. Hugh ordered an iced tea to temper the warmth of anticipation.

Hugh looked through the lens of the restaurant's front window to the scene directly across busy Cách Mạng Tháng Tám Street. He saw another person waiting at the Cathay Hotel. A bride was dressed in a western style, white wedding gown, but her groom was nowhere to be seen. She must be waiting for the bridegroom to arrive, he thought. Marriage parties usually arrive at the same time, but perhaps something else has happened. Hugh wondered if he was caught in the same traffic as the girl for whom he waited. Both he and the bride wedded to each other in their wait. Bride to the groom and Hugh to a dream. The old, streaked and faded snapshots in his mind are not as clear as the photographs being taken across the street. Future in-laws eagerly and nervously waited for the groom to arrive – father in his western-style black tuxedo, mother in her long, red mandarin-style tunic trimmed in gold, and grandmother in her elegant black velvet dress and white pearls.

The digital stream of Buddhist chanting kept Hugh calm. He was apprehensive and hoped she would soon arrive. He was told to look for a girl who will be wearing a yellow hat. Flashes of light from the camera at the Cathay Hotel froze moments in time. Flashes of yellow taxis froze in Hugh's mind for the moment. Hugh pondered; is she delayed by traffic, or delayed by the apprehension of meeting a foreigner with whom they share something extraordinary, or simply nothing at all? The heat wasn't too oppressive for Hugh, but he still appreciated the fan that forced cooling air across his back and neck. The fan mixed the air and kept things cool, but he begun to sweat, and the condensate from the iced tea glass formed a puddle with which Hugh could draw figures while he thought.

Hugh waited. The bride and family waited. The young ladies and the baby, who came into the restaurant shortly after Hugh, had already ordered their meal, eaten, paid, departed and the table was already cleaned, just as though they had never been there. They had no need to wait like the foreigner sitting in the back of the restaurant.

It was fifty minutes past the hour and Hugh was ready to surrender to the gods and leave empty of answers, empty of dinner, devoid of hope. Buses filled with workers slowly worked their way through the endless throng of motorbikes on their way home to the countryside. Buses filled with foreign tourists passed in the other direction returning to the city from the countryside. Hugh observed occupants from each look at one another through windows not understanding the world in which the other existed. Flashes from cameras momentarily brightened the faces of the workers, but not their lives or expressions. At the Cathay Hotel, flashes popped as guests still arrived for the wedding party. Will he arrive, they wondered? Will she arrive, he wondered? The nervous anticipating bride and Hugh have waited across the street from each other for over 50 minutes. Hugh benefited from an electric fan over the table to cool him. He saw the father of the bride had but a handkerchief to dry his perspiration. Everyone was waiting.

The Cathay Hotel was gaily decorated with fresh flowers, red and gold banners and a blossoming arch marking the wedding party entrance. A large banner above the arch depicted a brightly painted dragon facing an elaborate phoenix, separated by a flame-enshrouded egg. Traffic thickened and almost congealed to a gooey consistency outside the restaurant. A pregnant woman in a beige sun dress sat sidesaddle behind a man Hugh believed was her husband. They paused in the coagulation and she looked at Hugh with penetrating eyes and black hair trailing behind her. She pensively looked at the foreigner in the restaurant and he returned her gaze somehow understanding what her life was like; keeping house and home, bearing children, satisfying her husband. Camera lights illuminated behind her providing a glowing halo. *L'Indochine Madone*. She was posed just so on the back of the motorbike with her elegant posture that could have been sculpted by Rafael. She seemed a much better model for the Blessed Mother, Hugh thought. Camera lights continued to pan at the Cathay across street and illuminated traffic that begun to melt and ooze forward again in the new darkness of night. Hugh saw an enigmatic smile on the pregnant woman that Da Vinci could not replicate, or was it merely the vibration of the motorbike beginning to move again and a grimace possibly connected with the moving treasure carried within her womb? Hugh grimaced as more camera lights were lit and people became excited. The groom arrived. Hugh's girl in the yellow hat had also arrived.

Lieutenants Emerson and Campbell were becoming fatigued from their rest after the operation. They had been waiting at the Rex for two weeks for orders and each day, by five o'clock, none came. They knew the day duty clerks wouldn't do any work after three o'clock in the afternoon, as they would begin to wind down their day and talk about plans for the evening; which bars to visit, which to avoid, and which had the best protection from sappers who lobbed grenades and satchel charges through front doors. The clerks knew that at five in the waning heat of the afternoon they would be free for the night, freed from the toil of their own battles of office politics and battling time until their return to the states. Whitman had struck up a lukewarm friendship with a public information officer and would sometimes go out for a beer, dinner and a movie.

Hugh, ever cautious of being followed, walked off by himself some nights after five o'clock taking circuitous routes around downtown that would eventually return him to the labyrinthine alley behind Hai Bà Tr□ng Street. He took comfort in now being able to smoke five or six pipes in one night; the same young girl as his first visit, ritualistically prepared each pipe. Each night he would come to her and she would be wearing the same flowered robe of yellow hydrangeas set against a lavender background and embroidered designs. Each night she would sit beside him, sometimes immediately placing her small, childlike hand inside his pants feeling the warmth in his groin. Hugh allowed her to fondle him and when she would fill his second pipe, he would find the nerve to gently stroke the soft, delicate strands of soft, silky, black hair that covered her soft *mons veneris*. His fingers traced down the side of the triangle of hair and felt the small area between her leg and the rising, fleshy lip on the side of her small vulva. He would use thumb and forefinger to slowly feel down either side of the fleshly lips and his fingertips would move across, but never entering, the slight opening, moist and warm from his touch. When she warmed the small bead of opium, he would watch her lit by the amber glow of the lamp and move his hand to cup her small breasts while his other arm wrapped around her tapered waist.

She would nod a silent approval to Hugh, signaling her own enjoyment at the gentle caresses he gave her. It wasn't like the forceful grabbing and insertion of fingers by the other customers, she thought. This foreigner was kind to her. She wanted him to do more with her, but she knew he restrained himself. Usually, after his fifth pipe, yes, she thought, he is now smoking five pipes in the night; he would relax and simply hold her next to him while he idly spoke to her in her northern dialect. She liked this foreigner. He was kind to her, considerate enough to use her own native language and he was generous with his tips. She thought he always took an

interest in her by having her talk about herself and her family
and the countryside where she grew up and her customs, but
he would never talk about himself or his home country. She
looked forward to his arrival each night around six. At five,
she would take a rest, with the approval of her boss, and she
would bathe. After washing off the dirt of daytime customers
and removing their ugly touching, she would put on her best
robe, the clean one she had just bought at the new clothing
store further up Ha Bà Trưng Street, across from the Mạc
Đinh Chi Cemetery, where the important old-timers and the
Europeans were buried. She sensed the foreign soldier liked
her robe, so she would prepare herself for his return solely
because she wanted him to be happy. She only wore it for
him and discovered herself missing him when he did not
arrive.

Hugh looked up at her. He asked the one question he
didn't want to know, but his curiosity grew after he smoked.
"*Em bao nhiều tuổi?*" he asked, wondering her age.

"*Dạ, em mười sáu tuổi,*" she replied matter-of-factly in
a voice just above a whisper that Hugh could barely detect.
Sixteen.

Hugh didn't feel disgust. He knew he shouldn't have
asked the question; he shouldn't have surrendered to his
curiosity which now held him a prisoner without knowing
what his rights were. There was a war going on outside,
he thought. There are no more rules of engagement when
the lines of morality and ethics are fogged, or completely
disregarded by the powers. When your own side becomes
your enemy, Hugh thought about the bombing again. All the
rules of propriety were tossed out the window like effluent

water thrown towards the sluice running down the middle of the passageway. Sixteen, he thought again. He knew after another pipe it wouldn't matter and his conscience would forget it the following day. Then he would return to her comforting touch once again. He didn't want to have to carry the burden of morality for his country anymore.

Hugh lie on his bed at the Rex and felt himself getting weaker as the days went by without orders. He wondered what the Army was waiting for. He wanted to stay in-country, to stay forever in Việt Nam, but he also wanted to leave the lies, the plotting and the deception behind. He didn't want to leave the girl in the opium house behind. He wished he could take her with him anywhere and everywhere he went in the world. He wanted to transport the small chamber they rested in, and where each night she would prepare his pipes while he spoke with her and she would whisper to him in her soothing, melodic voice. He wanted to take the feel of her body with him and, every night while still in Việt Nam, he would memorize her face so he wouldn't forget. He touched her face, traced the lines of her nose up to the fold of skin on the inside of her eyes and softly moved his fingers over her eyelids, eyebrows and down her cheeks to her full, pouting lips, memorizing each feature with his finger tips. He wanted all of it and all of her. During the day, it saddened him that he would someday have to leave all this and leave her behind, as well. The town was becoming his "Beloved Saigon" and he wanted to cherish and remember each moment, taste and feel it the rest of his life. He came to the realization that Việt Nam was not merely a location on the map, but it was "a feeling;" it was "his experience."

The knock on the door brought Hugh back to the present and he answered it in his underwear. "Lieutenant Campbell, sir?" the corporal asked while saluting the unclad officer.

"Yeah, that's me," Hugh replied while half-way returning the salute.

"I have orders here for you, sir." The corporal handed Hugh the single sheet of paper, saluted again, turned and walked down the corridor and stopped at Whitman's room. The corporal went through the same routine he must have done hundreds of times before. Just like the lieutenants, he was another errand boy in the war, but his tasks were safer.

Hugh looked at his orders. He was going back to the States. The normal tour of duty in Việt Nam was twelve months, but he was going back early. He looked down the hallway at Whitman who was reading his orders also.

"Where ya' going?" Hugh asked.

"Fort Benning. OCS training. Shit, we haven't even done a portion of our tour of duty here. How about you?" Whitman asked.

"Same. Fort Benning," he said with a resignation that betrayed his yearning to stay.

Hugh walked down the hallway in his underwear, not particularly caring since the Rex was for officers, anyway.

Hugh asked, "What do you think is up with this? Why do you think we're going back to the States? We haven't even done our tour yet, and I'm sure they wouldn't want to waste all that money on our training by sending us back."

"All I can say is that this last op was a 'make it or break it' for us. They don't trust you anymore, Hugh," Whitman pensively admitted, "and goddamit they now apparently don't trust me, either. I'm considered guilty by association. I knew your questioning orders might fuck things up for us. Why can't you simply play the game, goddamit? You know, Hugh, that's all this is, it's a big fucking game between the US and the Soviet Union, man, but we've got a patriotic duty and as officers in the Army, we have to play the game. I'm afraid that my Army career will get dogged because of you. What'd you do with that pouch, man?"

Hugh was surprised at Whitman's outburst, accusations and blaming. He knew Whitman wanted to have a chest full of war medals and ribbons like his own father, but in the long run did it really matter, he thought rhetorically. It's a game when your piece gets taken by the other side. It's not a game where you live to play again. It's a game and the end of the game for the loser is the end of life.

"It's not a game, Bud," Hugh exclaimed, reverting back to a familiar nickname. "People are dying. Americans and Vietnamese are dying every fucking day, every fucking moment. This isn't a game like chess, checkers or cards. These are real lives that are ending in this country. We have a moral and ethical duty to question orders. It's the politicians that get the military involved in war and they keep it going. When will you realize that we were manipulated? I've already used my arguments with you and nothing's changed, but think back about the timing of the "Arc Light." Morgan assured us at the beginning all bombing strikes would be held in abeyance while we were in the target area. You know, thinking back, if the VC knew about our mission, then there's someone overseeing the whole game, as you put it. And if so, they knew we'd probably be near VC leadership, so why not

order us to terminate them beside the NVA captain, huh?"
Hugh retorted.

"Keep your voice down, Hugh. This hallway isn't secure
and," he couldn't finish the thought.

Hugh interrupted. "You know what, fuck this war, fuck
this hotel and fuck the bullshit they tell the press every
fucking day during their briefing. You know, Bud, this was
all bullshit. We're nothing more than prostitutes for the brass
and the politicians. They fuck us then pay us," he paused.
"So when're you leaving?" Hugh asked, finally giving up
and changing the subject. He only wanted to quickly end the
conversation and go back to the den, back to her arms and
smoke.

"I leave in four more days from Tân Sơn Nhứt. How
about you?"

Hugh looked at his orders. "The same. Look, I'm sorry
that I've got this side that should question things that don't
add up or seem right. It's a survival thing for me. I don't want
to fuck up your career. I won't stay in, anyway, so you won't
have to worry about the extra baggage. I'll do my time and
then resign my commission. You'll be free of me and you'll
manage to get some sweetheart assignments. You're a good
officer and a damn fine Special Forces officer. Look, you
survived a B-52 bombing and you've got a Bronze Star in
your file. You'll survive anything, Bud. Still friends?" Hugh
asked extending his hand to Whitman.

"Sure, asshole. We'll get through this and it'll get better.
This war isn't going anywhere for awhile and I'll try to
get back – without you, *ass*-hole," Whitman exclaimed,
emphasizing the anal reference humorously.

The two lieutenants had lunch accompanied by a couple of ice cold Schlitz beers at the rooftop bar and then went their separate ways to prepare for departing the country. Hugh went to nap so he could be more awake at the opium house. Since he now knew his future, he wanted to spend as much of the next few days as possible exactly where he wanted to be; in the company of Somnus and the young girl.

A little before four in the enduring heat of a Saigon afternoon, Hugh again took a circuitous route to the opium house; he never repeated a random route twice. The opium didn't make him paranoid, but he was beginning to believe that sometimes he was being watched. The interruption at the opium house on his first visit by the MPs and the White Mice gave birth to those suspicions. He didn't want to take chances. He took to hiring different cyclos to take him to the Bên Thành Market and he'd slip through the other side of the large, steamy cauldron of the covered market and hail another cyclo driver to take him elsewhere and then he'd walk. He used the windows of storefronts to watch behind him and across the street. He'd pause and look at the scenery wondering if others were doing the same. Each day he would leave earlier to get to the house around six, just when she – he suddenly wondered what her name was – was returning to work.

The same wizened old man opened the door each day and welcomed Hugh. Hugh told him that he received orders to leave Việt Nam in a few days; something he'd not wished for. He told of his leaving more as a doleful courtesy than as a boasting. The old man turned towards Hugh and looked at him with dark, pinpoint eyes that seemed to bore a hole through Hugh's pupils. He took Hugh by the hand and led him back to the usual cell protected by the phoenix and dragons where the girl sat on the side of the bed patiently waiting with her black tresses pulled forward over her shoulder and covering the left side of her face. He saw that she was in her lavender robe again, the one he liked. Her slender legs dangled over the edge of the wooden pallet; her feet suspended inches above the old red and black tiled floor. Her hands were folded on her lap and she looked as though she could have simply been waiting for a bus or a train to god-knows-where, thought Hugh. The old man said something in Chinese that Hugh could not understand and left him alone there with her. She sat and looked at him. She smiled and said, "We wait."

Moments later, the old man returned. He led Hugh and the young girl down the corridor of cubicles, the Paradise of Opium-smokers, and to the stairs at the end that led to the upper floors. He whispered something to the girl again in Chinese.

"You know many things that we will never know and you must know that the saddest thing is the death of the heart," the old man began. "There is a hurt we see inside your eyes that you cannot see. You have ghosts that have already moved in and are residing in your house; ghosts that need to be comforted because their souls are not free. Only you can do that; only you can free them. The pipe can only keep them quiet but they will always come back and visit you. Someday you will be able to face your ghosts alone and tell them to be at peace and go home. Until then, I am offering you a gift.

"My granddaughter here is special to me. She is unlike anyone else I have known and she is much help to a tired old man, like me. She says you are kind to her, that you are kind to your ghosts and you only show interest in her, not your own pleasure. She says you have a gentle touch and a good nature," he paused to catch his breath, "and a good heart."

"Please, I simply want to fade awhile before I leave," Hugh said.

"Please wait a moment. Allow me to finish. You say you must now leave our country and I know how much this country has entered your soul and has become you. So, I offer you a gift. You will not worry and your needs will be taken care of. The top of this stairway leads to a hallway and at the end is a room. It has a bed, a closet, a private toilet and a small table for preparing food and a small fridge. I offer it to you as a gift for the time you have remaining. My granddaughter also has a gift for you, which she will explain when you reach the top of the stairs. It is something she offers and I have nothing to say about it," the old man concluded. He looked at Hugh and took the foreigner's large right hand into the two of his frail, bony hands and held them for a moment and peered into Hugh's eyes. He then went back to work.

Without a sound, the young girl took Hugh by the hand and led him up the stairs. They passed the first, second, third and fourth floors and finally arrived where the stairs could climb no further. A water-stained hallway, illuminated by a single bulb hanging in the center, had faded green, wooden doors on either side. Hugh thought they must be private residences. The barefoot girl, still holding his hand, led him down to the room at the end of the dank, humid corridor that kept the heat hostage. She produced a tarnished brass key from inside her robe and unlocked the ancient mechanism, freeing metal that was consuming itself, like the men downstairs, and rusting. Inside it was as the old man had described. The room also had a window on each of its three walls and Hugh saw it towered above the other narrow houses in the area. He looked out each window, more out of habit of training than curiosity and examined the rooftops nearby and those which protruded through the canopy of trees planted long ago at the behest of the French. Off in the distance, he saw the lights of the shipyards and the funnels of ships tied up to the docks alongside Bạch Dằng Street. After examining the area and the sights, he closed the old cotton curtains and looked at her.

She bade him to sit down on the bed next to her. His medium American frame was large in comparison to her small, sixteen year old body. As she knew only a few words of English, she whispered to him in her native language, her voice sounding soft and airy, "It is a tradition for a Vietnamese woman to save her body for the man she loves. She will not want to be with anyone else. You have been the only man who took an interest in me and did not try to take more. You have been respectful, kind and understanding. You have also taken the time to speak to me in my own language and have made me comfortable while I have wanted to comfort you.

"Grandfather says you will soon leave our country. My grandfather is wise and has seen many things during the time when the French were here. As a young boy, his family had a large farm, but it was taken over by the French for a rubber tree plantation and his father was forced to work as a slave on his own land. My grandfather has seen few acts of kindness in his lifetime of war. He says that you have shown much kindness and he feels compassion for you.

"I have a love for you, even though we do not know each other's names. You should know two things; my name is Hoa Hồng (Hugh knew it meant 'rose') and the other thing you should know is that I have never been with a man, a man like a husband.

"I have worked here for my grandfather since I was twelve years old. Many have wanted to touch me and have offered my grandfather much money. He has always refused and when a man tries to do things, grandfather does not let them have me prepare their pipes. You have a soft touch. I want to be with you as a wife would lie down with her husband," she ended.

As they sat, Hugh looked at her with a deepening affection for her. He disregarded her age while she listened to her because of the maturity in her voice. As she spoke, the beginning sound of rain was heard on the tin roof of the house. The faded floral-patterned curtains fluttered in the cooling breeze. Hugh said nothing and did nothing as she began to undress him. When she was done folding each piece of clothing and placing them neatly in a pile on a chair, she came over to him and bade him lie down. She began to prepare a pipe for him, paying careful attention to the opium bead being held over the flame. He held her wrist as she gently twirled the bead slowly, allowing it to bubble. When it was ready, she plunged it into the bowl of the pipe, held it over the flame where it began to smoke and offered the other end of the ivory-tipped bamboo pipe to Hugh. He took about three full draws on the pipe and lay back down on his back, staring at the ceiling. He thought about the ghosts the old man spoke about. He knew there were ghosts, but he also didn't know where they resided. His ghosts were as elusive as truth in war.

Hoa Hồng put the pipe down on the tray and gently placed it and the oil lamp on the table centered in the room. She placed her body on top of his and used her hands to caress his face and massaged his chest with her delicate hands. He took her hands in his and saw they were half the size of his own. Her fingernails were trimmed and extended slightly over the elfin-like tips of her slender fingers. He saw her arms were completely devoid of hair, as most Asian women's arms were. He untied the belt of her robe and let the material fall to the sides revealing her slender, graceful body. He felt the urge for her and she felt it also. They both began to ache for each other. They moved slowly, deliberately and gently. Hugh was ever so cautious of hurting her frail body. She wanted to enjoy the foreigner inside her, slowly advancing upwards, not causing any pain, as some girls complained their first time with a man.

Hours later, as it seemed to Hugh, they still lay there consumed, drained by the intentional and almost ceremonious slowness of their lovemaking. Hugh reflected for a moment that there was a pause during their act; a ghost who wanted to make itself known, a ghost that almost begged to be recognized. When Hugh began to pay attention, the specter faded and he was again lying on his side still coupled with Hoa Hồng. He looked at her gentle, soft facial features and noticed the strong Chinese bloodline in her cheeks and eyes. He looked at her tender, young body, offered to him and which he gratefully and carefully accepted. She looked at him and felt his sadness and made love to him again, taking the last of the day's seed he could produce. Alone and together in that room, they ignored the ghosts and loved until it was time for Hugh to leave Việt Nam.

When the time came, Hugh was packed and ready to go, the few souvenirs he purchased filled a portion of a suitcase purchased for that reason and his clothing and uniforms were packed into a B4 bag, also purchased. It was much easier than the duffle bag he had been issued at Officer Candidate School. A sedan from MACV Headquarters would be picking the lieutenants up shortly after lunch, so Hugh took the time to get to the local branch of the Bank of America and withdrew his cash.

With the money and a greeting card he bought from a street vendor near the Rex, Hugh took no bother of anyone following him and walked directly to the opium house where he had been residing for the past few days. The door was opened, as usual, by the grandfather. Hoa Hồng was busy washing clothes as most customers would not be arriving for a few hours or more. Sometimes the business of war took priority over the business of pleasure. Hugh took Hoa Hồng aside and sat on the edge of a bed in an unused cubicle downstairs. He gave her the envelope containing the card and cash and told her to save money for herself and maybe some day she will be able to make another life for herself that did not involve men and their prying little hands and fat, greasy fingers. He kissed her once more and she returned the kiss with her gentle Asian passion. He left her sitting on the edge of the bed by herself as he exited the house, saying goodbye respectfully to the grandfather. When he had gone, she opened the card and read, *"I only wish we could have met sooner. You will always be in my heart. Hugh."* She cried when she counted the money. It was much more than she had ever known existed in the world, so she hid it.

The two lieutenants departed Tân Sơn Nhứt Airbase; the chartered Boeing 707 rose rapidly in the air and turned quickly left over the city to avoid the potential small arms fire from northwest of the airfield that was not always secure. Hugh sat in the window seat on the left side of the aircraft and watched his Beloved Saigon slipping away underneath. He suddenly felt as though the world was being pulled out from underneath him and he felt a longing and a choking sensation in his throat. As the plane gained altitude and continued to bank, Hugh saw the downtown area and from the orientation of the Rex, he was able to quickly spot the opium house, easily identifiable from when he looked out the windows days earlier to get his bearing. He saw a lone girl in a lavender robe hanging laundry out on a roof. Then as the plane continued to climb, Saigon and Hugh's world no longer had support and they fell away from underneath him.

"Sir, I believe the situation is over, at last," Paul said.

"What do you have for me? Make it quick so we can get to the meeting on time," the Chairman demanded in his usual gruff voice.

"My contact says that the officers had been followed all the way from Saigon to Travis Air Force Base in California. Spot checks were being conducted for drugs and it was arranged that the two lieutenants would have their belongings thoroughly searched and nothing was found. In my last conversation with my contact in Saigon, he reported that he believes the document does, in fact, no longer exist. He said that the suspected lieutenant's story has been consistent all along and that if he did have it, he would not have left it behind for someone else to find. Now that they're in the States and their belongings thoroughly searched by trained men and nothing found, I believe the situation is over and nothing else needs to be done," twanged the enthusiastic Paul.

"Good work, Paul. But just for argument's sake, what if he did leave it behind, someplace he knew nobody would ever look for it. Someplace he thought would survive the war. Don't you think he may try and return to Việt Nam *someday* when it's safe to recover it?" the Chairman posited.

Exasperated, Paul thought for a moment, but dared not show a frustration with the Chairman. If it were up to him, he would have the two lieutenants assassinated. He pushed it with the B-52s, but assassination would be a different card to play in order to protect the Chairman and his ideals. Paul said, "That is a possibility, but my contact doesn't believe that possibility exists any longer."

"But, Paul, for argument's sake," Paul heard the Chairman's mounting frustration with him now, "let's say he did hide it. We don't know where it is. It could be in Saigon; it could be anywhere. What can we do to make sure that if he does return, we're able to be there if he picks it up?"

"Well, for argument's sake, sir, the one lieutenant is very trustworthy and had doubts about his friend. I also believe, from contacts in the Army press in Saigon that the one lieutenant is upset that his career may be marred by the suspicions surrounding the events. This lieutenant is the son of a career Army officer and resents the other lieutenant. Of course, arrangements, sir, can always be made to ensure the two of them are assigned to the same units, which has already been done."

"But, Paul, again I don't think you are completely understanding my fucking point," the Chairman said, now freeing the frustration with the aid. "What if the one lieutenant decides to leave the Army and he decides to return to Việt Nam someday. It could be whle the war is still going on. If afterwards, not matter who wins, it could still be sensitive. What can be done?" the Chairman asked looking at the aid with a peculiar look.

After thinking for a moment, he said, "Sir, if he applies for a passport, it can always be flagged for notification. If he applied for one, he would still receive it and not know that others will be notified of it. It is my firm understanding that resources can be used to monitor people's lives from time to time here in the United States in exceptional cases and it can be arranged, I believe, to have this lieutenant become one of those exceptional cases, sir. We would then be absolutely sure," Paul finished.

"Good, Paul. The council would certainly hate to have the information rediscovered, if it does still exist, and destroy our country and its way of life, you understand that, don't you, Paul?"

"Yes, sir. I will ensure protective measures are in place."

The Chairman walked out of the room to prepare for a talk to a group of stockholders he had to give out of state. Paul sat in the Chairman's leather swivel chair, imagining what it was like to be the Chairman, to wield power over people's lives and an economic system. Paul wanted to be like the Chairman, no, he wanted something more powerful so people like the Chairman would call him "sir." That's what Paul wanted and he had the contacts to help him in the future.

III

The girl in the yellow hat walked into the restaurant, peering around the room as though looking a table for herself. She still had her blue flowered mask on, more out of habit, and though the brim of the hat met her eyebrows, Hugh felt a tinge of recognition.   gracefully walked over to the table and motioned to the empty chair opposite Hugh. He rose, not only as a courtesy, but to offer her the chair and to shake her hand while she began to sit. She took off her hat and when she removed her mask Hugh could not believe what he was seeing and thought he had been taken back in time by nearly thirty-nine years. Images held back by a damming brain began to flood into his mind, suddenly unlocked after years of hiding in the depths of his dreams and desires. He stood there stunned, looking at a woman he loved for the first time many years before. He knew she was the same woman who saved him during the B-52 bombing, the same woman he made love with in the crater and in a hut alongside dark rice paddy and who washed his clothes and brought him his meals. Suddenly, the name Thu Lan came into his mind and he began to cry. Embarrassed, he immediately sat down and put his face into his hands and sobbed; thirty-nine years worth of tears poured from his eyes and Hugh quickly fled the table and went out the back of the restaurant to find a restroom to control his sobbing, if he could. He cried out to a godless world, cried out in pain, cried out in happiness, cried out for the loss of love he wanted so long ago, cried out for the failed loves that he hoped would replicate what was lying hidden inside, locked inside his memories and in his heart. He heard a knock on the door and a diminutive voice asking, "Are you alright?" she politely asked through through the thin, blue door. *It was her*, he thought. He calmed the sobs of his body for a moment and muttered, "Please give me a few moments."

Hugh looked in the mirror and saw a face swollen and red with years of pain and with tears, eyes bloodshot. At the age of sixty-one, it was difficult to recover after releasing emotions and memories that had been blocked for decades, but he knew he must. He could not believe the apparition sitting at the table waiting for him and begun to again doubt his sanity; this girl in the yellow hat. Hugh eventually settled himself down, washed his face and made himself presentable to return to the table.

"Miss Phạm Thị Thu Hương, I believe," said Hugh, recovered but showing the signs of the strain of the moment.

"Oh, Mr. Hugh, you remembered my name. I think you and I have much to talk about but first, we should order food, and please, call me Hương. It is much easier. I have just come from my countryside in Tây Ninh and I am hungry. It was a long ride on the bus. Do you mind?" she asked.

Hugh replied, "Please, no, I do not mind. Please order," and he handed her the menu that he read five times over while waiting. He could not divert his attention away from her and he was beginning to become self-conscious about his staring. Hương was an exact image of Thu Lan, the colonel's housekeeper; the enemy loved. He felt another surge of emotion in his chest and quickly grasped control of it and changed his thoughts by looking at the menu. At first, they limited their discussion to the food they should order. Hương was not a vegetarian, but offered to eat whatever Hugh suggested. As she looked at the menu, she used her slender index finger to scan the entrees, and then put her finger to the ridge of her nose while contemplating the selections. When the table server approached the table, Hugh ordered fried straw mushrooms, spring rolls, soya-based blue fish in lemongrass seasoning and a hot pot; a soup mixture heated at the table with different vegetables put into the pot and served over vermicelli noodles after it comes to a boil. She ordered a melon drink to cool the heat down inside her and Hugh had his iced tea refreshed for the fourth time. While ordering, Hugh couldn't look away from Hương. Hugh felt as though he was still in shock.

Hương broke the silence first. "Mr. Hugh, do you believe in fate? Do you believe people have destinies they must follow?" she asked sincerely.

"Yes, I do, Miss Hương," Hugh replied, "I believe that people's lives are intertwined in certain ways and I also believe the universe prefers order instead of chaos and confusion."

"Mr. Hugh, the day you had to travel in the ambulance, I was supposed to be at home to care for my younger sister, but there were no other nurses to come to Hồ Chí Minh City. I was offered an extra sixty thousand đồng in my salary to make the trip with you and return. As you know, we are a poor country and Tây Ninh is much poorer than here. My family needed the money because of my younger sister, so

I decided to accept the work that day. That decision put you and me together, but I see your reaction to me is much more than I would have expected. I feel there is much more, and I believe I quite possibly have information to share with you, is that correct, Mr. Hugh?" she pleaded.

"Yes, but I don't know the connection between you and Miss Mai who contacted you," he said with a puzzled look.

"Miss Mai is my father's wife's cousin. That is how she knows me and knows my family."

Hugh looked even more puzzled for a moment. "You said Miss Mai is your father's wife's cousin. Wouldn't you refer to your father's wife as your mother?"

"My real mother died shortly after my younger sister was born. Mother died in 1986. She was working as a nurse and called to Đắc Lắc Province to help with a new hospital. She was killed by some revolutionaries from the mountain tribes who wanted to be independent. They didn't know my mother was a nurse. My father married again and together they had our youngest sister who stays at home. She is the one with, I think the term you said was 'Agent Orange'," she explained.

"Yes, Miss Hương, that is the exact term. You have a very good memory," Hugh said complimentarily.

"Mr. Hugh, you can call me Hương. My father sometimes calls me 'Lệ Thu,' Autumn Tear, because I remind him of my real mother." Hugh's mind retreated back to the night in a dark hut when he thought about precious Autumn Tears from an Autumn Orchid and felt a choking sensation welling up in his throat like he was about to cry. He tried to abate the feeling and it felt as though he was choking as the emotion welled in his throat. He paused a moment to regain his composure.

"Yes, I need to ask you. Hương, who is, I'm sorry, who was your mother?" he asked needing to confirm all he now knew.

"My mother's name was Võ Thị Thu Lan." Hugh's heart stopped at the name, a name he hadn't heard spoken in thirty-nine years. "Did you know her?" Hương asked.

"Yes, I did, my dear. I knew her very well."

"What can you tell me about her?"

"I can tell you she was a housekeeper for an American Army colonel who was kind to her and she did a very good job of keeping house for him. I stayed at his house with another lieutenant. She was beauty and grace, she was delicate and kind. I knew her footsteps on the wooden floors and her knock at the door with the breakfast tray and coffee. I knew her soft voice and her passion to help the Vietnamese." Hugh paused to keep his emotion in check. "You know, she saved my life," he said not wanting to go into detail about the bombing.

"Mr. Hugh, I have to ask this question because of things my father told me when I was young. He said my mother was a patriot who fought courageously with the National Front for Liberation in Tây Ninh. He said to me long ago my mother had been in love with an enemy soldier. My father loved my mother, but she had been with another man, this American soldier, but my father loved my mother very much and accepted her anyway because she was the most beautiful and kindest woman he had ever known." She paused for several moments to collect her thoughts and to gather her emotions before they burst out of her body.

"I also have to tell you my mother used to tell me a story about courage. She told me a story about a woman hero of the National Liberation Front's 9th Division who helped her people, but her compassion also helped an enemy soldier. Mr. Hugh, can you tell me some things more?" Hương was now full of questions as Hugh had been.

"Hương, I was in love with your mother when I first saw her. Yes, she was with the National Liberation Front; Việt Cộng, as we Americans called them. She told me that when she contacted me on the road between Tây Ninh and Xóm Mát."

"Mr. Hugh, it is called Xã Mát now," she told him as a matter-of-factly.

"Thank you. She contacted me and we both realized we were in love with each other, but we were both in impossible situations. She was Việt Cộng, I'm sorry, National Liberation Front, and I was an American Special Forces officer. But, Hương, believe me when I say this, we loved each other and I buried that love for the past thirty-some years because of all the painful events. You should know your mother has been haunting my dreams almost nightly for all those years. I have tried everything I could to find out who she was. I see her every night and try to kiss her as she walks out of the rice paddy on the road to Xóm Mát, excuse me, Xã Mát," Hugh explained.

The two sat in silence as the waiter began bringing the food to the table. He placed small dishes of sliced red peppers, salt and lime, and bowls of vegetarian fish sauce on the table and walked away oblivious to the strange reunion.

Hương and Hugh looked at one another. Hugh still could not believe that he was sitting with the daughter of the only love he knew and yearned for; so much that he pushed her further into his mind to hide her there from everyone and himself. Here was her daughter; the exact image of her mother and Hugh felt pangs of agony in his heart and aches of longing. He remembered her parting words in the ambulance recently; *"You don't have to leave Việt Nam, if you don't want to."*

Hương sat there looking at Hugh. This American, this foreigner she cared for in the ambulance from Tây Ninh Hospital to the Franco-Vietnamese Hospital is the very same man her mother loved. Fate is a mystical companion, she considered; for the hospital to call her and charge her with his care to Hồ Chí Minh City was an arrangement only the gods could manage. Here he was, the very same man, the foreign soldier in the stories of her mother and father for those years until her mother died. Now he had returned to Việt Nam, Tây Ninh, and her family. She looked at him and could see why her mother, Thu Lan, had loved this man. Even for his older years, he was very handsome, healthy and he had a look of compassion in his eyes that she had never seen in any other man's eyes before. She now wondered what it was her mother felt. She had heard that mothers and daughters can be more alike than anyone could suppose. Hương wondered if she would have felt the same as her mother when she was eighteen years old, so long ago in Tây Ninh.

Hugh thought to himself for a moment how much Hương sounded like her mother and her mannerisms were like her mother's. His eyes unconsciously begun again to feast at her visage and he became uncomfortable with himself for wanting to look at her constantly. She was every bit her mother, yet she was a different woman in her own respect. Hugh recognized a potential conflict building in his heart and forced himself to remember Thu Lan and Hương may be mother and daughter, but they are two entirely separate persons; or were they?

They sat in silence, unaware of the questions they needed to ask, yet wanting to ask so many things of each other. Hugh tried to phrase a question and discovered each question would eventually answer itself, or it was a completely unsuitable question to ask a beautiful, young Vietnamese woman. There were so many uncertainties, so many things he wanted to know, but he could not enquire about them in a public restaurant, and so the two were silent until after the hot pot course arrived. They watched as the table server in his soy sauce-stained, white shirt placed the small stove on the table, positioned the small white square of paraffin inside and set a match to it to start it burning. He then placed the pot with the vegetables and stock on top of the burner. They waited for it to boil and she then placed the remaining vegetables in the pot along with the vegetarian shrimp. The paraffin and the pot were like his emotions, he reflected, unfeeling, and then when conditions were right, the wax square was heated and set aflame. The vegetables were like the questions we held inside, turning, roiling and boiling; questions he was afraid to ask and, more so, afraid to know the answers.

"Hương, have you ever been married?" Hugh broke the silence first.

"No, Mr. Hugh, I haven't. You asked me when we were in the ambulance, but maybe you forget because of your pain," she replied.

Ah, yes, the pain; the pain of the body and the pain of betrayal in the heart, Hugh thought.

"I have yet to meet a suitable man for me, and I have not looked for a man because I have been helping my father's wife, my new mother, with my younger sister. Because of the Agent Orange, she needs extra help. I think you would like to meet her. She's very loving and a kind sister. It is uncomfortable for some people to meet her, but maybe you are different. Yes, I think so," she said turning her head to the side and looking slightly down, allowing her black hair to fall in front of her face. Hugh wanted very much to move her hair to the side for her and to touch her cheek, but he managed to restrain himself.

"Hương, I would be honored to meet your sister," Hugh replied.

"Mr. Hugh, I would like you to meet the other people in my family."

"Hương, I don't know if that would be a good idea or not. You see, your father may have anger towards me and…"

"Mr. Hugh, I'm sorry," Hương interrupted. "If my father knew you were the man who also loved my mother and would have taken care of her, he will be honored to meet you. My mother and father had a special love and it was because you loved my mother first. My father will not be angry. He would welcome you as family. You remember in the ambulance,

I told you Vietnamese people know how to forgive. It was simply fate that returned you to America and fate that led my mother to my father, a comrade in the National Liberation Front. Please, Mr. Hugh?" she pleaded.

"My dear Hương, you do present the invitation in such a way that I cannot refuse. I would be glad to meet your family. They are all in Tây Ninh, as you said before, correct?"

Hugh needed the clarification because in the back of his mind he was still trying to determine how he would return to retrieve the document without arousing the suspicion of the police. He also didn't want to be followed, but perhaps he would be able to have "Bác" help him once he did get to Tây Ninh. However, he didn't want to think he was using Hương and her family and he started to feel conflicted. He looked intently at Hương sitting across from him, a picture of innocence and beauty. He watched her mannerisms and saw the influence of her mother. The way she would tilt her head and her eyes would glance to the side; when she looked down gracefully when she picked up her iced melon drink; the way she would raise her index finger and align it with her nose and forehead with eyes half-closed while looking for a word or phrase in English. Hugh remembered Thu Lan for all those things, yet, Hương was very much an individual separate from her mother. Hugh wondered, does she have a double life like her mother? He doubted it, but suddenly his curiosity again held him captive and he was forced to ask to escape the torment of his silent questions,

"Hương, I'd like to ask you a question."

"Yes, go ahead," she replied.

"This is difficult, but your mother worked for an American officer while she was Việt Cộng, or I should say, National Liberation Front, and kept that as her secret. Do you have any secrets that I should know about?" he asked reluctantly.

Suddenly, he cursed himself for asking and wished he could take the question back as it would cast doubts in her mind not only about him, but he also thought that she was innocent and would not have a double life to keep from Hugh. Her mother revealed her secret out of love. Asking for Hương to love him was too much, she was much too young for him, he thought, but many young Vietnamese women are sometimes like children and will tend to trust others blindly for the love and security it brings. Others who have been hurt will not trust as willingly.

"Mr. Hugh, I do not know why you would ask a question like that." Her answer confirmed his belief that he erred in asking. "I am a nurse and I care for people. My mother had to have a secret life because our country was at war and people had to make sacrifices of their private lives. My mother revealed her secret to you and her other secret of you to her husband, my father, and to me. Mr. Hugh, I think it is only foreigners who have all the secrets and play games with them to harm other people."

Hương looked pained by the question and Hugh felt agonized that he asked, and he was now at a loss at how to mend the hurt. He looked at her as she looked down into her soup and dabbled at the vegetables and tofu with spoon and chopsticks and her dark, silky hair slightly slipped forward across her right eye and cheek again.

"Hương, please forgive me. If you knew what my life has been like, perhaps you would understand why I asked. I need someone to trust. I haven't had anyone in my life to trust since I've trusted your mother. The only people I've met since your mother have calculated, plotted and cheated to advance their own careers and were only interested in themselves and hiding things from me," Hugh recalled several of his lovers and one he was engaged to until she ended the relationship telling him about the 'other man.' "Hương, I have a need to trust someone and need that someone to trust me," Hugh finished.

"Mr. Hugh, if it is someone you need or want to trust, I believe you should trust me. Why? Because I am like your family. I don't know much about you, but many people say I am like my mother in many ways, not just in the way we look. If you and mother trusted each other, Mr. Hugh, then I am one you can also trust," she said in a delicate voice that softly floated over the nearly-empty hot pot and settled into Hugh's ears, begging him to trust her.

"Mr. Hugh, my mother once told me, when I was a young girl that someday I will meet someone like she did and I will feel something in my heart that feels right. This is not traditional for me to say this, but Mr. Hugh, there is something about you that makes you special. I knew that when you were in the ambulance. I kept looking at you and wishing to care for you for a long time. That night, I remembered what my mother had said to me and my heart felt right that night. I know it is strange, but sometimes I believe my mother watches out for me and guides me sometimes. It must be our Confucian heritage, but I feel her spirit, at times and I do believe it. What do you believe, Mr. Hugh?" Hương wanted to know more about this foreigner whom her mother loved.

Hugh took a few minutes, causing H10.5ng to repeat her question. He asked her, "Can you give me a few minutes to think about the answer. What you have told me is very personal and you have the right to have honest answers to your questions."

She nodded and went back to the remaining bits of her soup as though she had forgotten her own question and Hugh tried to divine the answers in the floating vegetables in the bowl in front of him like tea leaves in a cup. He paused for a moment and picked up a fried spring roll with his chopsticks and dipped in carefully in the vegetarian fish-flavored sauce. He contemplated his answer and her question as he bit halfway into it, then dipped the other half in the soy sauce and minced chili pepper mixture. Hugh mulled over the flavor of the spring roll as he chewed over the flavor of his answer. He wanted his answer to be genuine, yet it had to be careful. He thought Hương had been waiting a lifetime to tell someone how she felt, and now that she had spoken her innermost thoughts, he needed to be careful and not have his answer be considered trivial and trite. He had instantly felt a deep connection with her in the ambulance and when she arrived at the restaurant, and perhaps now she should know the truth about him. He loved her mother and she had been his constant, spectral companion for all these years. She was always the faithful woman in bed with him every night. She had been his fantasy lover for thirty-nine years, and it seemed here was the incarnation of that dream – his second chance.

A flash of lightning caught his eye and he looked past her just as he heard the instantaneous thunder and saw motorbikes quickly pulling over to the side of the street and drivers donning raincoats; poncho-type coats that protected the driver, the front of the motobike and usually a passenger behind who could hide underneath. Another flash of lightning, the booming of thunder and an early evening downpour had begun. Hugh loved Việt Nam and he loved the dynamic weather of the monsoon season. The rains would clear the air of dust, dirt and other pollutants, cleaning, cooling and ionizing the night air. The thought of rain helped to remove the dirt and pollutants from his own mind and he finally broke the silence and answered Hương's question.

"I believe that fate can control people's destinies. But the people should be willing to 'let go' of their lives and not hold on because of other reasons. My dear, sweet Hương, fate has brought me back to Việt Nam, but something else also brought me back. The work I did in 1966, when I knew your mother, started a chain of events that have returned me to Việt Nam to finish the work. I believe that sometimes fate isn't completely in the hands of the gods, but sometimes it is in the hands of other humans, for whatever purposes they may have. It could even be to provide entertainment for the gods. As a child, I once thought there was a god who planned everything for people and I was led to believe he was a kind and loving god. Hương, early in my life, I discovered that god to be a superstition created to have people's minds diverted and to give humans a reason for remaining loyal to political controls in a country.

"Hương, I have no religion. I only believe that a person should be as kind as they can possibly be, even if it hurts, and they should practice good deeds. I believe that fate has led me to you, your cousin, Mai, and her cousin, the police inspector who has been questioning me about the death of my friend. People in America sometimes like to say 'it's a small world' and I must agree. I think you and I were meant to meet that day in the ambulance and tonight. What may happen past this night is beyond my understanding. I can only assure you that I will keep my mind open to anything. Maybe I have said too much," Hugh ended with a short gasp.

"Mr. Hugh. You have been through many difficult times and you were nearing death from the knife wound you received in my home town. Your friend was not fortunate and it was his destiny to die in Tây Ninh that night. I have only revealed a little of my heart to you and you have told me much. Let us finish dinner and we can go somewhere for *cà phê* afterwards."

Hương and Hugh continued eating; pausing only for small talk. Mostly, it was Hương who had questions about America and its way of life; the customs, the economy, the culture. Hugh responded by talking about how Americans have no idea of who they are working for or even why, and they have become slaves to a rigged economic system that continues to make the poor poorer and the rich richer. She was surprised to hear that America had homeless people and many were poor and without good medical care, and she also questioned why America continues to fight wars in other countries after the American war in Việt Nam should have been a good lesson to learn from. Hugh could only offer that, and he remembered Whitman quoting General George Patton, that "Americans love to fight. Americans love to win." Hugh could only tender the explanation that America still has much to learn from the rest of the world. As a still-young nation, America's arrogance is becoming boorish to the global community and that has gone to the detriment of the people who live in America, and they are generally ignorant about the rest of the world.

When they were finished, Hugh called the waiter over to pay the bill. They walked together outside, arm in arm, into the drizzle that cooled the air and Hugh called the taxi that hovered in front of the Cathay Hotel waiting for another fare. He told the driver to take them to Cafe Thềm Xưa on Nguyễn Cảnh Chánh Street, at the western edge of District 1. They sat quietly in the green and white air-conditioned taxi, holding hands like teenagers. For Hương, this was the first time she had held hands with a man, and realized it was compounded by the fact he was a foreigner and her mother's first love. Hugh looked out the window at the rain slick streets and traffic circle as they transitioned the traffic circle from Cách Mạng Tháng Tám Street to Nguyễn Trãi Street. Even for a rainy night, the streets were still crowded with cars and motorbikes going in every direction. They slowed for a collision between a motobike and another taxi in front of the Zen Center department store and it took considerable time to maneuver around a crowd that grew larger and impeded traffic – everybody loves to look. Several minutes later, they arrived at the cafe. They walked inside the gate of the eight foot high wall and were greeted by two waiters in white shirts and black trousers. Inside the gate, one could be directed to the right patio dining area or remain in the left courtyard for drinks and soft music. Hugh and Hương opted for the left side and requested a quiet table for two, preferring a table away from the music speakers that Hugh could hear were playing the music of Trịnh Công Sơn, a famous Vietnamese music composer.

They were seated in a far corner of the front garden area. The inn had once been a French villa and had been converted into a romantic theme cafe. Hugh sat with his back to the wall. Even in peacetime it was a difficult habit to break. He looked up and over the wall towards the eastern sky to watch the flashes of lightning highlighting the clouds of the distant storm that had just expended most of itself over the city. He looked around the cafe, out of habit, but now more for curiosity. He already knew his followers were sitting outside on their motorbikes, feeling safe that Hugh was with a woman and wouldn't try to evade them.

The café's courtyard area was separated into secluded private areas by lush, green, flowering plants and walkways. In the corners of the courtyard, and on poles stationed in the middle, small, quiet, electric fans swirled the air, giving a shivering touch to the moment. Tendrils of flowering vines inched their way towards their small table yearning to be nourished with love, like plants that face the sun. The waiter returned and removed the red shade of the oil lamp, which resembled a lotus, and set two coasters with small glasses of iced green tea on the table. He placed two napkins down before he walked away and another server appeared with a menu. Hương and Hugh sat silently as they read through the menu. She ordered a salted plum drink and Hugh ordered an iced jasmine tea. The waiter returned with their drinks and after serving them, went back to sit down and talk with his friends near the old, wooden gate.

Hương started the conversation and asked Hugh about his life. Hugh betrayed his contempt for his homeland but couldn't help taking the lion's share of responsibility for himself. He admitted the lost loves and lost jobs, how people reacted to him and how he developed the habit of always looking over his shoulder.

She listened intently to him, being mindful that he was speaking slowly for her so she could understand everything he said. His speech was deliberate and clear. She appreciated the time he was taking and she enjoyed his company. She also felt sorry that Hugh's life was fraught with mistakes and unfortunate times, but she also felt sorry that he believed people were watching him or influencing his life. She knew that had happened in other countries, in dictatorships, but in America, it was a free country, she thought, and nobody would worry about one person.

"Mr. Hugh. Have you thought about what I said to you in the ambulance?" she asked changing the subject.

"What was it you said? We spoke about several things."

"That you don't have to go back if you don't want to. You could stay here in Việt Nam. There are jobs you could get here and you could stay if you want. My country is beautiful and peaceful. We are not rich, but we care about people and families always help each other. We do not have high salaries or many things like America, but you may find living here to your liking," Hương suggested.

Hugh thought for several moments and said, "You know, you present me with a valid argument. I do not have to return, but I still have business in America to finish if I were to decide to make a life here. I'm not young, but fortunately, there is a small annuity I receive that would go a long way here so I wouldn't have to struggle. I'm sitting here with you and I think to myself that I really don't want to go back. A moment ago, I remembered another rainy night many years ago, before I left Việt Nam the first time, and I didn't want to leave then. I remember sitting on the plane going back to the states and wishing I had never got on board but stayed here. Hương, it was because of the war here and the things I saw and knew that kept me from staying in the military and supporting a government that catered to, what many would call the 'military industrialized complex'." Hương didn't understand the term, but let Hugh continue. "You are right. I don't have to go back. But if I stay, what could I do? Where would I live? Most of all, what about love?" he hated to use that word as it had become so hackneyed in the States.

"Mr. Hugh, do not worry. If you decide you wish to stay in my country, it would be my duty to my mother and to me to help you in any way I can." Hương sat there like a precious, scented flower floating in a bowl; demure and allowing the barest current to let her drift within the confines of her life. She was thinking in her innocent way about life; thinking what being married to a foreigner would be like. She felt as though she had known him all her life and, suddenly, she was finding that she didn't want to be away from him. She couldn't fully understand the unexpected feelings that were quickly welling inside her.

Hugh couldn't believe himself and what he was beginning to feel. It had been a very emotional day for him. The anticipation of the meeting and discovering the long secret of his memory loss and having it reawakened in the way it did at the restaurant had drained him physically, besides emotionally. He wanted to impetuously say to her, 'let's forget everything and let's make a life together,' but he could not. He was thirty-two years her senior. He couldn't cheat her out of a long married life at that great of an age difference. Hugh began to realize that he was thinking the crazy thought that she would ever want to be with him. Then he recalled another time, long ago in an opium house and he was with a young girl who was six years his junior who wanted to be with him. He remembered those moments very fondly after returning to the states, but she, too, what was her name? Oh, yes, Hoa Hồng; she also wanted to be with him. He had also wanted to keep her forever, but her youth imprisoned her in Saigon.

Time was certainly relevant. He continued to look at her in the soft light of the oil lamp and thought again about Hoa Hồng in the opium house that had been on the other side of town. He recalled how her skin also reflected the amber glow of the oil lamp as she prepared his pipes and he would gently stroke her soft, golden skin. He had slowly forgotten about her over the intervening years; only remembering her a few times, but tonight everything came flooding back. When he was hired to be a police officer, he was asked the pre-employment question, "Have you ever committed a felony in this state, any other state, or in any country where an act would be legal but considered a felony in this state?" Hugh simply replied "no" before he had a chance to think about the opium house and the sixteen year Hoa Hồng. The distant rumble of thunder brought Hugh to the present. Hương was the exact image of her mother and Hugh could not help but feel a strong love inside; a love that has haunted him through all those long, dark nights.

As soft as the distant thunder, Hugh said, "Hương, I have never really ever been happy in America since I returned in 1966. It is only here that I feel human, feel worth something and feel like I belong. I have been to many countries when I was in the military because of my job, but it is only here that I feel like it is truly a home for me. I trust your word and trust that you would help me. I do have to return to America, once all this is over, and take care of personal matters. It may take a few months or so, but I shall return. I can promise you that much."

Hugh saw her small, dark eyes beginning to glisten with moisture. She was looking downwards at her drink and the oil lamp when he said this to her. He saw her full lips rise faintly at the corners in the slight trace of a smile. Her head rose slowly as did her eyes and they met Hugh's and he saw tears forming in the soft inner fold of her eyes. Hugh shifted closer to her in his chair, took her hand and gently moved her head to his shoulder and she cried silently and gently. He saw her tears were as delicate as dew on a jasmine blossom. 'How can I ever leave this country' he thought, and he felt sad inside. Not for her, but for all the lost years roaming in the wilderness of capitalism, greed and the self-serving, instant gratifying motif of the developed world and the vacuous space of failed relationships. He had now found genuine life and a humanity that couldn't be understood in the west for all its education, money, technology, sophisticated medications, psychology and its unrestrained weapons of war and desire for global economic domination. Here in a poor country, here in Việt Nam, Hugh found life and humanity gathering in the inner corner of the eyes; in the soft tears of a Vietnamese nurse, a woman whose deceased mother he also loved and still lives in his dreams.

They finished their drinks and Hugh saw her back to where she was staying while in the city. She was staying with not-too-distant family members; people she called "Aunt and Uncle" in District Five, near Chợ Lớn, the China Town area. The small house was situated along Kinh Tàu Hủ, the canal that eventually wends its way to the Saigon River. They promised to meet the following morning and spend the day together sightseeing and getting to know more about each other. Hugh had the taxi driver take him back to the police house, paid the fare and went inside, first nodding to the guards and to Thảo, the guard whose grandmother recently passed away. He went inside the house and saw a package waiting for him.

Now there are more voices, voices that are different, but friendly voices anyway. Gosh, I'm still full from eating. I like to eat, but they never let me eat in the light. I can sense the light outside the doorway but it never penetrates this room. That's alright, I have much to do anyway. I have to comb my hair, wash my face, change my clothes, trim my nails and brush my teeth. At least they let me do that much for myself. Some other things I can't do. I go to the bathroom, but someone else takes care of the flushing or disposal, whatever it is they do. For now, I'll tend to other work and other things that have to get done, and then I'll call for someone to help me again. I don't like asking for help, but sometimes a person has to, that's just the way it is. Everyone has to help. I even help at times doing many things for other people. People say I make them feel good; they say that without me their lives would be dull and meaningless. You mean I bring enjoyment to other people? That's wonderful. I wonder how I do it, though, locked in this dark room all the time.

PART VI

I

Paul was in charge now. He remembered those nasty days, months and years he spent with the Chairman, under his tutelage and learning the ways of the world. He had made his own in the world now and he felt he was on top. He was better than the Chairman could ever have been. He no longer worried about the lieutenants, the Special Forces or Việt Nam any longer and in fact, he had since long forgotten those days. Those were the affairs of the Chairman and he was far too distant from those days now. In those earlier times, Paul could use cocaine and drink as much as he wanted. It made him powerful, he could get work done, and he could make snap decisions without having to consult the Chairman. Sometimes, when he was reading about Việt Nam or the military, or even thinking back about the economics of the capitalist system, he wouldn't remember for a moment any of those circumstances. After their return to the States, he never heard about the lieutenants again, nor did he care. He had his own career to look after and ambitions to attain, and a goddamn good job he did of it, Paul thought.

A direct line rang into his office and placing a folder on the near-empty desk in front of him, Paul picked up the receiver and said "Yes, Carla." Just like the Chairman, Paul also had direct lines and didn't have to ask who the other person was.

"Sir, I received an interesting message a few days ago. I don't know what to make of it. It sat on my desk until I returned and it seemed odd, so out of curiosity I returned the call. I believe you have some free time now and I'd like to drop in to talk to you," Carla said without waiting for approval.

Carla strolled into Paul's office confidently without knocking. She had that privilege. She and Paul had known each other for many years and they dispensed with the usual rituals, unless in the company of others, when situations demanded protocol.

"Paul, I received this unusual message from CIA. Seems a specific name on a passport application had been flagged many years ago with no action being taken. Someone at the State Department caught it and saw that CIA was to be notified if this person ever applied for a passport. These people were confused and didn't know what to do but a check of the files indicated that they were simply to monitor this individual should he leave the country. I understand that is what they have been doing, just monitoring. After discussions with supervisors, though, and monitoring activities overseas, it seems there is a need for additional information and focus. Because of the nature of it, and a certain event, word has now slowly made it up the chain so that you should be notified. Seems you are the contact person should this occur, or at least, someone who shares the same name as you. Our people want to know what it's about," Carla now expressing her own curiosity. "Hugh Campbell is the name."

"I have no idea who he is. Who is he, anyway, and why would I want to know?" Paul asked, completely forgetting the incident nearly four decades before.

"Sir, I have no idea. We'll get some more background on the individual. We'll also cross check files to see if there is anyone else with your name who should be getting this information instead, but the clerk who caught it believes it was intended for you because of mention of specifics in the past."

"Okay, Carla, check it out. And find out about that clerk and what he or she knows. How the fuck should I know that name anyway? Tell me now about the meeting this afternoon. I really don't understand why I'm meeting with this trade minister. Isn't there someone else to do that?" Paul asked.

Frustrated, Carla replied, "No, Sir, it's your job."

At 4 Lê Duẩn Boulevard, in downtown Hồ Chí Minh City, there are some single story buildings protected by twelve foot tall cream-colored block walls with sharpened metal pointed grillwork on top. It is watched by surveillance cameras and protected by Vietnamese Police carrying automatic weapons. This newer, smaller campus was built in 1999. The area is the former site of the Saigon US Embassy, which was eventually torn down. On April 30, 1975, the Americans finally and hastily left the building and the country, leaving classified material and American supporters behind as the North Vietnamese Army came in to finalize liberation of the south. Now, the sedate buildings stand as a mute symbol of a paranoid nation; a nation which feels that Vietnamese women seeking tourist visas or emigration as wives are considered "threats to national security," simply because they wish to travel or to accompany their husbands. Inside the "paranoia," a briefing was taking place in a secure room of the US Consulate. The participants had gathered, entering after hours through a different gate on Mạc Đình Chi Street, rather than the main entrance on Lê Duẩn. The meeting had been set for earlier in the week before, but the Station Chief had been called away to a secret meeting of the Office of Directorate's Office of East Asian Affairs in Tokyo. The meeting had gone on longer than expected because of the pirating crisis in the Straits of Mallaca, terrorism and the need for reeinstilling confidence in the CIA after the "yellow cake" and Iraq War fiascoes.

"Let's get this clear again, Anh. You lost your weapon, I should say *weapons*, and the secondary target is dead, killed with your weapon. And where is it?"

"Sir, I don't know. I had control of the environment and then lost it," Anh simply stated in his defense.

"It's caused problems, but apparently, no one is looking our way. Who was the man who freed you?"

"Sir, that I don't know either. He's apparently one of the Cao Đàists who look after the place at night. He seemed to be scared with police around and with me being restrained. He didn't appear to know anything and looked confused," Anh reported.

"What do we do now?" the other agent asked the Chief.

"I'm not really sure. We have fucking people running around a temple in the middle of the night watching each other and nobody knows what the fuck is going on. You say the primary target is in police custody?"

"Technically, yes, sir, but no. He's staying in a house owned by the police and guarded. He has a twenty-four hour tail, but everyone seems comfortable with the situation. We know he's not going anywhere and his return ticket has been changed to an open ticket for an indefinite return to the States," the other agent reported.

"Alright, there's not much going on around here anyway, just the usual expat shit and business meetings. Anh, make sure you simply monitor his whereabouts. This assignment came via State Department memo to Langley, but it sure sounds strange and I don't like it," the Station Chief concluded and the meeting dissolved into the cool of the evening.

There was a message from Inspector Quỳ next to the courier package when he arrived back at the house. It simply stated that he wanted to begin concluding the investigation and wanted to meet with Hugh the following day. "Crap," Hugh thought. He wanted to spend the day with Hương. He called the Inspector and asked if they could make it early for the next day and told him why. Quỳ was pleased and assented.

Hugh looked at the courier package. It had been sent to the Continental Hotel and the police were called to pick it up and re-deliver it. It now sat staring at Hugh. He picked it up and saw it was from his brother, his power-of-attorney in the US. Hugh had made arrangements with his brother to check things for him and to send anything important by overseas express courier. Apparently, his brother felt this was urgent so Hugh opened it and pulled out the contents.

He had forgotten that he had requested information about him under the Freedom of Information Act more than a year or so before. He saw the various sources he requested had sent him plenty to read, even though much of it was redacted. However, some clerk who had busily been blacking out information had missed several key sentences in a report that had listed Lieutenant Hugh Campbell and Lieutenant Whitman Emerson. Somewhere in State Department files, Hugh's name had been flagged should he apply for a passport, which he was now using. Hugh had always traveled to other countries, but it was on military aircraft under orders and no need for passports and visas. The partially-censored document gave the name of the responsible party to be notified. How this slipped through their censors Hugh couldn't even guess or try to speculate. The fact that he was now reading something simply meant that someone had unknowingly erred in a gravely serious way. The document had been de-classified years ago so that a clerk could enter his name into a long-ago forgotten computer. The document listed Hugh's name alongside Whitman's name and another name that had no meaning at the time for anyone. It had now been laid in Hugh's hands. He suddenly became nervous and thought back to the night that Whitman was killed in Tây Ninh. Where did Bác get the gun? Cao Đàists had their private army dissolved years before under the French and the weapon he saw in Whitman's and subsequently Bác's hands was a small caliber pistol and new. Hugh read further. For some reason, in another folder from the FBI, there was a comment about Hugh's employment history and two failed marriages. An obscure note was made, again referring to continued monitoring and occasional contact over the years for "national security purposes." Apparently, Hugh thought, someone who was to declassify and redact the information didn't feel, at the time, any of this was a national security issue as the US's foreign interests shifted to the Middle East and terrorism, and Communism in Southeast Asia had ceased to be a threat. Hugh now believed the Tây Ninh operation had long lasting effects and documents he now had, along with the CIA file, included some of the key players. He became nervous but felt relieved for once that he was in the care of the police and Quỷ was a "friendly."

Hugh could barely sleep through the night. His sleeplessness wasn't from the dreams, but from his anticipation of seeing Hương again and pondering all the possibilities for them that lie in the future. He also considered the drawbacks for her; an older foreigner with a much younger Vietnamese woman would certainly cause rumors and talk. He didn't want her to get hurt. Then he started deeply contemplating the startling revelations in the documents forwarded to him by his brother. He spent the night laying on top of the bed with a fan blowing on him, and putting all the pieces in correct order. Like a jigsaw puzzle spread out on a dining table, he meticulously put pieces together until they fit and in the morning and thirty-nine years after the classified operation he finally had the entire picture.

He rose early to bathe, shave and put on clean clothes and to get coffee prepared for the Inspector and himself. After getting ready, he went downstairs to the kitchen and put the kettle on to boil and withdrew two glasses from the cupboard. Into each, he poured about two tablespoons worth of *Ông Thọ* sweetened, condensed milk. He then put about three heaping teaspoons of ground Vietnamese coffee into two small metal coffee filters and waited for the water to boil. Once it did, he poured the water into the filters and sat and waited.

The Inspector arrived promptly at seven o'clock. His green uniform was pressed and he was sporting a fresh haircut. "Good morning, Mr. Hugh. I see you are up early. Preparing for a happy day, I believe. You are feeling much better, I hope."

"Yes, Inspector, and I can also tell you, that even though I didn't sleep much last night, I had a very peaceful and fruitful night. I have you partially to thank," Hugh said as he smiled at the Inspector, no longer feeling as though he were a potential adversary.

"Last night you replied to me and said we can begin to conclude this investigation. Please, go ahead," Quỳ asked Hugh respectfully.

"I would like to, but first, let me get our coffee. It should be ready."

Quỳ followed Hugh into the kitchen more out of a need for company and to practice his English than for any other reason. Quỳ said, "I understand you had a very enjoyable evening. My sources have reported to me that you and the young lady have made an instant friendship. That is good to hear. Mr. Hugh, Việt Nam has many good things about her. We may be poor, but we are rich when it comes to family and caring for others. Wouldn't you agree?"

"Yes, Inspector. As we say in the States, 'you've hit the nail on the head.' We did have an enjoyable evening, but more so, I believe my troubling dreams will stop. Do you know why?" Hugh inquired.

"Mr. Hugh, I could only make the guess as you had a very good evening with the young lady. My cousin has already told me. On the next matter, my cousin and I have been trying to solve this for a long time. Maybe you will now reveal some more information that will clarify some things. Be assured, we have trusted you and you have trusted us. I will report to Hà Nội only what Hà Nội will want or need to know. They are still very old fashioned there and I think it is because of the cold winters." Quỳ explained.

"Inspector, last night, as you already also know, I received a courier package from America that my brother sent me. About a couple of years ago, I had requested information about me from the US government. It has been so long ago that I requested it, that I nearly forgot all about it. We are allowed to do such things from our government, but that is rapidly changing under the current administration as they are becoming more secretive. I was surprised at the revelations that somehow got through the over-worked censors. I believe I can tell you things in confidence."

"You have my word, which you know I have already been keeping. Go on," said the mild Inspector.

Hugh began to tell him the entire story related to the mission, but omitted details of the hidden document that had been dispatched from the north. He also spoke about the past interferences with his life and the goading into returning to Việt Nam by Whitman. Hugh had discovered that his perceived paranoia had been vindicated by what he had read in the just-delivered package and in the file that Quỳ and Mai had given him. Hugh also mentioned the name, an obscure name years before, but a name that had slowly gained prominence and was now widely recognized. He had played a hand in all those events and had helped set everything in motion related to the operation in Tây Ninh.

Quỳ listened with interest, hardly believing what he was hearing, but then believing because not only was it plausible, but he knew America liked conspiracies. Quỳ laughed. Americans were almost better at it than the Asians, who were well known for plotting. He remembered a phrase from his US university studies, something about the truth being stranger than fiction. He wondered for a moment, and then Hugh was quiet.

"Mr. Hugh," Quỳ spoke after a silence, "I am now considering aloud new concerns for your safety and other matters, some of the heart. I first wanted to hear what you had to say. I did not tell you, but Mai spoke with Hương last night. She believes she is in love with you. Can you tell me how you are thinking about her?"

"This is an unusual form of questioning, Inspector. What business is it of yours, Mai's or Hà Nội's?" Hugh reacted defensively.

"The business I have made it is that Miss Hương is, by extension, a cousin of mine. We Vietnamese are always concerned about family. Now that you tell me about such information that reaches so far with conspiracy, I have concern not just for your safety, but also the safety of my family. I need to know what you are feeling."

"Inspector, now that you put it in that light, I can tell you that I have done nothing but think about Hương for the past nine hours. Those few hours we spent with each other at dinner and the cafe later convinced me that I do not want to leave your country. You should also know, if you don't already, that it was Hương's mother, Thu Lan, who had been in my dreams and troubling me every night for the past thirty-nine years. Hương is the exact image of her mother and I don't ever want to lose her again and I believe that I am in love with her, also. It's odd to say, but I've been in love with Hương for the past four decades through her mother. That simply cannot change. I will do everything in my power to correct what was done, Inspector, and afterwards, I want to stay here if Hương would have me. I want to stay with her. Is that understandable to you?" Hugh asked the surprised Inspector.

"Yes. My agreement with you is still good. Our family will be pleased and now, by extension, that almost makes you my older cousin. Now, we have a problem. The documents are in Tây Ninh, you say, but you didn't say where. And you have these other documents which reveal your government's concern about you and the documents are here. I also understand, Mr. Hugh, that you are the only guardian of the information contained in those documents, is that correct?" Quỳ's curiosity was continuing to grow.

"I believe so, Inspector. However, there was someone else who helped me at the time. That person may still be alive," Hugh said, not wanting to compromise an old man.

"Mr. Hugh, please tell me what the documents are related to. I will need to decide, for the sake of my country, you understand, just how serious this is. It may be that if it is something embarrassing to my country, then they cannot be revealed. Sadly, I cannot confide or consult with anyone else. This is a burden I will now have to accept, just as you accepted your burden over the past, long years."

Hugh explained in detail what the documents stated. He then explained the reason he now believed what the true mission was. The sole goal of that long-ago operation was the intended destruction of the documents at any cost. Even now, with the additional information from the files and the package, Hugh and Quỳ had the near complete picture and it was overwhelming to them. Hugh glanced at the clock and saw he still had two hours before he and Hương were to meet again.

The two men finished their first glass of iced milk coffee in silence and then assisted each other in brewing another. They sat down on the couch in the front room in silence. Hugh rose momentarily to put a CD in the player that the police had generously provided. It was a CD recorded by Khánh Ly, a Vietnamese woman singing the ballads of Trịnh Công Sơn. Quỳ said, "You have acquired a good ear for the music of our country. Trịnh Công Sơn is like a hero to many. His words are mystical, filled with double meanings and his music is, how can I say?"

"It's hauntingly beautiful," Hugh finished the statement for him.

"Yes, Mr. Hugh, you're right. Now, I have been considering the predicament, as you know. I believe the existence of the documents will not endanger nor will it cause my country to lose face. I believe the existence of those documents and the information you now possess will cause others in your country to lose face. That is now your decision. I believe it is correct to say that for Việt Nam, those documents are merely historical, such as they are. For your country, it is, I cannot think of the word to use; it is when someone is thought guilty and formal charges are brought forward in your courts."

"Indictment, Quỳ?"

"Ah, yes, Mr. Hugh. It is an indictment against those in your country. I have made a decision; I trust it is correct, that you shall bear the documents yourself and do with them what you shall. I shall do what I can within my limited bureaucratic powers to protect you here until whatever outcome of your decision is made. You will have the protection, as long as I can approve it, of the police here, but it cannot be forever. You will have to move quickly and I am afraid I can only justify your presence for maybe one more month, Mr. Hugh. You will have to be decisive and much sooner would be better."

"Thank you, Inspector. I believe I know what to do. It's a matter of timing. I do need to return to Tây Ninh, though."

"If it is to meet the family of Hương, as you have been already invited, that I already know, then you must return to Tây Ninh. It is a sacred duty and responsibility to pay respects to the ones you have carried in your heart for so long. Of course, you will be followed and Mr. Hugh, please do not evade those who are protecting you. I fear that what happened to Mr. Whitman, the same fate may befall you." How true the words sounded from the Inspector, Hugh thought.

The late-season football playoff game was being watched by millions of fans, including Paul, who sat with his wife on the couch. A typical late fall-timed television commercial for soup began to play, when suddenly Paul went flush and felt faint. His wife immediately rang for help; her husband was beginning to pass out again for an unknown reason. She told Paul to continue to lie down and a nurse, who was always close at hand, was summoned to check his pulse and blood pressure. As the nurse began to check Paul's vitals, he pushed her away and demanded to see Carla, his personal political advisor and confidant. Carla was a very aggressive woman and let people know it. Paul's wife wanted to know what was wrong. Why the sudden fainting spell?

"Is it from those drugs in the past again?" she asked. I know that happens to people, honey. If it is, we can cover it up again. Is it?"

"No" was his curt reply and Paul rose from the couch and went to his office. "I'll see you later."

Paul was sitting in his office when Carla walked in. They hadn't spoken for the past few days because everything seemed to be on autopilot for Paul. Carla asked, "You wanted to see me?"

"Yes, I remembered that name. I saw a soup commercial and suddenly I remembered that name. I think we might have a big problem. What other memos or documents have my name on them from almost forty years ago?" Paul demanded to know.

"There's no way to know. You'd have to tell me what you were doing specifically so we can backtrack and try to cover relevant agencies. We already know State and CIA had your name in some obscure files and quite possibly, the FBI; but that was when you were completely unknown."

Paul disliked her assessment of his earlier days. It made him remember that he lived in the shadow of his Senator father's shadow and that also of the Chairman. "Sir, you'll have to tell me everything you know so I'll know where to begin and what we need to do," she urged.

Paul told him his role in working for the Chairman. He also told him he believed that his name had never been used, but it must have, and now, yes, he does remember he assured the Chairman that he personally would be notified should anything come back to them and that the officer should be monitored. He didn't realize that almost forty years later it would come back to haunt him, not at this time, not in his position.

"Carla, we need to put a clamp on this now."

"Sir, it will be difficult to track down every last reference, but we have places to start at State and CIA, and maybe DOD. I believe we can catch up soon and take care of it. Why don't you go back to watching the game and I'll handle it," Carla reassured him.

"Gosh, that's great, Carla. You've been my most trusted friend ever," moaned Paul as he walked out of the office.

"Thank you, sir," Carla replied. Shit, she thought. How many fuckups has this guy had that I've had to save his ass and now this! Carla thought if it hadn't been for her own position of confidence and all the perquisites it allowed, she would have given up on this asshole long ago. But, now she had a job to do to save Paul's ass and her own job and power. She also thought she needed to start distancing herself from him – just in case of a disaster.

II

Hugh went out the front gate and looked down the quiet street on the chance there would be a taxi. There was none, so he walked. It was a nice morning for a stroll and he heard the idling motorbikes of his followers behind him. It hadn't b   get hot yet and the rain the night before turned to a light drizzle in the middle of the night. The streets glistened from the overnight rain and the sun's reflection was nearly blinding at that angle. As he neared the main road, he saw the motorbikes in their morning race to work, each with its own rooster tail of water thrown up by the rear tire as they continued to jostle for their positions as part of the daily traffic ritual. What did it matter, thought Hugh, everyone is usually late anyway. Out on the main road, away from house, he found a Mei Linh Taxi with the familiar white and green motif and it was vacant. The driver had been tweezing his chin whiskers when Hugh walked up to him, got into the taxi and gave him the address near Chợ Lớn in District Five. Hugh thought to himself, he didn't need to say District Five. Where else would Chợ Lớn be?

He arrived at her house, just a few blocks from Trần Hưng Đạo, the main road through the area named for the famous military hero who routed the Mongol army from Việt Nam in the thirteenth century. Hugh suddenly recalled Trần Hưng Đạo Street in Tây Ninh behind the Anh Đào Hotel where he stayed the last night of Whitman's life and the the street where the General Hospital is located. He paid the taxi driver and asked him to wait patiently for him. He was glad to because he wouldn't have to look for another fare out here in the predominantly Chinese area. The driver was *kinh*, a Việt, and had his own prejudices.

Hugh pressed the bell at the front gate and heard it ring somewhere inside. He heard numerous muffled voices coming from the open windows letting in the cool morning air; noises of hurry, noises of questions, though he couldn't make out the words. Soft women's voices sang to each other and an occasional male voice provided a counter-point filtered through the iron grates on the windows. A moment later, Hương appeared at the front door and came out to unlock the front gate and let Hugh in. The house was unlike the long and narrow houses that were so predominant in the city. This one had a small courtyard with potted flowering plants in the front and taller, potted trees as one approached the front door painted a glossy red. Yellow apricot flowers dotted the pathway to the door and Hương seemed to float on the petals as she walked out towards him in her áo dài.

She had white, silk trousers underneath the long tunic. The silk dress, split at the sides, was an elusive shade of lavender with pastel yellow flowers embroidered upon it. Hương, who stood a mere five feet tall and weighed less than ninety pounds, seemed the epitome of grace as she glided towards him. Her black hair was down this morning and it shone in the morning sun. Hugh recalled her having her hair in the typical 'chicken tail' the night before, the style that most Vietnamese women and girls wore their hair; pulled together and tied at the back of the head, rather than at the base of the hairline. She had the barest hint of makeup and a subtle coating of lip gloss. As she approached, her head was slightly tilted downward to watch where she was stepping and she raised her trousers' pant legs to keep them clean because she was barefoot. He looked down at her feet as she began to release the two locks on the gate. Her feet were also delicate like the rest of her; small but slender, long willowy toes, nails trimmed straight and veins pressing lightly against the amber hue of her skin at the ankles. Just like her mother, as he was remembering more. She let him in, relocked the gate and invited him to enter the house. He paused, turned to the driver and said, "*Một chút, Anh ơi.*" Just a moment. The driver nodded and returned to tweezing chin hairs loose from his skin.

Hugh entered the home, stooped to loosen the straps of his sandals and pet the tiger-striped cat that purred its way around his ankles. He was invited into the front room and Hương asked if he wouldn't mind paying his respects to the ancestors. As most homes in Southeast Asia, one will find family shrines, dedicated to the memory of the ancestors. Photos of the deceased share an honored place in the house and fruit and incense are offered to please them. Hugh was only partially familiar with the ritual from his experience at Thảo's grandmother's funeral several days before. She lit the incense for him from a small oil lamp that was kept permanently lit on the table and he remembered the long-forgotten passageway leading to the opium house he visited in the days before he left Việt Nam so many years before. Hương's lavender áo dài also struck the same memory chord of the young girl, who tended him those last few days, and he ached for the lost years spent away from a land that he truly loved; the only place he really felt comfortable and comforted. He looked into Hương's eyes and saw, yet again, her mother, Thu Lan. Suddenly Hugh ached to be with her, to share very private and tender moments and to share each other.

"Is something wrong? You look sad," she asked him demurely.

"No, quite the opposite. Those many years I spent away from this country left a large vacuum in my heart." She looked at him quizzically and wondered about the meaning of the literal translation of his words. He saw her puzzling look and decided to rephrase his sentiment.

"There's a big empty place in my heart because I have been away for so long and memories of your mother were buried by my mind. And now, being back here, being with you, the heat, the smells, the weather, everything, Hương, is flooding into that empty spot and filling it. It's almost like a newborn that is beginning to experience the new world and wants to take everything in at the same time."

"I understand. Be slow, Mr. Hugh. Please be slow and you must take care of yourself. I want you to enjoy your life here. If fate is meant for us to be together, we will have time," she offered.

"Yes, Hương, but at sixty-one, I have fears of growing old and being alone." He surprised himself at revealing a deep vulnerability.

"You will not be alone. Do not fear. I have spoken to my cousin and you should know I also know how you feel. We feel the same way, so do not fear," she said reassuringly and quietly touched his tanned and hairy forearm with her fingertips while allowing her straight hair to fall forward.

Hugh was briefly introduced to the Aunt and Uncle, who smiled courteously at the first foreigner to grace their doors. Hương and Hugh left the house soon after finishing their green tea and visiting shortly with the older couple. Hugh told the taxi driver, who had been napping, they wanted to go *Thảo Cầm Viên*, the Saigon Zoo. They spent a few hours walking around the zoo looking at the animals that spent their idle time watching the people from inside their dismal enclosures; the humans provided amusement for them. Walking around the botanical gardens, Hương reached for Hugh's arm for the first time, putting her hand at the lower part of his bicep, and they walked slowly in the cool of the morning realizing there was an entire future ahead of them. She thought about home and family. He thought about her and the immediate need to finish the task begun so many years before. He needed to get back to Tây Ninh. He was quiet, trying to formulate a plan and needed to do it without involving her. He needed to tell her the truth about the operation and the contents of the document and his other revelations. But he also knew if "they," select people in the US and possibly in Việt Nam, were aware of his travels, which he did not doubt after Whitman's violent death and the incident of the visit while he was having coffee, Hương could also be in jeopardy. He needed help and either the Vietnamese police or Mai would have to help. He wanted neither, and he felt vulnerable.

She watched him as he stared into nothingness, a place that frightened her and she asked, "Hugh," now becoming familiar and omitting 'mister' from his name, "are you okay? What is the matter?" her voice expressed deep concern.

"My dear, it's just that I still have important business to tend to here in Việt Nam before I can return to the States and clear up my business there. I also need to do it soon while I have the time. If I take too long, it may become too much of a problem," he explained.

She simply replied, "I know." He knew what she meant by those two words. He suspected Inspector Quỳ would have talked to his cousin, Mai, and she in turn would have spoken to Hương. They were all involved now, they were all family and he didn't want anyone hurt, but he was feeling supported for the first time.

She broke his thought by suggesting, "We should go to Tây Ninh tomorrow. I want you to meet my family. From there, I have a close friend who can help. I will help you through this difficult time. You have family now. Please do not worry for yourself. Let us plan to spend a peaceful day together and tomorrow we will work this out."

"My dear," he began, "you are incredible. I don't want to compare you to your mother, but you share the same traits. She was wonderful at being able to work under intense and stressful situations with grace and style. Even that last night we had together, she saved my life; I told you that. She was calm the entire time and supportive."

Hugh wanted to tell her he was in love with her, but hesitated because he feared she would think he loved her mother vicariously through her. He wanted Hương to know that he loved her for herself, but he knew separating the two would be as difficult as separating conjoined twins who shared a heart. His heart was wrenching. He now wanted to protect Hương as her mother, Thu Lan, had protected him, but how could he if he doesn't know what he is up against. He worried and wanted her out of harm's way, yet realized he did need her help. He had to remember that when a Vietnamese offered help, it is sincere and genuine and Hương may be aware of the potential dangers.

Several blocks away, without each other knowing about their close proximity, another meeting was being held inside the US Consulate. The CIA Station Chief was briefing his agents about the newest message that came in from Langley, Virginia, more than eleven thousand miles removed from the world of reality for Hương, Hugh and his deceased friend, Whitman Emerson.

"This only gets more interesting. The latest communication regards the primary target, Hugh Campbell, US citizen, currently located somewhere in Hồ Chí Minh City. Fortunately, we know where he is, but here's the kicker. Seems this guy has secreted highly classified documents during the war thirty-some years ago, let's see, back in '66, and they have the greatest potential to damage the reputation of the United States and her allies and will threaten any and all future relations with Việt Nam and other nations in Southeast Asia. I have no fucking idea what this all means, except the war's been over for more than thirty years, and someone feels something here will threaten the US. Alright, we've been watching the Muslim community in the Phú Nhuận and First Districts, but they're quiet, so let's pool our resources to figure this out.

"We know the two targets, target two now deceased, conducted a CIA-handled black op in 1966. That's almost forty years ago. We know there was a courier from the north carrying, what were considered, highly classified strategic and tactical battle plans for the south. But, we also know, there was a meeting to take place with a Vietnamese agent from the south's regime at the same time. From some old notes someone has in DC that were passed on, a pouch was apparently destroyed, but no proof of destruction offered or witnesses to it."

Anh, still embarrassed from the incident in Tây Ninh was the first to ask, "Sir, what can possibly be important from almost forty years ago. That's when the target was here last. We have incomplete information about the operation, but if the documents are old battle plans, there's no value to them. What's the real story?"

The chief newly assigned and still struggling with the heat replied, "Anh, I don't know. We've got orders to monitor the target, his activities and contacts and determine where the documents are and to destroy them ourselves."

The other agent had been sitting quietly sipping an iced tea brought to him by one of the women civilian employees. He asked, "Sir, this isn't another case of alleged, purloined, yellow cake uranium for nuclear weapons, is it?" he asked apparently referring to a fabricated incident that involved the Company to try and build a case by the executive branch of the United States to justify another war elsewhere in the world. "Sir, the Company has taken some pretty dirty shots by the Taylor administration and I'm just wondering if there's something else going on and we're being used for political purposes again," he posited.

"You bring up a good point. The fucking politicos in Washington have been using the agency for its own ends without concern and fabricating or editing information to suit their goals. Tell you what. We will do what we're told. Exercise caution, especially you Anh. You'll still be on this as only two persons saw you. One is dead and the other is a frightened old man. Be cautious, don't take chances and if the locals get involved, back off, but get the documents. My curiosity is building on this one. You guys are right. We might be getting set up. God, I hate those assholes in DC. I'm getting hungry. Let's go eat."

Hugh and Hương spent the rest of the morning taking in the War Remnant Museum on Vô Văn Tần Street, then decided to find an air-conditioned restaurant for lunch. Hugh had been told about another vegetarian restaurant that came highly recommended, Cơm Chay Nàng Tấm, at 79 Bis Điện Biên Phủ Street in District One in the Đa Kao Ward. Hugh remembered Dakow, as it was also spelled, as the place where Graham Greene's CIA character, Alden Pyle, was killed on his way to meet Thomas Fowler at the Vieux Moulin.

They arrived at the restaurant and waited in the car in the narrow alley while three men, two Caucasians and a Vietnamese, entered another waiting taxi and drove off. Hugh and Hương were led to a table by the lone waitress, clad in black skirt, a formless, drab green jacket and black shoes that appeared uncomfortable.

Quiet and reserved, she led the couple to a table, offered menus and set about pouring iced tea in the small tumblers. Without comment, she stood there, waited and then took their order, jotting down notes on the single pad of paper. Hugh and Hương were already tired from the emotions of the previous night and the jaunts to the zoo and museum. They sat quietly, each not thinking, but living in each other's company.

Quietly, the young waitress returned with dishes and carefully placed them on the table. Her long slender fingers gently placed small bowls with chili peppers on the table and then poured *nước tương*, soya sauce, over the peppers and removed the wooden chopsticks from their paper sheaths and set them lightly on the white porcelain cradles. She asked in her northern dialect if there was anything else she could get them. Hương replied, *"Không, cảm ơn, chị,"* no, thank you, ma'm.

Hương took Hugh's empty bowl and placed some fried rice in it, added two *nem rán*, the fried spring rolls that he liked, and some sauteed vegetables and then she served herself. Hugh was adept at using chopsticks and had already won Hương's admiration the night before for his skill. What little talking they did was confined to her extended family and how everyone was related. This fascinated Hugh. She warned him with a smile about meeting the entire family some day and having to share meals at everyone's house from Tây Ninh to Hồ Chí Minh City.

"We will have to visit the family's homeland in Nam Đình for Tết, southeast of Hà Nội," she included, mentioning the Lunar New Year holiday.

Hugh decided to finally broach the subject of returning as soon as possible to Tây Ninh, to meet the family, "yes, by all means," but to finish the work; for to let it pass any longer without action very well may threaten his well-being and quite possibly Hương's, as well. He had a difficult time trying to explain the depth and scope of the information he had and how it could affect so many people in America and that is why he was now beginning to fear for his own safety. Mentioning the gun that killed Whitman caused her to become frightened for, as she explained, "Việt Nam is a peaceful country. We have no need of guns here."

He also explained, "Hương, I believe that gun may have been brought by another person. I have been trying to piece that part of the puzzle together. Whitman and I came over together, went through the same airport security checkpoints and they should have caught the gun that killed him or the knife that cut me. I only saw a glimmer of the gun afterwards. I think there was another person, a professional, that either gave Whitman the gun and knife or, or," he stammered, "I just don't know. But, my dear, putting that information together with all the documents that were released to me and some quite by accident, this whole thing goes much farther than Tây Ninh, Hồ Chí Minh City and Việt Nam. It reaches all the way back to America and when something like that happens, nothing good can come of it, especially if powerful people feel threatened or believe they're backed into a corner.

"I don't know how much time I have, and I don't know how much other people know, whoever they are. I am absolutely positive there are people here already in Việt Nam who know about me. Quỳ told me about one person already, and they want what they think I might already have. I know it's a lot for you to understand at one time, but I ask you to trust me. I'm also asking you to help me. I can trust your cousin, Quỳ, but he does work for the police. I wouldn't want him to get into trouble because he has brought you and me together. He helped to unlock the nightmares that have bothered me for nearly forty years and I owe him so much that can never be fully repaid. So, I don't want to jeopardize his job or career. I need your help, Hương," he finished and felt relieved of the burden.

Hương was trying to understand everything he was saying, but he was using phrases she hadn't learned before and he was apparently agitated and spoke a little hurriedly. He was talking about people in America who might want to hurt him, she believed. It was all so much. She knew, however, that her position would be to help him and be at his side through whatever troubles he may have to endure. She felt that they already belonged to each other and it was her duty to be with him. After contemplating her role, she finally looked at him and replied in her gentle voice.

"I will help you. We must together return to Aunt and Uncle's house. There we can rest for the afternoon. We are both tired and need sleep. Uncle will let you sleep on his bed if he is not using it already. After some rest, we will begin to make plans. I can call friends in Tây Ninh who will help. They have a car and there are other places that will be safe to hide should we need that. I also have another Aunt and Uncle who can help. He used to be a Captain in the Army of Việt Nam, for the South, but he is very trustworthy. He broke his leg many years ago and is, what you say, crippled?

He knows everybody in Tây Ninh. Aunt is a school teacher and has taught many people who could not pay her and also will help if we ask. Hugh, we can do this together. I will do it for the memory of my mother. If what you tell me is true about the document, she would have wanted you to finish your work. But, first, we must rest."

It was nearing two in the afternoon and they were still at the restaurant. They had finished the meal long ago and the front door already locked for the employees' afternoon rest. Hugh looked for the waitress to pay and took his wallet out to look for some money. He remembered something he had kept in his wallets from many years ago. It was always transferred to a new wallet when the previous one had worn out. Placed behind his drivers license was an old paper twenty piastres note left over from the previous regime's currency in Saigon. He took it out and handed it to Hương.

She looked at it and said, "This is something we teach little girls; to fold paper money into stars and swans, like this one, with the heart in the middle. Who gave this to you?" she asked.

"I now remembered it was in my wallet and had been for many years. I didn't realize I still had it until now. Your mother gave it to me many years ago in Tây Ninh. I would like you to have it. Your mother made it and I have faithfully kept it all these years, not remembering where it came from or who gave it to me. Now I know and you should have it as a reminder of your mother."

"But, I believe you should keep it as a reminder of my mother. She gave it to you to show her love."

"You, my dear, are a perfect reminder of your mother, even though you are your own separate, beautiful woman," Hugh replied as Hương blushed and glanced downward in shyness for a moment.

The waitress came over with the bill and Hugh gladly paid her. The waitress saw them to the door and the doorman closed the yellow-painted gate after they left so the restaurant workers could continue napping before they began preparations for the dinner service. They found a taxi at the corner of two alleys, across from a middle school. The driver was dozing, but grateful to make some additional money. To him, a foreigner meant a good tip. She told the driver where to take them in Chợ Lớn. The economy-sized blue taxi easily wove its way down one-way streets through District One, as traffic was light at the tail end of *ngủ trưa*, the noon nap. Hugh began to nod off in the air-conditioned car; blinking his eyes, trying to fight the sleep that was overtaking him. The afternoon was warm and his stomach was full; a perfect recipe for being lethargic and needing the required time to sleep. Turning off Trần Hưng Đạo Street and into a hẻm, the taxi pulled up to the side of the residence in the alley. Hugh paid the twenty-six thousand đồng for the trip and tipped him an extra five thousand. This made the driver happy. He could now find a shady spot, tweeze his chin and then take another nap before workers began heading home.

"There's no sign of him. He's been gone all day," Anh reported to his Chief.

"What do your contacts say?" he asked.

"They're not talking now. I'm not sure what happened, but no one is willing to share information with me."

"Don't you have the twist on some of them? Don't some owe you favors?"

"That didn't work. It's as if suddenly they don't care or don't want to be involved, but I think somebody's pitched something to them and they're all quiet. Nobody's talking about anything. You can't even get the time of day, hardly," Anh clarified. He was at a loss to explain his few contacts' reluctance to talk.

"Perhaps if they had a different handler," the chief offered.

Anh interrupted his chief, something that surprised even him, "Sir, with all due respect, that's not the case. Any twist I have on them or whatever their need for money, they're simply not speaking. I've seen this numerous times before; it's like when a family starts protecting each other."

"Family, you said?" asked the Chief. "Campbell doesn't have family here." The CIA Station Chief realized he had used a target's name and wondered suddenly if he was becoming personally involved. He had been wondering all day about the Company being used and how the Taylor administration in Washington had outed one of their operatives in retribution for a whistle-blowing incident. 'God, I hate fucking politics,' he grumbled to himself.

"No, sir, you're right. He doesn't have family. I can't figure it out, but it seems that their level of protection has increased above what is considered normal. In fact, this level of security and protection is quite out of the ordinary. It is like he's become family. I know it's easy for Vietnamese to be protective of someone who is a foreigner and takes on the customs, traditions and language of the culture, but I just don't know about the primary target," the officer offered.

The second officer, Earl, offered a suggestion, "Chief, why don't I talk to a couple contacts and encourage them to break loose with some information. You know I've had success with it in the past."

The chief interrupted him saying, "That won't work. We can't muscle the locals. This is now a friendly government and that would work against the best interests of the United States. We've got orders, but the administration has been fucking with the agency for a long time. I'm almost tempted to say 'fuck 'em' but if we don't do a thing we can probably all kiss our asses and our cushy jobs here good bye. You know what they've done in the past; suddenly reclassifying officers as contractors and washing their hands of them. We'd all be written off. Let me kick it around tonight and see what sort of an operation we can come up with that won't piss off the locals or tip them off to what we're doing but at the same time, we won't be seen as sitting on our fucking hands either. I won't give those assholes in Washington any bullets to shoot us with. We'll meet at the 155 Cafe on Nguyễn Văn Trôi at nine in the morning. Most of the locals will be gone by then and we can sit upstairs without being interrupted.

The two officers left the US Consulate compound by way of the eastern gate on Mạc Đình Chi Street. They hated the current political environment that would use the agency for some larger global business plan than for national security. Once the officers reached the outside, they didn't make eye contact with the Vietnamese policemen carrying their automatic rifes, but continued walking. Reaching the sidewalk, they said goodbye and walked in opposite directions.

One of the unseen of Việt Nam, a tattered and tired, old man across the street with a sweat-stained ball cap tilted to shade his eyes, had just been resting in the canopied front seat on his foot-powered cyclo in front of the silk tie store and watched idly as the men walked away in different directions. He waited another ten minutes, lit a "555" cigarette with a wooden match, and pushed his antique three-wheeled vehicle to get momentum, then climbed on the seat and began cycling. He inched his way through motorbikes, cars and buses south along Mạc Đĩnh Chi Street and across the wide street, Lê Duẩn where the US Consulate fronted the street. He kept pedaling on further down and turned right at the corner, where the one-way street ends at Nguyễn Du Street and the hospital. Another block of pedaling and he found himself at the Asia Restaurant. He parked his cyclo in front of the inn that was decorated with an abundance of lush, potted plants. He didn't bother chaining it to a tree. Nobody in their right mind dared steal a poor man's weather-beaten and rusted cyclo with the old "PHX" license plate. He walked inside and went straight through to the kitchen and out the back. Seated in the secluded back was a pea-green uniformed policeman, his hat resting on a nearby chair. He was having an iced milk coffee in the afternoon and reading the newspaper. The policeman picked up his hat and offered the seat to the man.

"What do you have for me, Uncle?" he inquired.

"I'm not sure how long the meeting was, but they were in the compound from mid-morning until a little while ago. Three left before lunch time and returned about an hour later. It was the Station Chief and the two officers; one Vietnamese, the other American. The two agents left the east gate together but took different directions," he reported.

"Thank you, Uncle. What do you make of it?"

"The increase in their meetings lately, especially at the Consulate, is something interesting. I don't think their purposes are with our government but something else. We don't have anything, except for our offshore oil fields that would interest the Americans. Their businesses are here only because they see a chance to get in at a low price and get out later when the price is higher and send the money back to America. It's their history to exploit like that; like the French. So, it's not our oil, yet, that they want. They're too busy elsewhere in the world to worry about us. I think it may have something to do with one of their people, like you suggested," he said.

"Very observant, Uncle. You may be right. My other sources don't think it's anything about our country. It's about their citizen. As always, thank you, Uncle. I hope this small offering will help you through the next few days," the policeman said as he handed the cyclo driver an envelope. He opened the envelope and quickly fingered the cash inside.

"Thank you, very much, Nephew. I wish you happiness, health and good luck in your work. I believe you may need it. You may call on me anytime." The cyclo driver in the old rubber sandals, faded and torn blue pants and a green, button down, sweat-stained shirt walked out the front. He turned his cyclo around in the street, pushed it off and jumped on to take advantage of the momentum and he went looking for a fare. He hoped to get a western tourist because they tip the best, he thought.

Quỳ sipped at his soothing afternoon drink while he evaluated the information his uncle, and some others before, gave him. He was becoming concerned for Hugh's safety and would help see to it that he got to Tây Ninh to finish what was started by others so many years ago; a plan that was against the Vietnamese people long ago and for what he believed was evil. He went to a phone and called his headquarters to get a report from the followers who had cell phones.

"Inspector, they are not back yet. They are at your Aunt and Uncle's house in Chợ Lớn since they returned from lunch in District One. They have only been to museums, the zoo and lunch," the officer at the other end of the telephone reported.

"Thank you. Let me know if they move."

Inspector Quỳ decided that it would be better to discuss matters with Mr. Hugh at the Uncle's house rather than the safe house. He knew it was also being watched by others and didn't want to provide them with any intelligence. They would have to work for it the way he worked for his. He went out to the front, and without having to pay the two-thousand đồng parking fee, though he offered, got on his Honda Dream and pulled into traffic, heading west on Nguyễn Du Street. He knew it was faster, with fewer lights and much less traffic than the larger congested streets and he could make it to his Uncle's house in about twenty minutes. Time enough, maybe, to be able to be invited for dinner.

III

Quỳ checked his watch and noticed it did, in fact, take him twenty minutes to reach the District Five house of his relations. He rang the bell at the gate and waited. In a few moments, the housekeeper peeked through the red enameled door and came out to unlock the gate and let him in. She recognized him immediately, as she had always dreamt about this young police Inspector and about a life with him and having a family. Quỳ had also always noticed her, but was afraid to say anything to her for fear she would not return the affection he had for her. What a shame, he thought quietly. What a shame, she thought quietly.

She led the young Inspector to the front room and returned with a tray and on it were a hot teapot and small cups. She wiped the inside of a cup and poured the steaming liquid into it and offered it to him with two hands, eyes cast downward as he accepted it. She looked upwards for a moment and they looked in each other's eyes and let, yet, another moment pass without saying something to each other, except "*Cảm ơn, em nhé.*" Thank you.

The Aunt came in through the side door and asked the Inspector if he had paid his respects to the ancestors after he entered their house. Without replying, he set the teacup down and went to light the incense and offered it at the family shrine.

"Someday, we will be dead and would appreciate your honoring us, as once you're dead you will want someone honoring you, if you ever find a suitable wife," she admonished him.

"Auntie, I am sorry, it is because there are important things on my mind."

"What in heaven and earth could be more important than your own deceased ancestors and taking care of them?" she offered rhetorically to Quỳ.

"Nothing, but I am here to see the foreigner. I believe he is here and has been visiting with cousin Hương today."

"Yes, he is still resting; you know how foreigners have difficulty with our weather and heat. But, I think he may get accustomed to it soon enough."

The Aunt then called for the housekeeper and she arrived immediately. She had been around the corner listening to the sound of Quỳ voice. "Mistress, you called for me?"

"Yes, see if the foreigner is awake yet. Ask him to come in. He has a visitor. Don't tell him who it is as he may become frightened. You know how foreigners are," she warned her.

"Auntie, I don't believe he will be frightened of my being here. Mr. Hugh and I have become a bit more than friends," Quỳ said.

It was still several minutes later, after Quỳ heard muffled sounds of voices, water splashing and heavy footsteps on the hardwood floors, that he saw the figure of Hugh filling the doorway. Quỳ stood and invited Hugh to come in and take a seat on the wooden divan.

"Auntie, we do have some business to talk about. May we talk alone, please?" Quỳ asked the doting woman.

"Yes, it is enough to know my own nephew will forget us, so I may as well get used to the idea now," she said instilling guilt in the young policeman.

After the Aunt walked out, Hugh turned to Quỳ and asked, "What brings you out here. I am not surprised you know where I am and you know how I feel about your cousin."

"That is the exact reason why I am here. I am grateful for the two of you finding each other and I know how each of you feels about the other." Hugh looked at him; surprised, but elated. "You are becoming family and we help protect each other. Mr. Hugh, I have concerns that others may be planning things. I have no proof, but only suspicions. I cannot tell you how I know, which you would expect, but if you have made a decision of what to do, it must be done quickly before others become aware."

"Inspector, just today at lunch, Hương and I were discussing my need to return to Tây Ninh. As you know, I have something there that needs to be recovered and I am also concerned when thinking about all the things that have happened. I decided, though, that I didn't want you to know or to help because you may have problems over this later and I didn't want to jeopardize your job or career."

"Mr. Hugh, that is very honorable for you to think that, but I am a party member and my job is secure. All my ratings are very high and I have benefactors in higher places who have noticed my work. Did you not think it odd that I was assigned to your case for the investigation? When I heard your name, I went to my benefactors and asked them to assign the investigation to me. They did it as a favor. They will watch out for me as I have also watched out for them." Hugh understood what Quỳ meant. He may have had embarrassing information that was guaranteeing his career.

"Well, as your career is guaranteed, as you say, I will accept the invitation of your help. I need to get to Tây Ninh as soon as possible without anyone noticing. I'm not small and I don't have black hair, so getting me out of town may be difficult if others are watching."

Quỳ was quick to tell him, "Yes, we do know that you are being watched. But, it seems they were not serious this morning. But we believe they may be more interested as they are increasing pressure on my people and are having longer meetings. Mr. Hugh, I believe that it may have been an American agent who killed Mr. Whitman. Do you agree?" he asked.

"Inspector," Hugh suddenly stopped himself and thought a moment.

"Inspector, I believe you may be right," he said now using the chance to alter a fact to protect Bác, his old friend, as the outcome would never change: Whitman was still dead. "You see, I have been thinking about this all along. I didn't want to say anything before, and please forgive me, but I told people it may have been a robbery. Whitman didn't have a gun or a knife. We went through airport security in Los Angeles and they inspected our bags, x-rayed them and who knows what else they do, before they're satisfied the baggage is clear. It was a man who killed Whitman and who cut me after I knocked the gun free." Hugh was not above giving a different version to protect his friend. "It was dark, but my eyes had become used to the darkness. I'm sorry for not telling you before. I wanted to try and evaluate the information for myself."

"Mr. Hugh, we believe there may be a Vietnamese and an American who are part of the planning. Are you prepared to go to Tây Ninh immediately?" Quỳ asked.

"As a matter of fact, yes, Inspector, I am. It's only two hours, wait, at this time, we'd better add another hour, so let's say we get there around seven tonight, we may be back before eleven. Is that possible?" Hugh asked.

Quỳ thought for a moment and replied, "Yes, all I have to do is order a car and have it brought here to pick us up. Yes, that would work." The inspector reached for his cell phone in his pocket. He dialed a number, waited and then dialed another series of other numbers to obtain a secure line rented through Viettel Phone Company, which is owned by the Ministry of Defense. It took a few moments for the connection. He spoke into the phone requesting an unmarked, fast car with blacked out windows to meet him. He gave the address and pressed the "end" button, terminating the phone call. "It will be here momentarily." Quỳ noticed the lower portion of the housekeeper's red-flowered, yellow cotton pants around the corner near the door. "Mr. Hugh, you may want to take this time to visit with Miss Hương."

He then lowered his voice and called to the housekeeper, "*Em ơi, lại đây.*"

"Yes, older brother," she replied using the formal term for the older, unrelated Inspector.

"You have been listening to a private conversation. What business is it of yours and what is your interest?" he sternly demanded.

Beginning to cry, she said softly, "Older brother, I have no business or interest in what you say to the foreigner. I don't understand what you say in English and I have no care about what you say in Vietnamese. But, I think now that you accuse me of spying on you and I need to tell the truth in my own defense that it is only the sound of your voice I want to hear, it is only to see your reflection in the lacquered door of the cabinet behind you that gives me happiness. I am not a criminal and I am not a spy. Please forgive me for wanting to only hear and see you." She quickly turned away sobbing and ran down the hallway leaving the Inspector stunned.

The Aunt came in a moment later after seeing the young girl running past her room and crying. "So, Nephew Inspector. Your are good at solving crimes but you cannot see when someone near you is guilty of having feelings of affection for you. How will you survive without a wife?" she asked in frustration.

"Auntie, I didn't know. I truly didn't now what she felt about me. Maybe it would make her happy to know that I have had feelings for her and have watched her also. Perhaps I should have a talk with her."

"Perhaps you should. She is sitting in the kitchen embarrassed and afraid that you do not respect her. I do not want to lose such a valuable housekeeper like her, but it is time for you and her to talk. Such a silly nephew; has to be told to pay respects to his ancestors. What are the young people coming to nowadays?" she complained as she turned away and walked back to her room to continue her rest. All this fuss going on in her house tired her and she then complained to her ancestors for leaving such ill-mannered progeny behind.

The Mercedes sedan arrived within a half hour of Quỳ making the request. The car had license plates with the black letter and number combination on a white field rather than a blue field that indicated the car belonged to the government. Such a car was only used for special cases like this when the police did not want their government-presence known to others. The windows in the back were tinted black and for extra protection, sunshades covered the inside of the windows so it would be difficult for occupants to see outside as well. The car sat idling in the alley and the driver stood outside, opened a "Craven" cigarette packet and took one out to smoke. The driver didn't mind smoking in a restaurant while he waited for his meal, oblivious to the smoke blowing onto other diners who didn't like the smoke with their meal, but he wouldn't smoke in the unmarked police vehicle. He stood near the wall, but didn't lean on it fearing paint dust would stain his black shirt and pants. He nearly finished the cigarette when the Inspector came out followed by a foreigner and a Vietnamese woman.

The driver observed the speed rules for most of the way. Nearing Trảng Bàng, Quỳ asked if he should take the back way into Tây Ninh. Hương, who had just been over that route a few weeks before on her return to Tây Ninh objected advising that the back way added another ten kilometers to the trip and the road was much more rough with many sections still under construction. Hugh, sitting with Hương in the back contented himself trying to look outside by moving the sunshades and trying to locate the remains of the old French watchtowers that were placed every kilometer between Saigon and Tây Ninh. Occasionally, he would see what seemed to be the remains of foundations of buildings that could have been the watchtowers. He saw the foundations were, as he measured, nearly a kilometer apart, but he couldn't be sure. He was fascinated by the French presence and the architectural heritage left behind, but he didn't like the French colonialism. Then again, he thought on that darkening drive to Tây Ninh, he didn't like the reasons the US went into Southeast Asia with its chemical warfare, napalm, white phospherous and carpet bombing. The damage to humanity, families torn apart, bodies ripped to shreds, burned or vaporized, inhumane and incorrigible acts of brutality against others, for what? he wondered. How senseless the horrors of the past. He looked metaphorically behind him and saw the caravans of ghosts, not just from Việt Nam, but from genocides in Cambodia, East Timor, Poland, Germany and humanity was powerless to stop its march to self-destruction. Hugh realized he had to finish what he started and to finally come face to face with the ghosts not only in his house, but the houses of countless others who died for no apparent reason, except....

"What are you thinking about, Anh?" Hương asked. She felt comfortable enough with Hugh to stop using his first name and used a more familiar term.

"Nothing, just this and that, trying to think some things through. We should be there soon, won't we?" Hugh asked.

"Maybe another fifteen minutes. We passed Cẩm Giang Market a few moments ago. You had a very sad and lost look on your face while you looked outside. I felt sad also," she offered him in the form of compassion only in a way a soft-spoken Vietnamese woman can.

"Where are we going to stop first?"

"We are going straight to my father's house while there is still some light remaining in the day. He wants to show you something because he is not sure when he will see you again. My father and you are nearly the same age, did you know?"

"No, I hadn't thought about it, but that would make sense."

They arrived on the outskirts of Tây Ninh almost to the minute as predicted by Hương. In a little area a short drive from the main highway leading into town on the west bank of the river, the car pulled onto a dirt road, pitted from years of rains and subsequent refilling of the red dirt in the holes. Hugh believed this area was near the site of the old Tây NinhWest where it all began, and he remembered the days at the colonel's house and the girl he fell in love with. Now he was sitting with her daughter who was dressed in a beautiful, baby blue áo dài. The sun was just setting as they pulled onto the hard-packed dirt street and stopped at the yellow, aged, plaster and cement house. An inscription above the door read "1960" indicating the year it was constructed. A man who looked much older than his sixty-two years stepped off the front porch of the little house and walked out to the car. He had been anticipating their arrival and had wanted to meet the man who had carried his wife's heart with him. He had his wife's body, but this foreigner had her heart. Would he also take his daughter's heart, he quietly wondered.

"Father, I am happy to see you again. You have been well these past few days, haven't you?" Hương asked.

"Daughter Lệ Thu," using the name he preferred to call her at home, his *Autumn Tear*, "I've been very well. The cough has returned since you've been away, but I feel fine. I wish to meet the foreigner, please," her father quietly asked.

"Anh, this is my father, Phạm Đào Minh," she said as she held her hand on her father's back.

"Father, this is Mr. Hugh Campbell. You may call him Mr. Hugh, if you want. He has had many sad times in his life and he is happy to meet you."

Hugh began, "Sir, I wish there were words to say. I am sorry for your losing your wife, Thu Lan." He found her name difficult to say to her husband. "Your wife's memory has been with me, although I could not remember who it was. Those days so many years ago were very difficult for many people. I am sure you remember those bad times during the war."

The old man interrupted him, "I am sorry to speak, but those sad times are only memories now. There are too many of the days that have passed us, and much less of days to come for men our age. Let us not waste what is left. I am also very pleased to meet you. You were a companion and a brother of mine in a different manner. But there is something you may wish to see. There is not much of the waning daylight left. We must hurry. *Em ơi*," he called into the house, "bring the lantern. We may need it later."

A lovely girl younger than Hương came out from the house in black pants and a white, long-sleeved blouse carrying an old, tarnished oil lantern that has brought much useful light to the dark. This was another appropriate night for the lamp's use. The flame from the lamp played on the younger sister's face and Hugh saw the likeness of Thu Lan in her face, also. A quick introduction with the younger sister was made and they walked down a red dirt path to the rear of the house. They walked about a hundred feet or so, by Hugh's reckoning, and after passing through a cospe that escaped the war, they came to a gate. Beyond the gate were the above ground tombs of white, blue, black and red marking the location of those who are finally resting, in no particular order. Many of the tombs featured a photograph of the deceased person, including the age, date of their entry into the world and the date of their beginning journey to join the ancestors. Before the old man had a chance to indicate their purpose for being there, Hugh saw Thu Lan's etched photograph behind glass on the elaborately decorated tomb and adorned with the remnants of incense sticks, fruit and dead flowers. Hugh stopped dead in the cemetery and began to weep inconsolably, realizing after thirty-nine distant years, fraught with heartaches, sorrow, and a smattering of happiness and nightly hauntings, he was again looking at Thu Lan, but more so, he was only feet away from the enemy he had loved in war. But, she was never his enemy. That term was meant for those whom one fought against, not for one whom love was a tendon of strength between two people. Hugh was left alone to face, yet, another ghost in his house. Others watched him as he knelt down and sobbed at her grave. Quỳ, a toughened policeman could not hold back his emotions, nor could the old man. The sisters looked across the tomb to their aging father, seeing him age even further in the light of the lamp and in the fading light of day. Here in the graveyard, replete with tombs from many years past, some from the French war, they noticed how their father looked much older than the foreigner, though they were only within a year different in age. The girls held each other around the waist in the garden of tombs and it was eerily quiet, save for the beginning few chirps of crickets in the nearby knee-high brush and Hugh's subsiding cry. The lamp's flame flickered from a bit of wind entering through the chipped and blackened glass and it danced on the photograph and on Hugh's face as a slight rain began to fall. Raindrops began to fall across the face of the tomb and in the sputtering light Hugh imagined he saw Thu Lan crying with him. The two lovers had been reunited. He sensed her presence and was assured everything would be alright.

Hugh felt someone beside him and saw Hương kneeling at her mother's grave. She had also been crying not for the loss of her mother, but at the release of years of sorrow dammed up behind repressed memories and she knew happiness would remain trapped in the weirs of Hugh's heart. She reached for his hand that was resting on his upper thigh and she squeezed hard reassuring him he was no longer alone.

After several moments, the entourage slowly ambled back to the house in the dark. A gibbous moon was rising in the east underneath the clouds to light their way back to the house. As they walked back, crickets chirruped and chirped while safely hidden in the undergrowth. The band of people carried their songs back to the house with them.

Once back, Hugh was formally introduced to the lantern-carrying sister immediately younger than Hương, a lovely young lady named Ngọc, and her skin was a cream color of rare jade, like her name. After everyone removed their sandals and shoes, they entered the house and sat in the small front room, unaccustomed to having so many visitors. A few extra red plastic stools were brought out from the back of the house, and from his seat, Hugh saw another figure in the back quietly sitting outside the kitchen rocking slowly back and forth. He looked at Hương but said nothing. She rose and went to the back and brought the youngest sister out to meet Hugh.

"Hugh, this is my sister, Sương." Hugh knew it meant *mist* or *fog*. Hugh saw immediately why. Where there should be two eyes, Sương had only skin covering that area. "She is my sister I told you about who was born without eyes. The doctors in Hồ Chí Minh City tested her and said it is because of *chất độc mâu da cam*, or Agent Orange, as you taught me. Her mother, my father's second wife, lived in a village as a young woman and the forests nearby were sprayed by airplanes when she was a little girl. She said there were many animals that also died along with the trees, and the village water after that always tasted different and bad. They were all afraid to drink it, even after boiling, but had no other choice; fields had to be watered, babies bathed and water to drink. Mother now has cancer and is not well. You will not meet her because she does not want people to see her condition. You will understand, yes?" Hương asked.

"Please don't worry." Turning to Sương, Hugh gently took her hand and said, "I'm pleased to know you, *em*," preferring to call her in the tradional ranking of an older to a younger person.

Speaking in English, he asked Hương, "How does she spend her days?"

"Usually she sits in her room very quietly. Sometimes she will speak with us about strange things, but it seems she prefers the solitary life. She did not like a special school and we could not also afford it. We are happy to have her here. She inspires us." She thought for a moment and then began to speak in English to Hugh again, "You should know that my father and my mother, if she survives much longer, will reach an age or their health will not allow them to care for her anymore and my sister and I have promised to take care of her."

Hugh looked at her with kindness in his eyes. He knew what she had meant. If they were to be together, they would eventually have Sương to care for. She would become part of their family. Hugh said reassuringly, "I fully understand and accept." She smiled at him, looked slightly downward and a small tear formed in the corner of her eye and fell to the earth with happiness. The father's pet name for her, Autumn Tear, was apropos, he thought, as he saw another tear fall slowly from her cheek.

Quỳ had been silent the whole time and then deemed it necessary to speak. "Mr. Hugh, I believe it is time. You must act now so that you will still have time on your side. I fear spending more time away from your duty may provide time for others, should they be aware of what we do."

"You're right. We need to begin to recover those documents right away." Hugh, Quỳ and Kim went to another part of the house to discuss their plans.

Driving north on Highway 22b, just past the Củ Chi Market, were two others who had at least one contact come through with some useful information, though it meant having to pay him with two crisp, clean, United States one-hundred dollar bills. It was more than a couple of month's salary for their contact, but the two officers didn't care. They learned earlier that their target, the former Special Forces officer, was possibly already in the Tây Ninh area, having been picked up elsewhere in the city by an unmarked police car. They were told he may be accompanied by the police Inspector. They were still oblivious to the relationships that had developed. They only knew what Langley had told them; the target is a threat to national security and must be stopped, but not until after he has retrieved documents said to contain highly classified information injurious to the prestige and integrity of the United States of America and her allies. Once confirmation is obtained that he has the documents, he is to be terminated and the documents properly destroyed in accordance with agency directives.

"Earl, once we arrive, I think it's probably best if we park the car on Cách Mạng Tháng Tám Street just past the Toà Thánh Tây Ninh," Earl interrupted his partner, Anh, and asked what he meant. "It's the Cao Đài Temple. It's where those two were the night I got knocked out," he hated to say that, "and the one target died. I believe that is where the suspected documents are located, somewhere in the compound, otherwise they wouldn't have been there late at night."

"You are probably correct. You know, I missed dinner and I'm hungry. I know, we're supposed to be professionals at this, but everything here in Việt Nam is so," Earl hesitated for a moment, "so laid back. If it wasn't for this op, I'd be hanging out at one of the expat bars in downtown Saigon," he explained, incapable of acknowledging the hero of Việt Nam, but persisted in using the city's old name.

"There're several small restaurants not too far from the temple. We can park the car at one of them and they'll watch it for us. Then when we're done, we can slip out of town the back way through Trảng Bàng without being noticed," Anh offered.

"I don't care. I want something to eat; I want this op over with because I'm beginning to think it's all wrong. Tell me, Anh, who really gives a shit about some old documents from thirty-nine or forty years ago? Nobody. I think somebody fucked up royal when they were young and got involved over here somehow and didn't realize that he or she would make the big time. I think we're here to save someone's ass in Washington and I don't like it. If we weren't under orders, I'd simply walk up to the target and ask him 'what's up' and go from there. I think you and I are going to get fucked on this one, buddy, and like I said before, I don't like it," Earl complained.

Anh kept driving the car without commenting. After several kilometers, Anh finally spoke, "I think you're right. I was uneasy about this when I saw those two guys in the dark that night. I think people high up in the Taylor administration are covering their asses, but we have orders." Suddenly, Anh had to slam on the brakes from hitting some people in the dark of the night on the unlit portion of road ahead. A bus traveling south marked "HCMC" in the front window had skidded in the light rain in order to avoid a motorbike carrying a family of four and ended up rolling onto its side and sliding across the lanes of traffic, blocking everything. The shoulders of the road were embankments for the rice paddies, several feet below the road elevation. The officers cursed their fortune and sat.

Hugh told Quỳ about the old man named Bác. He didn't mention it was him who had killed Whitman because he believed that revelation wouldn't serve any purpose, except to get the old man in trouble. After all the years of protecting the secret, Hugh wasn't about to compromise the old man's identity for the sake of appeasing the curiosity of the police, no matter how close they were becoming. Quỳ, Hương, Hugh and the driver left the house and drove the distance across town to the Great Temple. It was already dark and the lights in the car park across from the monkey's reserve were turned on. They pulled into the gate immediately north of the temple at the road which leads in the opposite direction to Núi Bà Đen, Black Lady Mountain. The car turned into the large square in front of the temple, drove past the elaborate façade and aimed the car into the dirt lot south of the temple, as suggested by Hugh. Quỳ and Hương got out of the car and looked around and waited. Hugh also got out and stood, remembering events from so many years ago and from a little more than two weeks ago when his only friend died. Hugh knew they didn't get along, but he was the only one who understood what they had both survived. The evening quietly took back its night sounds of crickets and the myriad insects calling to each other in response to pheremones unknown to the humans standing nearby. Across from the parking area, all four heard the rustling in the trees as the monkeys shifted themselves in their nests high off the ground to get a better look at what the humans would be doing this evening. They lived in harmony in their own natural temple of branches and foliage, kept neatly tucked away from further human encroachment. Hugh wondered what it would be like to live naturally without the complications of human existence, unencumbered by plots and conspiracies. He knew he'd never know, but his immediate task at hand was to ensure some individuals would pay for sins committed. Hugh knew that Bác was still around, but he didn't know where he was residing or how to find him. He knew if everyone waited, Bác would find him. Hugh's instincts, based on knowledge and buried in the subconscious were working this night. Within five minutes, the old man, dressed in a white shirt and matching pants and a white cap appeared from around the corner. He arrived quietly and caught them off guard. This was the old man's territory, thought Hugh.

The old man was hesitant about the extra people, at first, but when Hugh told him what he planned to do with the documents, the old man was relieved to be relieved of the responsibility and finally relented and trusted Hugh's decision to involve the other people. He had no choice, but he was intrigued by Hugh's plans. He was also content that the temple would not be revealed as the refuge of the documents. The old man also recognized Hương, and she him, simply because residents of Tây Ninh have come to know everyone in their city through contacts at markets, hospitals, pagodas, schools and a myriad of social groups. Tây Ninh hadn't become too big a city yet.

The six o'clock service had already ended long before the party arrived and the Great Temple was empty. The Divine Eye had no one to look after until Bác, Hugh and Hương entered the cavernous hall with the ornately, decorated dragons still standing guard over its treasures. Quỳ decided to remain outside with the driver, another specially trained policeman. Each positioned themselves at a corner of the temple so all four sides could be observed.

In socks and bare feet, the trio padded softly over polished tiles still reflecting the mysteries of the Cao Đàis. The grill work over the windows allowed a trace of a breeze in to cool the tension growing in Hugh's body. Hương sensed his apprehension by watching his stiffened shoulders as he moved slowly in front of her. She offered her hand to him to withdraw some anxiety. He smiled reassuringly at her but she still sensed the stress increasing. To Hugh, the quiet in the temple rang in his ears and he imagined the cilia in his inner ears laying flat as a result of his age and and it provided that ringing; an impudent distraction to his task at hand. With Hương's hand in his, he stared back at the Divine Eye set atop the altar, a mere twelve steps away, protected by a squad of open-mouthed, green, imperial bearded-dragons, with their orange, yellow and red scales warding off evil; protected under its blue sky with wisps of clouds and stars and portents.

Hugh slid his sweat-moistened hand along the yellow tiled wall, hoping the foundation of the building would uphold the foundation of the faith in Hương, himself and the information the documents held. Slowly, they approached the rear of the huge orb of the Divine Eye, at the back of the grand hall. At the bottom of the twelfth step down from the polished hardwood altar rested the stone slab recessed into the polished tiled floor and locked with two thick and strong locks. Bác looked at Hugh as though requesting permission to open the vault where the truth lay hidden for nearly four decades.

South of Tây Ninh, Earl and Anh felt the frustration of waiting for the road to clear and they weighed their options. They discussed turning around and doubling back to Trảng Bàng, waiting on the road, or heading back to the last village and getting something to eat. Earl's stomach had been rumbling for the past couple hours since leaving Hồ Chí Minh City. Anh speculated that if they had gone to Tây Ninh to recover the documents and if they were located somewhere near the Cao Đài Temple, the target may wait until after midnight, perhaps, to retrieve them on his own. They couldn't imagine Hugh gaining the trust and assistance of Vietnamese. The men decided to turn around and find a place to eat while the road was blocked and would be for another hour, at least.

Bác took the ancient brass key from its resting place, now secured to a safety pin inside his white shirt. He looked at Hugh and offered the key to him, but Hugh refused, and instead asked his old friend to unlock the mechanisms that would bring them closer to the truth. The old man squatted down, sitting on the back of his calves, knees like outriggers to keep his balance and inserted the key into the first lock and the hasp was released. He took the lock and quietly set it aside. He scuttled across to the other lock while still squatting and went through the same motions. At last the locks were out of the way, but these two men were much older now and had lost some muscle while the stone seened to gain weight over those intervening years. It took the two of them to try and pry the vault open and it was difficult. Hương suggested that she fetch Quỳ or the driver to help. Hugh immediately said, "Quỳ." She returned a moment later and they heard Quỳ's footfalls. Hugh thought it typical for police not to remove their shoes when there is no need. The sound of his leather shoes became louder and quicker as he approached the two older men sitting on the steps leading up to the altar.

Hugh explained, "Quỳ, we need help. The stone has become heavier since I helped lift it years ago."

Quỳ laughed and suggested the "older" men pull on the stone's hasp at one end while he pulled on the other. They were able to finally free the slab that had been trampled into place from decades of foot traffic, cementing the dust and moisture in the seam to floor and slab. When it was free, they set it on the tile to slide it until Bác objected, fearing damage to the old tiles. With care for their backs, as well, they maneuvered the slab completely free from its resting place and peered into the darkness with apprehension. Quỳ excused himself to watch outside. Hugh slowly inched his way down the stairs and turned on the flashlight. He peered around the walls of the room, filled with dogmatic clutter of more than eighty years. Clutter that bore witness to the birth of Cao Đàism; old private army uniforms, wooden poles, musical instruments, several dusty wooden cases containing planchettes, urns of priests and popes and then Hugh looked around the crevices looking for the one that contained the waterproof pouch he concealed in 1966. It took a moment for him to find it as the tectonic plates in his memory shifted over the years and it seemed as though the crevice had shifted also. Bác explained, remembering, "Cậu, I remember now that I moved it. I don't know if I told you. It had to be moved in February 1975 as I believed we would not find favor during a change since we did not support the communists. It was safely hidden for a few years outside of the temple. It was the monkeys across the way that protected it, safely buried in their enclosure. I only put it back when everything became stabilized. You also must know that from my own curiosity, it was read. I only did it to ensure that if you never came back in my life time, I would know the importance and would have someone whom I could trust take over its safeguarding. I hope, Cậu, you are not upset with me."

"Bác, to the contrary. You did what I would probably have done also given your position."

"Yes, and I know only a portion of your secret, but I sense you have much more. Hurry, I hear other sounds."

"Yes, hurry, there are foreigners entering the temple from the back," Hương said urgently.

Hugh pulled the old packet out from the crevice and examined it, not for damage, but examined it as an indication that all that has happened would be corrected. Those responsible will be held accountable, if they could ever be touched where they now reside. Hugh found his footing on the steps leading back up to the main floor and handed the pouch to Hương. While the two men replaced the heavy stone slab, she put the pouch into her purse, as innocently as she would a wallet, keys or a photo case.

Cautiously and with a heightened sense of urgency, they walked to the north side door as several foreigners began to enter and mill about at the southwest entrance. Hugh could hear them speaking in German and he guessed, correctly, it was a tour group that had returned very late from visiting the mountainside pagodas on Núi Bà Đên and were visiting the Cao Đài Temple before spending the night at the Hoà Bình Hotel on 30 Tháng 4 Boulevard. As the tourists began to walk down the southern corridor inside the temple, Bác, Hương and Hugh left out the north side door and met with Quỳ and the driver and returned to the car.

"Bác, I don't know how to thank you. Your loyalty and trust for all those long, dark years is unimaginable. I know that your help here so long ago will help correct a history that is filled with lies, deception and plots. I can never repay you for your decade's long dedication. Someday, very soon, I will return again," Hugh said, unsure of really what to say in a situation like this. He thought of the man who safeguarded the documents and when he was unsure of the pouch's safety, had gone to the extreme of burying it when the political situation had changed. He conjectured that some may have used the pouch to their advantage had they known of its existence, but how could they without all the pieces that went with it. Like a jigsaw puzzle, the document alone is nothing without the other pieces that Hugh has back at the safe house in Hồ Chí Minh City. Suddenly, Hugh felt of twinge of anxiety and worry over the security of the packet he received from his brother in the States. Hugh thought for a moment as they began to enter the blacked out Mercedes-Benz.

Hugh thought of Quỳ and the proficiency of the police and he then felt a calm return to him. He felt assured simply by Quỳ's presence that everything would be alright. He felt Hương place her hand on his as it rested on the seat next to him. He knew everything in his life was turning and he had her to thank. Here was a young, beautiful Vietnamese woman, thirty-two years his junior, and yet it did not matter to her. He imagined a part of Thu Lan's heart had passed into her; mother and daughter becoming one. He looked into her dark, penetrating eyes and saw them smiling back at him with confidence and encouragement. All were silent on the way back to the family home.

At the very large, and somewhat confusing, off-center traffic circle connecting four main highways in the center of town, they were nearly hit by another car driving in the wrong direction around the circle. The car was being driven by a foreigner and the Vietnamese passenger was arguing with him, too busy to notice the other vehicles. The police driver of the Mercedes simply commented without emotion about how foreigners don't know how to drive in Việt Nam and shouldn't. Quỳ agreed, simply from his policeman point of view.

Once they returned to the house, they were greeted by the older Minh, who was taking a break from the pile of khaki trousers and his sewing machine set up in the front room. They came in, removed their sandals and shoes and took their places on the sofa and the chairs that were offered. The driver pulled the car around the back of the house where it could not be observed from the road and serve as a temptation to any hooligans who may wander past in the dark of night. After securing the car for the evening, he was invited inside and offered a seat with the others.

"You idiot, at least as a Vietnamese, I know how to drive on these roads!" Anh exclaimed.

"Look, if the traffic circle had been designed better to be in the *middle* of the intersection rather than off to the side, we wouldn't have nearly hit those other cars and the truck. Just let me drive and who are you to talk? Your navigation isn't worth shit anyway. Where's the fucking temple?" Earl asked.

"Okay, you should have turned right back there where the park is, instead of turning left. We have to go back now out Cách Mạng Tháng Tám to take us to the temple. It's not that far. Probably about five or so minutes in this traffic," Anh added.

"Well, let's get there so we don't miss them." If Earl had known their target had already retrieved the documents, he probably would have been much angrier at Anh and headed back to the city without him.

At the house, Quỳ, Hương and Hugh went to a back room that was generally used for cooking, bathing, food pantry and storage for an old treadle-operated sewing machine. They moved some plastic stools into a triangle and Hương removed the pouch from her purse. Apprehensively, Hugh took it from her and began to undo the waterproof wrapping around it. Hugh took the envelopes from the pouch and handed them to Hương. She carefully opened one envelope and on a specially made paper well known in the north was a letter written in beautiful handwritten English, which she quickly scanned and then read to Quỳ and Hugh.

Ambassador Henry Cabot Lodge

September 2, 1966

Dear Excellency Henry Cabot Lodge

It is with great hopes for peace between our countries that I am sending the letter to your President Johnson through your office. We have attempted other means of delivery of peace proposals to your country, but each time they have been unsuccessful. We find it necessary to use an unconventional means of delivery and will hope you understand.

Your predecessor, Ambassador Taylor expressed grave concerns about your country's involvement in the jungles and forests of Việt Nam. Even he told your President that America was about to repeat the same mistakes of the French by sending more foreign soldiers to our country.

We want you to know that we are trying to make every possible approach to ending America's presence here in our region of the world, a region thousands of miles away from America. Our only desire is for a unified Việt Nam. Towards that end, we are proposing a peace that is written out in the letter to your President. I am asking you deliver it to your President Johnson and let him know we are sincere in ending this war before more lives of Vietnamese and Americans are lost.

Sincerely,
Ho Chi Minh

———

Quỳ and Hương looked at each other and then at Hugh. For them, this was only part of the Vietnamese history that was over long ago. Quỳ was curious about Hugh's feelings. He glanced at Hugh and saw he face becoming a little red. Hương took the second letter from its envelope and read it also.

September 2, 1966

Lyndon Johnson
Washington   D.C.   United   States   of
America
Excellency,

    Việt Nam is a country many miles from
the United States and we are incapable of
posing any threat to your country. The
Vietnamese have always wanted to live in
peace, but our history has been one of war
with our northern neighbor the Chinese and
then the French. We have been at war for a
thousand years and we can continue to fight
for independence, but at what cost? I believe
the cost in lives to my people and your people
will be very high. For the past few years, we
have seen your presence increase, and we
are concerned about the great loss of life that
has taken place in the south with bombings
from your planes, defoliants in the forests
and jungles and the mass of troops and
weapons you have placed in the Tây Ninh
and Bình Dương Provinces. We no longer
want the intervention of the United States.
But, thinking about the large loss of human
life already, I am proposing the following

to you for serious consideration to end this war at the earliest possible time.

In her desire for peace, and upon your acceptance of this letter and its proposals, the Democratic Republic of Việt Nam will immediately and unilaterally cease all military operations in South Việt Nam. We will cease all transport of supplies and soldiers and we will order our military and political units in South Việt Nam to begin a peaceful discourse with local governments to return democracy to the Vietnamese. We are also urging the use of a representative of your country and a neutral country to monitor and supervise our activities as a gesture of good faith and our intentions to prevent more deaths. We only ask the United States also cease military operations at the same time as a gesture of good faith, and cease all shipments of war materiel to Việt Nam.

We ask the United States to sit with us and work on details of the four-point position of the Government of the Democratic Republic of Việt Nam, such is the statement of the essential principles and essential arrangements of the Geneva agreements of 1954 on Việt Nam. It is the basis for a correct political solution of the Vietnamese problem. We urge you to accept our sincerest offer to immediately end this war.

Your acceptance of our apologies for sending this communique through unconventional means is requested. We do apologize as we have attempted to address our unconditional cease-fire for the sake of peace twice before, but both times have been met with interceptions. I hope this letter will make it to your personal presence.

Excellency, it is the desire of the Government of the Democratic Republic of Việt Nam to immediately cease fighting, discuss terms of the Geneva Accords and to comply with future mutually agreed amendments in order to save the potential huge loss of human life and environmental destruction that accompanies a long war.

I await your word.

> *Sincerely,*
> *Hồ Chí Minh*

Again, Quỳ and Hương looked at each other and then at Hugh. Quỳ spoke, "This is what your friend, Mr. Whitman was killed for?"

"Yes, this was the exact reason, Inspector," Hugh replied sounding angry.

"I do not understand. These are interesting original letters with Uncle Hồ's signature, but are they worth the death of a friend, a death in exchange for some artifacts of a war long over?" Quỳ was perplexed. Hương remained silent believing her love would provide a reasonable answer.

"Yes, Inspector, that is the exact reason and now you need to know about the rest of the puzzle that you haven't known, but now you will, Inspector, now you will.

"The documents back at the police house provide much more detail. These letters were intercepted by Whitman and me. We killed the courier, a North Vietnamese Army Captain. That was our orders from the CIA. We went into the heart of the Central Office of South Việt Nam, COSVN as we called it. You know that organization by the name *Trung ương Cục Miền Nam*. We were to destroy the documents. We were told that they were tactical and strategic plans by the North Vietnamese for conduct of the war in the south. It was difficult to believe we'd be ordered to destroy documents that were highly valuable as intelligence products. Whitman didn't agree. He said we had to comply with orders and destroy them. I told him we were being used and when we advised our radio contact the pouch had not been destroyed, we were bombed by B-52s. I mean, we were on the same side, I thought.

"My life since the war hasn't been quite normal. A couple of failed marriages, couldn't stay in one job too long; burned relationships, you name it. I always felt like someone was messing, I'm sorry, interfering with my life. Well, that packet I received from America confirmed what I thought and combined with the folder your family retrieved during the fall or liberation, whichever you like, of Saigon back in April '75, I realized there was a conspiracy, a plot to keep the war continuing for business profits. That war could've been ended in 1966!"

"Mr. Hugh, if there was a plot, what can be done about it now?" Quỳ asked.

"Plenty. I need to get back to the city and get to a western press contact; anyone from the media. Those documents place the current American president, Paul Taylor, and several others smack in the middle of it. His name is repeated in several places as calling the shots and contacting SACSA, that's the special assistant for counterinsurgency and special activities, or I should say, ordering things to be done through SACSA, including the bombing," Hugh said quietly though he had no reason for the subduing of his voice.

Hương spoke in a soft voice, "Anh, will it be safe for you? I am now worried. These papers, as you say, are true and others will want to come after you."

"They already have, my dear. Quỳ has told me that the CIA already made a contact with me near the police house and I am sure that the weapons that killed Whitman and injured me were CIA weapons. They've known about me.

"Here's the troubling part. Apparently, from writings in the file from the Saigon Embassy and the information I recently received, President Paul Taylor was a young upstart; son of a United States Senator, and working for George Planter, one of the most powerful men in America at the time. Planter was the president and chairman of International Global Industries. You may not know it now because it's changed names a couple times to protect themselves from consumer and class action lawsuits over the years, but IGI was one of the biggest players in the startup of the war here and they posted record profits from bloated Defense Department contracts during the entire time of the war. They had their hands in armaments, aircraft, base construction projects and commissary contracts. They had retired Pentagon generals and colonels working for them as consultants and their stock soared during the war. That's where everything started. There were always rumors in the papers that Planter literally pulled the political strings of Congress and the President's office for years. He ran America for his own profit, and it looks like he's still doing it, though he's been dead for over ten years. He's doing it through his former protégé, President Paul Taylor. He worked for Planter and somehow they found out that Hồ Chì Minh was trying to find a peaceful resolution as the war began to turn very nasty and they knew about these letters. These weren't the first ones, as you can see. Whitman and I weren't ordered to kill an NVA officer and destroy tactical and strategic documents. We were ordered to protect fucking American businesses to make profits from all the deaths over here from a long, protracted and senseless war." Turning to Hương, Hugh apologized when he realized he had used harsh language in front of Hương, who did not understand the word. Quỳ sat absorbing the information.

"So, apparently then-aid to Chairman Planter, now President Taylor, ordered the operation, or at least relayed word of it and was the contact who apparently ordered the B-52 strike. That'd be a tough one, but there's record of Morgan, the CIA officer in Saigon at the time, calling Taylor after learning Whitman and I didn't destroy the documents, and as Morgan pointed out in his notes, 'Paul Taylor says he'll take care of it.'

Hugh waited for them to let the information he'd given them to sink in, and he became quiet for a few moments; he needed the moments to settle down.

"Now, they're on to me being back here and they're sure I've hidden the documents, but they don't know I have them yet. That's why I need to get back to town immediately, get to the house and get the package and get to some credible international news media contact to get this information out. That asshole of a President needs to be out of office. As far as I'm concerned, his tinkering with all those lives to keep a fucking war going for no fucking reason, except for war profiteering, makes him a mass murderer, a war criminal and nothing less," Hugh finished, again apologizing to Hương for his passionate feelings and use of harsh and offensive language. She looked at him and realized she was seeing a side of him that wanted things right in the world. He wanted good things and to rid governments of the bad people. Suddenly, she realized his anger had aroused a spark of intense desire for him. She also unexpectedly began to feel a tingling, ticklish feeling in an area she only referred to as private.

Quỳ was silent for several moments taking in all the information he had just heard Hugh relate.

He then spoke, "Mr. Hugh, now I think I know the reason why my student visa was quickly cancelled and I was asked to leave America. I had started to ask questions about things I knew in your file. Someone must have sensed that the questions I asked led to your country's leadership. I, like so many others of my countrymen, have long believed that America likes to make war and that your president, Paul Taylor, likes war and he does it for business purposes. We read the papers and know that your current war has benefited only a few American businesses by tens of billions of US dollars and left out European business companies. Even your own defense department does not allow tenders, or bids, but will award large contracts to friends of your government's administration. Even when there are complaints of overcharging, your government is unwilling to pursue the matters with the corporations. What can I do to help you, not as a representative of my government, but as a person who also demands peace, like you?" Quỳ asked.

"I need to get back to Saigon now," Hugh said, slipping back to the former name of the city. "I don't want to wait any longer. I have the advantage of knowing what I know and having all the evidence to offer the American people and the world. Let them decide what to do with President Taylor. He's the criminal in this whole matter. He's the one who helped keep the war going for profits, which, mind you, he used to almost independently finance many of his campaigns leading up the presidency. Evil men like him need to be brought down and Truth is the only one that can do it," Hugh finished. He felt tired now from the emotions that had been coursing through his body. He looked at beautiful Hương and saw in her face affection for him, at least that's what he believed, but he could only concentrate on returning to the city.

"I'm sorry to bother you," Ngọc said as she quietly rapped on the door jamb and bowed slightly at the waist, with her arms now folded in front. "Some neighbors know we have visitors and have brought food over to share with us and our visitors. Please, join us in the front room again, if you are almost done. I'm sorry, but father didn't want any of you to get hungry, especially Mr. Hugh. He's afraid that foreigners need much food because they are larger," she said innocently and providing an additional explanation for interrupting.

"*Không sao đâu*," Hugh replied. Hugh took charge of the letters and returned them to the pouch and held on to them. Throughout the meal, Hugh had the pouch tucked under his leg. It wasn't as though he mistrusted the people that fate had thrust into the middle of his life, it was simply he had a strong attachment to the documents that had changed his life and those of countless thousands and millions of others. This was his entire past; a past that others called paranoid, sad and pathetic. He had done his best, but there were those who didn't deem Hugh worthy of having the "American Dream."

After dinner, preparations were made to return to Hồ Chí Minh City immediately. Hugh wanted to make contact with people, but Quỳ told him to wait. Most telecommunications in the country were still under the auspices of the military. Hugh had waited almost forty years, another few hours wouldn't matter.

In another part of the house, Nguyễn Đào Minh and his daughter, Hương, were having a private conversation away from listening ears. "Father, I believe this is my destiny. How else can one explain that I was called and accepted the work to go on the ambulance with Mr. Hugh? How can it be explained that he has now returned to us, and the family connections with mother and our cousins have linked us all together?

"Father, I am having strong feelings for this man, feelings that make me feel happy. I believe he feels the same way. We spoke only briefly about feelings. Father, I promised you always to be traditional, and I am keeping that promise," she told her father with only a trace of emotion.

"You have always been my Autumn Tear, like your mother was an Autumn Orchid. There was something special about you when you were born. Your mother loved you while you were still inside her womb. She also carried the love from the foreigner. I am not sure what it was that the woman I loved also loved this man. Yes, daughter, there are mysteries in life we cannot answer. I have prayed to Buddha for guidance for many years because of the foreigner who entered our house years ago and left his presence behind. Now he has returned, I cannot argue with destiny, those gods are far from me. If you feel it is your destiny, you shall have my blessing," he told her stoically.

"I never told you this, but years ago, I went to the fortune teller," he began to confide in her. "I was worried you would not find a husband and would be left on the shelf," he said, worried that she would forever be unable to find a husband. "He said for me not to concern mself. Someone from eastern lands would be your husband; someone who would be older than you, but would keep you safe, protect you from the world, and would forever be faithful. Earlier, tonight at mother's tomb, I remembered the fortune and knew all would be alright." He looked at his daughter who amazingly looked like her mother. He ached that he was losing the heart of another woman to this man, but it was alright. She would not leave him as her mother did in death.

"Thank you, father." She hugged him tightly, and he returned the hug. It was something they hadn't done in years.

"Before I forget, father, I want to show you something." She left the room for a moment and returned carrying a paper fold   two swans kissing made from an old piastre in hand; their bodies forming a heart. "Hugh gave this to me. It is something mother made for him."

"Your mother was remarkable. I have a small box in my room where I have kept many of these she also made for me. Now I know you will be safe." At the sight of the folded bill, father and daughter cried, adding to the river of tears of Tây Ninh.

IV

Things feel much better now. I had this dream that I was looking for something, what was it? Oh yes, it was a box that had a ring in it, but the ring was missing. I was looking for it, feeling under clothes and behind the furniture wondering where it had gone to. Where was that ring, anyway, I dreamt. I looked everywhere. It was frustrating. I knew it had been in the box a long time ago, but I put it away for safekeeping, but I think someone else took it. Finally, after a long and thorough search of my room and my home, I found it. I was very happy to have found the ring again and could put it in the engraved box right where it belonged. In my dream I wondered who could have taken it, but now it was found, it did not matter. What was lost had now been found and was in the right place.

Now, I am still asleep and it is dark. Some say people can control their dreams. There are names and terms for that practice. It is easy to do. If I don't like the way my dream is going, I simply make it stop and change the dream to the way I like it. My mind likes to play tricks with me. At times, I think my mind is the only friend I have, but I know better. The ones who care for me, the ones in the other room, do care and I love them. Something is changing with them but I don't worry. I don't worry at all.

Two men sat in the dark wondering what the other one was doing. They arranged to wait until three o'clock at the latest. If the target didn't arrive by then, they would return to Saigon and make their report. They didn't have the motivation for this operation as they had for other operations. They both surmised that they were being used and when that happened, it compromised an officer's safety and the integrity of the Company. They discussed the 'outing' of an officer by a Taylor administration official that reached to almost the president, but he was protected. Someone kept him distanced. There was a lot of resentment for the politicians by operatives and officers. Earl and Anh agreed that politicians feared the safety of their own political careers more than the integrity and safety of the United States. Swearing to uphold the Constitution of the United States meant nothing to a politician. It was a mechanical ritual; an obstacle to overcome to access the political contributions that would ensure their power, wealth and control.

So, they sat in silence, quietly waiting for three o'clock to arrive when they would head back to Saigon. They'd file their report tomorrow and go back to their regular work of developing and handling their contacts. In Việt Nam, there wasn't a lot of hard work for them. There wasn't that much capitalistic intrigue in the old Indochina any longer. They hadn't learned that much from the west; yet.

Hugh, Hương and Quỳ returned to the city that night. The driver dropped Hương off at her Aunt and Uncle's house in Chợ Lớn, and then drove to District One to leave Hugh at the police residence. As usual, the guards posted were wide awake and watchful. They knew their charge wasn't there, but it did not relieve them of their duty. Vietnamese are like that, Hugh thought, as they drove up to the locked gate and parked next to the small, aluminum-sided sentry box. A block away, another man sat half asleep under the canopy in his cyclo, watched the car arrive, noted the time, and went back to sleep.

The next morning arrived much too early for Hugh. He had been sleeping soundly. The woman who emerged from the rice paddy nightly, now arose without her limpet hat and scarf covering her face. Now the visage was that of Hương, or was it Thu Lan still, Hugh wondered upon waking. It no longer mattered as the two of them were exactly alike in their facial features. He lay there at some length thinking about her and wondering what their future held. He knew she had feelings for him, but how intense were they and was it possible that she only saw a father figure in him? After all, he was twice her age and it was wishful thinking that he could be in love with a much younger woman and she in love with him. Those thoughts plagued him. He wanted to know exactly how she felt, but was afraid to ask, afraid of the rejection, and now afraid for her safety until this whole matter had been seen through.

The phone rang.

"Mr. Hugh, I would like to come over, please. We need to discuss matters. I will be there in fifteen minutes." Without time for a response, Quỳ hung up leaving Hugh holding a phone connection to the world went suddenly dead.

When the Inspector arrived, he asked if he could make the coffee for them. Hugh let him.

"Mr. Hugh," started the Inspector as he began preparing the glasses, filters, coffee and condensed milk, "while you have been asleep, I have been thinking about the importance of your task. You know that once you reveal all that you know and the documents you have, your safety may be in peril, perhaps not here, but when you return to America. Many may be angry with you. You are reaching all the way to your President and he is very po⌐⌐⌐⌐⌐l and has many people who will do anything to protect h⌐⌐⌐. You already know that he had the power to order that bombing strike, and to interfere with the intentions of our president and yours, even as a young man. Men like that do not give up easy and to them murder is something that simply must be done. To them, it is like killing a mosquito that flies near your head, without thinking about it afterwards. I fear, not for the information you have, but for you, *my cousin*." The Inspector emphasized the word, "cousin."

"Well, then, Inspector, I believe it sounds like you are inviting me to stay longer in your country, is that correct?" Hugh asked directly.

"I have also been speaking with cousin Thu Hương. She also believes that you may be in danger here, but more in the America if you return. You should know that she feels very strongly about you and concerned you do not have a wife. She is hoping that you would want a wife here in Việt Nam," he paused. "Mr. Hugh, do I need to be direct with you, or do you know what I am talking about? You know we Vietnamese like to arrange for marriages."

"The point, Inspector, is that you are assisting in, what we call, match making. To be more direct, let me ask you.

Is Hương interested in marrying me? A simple yes or no, Inspector," demanded Hugh.

"Yes, she is. She spoke to her father last night about her wishes to be with you. Without details, he has given his permission."

"Well, then, cousin, let's by all means plan a wedding," Hugh said with his excitement betrayed by his voice. "But first, I have urgent business. I need to speak with someone at International Communications Satellite Broadcasting. I have no idea who to contact, but I need someone of a high profile who I can tell the story and get this information broadcasted immediately. What can we do?"

"I have contacts with VNA, Vietnam News Agency. They know the people at ICSB. I will call. My phone is more secure than the line here." Hugh knew he meant the telephones were constantly monitored when the house was occupied. Quỳ walked into the other room to get better reception and pressed in the numbers to transfer him to a secure line at the police dispatch on Nguyễn Cảnh Chánh Street, across from Thềm Xưa Cafe where Hương and Hugh had gone for coffee the first night they met. After a series of beeps, he dialed an outside line to his friend at VNA. A very brief discussion ensued and Quỳ was told to call back in fifteen minutes. 'Excellent,' thought Quỳ, 'enough time for a good drink of iced milk coffee. He told Hugh they had to wait about fifteen minutes for contacts to be established.

The men now considered themselves cousins, although the marriage had yet to take place. That would eventually be a formality conducted at the government offices when the couple would sign the marriage register. The only problem, that Hugh and Quỳ could foresee, had to do with obtaining permission from the Vietnamese government for the younger Hương to get married to a much older Hugh. That would entail Hugh having to go into the US Consulate compound to obtain notarization of his paperwork. Quỳ and Hugh put that off for the moment, as Quỳ mentioned, some procedures can be handled in some other ways which would be safer for his cousin. Quỳ mentioned that going into the snake's den was much safer after the venom has been removed from the snake. The bite still hurts, but it is quite harmless.

The fifteen minutes passed quickly for Quỳ, but not for Hugh. Quỳ again made the connection on his cell phone and reached his friend at VNA. Quỳ jotted down a name and a private phone number and was told it was okay to call.

Going through the secure router again, Quỳ called the number at ICSB, located not far from the house in District One. It was located in a tall building off Hai Bà Trưng Street and had the entire roof covered in satellite dishes. Quỳ's phone call was answered by a woman's voice that identified herself as Paula Alden. Quỳ thought that would be appropriate as she would want an important news item like this to propel her career. Quỳ didn't tell her what the requested meeting would be about, but told her it would be very critical for them to meet discretely and quickly. Arrangements were made for them to meet Ms. Alden at eleven o'clock, just before she had to provide her feed to network headquarters in Los Angeles, currently eleven hours behind Việt Nam's Indochina time.

"He's on the move," the Station Chief said into the cell phone. "Just got word he entered a Mercedes, like the one he returned in last night. It's headed somewhere downtown. How fast can you intercept?"

Anh replied, "Earl and I are over here on Võ Thị Sáu Street near Trương Định, near the police barracks. We're waiting for a contact. We can make it there in about ten minutes, depending on the traffic at this hour."

"Fuck your contact, get moving now. You didn't find him last night and wasted a trip to Tây Ninh. He's with the police inspector but I have no idea where they're going."

"We're leaving now," Anh said as they jumped onto their motorbikes, Anh preferring his newer Honda Future II to Earl's SYM Attila with the automatic transmission. The officers wound their way down to Điện Biên Phủ Boulevard, turned on to the one-way boulevard and then turned south on Nam Kỳ Khởi Nghĩa. Once they reached Lê Duẩn, in front of the former Presidential Palace, now named "Reunification Palace," they turned left and headed towards an intercept.

Quỳ and Hugh were in the back seat of the Mercedes. Hugh was feeling agitated and didn't know why. Perhaps, he thought to himself, the years of anger was about to explode and he needed to be calm, he needed his focus back the way he had it in the Special Forces. He needed to be aware of what he would say, how he would say it and present the evidence he had in order to inform the American public about the criminal occupying the White House, their very own popularly-elected President Paul Taylor. He was nervous and began to feel a nauseous feeling in his stomach, which wasn't soothed by the quick driving skills of the driver as he wound his way around buses, motorbikes, pedestrians and food carts being pushed across the streets by old women, each feeling entitled to full use of the roads. They only had a few more streets to go when the light turned red and the Toyota in front of them stopped. The driver had no way to pull around them at such a close distance and was prevented from going through the red light. He apologized.

"It's not a problem," said Quỳ. "We are early, anyway."

The two officers on their motorbikes saw their informer with a cell phone to his ear, like so many others in the city, tailing the Mercedes. Once he saw the two arrive, he broke off the surveillance and went to find a coffee shop and relax. Earl and Anh saw the car; the Mercedes with blacked-out rear windows. They couldn't see inside. Anh was able to maneuver his Honda closer and the driver caught view of him looking in the car. Not only was he trained in evasive driving, but he also recognized the man on the motorbike as being an agent for the United States. Like mice in a Vietnamese house, where's there's one, there's always another, he thought. The driver quickly told Quỳ about it and as Quỳ was looking for the other officer, the light changed and the driver sped around the Toyota as it advanced into the intersection, weaving around the motorbikes that jumped the light to make their left turn. The beige-uniformed traffic police officer at the corner blew his whistle and waved his black and white baton at the Mercedes driver to pull over; unaware it was an unmarked police vehicle. The driver, understandably, ignored the signals and continued. The policeman, a member of *Cảnh Sát Giao Thông* – the traffic police – knowing that there may be a good take of money from someone who could afford a Mercedes, jumped onto his police motorcycle along with his green uniformed partner. He activated the red light and siren and chased the Mercedes, which was also being chased by Anh and Earl.

The car sped down Hai Bà Trưng Street and the car's horn was blaring at traffic to move out of the way; a woman pushing a three-wheeled cart hawking corn was nearly hit by the speeding Mercedes. She let out a string of profanities at the driver, and then calmly went back to wending her way across the busy street, quickly forgetting the incident; it was like that every day for her.

The ICSB building was coming into view as they kept speeding in the direction of the Saigon River. Hugh could now see clearly the large statue of Trần Hưng Đạo in the traffic circle at the end of the street, several blocks away, urging them forward to victory over their own battle. The traffic policemen, with red light flashing and siren wailing was driving his motorcycle madly down Hai Bà Trưng, the policeman on the back was reaching with the baton to force people out of the way and knock motorbike riders who did get in their way. Anh was one who was struck on the shoulder by the officer on the more powerful police motorcycle. Anh slowed down to let the police go by and Earl quickly caught up to him. He yelled at Anh, "Keep your distance. We were made, that's why they sped away." The two reduced their speed, but kept the speeding vehicles in sight.

Quỳ had placed a call during the chase, and saving time, he didn't bother using the secure channels but talked to Paula Alden directly. He told her about what was happening. She had been waiting on the ground floor for their arrival and learning about the chase, quickly called for a camera man to meet her. He arrived with the camera poised on his shoulder and began recording just as the Mercedes pulled up in front of the ICSB building, just in case she wanted an exciting lead-in for a story. As the car screeched to a halt, Quỳ and Hugh jumped out and ran to the front door. The police stopped his motorcycle behind the Mercedes, completely surprised by the two men running into the foreigner-owned building, but their concern was with the driver. He would have some money. Earl and Anh stopped their motorbikes several car lengths behind the Mercedes, bemoaning yet another lost opportunity. They looked at each other, not so much in resignation, but in relief. Once they saw the ICSB logo on the front of the building, they realized that their elusive target had whatever information he needed and would now be passing it on to the world. "Oh, well," they said in unison. Earl said, "Let's get something to eat across the street. We can watch from there," he said in resignation once again.

Paula Alden quickly ran up to the two fleeing men, noting the older man was in good shape and running hard even with materials in his hand and keeping up with the younger Vietnamese. She met them, introduced herself and they entered the building, dispensing with the formalities of introductions until they entered the elevator and pressed the twelfth floor button.

Turning towards the Inspector she said, "You must be Inspector Quỳ that I spoke to on the phone. And who is this, may I ask?"

"Yes, I am Police Inspector Nguyễn Văn Quỳ, Intelligence Unit of the National Police of Thành Phố Hồ Chí Minh.

This is Mr. Hugh Campbell. He is American and I believe information he has will be very interesting for you. It is, indeed, critical."

"Mr. Campbell, pleased to meet you." Turning to Quỳ she observed, "I'm interested, needless to say, that you arrived being chased by the police."

"Well, yes," said Hugh answering her question. "The police because of our traffic violations, but also because we were followed by others from my own government and would be very interested in what I have with me and with what I know. We need to talk where it's private," Hugh suggested.

"We can go to my office. May I tape this?" the lovely young brunette asked.

Quỳ interrupted, "Miss Paula, I must ask you not to mention the police involvement in this matter. At this point, although I am a police inspector, my government is not directly or indirectly involved in this matter. It is imperative that you do not include me, my name or any mention of the *Cảnh Sát* or *Công An*, is that understood?" Quỳ demanded more than asked.

"Yes, Inspector, I fully understand. I would like to hear the full story, though," she replied as the elevator reached the twelfth floor and opened its doors to an air conditioned hallway.

They entered and passed through the suite of offices that the young reporter shared with others, and she led them down to another office that was exclusively for her private use in times like this. It already had a camera set up, lights and chairs. It turned out the office was a complete interview set.

She asked if the two guests wanted anything to drink. Even though they replied, "No, thank you," she nonetheless had an office boy get a pot of tea and bottled water. Quỳ noted that she was aware of the cultural customs of his country, and he respected for her it.

"Now, let's get down to business. You have something important you want to get out to people. I need to hear your story and see what evidence you have."

Hugh asked, "How much time do we have?"

"Mr. Campbell,"

"You can call me Hugh."

"Hugh, if, as was already implied, that this is very critical, I want you to speak carefully and slowly. Catch your breath and tell me the story first. I'll take notes and we'll begin taping the interview afterwards. I see you have some old documents along with a courier envelope with you. May I see them, please."

"Not quite yet. I want to tell the complete story and present what I have to you during the parts of my story where they fit in. I'm sure you are fine with that?"

"Yes. Knowing that you were chased here by the police,"

"And others," Quỳ interrupted.

"Oh, yes, others, you did mention before," she commented.

Hugh replied, "Yes, two CIA operatives. The CIA has been interested in me since I returned to Việt Nam after a thirty-nine year absence."

"Why would the CIA be interested in you? Especially if you've been away for so long?" she asked now confused.

"That's the story," Hugh explained, and he began to tell her the events from 1966 and leading up to their sitting in the office at the moment. At different times, he gave her the documents that he had, like placing pieces of a puzzle onto a board that eventually became a picture that one could recognize.

Hugh had finished the story, leaving out the involvement of Quỳ, Mai, Thu Lan, Hương, and reference to the Cao Đài Temple. He knew those pieces were simply parts of the blue sky of the jigsaw puzzle and would not be missed. His story and the documents were the buildings, the bridges the streets and the key people that gave Miss Alden all she needed to know to see the entire picture when finally assembled.

"Mr. Campbell," she paused forgetting he asked her to call him Hugh. "Mr. Campbell, you realize this information is not only detrimental to President Taylor, but will more than likely lead to criminal charges against a sitting President, besides impeachment, you understand?"

"Absolutely, Miss Alden,"

"Please call me 'Paula'."

"Paula, yes, I clearly understand that. You have to realize that the American War in Việt Nam could have ended prematurely in 1966 or early 1967 without it having to be dragged on until 1973 when we Americans pulled out, or to the end of hostilities in 1975. This war was intentionally prolonged in order to continue record-setting profits that the industrialized military complex of the Pentagon, airplane, munitions manufacturers, and defense contractors were making. The My Lai massacre may not have occurred. The millions of tons of bombs would not have been dropped in the north, leveling villages, destroying hospitals, schools and infrastructure. The environment, and especially the hundreds of thousands of Vietnamese, American and allied soldiers damaged by Agent Orange, would have remained healthy. There wouldn't have been a *Tết* offensive in 1968. And, it would very well, not have led to the political situation in Cambodia that led to the genocide of about two million Cambodians, and let's not forget all of the deaths on both sides. I know these are all fallacious arguments, but consider what could have been if the war stopped years sooner," he posited.

"Yes, Paula, I completely understand the ramifications of all this information that you now know and especially that it directly implicates President Taylor. He is nothing more than a criminal, and as far as I am concerned, he ordered the B-52 strike to kill me and my fellow Special Forces officer, Lieutenant Whitman Emerson, but also is personally responsible for the estimated two million Vietnamese military and civilians that were killed, the more than fifty-eight thousand American lives and the desecration of the environment and the use of Agent Orange. To me, he and the deceased Charles Planter are like mass murderers," Hugh concluded in an angry tone.

"Hugh, that is a pretty strong statement. Let's take a break while I write some notes, formulate specific questions in a specific order and have Cường set the camera up. I'm going to go with this. I have another uplink to New York at one o'clock this afternoon, that's only one more hour. They'll get it at two in the morning, New York time, so they'll have it for their morning shows and it'll eventually get picked up by the other networks and media. But, I have to ask you; what's in it for you? What sort of money are you looking for?" she asked pointedly.

"Miss Alden," Hugh said returning to a formal way of addressing her to emphasize his sincerity, "I'm not looking for money, recognition or fame. All of that doesn't mean anything to me; nothing. Justice and truth is what needs to be served here. Those who are responsible for the atrocities because of their insatiable greed for war profits need to be held accountable and answer the charges, even if one of them is the President of the United States. I only want a peaceful life away from all the noise of consumption. I hope you can understand that, Miss Alden."

"Whoa, wait a minute; I'm on your side. I was just wondering where you're coming from. You could have gained a lot from taking these materials elsewhere and could have rested comfortably the rest of your life on a huge sum of, probably, tax-free cash in the bank. Is there anything we can do for you financially that can help?" she asked again.

"No, then the truth would be tainted. No doubt, your company will benefit from this story. I understand that. But people have to understand I'm not out for money. I only seek justice," Hugh concluded.

"You are the very definition of an American Hero. Why aren't there more like you, Hugh?" Paula asked rhetorically. "Ready, Cường? Let's get started soon," and with that she went to another office.

The taping of the interview took her almost to the deadline. She would upload the unedited, raw interview to the satellite, advising New York that it was on its way and it was a hot story. Before leaving, Hugh asked for a copy of the interview for a personal copy and Paula Alden was happy to provide him a digital copy, which he checked to ensure it contained the entire interview before placing it into his pocket. The documents were scanned and sent along with an affidavit that Hugh signed attesting to a chain of evidence that he was the sole person who had the documents and they were recovered in the same place as he left them in 1966. Hugh did not hesitate as the documents he recovered at the temple the night before were the exact same documents he hid years before. There was no need to bring others into this.

"Hugh, as you say, CIA was also following you. What will you do now? They will, no doubt, still be waiting. And what about the safekeeping of the documents you have?" Paula asked, concerned for Hugh now that she had her career-making, Pulitzer Prize winning story in the can. She suddenly felt qualms about his returning to America after hearing the story.

"Quỳ," Hugh not thinking about the documents' safekeeping, turned to his police cousin, "where can I keep these safe? No doubt many will want the documents. I know your government will because of the historical, and quite possibly, the political value of the documents, though I doubt the latter."

"While you were being interviewed, I placed a call to my superior and briefed him on the story. He does not believe our government will use the documents for political purposes. The war is over. The documents only have value now as historical documents, but you have been, technically, the sole owner, as an "agent' of your own government. Việt Nam would eventually like the documents returned, as it is in Uncle Hồ's original handwriting and carries his signature. We discussed your safety and he has agreed to allow you the use of the house and we will continue to guard your safety for at least another six months," he paused to let Hugh think for a moment.

"If you are prepared to stay voluntarily, we will extend your visa indefinitely for you, no problem. The same arrangements as before will remain the same. If you desire to stay longer and live here, the government will make special arrangements for you to obtain a permanent resident card, if you wish. You must keep the documents with you. I would not, nor does my superior, recommend you entrust them to anyone else until you feel it is appropriate. Miss Alden has scanned everything so we are confident that certified copies exist, but you must retain the originals," Quỳ concluded.

EPILOGUE

FOUR MONTHS LATER

"Do you think our wedding should be traditional or should we have a western style wedding?" Hương asked.

"It is entirely up to you, my dear," Hugh replied.

He sat in the swivel chair at the computer and watched her reading her magazines, and reflected on the last four months. He considered the difficult road it took to arrive at this point in time, practically unscathed and knew it was made smoother by her company. Without her support, life would have been difficult. He was still living at the police house, which the government had subsequently provided the use of for a reasonable amount of time. As Quý's supervisor had told them, "No problem." The government knew the matter would last quite awhile, but the positive effects of the revelations proved to be worth the use of a nice villa to Mr. Hugh Campbell.

Hugh thought about that day a few months ago, after the initial interview. Hugh was invited to stay around the ICSB building with Paula Alden until after the uplink to the satellite on the afternoon of his interview. Quỳ quietly spoke to his driver, via cell phone, and told him they would be occupied for several hours and to return the car and wait for further instructions. The driver told him he spoke to the traffic policemen, who apologized, and they left to look for other traffic offenders.

Quỳ sat absentmindedly thinking about his Uncle and Aunt's housekeeper. He finally had the time to think about what his Aunt had said, and what the housekeeper had said to him, as well. He realized he never knew her name, not that it mattered. He would continue to refer to her as *em* since she was a bit younger than him, but only by a couple years. Once this is over, Quỳ thought, he would visit with Uncle and Aunt again but he would also take the time to visit with the housekeeper in the kitchen; yes, that would be a great place to visit with her in her own environment and watch her as she meticulously prepares a meal. Quỳ had been worried more so for Hugh. He knew there was much at stake, and if his assumptions were true that the CIA was responsible for Mr. Whitman's death, then Hugh would also be in danger. He couldn't allow anything to happen to him while he was still in his custody and protection, so to speak. Especially now that this information would be the breaking news worldwide in another few hours, Mr. Hugh's life would be more in jeopardy. He needed to plan for more security and request additional officers.

Hugh sat looking at the documents in his care, once more, as if he stopped looking at them, they would disappear and he be made to look the fool. No, there were all there; original letters from Hà Nội and the certified copies of documents from the US government with the FOIA citations. He also looked at the CIA file marked "*DESSERT*" left irresponsibly behind in Saigon on April 30, 1975. He now had these documents. What would be the reaction when the

US government discovered their officers had committed gross errors in leaving documents behind in error that revealed sensitive information? Those were his concerns, but also the concern about any possible criminal charges of espionage, dereliction of duty or unauthorized possession of US Government secrets. Right now, he didn't think the government had any substantive arguments, but he knew that he had permanently burned a bridge and it would be very difficult to return to the States, that is if he had to. He knew things would work out, and who knew? Wasn't it Hương who said once in the ambulance from Tây Ninh to Hồ Chí Minh City that he didn't have to return to America if he didn't want to?

He watched Paula as she put the story together quickly with Cường delicately working on the full tape so words and phrases would not be cut or taken out of context, but presented in the full light of what had been learned and discovered. She had notified ICSB Corporate Headquarters that she had a lead story for the morning news program and they would be receiving it on time. When given a synopsis of the story, Corporate requested it be sent earlier for review by their attorneys, who would be woken up and brought in at the early hour in New York. Hugh worried that when the lawyers were called in the truth, once again, would be buried and ignored. His qualms were unfounded as Corporate finally gave approval. Apparently, they believed that Nielsen ratings were more valuable than pressure from a sinking presidency with very poor approval ratings. In addition, they had the exclusive story. Corporate didn't want the dollars to slip away to one of the competitors.

Hugh learned when the show aired in America, beginning at seven o'clock on a cold New York morning, that the story was picked up by the other networks, including broadcast, cable and satellite. Not one news media station wanted to be left out of the breaking story of President Taylor's criminal acts many years ago and the attempted cover up. By now, four months later, in a precedent setting ruling, the Supreme Court of the United States allowed criminal charges to be filed against a sitting president. The court had changed from the days when they would issue emergency rulings regarding disputed elections and they felt this was necessary for the judicial health of the nation. President Taylor was also facing impeachment proceedings and his conservative backing in Congress had eroded to nothing. The President has become a political pariah. President Taylor had exhausted all of his political capital and was bankrupt; politically, morally and ethically. He was faced with massive resignations from his own administration, those who didn't want to be buried in the landslide of negative opinion and be connected to his administration. Americans who had experienced the American War in Vietnam, either actively or passively, were all in agreement that the war was senseless and now the truth was out, they demanded blood for those who were killed needlessly.

It was a supposedly errant Secret Service agent on the POTUS detail who left his jacket with a non-descript pistol in the inside pocket hanging over the chair in the presidential secretary's office. It was not standard issue. The agent had secretly been a supporter of the President and had voted for him, believing him to be a fine president. President Taylor had spoken to him about the matters, quietly one Sunday afternoon, and how he didn't believe his Presidency would survive, and very likely, the Vice-President, whom he argued with constantly over domestic issues, would not grant him a Presidential Pardon. He couldn't stand to be housed with Manuel Noriega, or suffer the indignation as Saddam Hussein had. He needed another way out. The Agent provided that way for him.

While most Americans were talking about the beleaguered president during television commercials, a despondent and disgraced Paul Taylor, for the first time ever in his life, did what he believed was right for the country and his fellow Americans. He went to the jacket pocket that was left in his secretary's office, took out the weapon and walked calmly to the Presidential residence. His detail followed him and upon reaching the bedroom, turned to the agents, thanked them and told them he would need some privacy while he napped. After closing the door to the empty residence, he went to his dresser drawer and took out his container of cocaine, a habit he never kicked. After snorting the powder, he thought about his wife, the First Lady, who left on the previous afternoon and went back to her home state to seclude herself until the matter was completely cleared. She was accompanied by Carla Reeves, the President's advisor; both ladies feeling very much betrayed by the man they had trusted. When the football viewers returned to the game after half-time commercials, and at the kick off marking the start of the third quarter of play, a thirty-grain polymer tipped and copper-jacketed bullet exploded out of the barrel of the pistol, penetrating the bone through the palate of the mouth and began ricocheting randomly inside the skull of President Paul Taylor. Memories of George Planter, B-52s, Tay Ninh, his wife and his ascension to President of the United States, were randomly severed as the now-expanding bullet ripped through filing cabinets of information in his brain. The last memory to be eliminated was the jingle for his favorite soup. The American War in Việt Nam claimed another life, thirty years after the end of the war. This life taken, though, was very appropriate.

A few weeks later, at the Khách Sạn Anh Đào, a wedding party was taking place. This was the hotel where Hugh and Whitman were registered the night Whitman died. The small restaurant area, just to the left of the lobby, was festively decorated with a wedding theme. A huge sign with gold letters on a crimson field of cloth displayed Hương's and Hugh's names as wife and husband. A large ornate dragon and a multi-colored phoenix, separated by a flaming golden egg, were mounted on top of the wedding announcement sign. Pastel streamers and balloons decorated the room set up with twenty tables. It would be a small wedding, but no one anticipated the world press that would assemble in Tây Ninh a few days ahead of time to catch the event; the wedding of the man who brought down a politically powerful presidency; a man who unknowingly and quietly began a new era of morality and ethics in American politics. It was also a wedding that had caught the romantic hearts of Americans and others world-wide. Hugh had been viewed not as a traitor to his country, but as a hero, and a man who despite the dangers to himself, or even facing opportunities of vast financial rewards from either silence or disclosure, decided simply to let Truth be his guiding beacon. Hugh sought neither the fortunes offered to him, nor did he shy away from the dangers when they presented themselves. Hugh had inadvertently become a champion to many people. Oddly, enough, in addition to the awards and decorations he received from the military during the war and afterwards, the new President deemed it appropriate and fitting to approve Congress's vote to award Hugh the Congressional Gold Medal. Hugh was invited to travel to the United States for the presentation ceremony along with his new wife, Hương, at the government's expense, First Class of course, with an armed escort for their safety. But Hugh had other concerns than his future travel. He was being besieged by the press as he and Hương were at the front door of the hotel conference room where their wedding party was being held. They were receiving guests, as is the tradition, and the constant whirr of cameras blending with the constant hum of motorbikes on 30 Tháng 4 Street, the wide divided boulevard where the hotel was located, created a traffic jam as the curious wanted to watch. Quỳ was helping the local police with security and the police from neighboring Bình Dương Province were also assisting.

After the wedding party, Hương and Hugh said good bye to their guests and thanked them very much for their attending the party. It seemed that the 120 people who attended the party added to the hundreds of millions who would view it later on the news or read about it in the newspapers. Hugh felt it also important to thank the press who had come to cover the story of their wedding, for by now, the implications of the family relationships began to leak out, gossip what it is, and the world had become interested in the love story between Hugh and Thu Lan in 1966 and the fateful meeting of Hương, her daughter. Hugh had been besieged by film offers, but firmly stalled them until he could get his life grounded.

Hugh's priority would be to make sure the home for Hương would be comfortable. He also had to make sure the home would be safe for her sister, Sương, when she come to live with them, whom he would welcome and assured it would also soon take the strain from her father.

Someone's touching me again. Why is it always dark? The place where I am is different now. Smells are different and the walls and furniture are different. A huge hand has led me around this new place, and even though he speaks my language, he says it with a different sound. Sometimes, I hear him talking using different words that I don't know. How does he do that? My sister also talks with different words when he's around. I hear them use the words "Chát đọc mâu da cam is Agent Orange" but what does that mean. Is that the reason for my always living in darkness? Well, it doesn't matter. I'll return to my own world and my own stories that I create and I like. Let's see, where was I?

Oh, yes, that's right, Hugh and Hương wanted to live in their own home after the news people had left......

Made in the USA